THE TIDE & THE STARS

THE TIDE & THE STARS

DYLAN ROCHE

The Tide and the Stars
© 2024 by Dylan Roche

Editors: Marci Carson, Nöella Simmons
Cover and Interior Design: Emma Elzinga

Indigo River Publishing
3 West Garden Street, Ste. 718
Pensacola, FL 32502
www.indigoriverpublishing.com

Ordering Information:
Quantity Sales: Special discounts are available on quantity purchases by corporations, associations, and others. For details, contact the publisher at the address above.

Orders by US trade bookstores and wholesalers: Please contact the publisher at the address above.

Printed in the United States of America

Library of Congress Control Number: 2024904103
ISBN: 978-1-954676-84-8 (paperback)   978-1-954676-85-5 (ebook)

First Edition

With Indigo River Publishing, you can always expect great books, strong voices, and meaningful messages. Most importantly, you'll always find . . . *words worth reading.*

THE TIDE & THE STARS

CHAPTER 1

Marin knew he had to choose—would he keep arguing with the cruel old two-headed cow, or would he be on time and hope Ilth didn't punish him too severely? The very thought of being late made his heart thud. He'd never been late with his morning delivery before.

His reflection stared back up at him from the bucket under Prunella's udders, his dark eyes full of uncertainty. It was most definitely tea in the bucket, not coffee—and Prunella was supposed to be producing coffee today. Marin let go of her udder, watching the last few drops fall.

"Come on, Prunella, she wants coffee this morning, not tea." Marin patted her back, hoping he could coax her.

The cow stomped her foot. Marin knew what that meant. *Won't.*

"She's going to be furious if I bring her something else," he said.

Another stomp. *She won't have it.*

Marin sighed. It wasn't any use arguing with Prunella when she was in a mood like this. And she had moods like this more and more frequently in her old age.

"Why can't you just produce coffee like Ilth wants?" he said.

Prunella's head that faced the southern side of the barn bleated. "Is she being difficult again?" she asked.

"Oh, stay out of this," Prunella's north-facing head snapped back.

Now they would start arguing. Marin could handle Prunella when she didn't talk, but her two heads always liked to start talking—arguing—at the worst times. This was so like her!

Marin got to his feet and sidled over to the barn door. He looked out across the lawn. The orange glow of summer sunrise gilded the clouds on the horizon, bathing the fields in a warm haze. He couldn't waste much more time.

Maybe Ilth would forget she demanded coffee that morning. She'd been adamant, no doubt. But maybe by the time his wicked old mistress dressed and came down to the kitchen, she would forget.

The harsh sound of her voice still stung in his ear, even though it had been a quarter hour since then. Marin had been coming from the chicken coop, collecting eggs that had been laid by the red chickens, and on his way to the barn.

"Marin!" Her sharp voice came from above.

He turned his sunburnt face up toward her, shaking his shaggy mess of brown hair out of his eyes. She leered down at him through the decaying frame of her upstairs bedroom window.

"Yes, ma'am?"

"I want coffee this morning," she demanded. "Have Prunella milk coffee."

"As you say, ma'am."

The old hag grimaced down at him as if he'd said something offensive. It didn't matter how respectful Marin was. She always grimaced and sneered. He straightened his shoulders, drawing his lean form up to his full height, hoping it made him look less pathetic.

"And make sure it's hot this time," she said. "It was tepid last time, and that's putting it nicely."

"As you say, ma'am."

Ilth paused for a moment, maybe to come up with more cruel

2

words she could say to him. Her pinprick black eyes narrowed, nearly getting lost in the sagging wrinkles of her face. Marin sometimes got the impression she must have been a great beauty when she was younger because of the proud and haughty way she carried herself. But if that were true—if she had ever indeed been a great beauty—it definitely had never been true in Marin's lifetime. There was no sign of it now. The years had not treated Ilth kindly, and it sometimes seemed like her face and her mood were competing to see which of them could be uglier. As far as Marin was concerned, they both were winning.

After staring at Marin for several seconds, long enough to wrinkle her nose in disgust, Ilth drew the shutters closed with a bang.

Shaking off the memory, Marin turned back from the barn door and hurried to Prunella's stall.

"Please." Begging wasn't beneath him at this point. He sat himself on the stool beside her and looked her in the eye. "I'm not up for dealing with this today. I *have* to take her what she demanded. And I *can't* be late. I can't be!"

The north-facing head bellowed. "Oh, don't blame me," the north head replied. "It's not all my fault that I can't produce coffee today. These udders are just as much hers as they are mine." She tossed her head, glaring at south. "Or has the old nag forgotten?"

The south head scoffed. "Maybe you should remember the same thing before you go calling me an old nag."

Marin stood again, his skin prickling with anger. "Both of you—*stop it!* This isn't funny. This will be the third day in a row I've brought Ilth something other than what she wanted and she's going to be angry." His stomach twisted at the thought. He might be without meals for a week. He might even be beaten. He recoiled with the thought of Ilth's cane striking his back over and over again.

Prunella stopped bleating long enough to stare heatedly at him with both sets of mean, black eyes. "And you'll be late," she said. "Yes, you'll be late if you stand here and argue. Take the tea and deliver it to her. It's the only thing you're going to get."

A gruff voice came from the back of the barn. "Just give the boy what Ilth asked for, Prunella." Marin had practically forgotten Holdfast was still asleep in the hay, tucked away in the corner of the barn where morning's light had not yet crept in. The old farm dog stretched and sauntered over. "He's surely going to get the cane for this."

"Stay out of this," both of Prunella's heads chorused together, then erupted into laughter.

Holdfast lowered himself down beside Marin and looked into the bucket under Prunella's udders. "She's never withheld this long before, has she?"

"She always produces what Ilth asks for if you argue with her long enough. The last three mornings though…" Marin gestured at Prunella's two heads, both of them still laughing at his expense.

Holdfast nodded, understanding.

"But no," Marin continued. "Never this long."

Holdfast gave Marin a wink with one of his droopy eyes and nodded at the cow. "Want me to bite her for you?"

"That won't do any good. She's dead inside."

The north head stopped laughing abruptly. "Well, it's a lot better than being dead on the outside. Like your parents!"

Prunella's south head laughed even harder. "Ah, good one, dearie!" she said.

Marin clenched his fists and got to his feet. "You two are a curse!" He lunged and grabbed the bucket from under her udders.

"I can't deal with this anymore," he said to Holdfast through gritted teeth as he lifted the bucket and headed toward the door. "I'm late as it is. If I waste any more time, Ilth will already be down in the kitchen for breakfast by the time I get there."

But there was still time—there was still time if he hurried.

4

There was.

He rushed out the door of the barn, his lanky body moving with determined speed.

"Good luck," Holdfast called after him.

Marin looked over his shoulder to nod. "I'll need it!"

He stepped out of the cool barn and into the misty warmth of dawn. The rising sun had crested the horizon, making the dewdrops on the grass sparkle.

Yes, Marin definitely needed good luck. It had to be almost six o'clock, and Ilth's strictest rule of all, the rule Marin never dared break, was that he make his delivery of milk and eggs before six o'clock. Then he had to be out of the kitchen and out of sight.

The same rule went for delivering the crops and firewood in the evening—they were not to be delivered until after eight o'clock. Ilth had many times threatened to beat him bloody if he ever broke the rule.

"I don't want you around the house when I'm present, and I don't want your smell lingering around my kitchen either. You'll make your deliveries before I come downstairs and after I've gone to bed."

"Yes, ma'am."

"If you can't follow that rule, boy, you'll wish you'd never been born. After I'm done wearing my hand out on you, you'll be without supper for a week."

"Yes, ma'am."

"Don't think I am joking. Do you want to test me, boy?"

"No, ma'am."

And that was the truth. Marin never wanted to test Ilth, no matter what. He would keep to the fields and stables where he belonged. He would do as he was told, wouldn't disobey, wouldn't suffer the witch's wrath. She might beat him, starve him, even send him away to fend for himself. Or worse...if she were especially angry, she might turn him into a toad or a rat or a stone statue.

Maybe I shouldn't have spent that much time arguing with Prunella, he thought. But he had been so scared about being punished for bringing tea instead of coffee—and now he was going to be punished for being late. Either way, he lost. No matter what he did, he failed.

He hurried his way up the sloping lawn toward the ramshackle cottage. He hated the sight of the house with its boarded-up windows, its decaying shingles, its mossy roof. The fields might have been where he always had hard work to do, but at least when he was out there, he was alone. When he was out there, he didn't have to deal with Ilth.

How he hated her!

"You're lucky I tolerate you," she often told him. "An insolent, lazy, good-for-nothing servant boy like you. I wonder how I got so unlucky as to have you for a farmhand."

Marin had often wondered that same thing. Whatever had happened to his parents or his family, he had no idea. How he came to be enslaved to Ilth—a reclusive old woman who may or may not have practiced witchcraft—he didn't dare ask. He didn't expect he would get much of a truthful answer even if he did.

This was his life. He knew he should be grateful to have a roof over his head and food to eat. It could have been a lot worse for an orphan like him.

Halfway up the sloping lawn on his way to the house, Marin stopped. A pair of newts lay on a nearby rock, warming themselves in the morning sunlight. "You better make yourselves scarce," Marin said. "If Ilth comes out in the yard and sees you, she'll be hell-bent on catching you and using you in one of her potions."

The newts looked up at him, blinking their large eyes in unison. "Thank you, Marin," one of them said.

"Yes, thank you," said the other.

"Go on," Marin said. "Go."

The newts slithered down from the rock and disappeared into a patch of ivy.

Marin rolled his eyes. "I wish I could run away that easily."

He strengthened his grip on the bucket handle in his right hand and the basket in his left, then continued walking, dreading the confrontation he was likely to have with Ilth.

Holdfast was right. Marin probably would get the cane for bringing tea when Ilth demanded coffee, and for bringing the wrong thing three days in a row. Two days ago, Ilth had asked for tea, and Prunella had produced coffee. Yesterday, Ilth had asked for cider, and Prunella had milked juice.

And if he were late? He didn't even want to think about that.

It wasn't the pain of the beatings he hated so much. He'd gotten used to that a long time ago, accepted that it was only temporary. It was the sense of shame he hated. He was no longer a little boy and was nearly a man grown—seventeen years old—and it degraded him every time the gnarled old woman put a cane to his back for offending her in some minor, stupid, little way.

"You wretched brat," she always said. "Worthless! Insolent! No wonder your parents died. They must have been so ashamed of you."

That was how it had been his whole life. And that was how it was going to be for all the years ahead of him. Only Marin, his chores, and his feelings of worthlessness.

Legends and ballads often told of orphans who grew up as insignificant little nobodies but went on to prove themselves worthy heroes. They became kings and warriors, respected and admired by all. It was too much to expect anything like that to happen to him, Marin knew. This was real life, and real life wasn't like epic legends and ballads.

But still—one could dream, right?

He reached the porch leading to the kitchen door and wiped his feet on the calfskin mat. It wouldn't help him any if he tracked mud and dirt into the kitchen. Pressing his ear up against the door, he listened for any sounds within. Quiet. Ilth must not have been down-stairs yet. He wasn't late. He could still slip in and drop off his delivery.

He became suddenly aware of how hard his heart was pounding. So much stress, and it wasn't yet much past dawn. He set the basket and bucket down, wiped the sweat from his palms on his trousers, and took a moment to adjust the sleeves of his tunic to cover the birthmark on his inner forearm. ("Keep that hideous birthmark covered up," Ilth always told him. "I don't want to see it, not now and not ever—do you understand?")

He ran a hand over his sharp jawline, his callused fingers feeling a trace of stubble. He had not shaved this week, but there wasn't much he could do about that now.

When he looked presentable, he lifted the latch.

The door creaked open, revealing a motionless kitchen steeped in shadow. Only a thin stream of light came from the boarded-up win-dow across the room. The potbelly stove, butcher's block, cupboards, and wash basin were silhouettes among the dreariness.

Marin picked up the basket and bucket, tiptoeing over the thresh-old. His nerves tingled with the thought that he was so, so, so lucky he wasn't late.

As if prompted by this thought, the sound of the Bluniawood cuckoo clock in the hall chimed. Six o'clock! His presence was formal-ly no longer welcome in the kitchen—nay, it was no longer allowed. If he made himself scarce, Ilth might be lenient about the tea.

Spurred by the sound of the clock, he dashed across the room toward the table and set the bucket and basket down.

The sixth chime sounded, leaving nothing but overwhelming si-lence. Marin wheeled around and darted back toward the door.

And then the silence was broken—footsteps in the hallway, coming closer. Marin's stomach lurched. Ilth, only seconds away from catching him in the kitchen.

8

He had barely reached the threshold to the porch when the hall-way door swung open. Ilth would surely beat him for this.

He whirled around toward the door.

But it wasn't Ilth standing in the entry to the hall.

Instead of a scowling old hag, there stood a boy about his own age. Marin froze.

The other boy looked back at him, the expression on his face one of dumbfounded amazement.

Before Marin could say anything, Ilth's voice came from down the hall. "Aster! What's wrong with you, boy?"

CHAPTER 2

Still trying to gain his composure, the other boy stammered. "Huh?" He never took his eyes off Marin and the shock never left his face.

Ilth's voice came again. "What's the matter, Aster?"

The boy—Aster, his name was—shook off his amazement. "Nothing," he called over his shoulder to Ilth. "It's just…I'm just tired. I've got work to do and I'm trying to decide what to do first."

Aster met Marin's eyes with a pleading expression and nodded subtly toward the porch door. A warning to leave.

Ilth barked again from the hall. "Well, think while you move, lazy thing! I don't need you to take all morning to make my breakfast."

The chance for escape wouldn't last long. Marin tiptoed over the threshold, then turned back. "Thank you," he mouthed.

The boy responded with another subtle nod. He ran his hand across his tunic, straightening his belt, as if readying for work.

With a deep sigh, Marin pulled the door behind him, dropped the latch, and ran. He didn't even realize he was running until he collapsed on his knees at the edge of the cornfield.

Another servant! There was another servant living inside the house! And Marin had never known about him.

Why? Why hadn't Ilth ever mentioned there was another servant working inside the house?

This explained a lot—why he had never been allowed inside, why he had to make his deliveries at certain times. Why every window to the decrepit shack was boarded up. How could Ilth hide something like this from him all these years?

"What in the cursed underworld?" he swore.

He climbed to his feet, taking a moment to steady himself. One deep breath, then another, then another, and his raging heartbeat slowed a little. Across the fields in front of him, flecks of gold gleamed on the cornstalks from the rising sun in the sky.

You've got work to do, he thought. *Work won't wait simply because of… because of all this*. If he didn't do his chores, then Ilth might suspect something. Bitterly, he trudged toward his shed to fetch his scythe, then made his way to the wheat field.

Questions raged through his head. Who was this other servant? Why would Ilth keep such a secret? Sweat dribbled down his brow, his entire body shaking as he slashed at the wheat over and over again with his scythe. Realizing how aggressively he was working, spurred by the questions racing through his head, he stopped to catch his breath.

He rolled up his sleeve and glanced at the birthmark on his inner forearm. It was a small diamond-shaped mole just above his wrist. Could it be that Ilth found the birthmark so offensive because it would make him recognizable to a long-lost family he knew nothing about? The thought had never occurred to him before. Maybe she didn't want him to know. *But why?*

He spent the morning reaping wheat, which he carried to the mill on the edge of the yard, then tended to the vegetables, and chopped wood in the afternoon. By the time evening set in, he had exhausted himself too much to still be angry about the morning's discoveries. Anger and shock had given way to something not unlike acceptance.

He couldn't confront Ilth about this. He didn't dare. *But maybe,*

he thought, *there's a way I can talk to this other servant. Find out who he is.*
Another servant on the farm meant Marin was no longer alone.

So, why did he feel lonelier now than he ever had before?

As the sun set over the forest beyond the farm, he pushed the heavy wheelbarrow full of firewood and freshly picked vegetables toward the house. Parking the wheelbarrow on the porch, he unlatched the door to the kitchen and went inside.

The kitchen looked the way it always did in the evening. Empty, with the swept floor and dying embers in the fireplace, the clean cooking tools hanging from pegs on the wall, the table and butcher's block still gleaming with a trace of wetness from being scrubbed down. *Scrubbed down by the other servant,* Marin thought.

The stillness had an eerie quality it never did before. He turned back to grab his basket of vegetables off the wheelbarrow. *Creak* went the floorboard just beyond the threshold. He'd heard it creak a thousand times, but it creaked so much louder now. The sound filled the emptiness of the dark kitchen.

After the vegetables, Marin set two logs on the hearth beside the fireplace, where Ilth's cauldron hung. There was still one log left from yesterday's delivery, and the rest he would stack on the woodpile in the garden.

He turned to go. Halfway across the kitchen, an ever so slight *creak* stopped him. He turned toward the corner of the kitchen where it had come from.

The door to the cellar stood ajar, nothing visible in the shadows just beyond the jamb. Had the door been open when he came in?

Marin paused. *No, that door was closed when I came in. I would have noticed if it had been open.*

He had a suspicion—a very strong suspicion—that somebody might have been standing a few feet down the cellar steps, hidden in shadow, watching him.

His urge to whisper, "Hello?" was so strong. But he caught his voice as he drew breath to speak. He couldn't. If Ilth came in—if she caught him—

He gulped. No, for all he knew, the door had been open the whole time.

Giving one last look at the empty, quiet kitchen, he stepped out to the porch and pulled the door closed behind him.

CHAPTER 3

After Marin stacked the rest of the logs on the woodpile, he parked the wheelbarrow in its usual place in the lean-to around the side of the house and made his way across the lawn to his shed.

Night had fallen, and the stars shone bright. Even on the worst of days, even when the work was its hardest or Ilth had been especially cruel to him, Marin loved the simple joy of twilight in early summer, when he could walk back to his shed, smelling the grass and earth, listening to the crickets chirping and frogs croaking. None of it gave him any comfort tonight.

His little shed awaited him. He stepped inside and pushed the windows open to let in the cool evening air, then went around and lit each of the lanterns to fill the place with a comfortable orange glow. He flopped down on his bed of straw and stared at the ceiling. "Why?" Saying it out loud took some of the weight off him. "Why did I never know?"

Quiet down. Holdfast might hear you talking to yourself. He went to the window and looked around. No sign of the old barn dog anywhere.

Turning away, he crossed to what he often called his "belongings." They weren't much to brag about, but it wasn't as if he had anyone to show them off to, living out here in the shed the way he did. His belongings were castaway items and pieces of junk that he had collected over the years. Ilth never deigned to give him anything of his own, and there wasn't much room to keep very many worldly possessions. But every so often, usually in the spring, she would leave a crate of books and knickknacks and other oddities on the front porch and tell him to take them out to the roadside for any passing caravans to salvage and carry off with them. Marin had always done as told, but not before choosing items from among Ilth's throwaways to keep for himself.

So his modest pile of belongings had come to be one of his few joys in life. He picked up a book and carried it back to his hay bed for some reading. It didn't matter what book it was, only one that he had never read before. Maybe it would take him away from all the thoughts racing through his head.

Ilth often said books were trash and a waste of time. That was part of the reason Marin liked to read so much, poring over book after book from a young age, trying to learn as much as he could about the world beyond Ilth's farm. History and theology and philosophy. Stories of brave adventurers and wonderful romances. It seemed to him that there was a very exciting world out there beyond Ilth's farm. Not that he would ever get the chance to explore it.

The sound of approaching footsteps drew his attention. He perked up, staring at the door of his shed. Somebody was right outside. His skin prickled.

For a second, everything was still. He held his breath, waiting. Then the door to the shed creaked open.

Standing just outside, barely illuminated by the light of the full moon overhead, stood the other servant. Aster.

Eyes wide, the boy stared at Marin with nervous apprehension. "Hello."

Marin struggled to find his voice. "Hello."

But if the apprehensive look on Aster's face gave any indication,

Aster felt as confused and self-conscious as Marin did. He shifted nervously from one foot to the other, then looked over his shoulder at the wide expanse of shadowy yard behind him.

"Are you...Ilth's servant?" Marin asked. The boy had the same lanky frame as he, though slightly smaller, his skin fairer. His brown hair had the same unruly shagginess as his.

"Aye," the other servant said. "Are you?"

"Aye. I'm her farm boy." It was awkward calling himself a boy when he was nearly a man.

"I'm her kitchen boy," Aster replied.

Marin nodded. "What's your name?" He already knew it, but this was the polite thing to ask.

"Aster. What's yours?"

"Marin."

Crickets chirped outside the shed. Marin shook his head, remembering himself. "Won't you come in?" he said. He stood, trying to appear welcoming. It was all so strange. He'd never had visitors out in his shed before. Even Ilth never came out to visit him in his shed. It wasn't a comfortable place, yet here he was, trying to receive a guest.

How pathetic his little home must have looked, with its pile of straw for a bed and all his shabby belongings piled in the corner. "I know it isn't much," he said.

Aster came over the threshold and looked around with a friendly expression. "No, no, it's right fine." He shrugged. "I sleep in the garret."

Marin couldn't decide whether that made him feel better or worse. Aster must not have had a much better life than Marin himself did—and Marin knew how bad that was.

"Are there more of you inside?" Marin asked.

"No, only me." Aster sat himself down on the milking stool up against the wall. "Why? There aren't more of you out here, are there?"

"No, only me. I tend the fields and livestock by myself."

16

Aster nodded. "I take care of the house all by myself. By the way, I'm sorry I didn't say anything when you were making your delivery tonight."

Marin struggled to hold back a laugh. "I had a feeling you were there. On the stairs to the cellar, right?"

"Aye!" Aster started to laugh too. The sound of his laughter lifted Marin's spirits.

"I'm sorry," Aster continued. "But I was so shocked when I first saw you this morning. I almost couldn't believe it. That is, it didn't seem real. But when I saw you come back to the kitchen in the evening, I knew for sure I didn't simply make it all up in my mind." He paused. "I couldn't say anything to you then, or Ilth might have heard me. Then she likely would have beaten us both."

That was no exaggeration, Marin knew. "So, she's awful to you too, huh?"

"I hate her."

Marin reclined back, looking Aster up and down. His clothes were tattered and ragged, but they had none of the soil of field work that Marin's tunic and breeches had.

"How did you come to work here?" he asked.

"To be her servant, you mean?" Aster replied. He flashed Marin a wry expression. Aster didn't seem like someone who was going to hold back the truth about anything. "I have no idea. Trust me, it wouldn't have been my choice." He stood and paced across the barn, taking in the sight of all of it. It was funny to think he had never been outside in his whole life, just as Marin had never really been inside anywhere except for a shed or barn.

"Same with me, I guess," Marin said. "I've been here as long as I can remember."

Silence hung between them. It was comfortable. It was enough merely being around someone else who understood.

17

Marin cleared his throat. "Would you like to play a game of cards?"

"That would be great."

Marin crawled over to his belongings and pulled out the old tin where he kept his rumpled deck of playing cards. Then the realization hit him. "I…I only know games for one player. Not two."

Aster smiled and shrugged. "That's fine. We'll just talk. I didn't come out here for anything special."

"All right."

Marin put the cards back down among his belongings and sat down on his pile of straw. "Sorry, I'm still a little confused and surprised by all this."

"It's all right. So am I."

"I had no idea there was another servant."

"Neither did I."

"I mean, I always wondered…"

"Did you?"

"Well, I knew there was no way that Ilth was doing everything herself."

Aster grinned at that. "No, of course not."

"Did you ever wonder where the firewood came from? Or who picked the crops out in the field and delivered them to the kitchen?"

"No. I guess I accepted it as normal because that's the way it had always been."

Marin nodded. There were certain things he himself took for granted because Ilth and the farm had been all he had ever known. What else had he taken for granted about the world?

His stomach rumbled. "Would you like some fruit?" He reached for a basket full of berries he collected that afternoon.

"Aye, please."

Marin handed the basket to Aster. It felt good to have someone to share with. Someone to talk to.

The hours pressed on, and their conversation flowed more easily. The two of them detailed their daily chores, exchanged stories about their childhoods in servitude, anguished over the awful punishments Ilth inflicted on them. When they laughed, it was shared laughter; when they complained, they united in each other's angst.

By the time their conversation lulled, it was past midnight. "I should probably go," Aster said, staring at the fire. "It's getting late."

Marin nodded. "It is." He knew he had to sleep at some point, but this—this had been good. This had been a reprieve from drudgery and degradation. It was the one time he wasn't miserable.

Aster stood and headed toward the door to the shed. "Will you be all right getting your chores done tomorrow?"

Marin shrugged. "I think so. I might be a little tired. You?"

"Oh, I'll be fine. I'm sorry I kept you up so late."

"No, no, don't be sorry. I'm glad you came out to visit." Marin stood. It seemed the polite thing to do when he was seeing a guest out. Not that he had any way of knowing proper manners except for what he read about in books. "Will you be safe sneaking back into the house?"

"Aye, not to worry." Aster looked out the door and gazed up at the house. It was all in shadows, not a single light coming from any of its boarded-up windows. "Once Ilth passes out for the night, there's no waking her. You can hear her snores echoing through the whole house."

"Ha!" Marin could only imagine. "Do you…do you want to come visit tomorrow night?" As soon as he asked it, he realized how stupid a question it was. Two late nights in a row would be bad for them. But still, Marin wanted to do this again. He *needed* to do this again.

"Of course," Aster said. "When Ilth is asleep, I'll come back out. It's all right that we visit here, isn't it? I would invite you up to the house, but—"

"But it would be too risky," Marin said quickly. "Out here is fine."

"Well, then. Goodnight."

"Goodnight."

Aster slipped through the door. Marin watched him go up the sloping lawn toward the house, his shadowy form gradually disappearing more and more into the dark until he vanished completely.

For a brief moment, Marin's skin prickled with the thought that Ilth would be waiting up for Aster when he came back through the door into the house.

She might catch him, and then they both would be in dire trouble.

This is risky, what we're doing, Marin thought. It was nice to have a friend, but still…

Marin crossed to his straw bed and lay down, his stomach all tied up in knots.

Was it worth it though? For the first time in his life, he wasn't going to sleep in despair. His entire existence wasn't all work and hopelessness and abuse. He had a friend.

And maybe—*maybe*—there was hope that things were going to be different.

CHAPTER 4

Moonlight streamed through the gossamer silk draperies as Tsema stirred from sleep. The prophetess drew herself up and climbed from the gold cot, smoothing the wrinkles in her white robe as she reflected on the vision that had woken her. The boys had met—they'd been reunited. After so many years.

Tsema strode to the table and lit the oil lamp. "Zareen!"

It took only a moment for her handmaiden to appear at the entryway, emerging from the night outside as she pushed her way through the silk hangings. The girl had a graceful, ethereal quality to the way she moved, her tall, lithe body seeming to walk on air. "You called, my lady?" She glanced at the disturbed blankets and pillows on the cot. "What is it that rouses you?"

Tsema sat triumphantly in her chair. "The boys. They have met one another."

Zareen hesitated, then arched an eyebrow in surprise. "You don't mean—"

"I do." Tsema smiled as she reached for a crystal decanter of summer wine and poured herself a glass. "And now I wonder what this means for the kingdoms of Grythium and Blunia." She said this half to herself, half to her handmaiden.

"I imagine it is a blessing, is it not?" her handmaiden said. "This promises of greatness and glory."

Tsema raised her glass to her lips and took in the smallest sip of wine. "Perhaps." She turned, glancing at the small gap between her draperies where the moon shone through. "But that will be up to them."

With those words, she stood and went closer to the draperies. A gentle breeze came through with the moonlight. Tsema reached forward and pulled the gap ever slightly wider, taking in the expanse of deep purple night sky beyond the shadowy trees. Stars twinkled, almost as if begging for her to read them and interpret. She refused.

"It will not happen by accident, that's for certain," she continued. "Though even I can't say how it will come to pass. They will certainly have an adventure ahead of them. I hope they are hardy young men."

She paused, closing the drapes, and turned back to her handmaiden. A moment of silence hung between them, each reflecting on this revelation that had wakened Tsema. How long had they been waiting for this to happen? Tsema had to admit she was impressed by the witch's ability to keep the boys apart all these years, to hide their existence not only from each other but also from the outside world. "We will have to wait and see, however," Tsema added. "It may be a while before they even leave the farm."

"But you're confident they will?" her handmaiden asked.

"Oh, I am." Tsema glanced at her reflection in the shining bowl of her wine glass and saw the twinkle in her own eyes. "Now that they know about each other, it's only a matter of time before they become curious about who they are and where they came from." She smiled, hesitated, then said in a calm, matter-of-fact tone, "Ilth's secret is about to unravel."

Her handmaiden gently closed her hands together and nodded. "Aye."

Tsema sat again, laying the tiny fingers of her plump hand on the surface of the gold table. "They will have to prove themselves, of course," she said, raising her glass of wine to her lips. Now she was talking to herself, almost as if Zareen were not even there, as she tried to imagine how it would play out. "A prophecy alone is not enough to make a hero. They'll have to find out what their destiny is and fulfill it."

Zareen took a step closer. "In that case, there is other news you should hear—news, I imagine, you have not seen with your dream-sight," she said. "Princess Elspeth of Blunia has been taken captive by the goblin army. She and her sister, Carys."

Tsema looked up. "Have they?" She didn't like the news—she didn't like it one bit. The kingdoms of Blunia and Grythium were already in a dangerous condition.

"They will need heroes to rescue them," her handmaiden offered.

Tsema shook her head, then took another sip of wine. "Most unfortunate that the royal princesses of Blunia would need heroes to rescue them," she said. "I always thought them stronger than that. If anything, I expected that they would be the ones to rescue boys who were in distress." Some tricks never grew old—when would villains like the goblin army ever learn to stop capturing princesses and using them as ransom against the kingdom? Tsema grew tired of it many years prior. "Well," she said in the sweetest tone she could, "this may be a worthy task."

Her handmaiden nodded. "Yes. And it will bring them together with the princesses of Blunia." She hesitated, then seated herself in the chair next to Tsema. "But, my lady, will it be enough?" Rarely did Zareen ever act this familiar—but Tsema understood. The girl felt the same excitement she did. She could excuse the informality from her most loyal adviser and confidant.

"What I mean is…" her handmaiden said, "…is that enough of a deed to unite the entire realm of Monte Prospera?"

"I'm afraid not. There will be greater challenges than that." Tsema stood and paced around the room, drumming her fingers on the bowl of her wine glass as she thought. "And the sacred relics of Grythium remain hidden for now. They will need to seek them out and put them to use. That will be a much bigger challenge than simply overcoming a goblin army." She stood for a moment, thinking. "I do hope the boys manage to find the pouch of fairy dust that Ilth has been keeping all these years."

A moment of quiet filled the tent as both of them reflected on the thought. When she got the sense their brief council had come to an end, Zareen stood, nodded, and made her way toward the entryway. She paused. "Will you know when they finally decide to run away?"

"Mayhaps," Tsema said, setting her glass down. "When they do run away, I would like to talk with them."

Zareen nodded, understanding the instruction.

"I cannot tell them too much," Tsema concluded, "but I would like to offer some wisdom before they seek out their destiny."

CHAPTER 5

An unseasonable chill crept into the air after sundown the next night, and Marin prodded at the small fire he had built to bring some warmth into his little home. Summers didn't often get hot until at least several weeks past the solstice, but even this coolness was unusual. Yellow flames crackled as he turned over some of the dry sticks he'd piled inside a circle of stones on the dirt floor.

A knock came at the door of the shed. Aster, of course. "Come in," Marin said. It was polite of Aster to knock, though Marin didn't think such formalities were really necessary out here in a shed.

The door cracked open and Aster's face peered in. "Evening."

Marin stood, setting down his fire stoker. "Aster. Good to see you again." And it *was* good to see him again—very good indeed.

Except as Aster stepped across the threshold and into the light of the shed, he looked tired. His eyes had a sad look to them they didn't have the night before. The first thought that flashed into Marin's head was that Ilth must have done something. "Are you unwell?" He hated to make such a personal remark when he still didn't know Aster, but he couldn't help himself. "You don't look so good."

Aster hesitated, then sighed. "Listen, do you have anything to eat?" He stepped closer, swinging his arms casually. "I'm sorry to trouble you for it, but I haven't eaten anything today."

Something protective surged up in Marin at that thought. "What?" He turned and went to a basket of fruit he'd collected earlier that afternoon. "Yes, here, have some fruit." He held the basket out, gesturing Aster toward the stool where he'd sat the night before. "Sit down."

"Thank you." Aster accepted the basket with one hand, grabbing for a pear with the other and biting into it. He sank into the stool.

Marin surveyed him, understanding exactly what happened. How often had he experienced the same thing?

"She sent you to bed without supper, didn't she?" he said. He felt a pang of anger at Ilth, then sympathy for Aster, then more anger at Ilth as he thought about it. He knew the gnawing ache he endured in his stomach when Ilth decided that going hungry would teach him a lesson. He knew how hard it was to complete his chores when was working on an empty stomach.

Aster nodded. "That wicked old shrew," he mumbled through bites of pear.

Marin kicked at some stray hay by his feet and paced across the shed. "What happened?" he asked.

Aster shrugged. "I just slept in was all. Not by much." The confession made Marin laugh, remembering how he himself had been tempted to sleep in that morning after he and Aster had been up talking half the night.

"But," Aster went on, "I was late to light the fires in the kitchen and in her spell room." He rolled his eyes. "I don't know why she even bothers having me light the fire in the spell room. It's been years since she's brewed a potion."

Years since she's brewed a potion. That caught Marin's attention. He sat down in the hay, suddenly intrigued. "Does she...does she actually practice witchcraft?" Ilth had often threatened him with magic if he disobeyed, but he'd never seen her perform any of it. How he'd lived in fear of it since he was a child!

"She used to," Aster said. "I haven't seen her really do anything in years."

Marin hesitated. Did he dare open up about this? "You know, she used to threaten to turn me to stone if I didn't obey her," he said. "When I was little."

He would always be able to hear her shrill tone and see the fury in her dark eyes. He couldn't even remember what he had done to upset her half the times she'd screamed at him, but he could always remember the way he cowered in fear—how he was ashamed of his timidity, throwing his quivering arms up in front of him as if they might be able to protect him from whatever it was she intended to do.

Stop flinching like that, you pathetic brat, she would scream when he would do that. *Take your punishment like a man. Worthless. Good for nothing.*

And when the job wasn't done to her satisfaction, she made it clear she wouldn't hesitate to hurt him. *If you disobey me, I'll make sure you regret it,* she warned. *You know what I'm capable of.*

There'd been the days when she refused to bring any meals to him out in his shed, of course, withholding meals as she had done to Aster on this day. Then there'd been the beatings—often with her cane, though sometimes with a leather strap.

And of course—though Marin had never been completely sure whether this had been Ilth or not—there had been the time when he was very little and he'd rescued an injured bird that had fallen from its nest and separated from its mother. Marin nursed the poor little creature back to health, feeling fiercely protective of it in a way that he always wished somebody had been able to be for him. "I won't let anyone hurt you," he'd told the bird. "I'm your friend, and you're mine."

Despite the strength the bird regained thanks to Marin's care, it suddenly died the next day and crumbled to dust right in Marin's hands. There was no way to know for sure whether it had been Ilth, but Marin never had any doubts.

Reflecting back on the memory, Marin stared at Aster. What would Ilth do if she found out they had met? That they were becoming friends?

Before he could think too much about it, Aster spoke. "How did you learn to work the field all by yourself?" He tucked the core of his pear away in the pocket of his tunic.

"Oh," Marin said, pushing his thoughts of Ilth away, "there were hired hands when I was very little. They would come by and show me what to do. I don't remember them very much."

The only thing he remembered was that they had always been kind to him.

"As soon as I could hold a tool, she dismissed them," Marin said. "They were also the ones who taught me how to read." He nodded toward the corner of his shed where his books stood stacked.

"You like to read?" Aster asked.

Marin felt a surge of excitement. "Aye, of course," he said. He jumped up and went to grab one of the books off the top of a stack, one of his favorites about a band of knights on a quest to rescue the king's daughter from a ferocious monster. He held the book out to Aster. "I read as much as I can. I want to know everything there is about the world, even if I'll never see it with my own eyes."

Aster accepted the book from Marin's outstretched hand and flipped it open. He traced his fingers across one of the illustrations. "Why don't you think you'll ever see the world?"

Marin shrugged. As if that question needed answering! "Well, because we're just servants," he said. "We'll never be anything more."

Aster nodded and gently closed the book. "Right."

Marin accepted the book back from Aster and returned it to its stack. All the wonders of the world written about in those books seemed exciting indeed, but it wasn't for the likes of him. Ilth had made him understand from a young age he wasn't cut out for such. *If you leave me, you'll never survive on your own*, she always said. *You're too weak to make your own decisions.*

Aster scooped a handful of nuts from the basket. "Thank you for the food. I was starving."

Marin hesitated, not reaching to take the basket back right away. "Did you have enough?" He wanted to make sure.

"Aye." Aster took the basket and held it out to Marin. "I don't want to eat all your food."

"I can take more from the garden tomorrow."

Upon hearing that, Aster paused. "I might have an apple if that's all right," he said, helping himself.

Marin laughed. "I'm glad you came out again," he said. "The only person I have to talk to during the day is Holdfast."

"Who?" Aster asked.

"The barn dog," Marin explained, going to the window to peep out at the yard.

"Do we need to worry about him?" Aster asked. "What if he catches us?"

Marin shook his head. "Don't worry, he sleeps in the barn," he said as he surveyed the dark yard, making out the shadowy form of the barn beside the vegetable fields. All was still and quiet. "And he never comes around my shed, especially not at night."

Aster shifted on his stool. "Ilth used to have a talking rat she kept in an iron cage," he said. "But then one day she killed it. Back when she was still practicing witchery. Drove a needle through its heart for one of her spells."

The thought made Marin's stomach lurch. "That's awful," he said. He couldn't help thinking of his bird. It must have been the same for Aster and this rat.

"I was little at the time," Aster said, though his tone suggested the memory still haunted him. "I remember how sad it was. Ilth burned it in the fireplace. I've never forgotten that."

Marin stepped away from the window and looked Aster up and down. Marin hated working out in the fields, doing hard labor under the blazing sun, enduring wind and weather day after day, but at least Ilth rarely came outside. "It must be terrible being inside with her all day," he said.

Aster swept a strand of his hair out of his face. "She keeps to herself mostly," he said. "And I'm always busy with chores." He stood, turning to stretch one arm in front of him, then the other. "Oh, my back is sore," he winced, giving a nervous laugh. "She had me scrub the floors today. I must've spent hours bent over on my hands and knees."

Marin nodded. "The life of a servant," he said in a sullen tone.

"I hate it," Aster said, twisting one arm up to massage his own shoulder.

"So do I."

"And you're sure you don't know how you came to be here on the farm?" Aster asked, sitting himself back down on the stool.

Marin grabbed his stick and prodded at the fire to give it a little more air. "I wish I did," he said. "I wish I knew something about myself."

Aster looked at him. "Say...you don't think we could be brothers, do you?"

Marin shrugged. Did they look anything alike? Maybe. A little bit. "I...I don't know," Marin replied. "I guess we could be."

"We really have no way of knowing," Aster said.

"No, but we could say we're brothers," Marin offered. "Just for the sake of it. Because we can."

It was a nice idea, having a brother. "What I mean is," Marin went on, "we might as well be brothers. Our situations are the same. We're both servants." He hesitated, then added, "And I don't have anyone else."

Aster smiled. "You're right. That's close enough."

Marin suddenly thought of something. "Come on," he said, standing and moving toward the door of the shed. "I want to show you something."

Aster got to his feet and followed. They slipped out into the open air of the yard, the cool clamminess of the night surprising Marin after sitting so close to the fire in his shed. He gestured for Aster to follow, leading him down the sloping hill toward the gate that looked out on the road. Moonlight illuminated the dirt track that cut its way along the fence in one direction, turned, and led off into darkness beyond.

"This is the farthest I've ever gone," Marin said, resting his hands on the fence pickets and staring at the road. "This fence marks the edge of the yard, and that road—well, that leads somewhere." He shrugged. "The hired hands used to arrive along this road every morning when I was little, and they would leave the same way."

Aster's eyes were wide. "Do you ever think about leaving here? Following along that road and seeing where it leads you?"

Marin balked, stepping back away from the fence at the thought. "It would be too dangerous," he said, shaking his head. "I should tell you about some of the things I've read about in my books. Fearsome beasts and malicious people who do you harm for money or clout." He faltered. "Don't get me wrong, there are also heroes who stand up for the poor and helpless, but they don't often have an easy time doing it," he said. "And you don't always know that they're going to succeed."

A look of something like disappointment crossed Aster's face. "I thought you wanted to see more of the world though."

"If only it weren't so dangerous," Marin said. Feeling a little embarrassed, he nodded at the road beyond the fence and shrugged. "I wanted you to see it." He stared around at the yard shadowed in darkness. "I wish you could come out here and see everything during the day."

Aster nodded. "So do I."

They walked back up the hill in silence, Marin quickly forgetting the feelings of self-consciousness that had overcome him the night before. When he and Aster said goodnight, he addressed him, "Brother?"

Aster nodded, smiling. "Brother."

CHAPTER 6

A s the summer wore on, and the long days wore the two servant boys ragged—Marin toiling in the fields and Aster trying desperately to keep the house clean despite the season's inevitable mustiness—they had agreed to meet only sporadically, at least until autumn came. As Marin had put it, "We need at least a few nights of good rest if we're going to do our chores the way we're supposed to."

That was Marin—always so responsible.

But on one particular night in late summer, Aster wasn't getting any sleep.

The oppressive heat hung in the air, and even by midnight, his garret bedroom had not lost the humid stuffiness built up during the day.

He sat up in his rickety cot and found himself staring at the trapdoor that led down to the hallway below. *I wonder if Marin's still awake. He probably is...I might as well go see what he's up to.*

Aster lifted his tunic and a pair of trousers from the crumpled heap where he left them on the floor and slipped them on. The tunic still had a sweaty dampness to it from when he'd scrubbed the pots and pans in the kitchen after cooking Ilth's dinner. At least it didn't smell of sweat, the way some of his clothes did before wash day.

Holding his breath so as not to make any noise, he crept down the ladder into the hallway below and padded his way along through the darkness.

In the kitchen, the dying embers of the fire left a soft orange gleam on surfaces around him. When he went out the door onto the porch, the orange embers gave way to silver moonlight that shone on the wide expanse of yard.

Now that he was outside, he could finally breathe. No matter how many times he snuck out of the house, it never got any less worrisome. He stared around, taking in the expanse of the vast sky overhead with the twinkling stars and glowing moon. The grandeur of it still hadn't worn off after so many weeks—he could still remember how much it had overwhelmed him the first time he'd crept out the kitchen door and stood there on that porch, looking at the outside world for the first time after so many years of only seeing it through a crack in a boarded-up window.

Life was so different now than it had been before he and Marin had met. There was a world outside the decrepit cottage, even if he had not seen any of it beyond the yard. It was an outside world where he had a friend.

Let's hope that friends of yours is still awake, he thought. *You agreed you wouldn't visit tonight. You agreed you both needed rest.*

He made his way across the grass, feeling the freshness of the air on his face, listening to the chirp of crickets that welcomed him, almost saying, "We knew you would make it here tonight. We knew you would come."

Light shone from the window of Marin's shed. Aster approached the door and leaned his face up against it. "Marin," he whispered. "You up?"

He lifted the latch to let himself in, revealing Marin reclined on his straw bed, propped on one elbow, reading a book by the light of a flickering candle.

Marin looked up. "Wouldn't you know it. I had a feeling I'd see you tonight."

Aster shrugged and stepped over the threshold. "Sorry. I couldn't sleep."

Marin closed his book. "Neither could I. What's bothering you?"

Aster bit his lip, unsure of where to start. "What's *not* bothering me is the better question," he said.

"What happened?" Marin asked.

And that was it. Aster heaved. "Oh, I hate her so much!"

Marin picked himself up from the straw and moved to seat himself on the nearby stool. "Come on. Talk."

"I can't deal with it anymore, Marin." Aster moved closer. "I mean, can you? We don't deserve this."

Marin shrugged. "That's good to know. I'll send a message to the gods and let them know what I've gotten in life is unfair."

Aster huffed. "Don't philosophize, Marin. Not tonight." He vaguely knew the pantheon of the ancient ways, full of gods who mercilessly used mortals for their amusement, putting them through suffering and torment at a whim.

Marin shrugged. "Well, it's true, isn't it? I mean, who's to say that one person deserves misery and another person deserves joy? And besides, who's to say that we don't deserve this?"

"Don't say that." Aster leaned against the wall. They didn't deserve this. They didn't. Unless the cruelty of the gods went far beyond what either he or Marin could imagine.

"All right." Marin got up again and reached for a basket of fruit and nuts. "Hungry?"

Aster accepted an apple and bit into it. His aggressive chewing sent flecks of juice spraying in all directions. "That's just the thing. She told me we *did* deserve it—or that I deserve it, at least. I'm sure if she had any inkling we knew about each other, she would have told me you deserve it too."

Marin stared intently at one of the flickering candles. He drew a breath to say something, hesitated, then exhaled and sat quiet instead.

When Marin didn't reply, Aster raised his half-eaten apple. "Did you pick these yesterday?"

That got Marin's attention. "Aye, I did. Why?"

"Deliver them to the kitchen last night?"

Marin nodded.

"I thought so. These were the apples she wanted me to make for dinner. She demanded a galette stuffed with roasted apples and caramelized onions. Not an easy thing to make, mind you." Aster took another bite and continued to rant as he chewed. "She said it was dry. I didn't expect her praise, of course, but she took one bite and sneered, 'Oh, it's dry.' So, she demanded I make it again. And while I did, she sat there and continued to eat the first one I made.

"'You're so worthless,' she kept muttering the whole time. 'Can't get a simple recipe right. What a good-for-nothing, lazy, hopeless little sloth you are. This pastry is dry—it's completely dry. You'll never amount to anything.'"

Marin shook his head. "I'm sorry."

"She ate the whole cursed thing while I made the second one." Aster shook his head at the absurdity of it. "She stood up and said, 'You took too long. I'll just have to go to bed without a proper supper.' And just like that, she wiped her crumbs onto the kitchen floor—which I had just scrubbed a few hours before—and sneered, 'Clean it up.' Can you believe that?"

Marin sat still. "Of course, I can believe it. I guess that makes two of us she's wronged in the past day."

Aster winced. "What did she do to you?"

"These apples, actually," Marin said. "I was carting them back from the orchard, and I had overloaded my baskets with too many of them, and that old wheelbarrow is wobbly when there's too much weight on it."

Marin's face twisted up as he reflected on the memory. "Anyway," he went on. "I was coming down the hill back to the yard, and I lost control of the cart. It tipped over, and apples spilled everywhere. Before I could even start picking them up, I heard this awful laughter, and Ilth was standing on the other side of the yard, cackling uncontrollably. 'Clumsy, clumsy, clumsy,' she shouted at me. 'I hope none of those apples is bruised.'"

Aster's jaw dropped. "She was just standing there, waiting for a reason to taunt you?"

"I was so angry, Aster. I stood right up and shouted at her, 'Why don't you make yourself useful and come help me pick them up instead of standing there laughing?'"

"You didn't!" Aster gasped. "Did you really?"

Marin nodded.

"Good for you! But Marin, what's gotten into you?" It wasn't like Marin to be so audacious.

Marin raised trembling hands. "I don't know. I was so angry, and it was almost as if I didn't care. I didn't care whether I made her angrier, or if she even tried to punish me. I just wanted to shut her up and stop her laughing."

"So, what did she say?"

"Well, she did shut up and stop laughing, and she just stared at me for a heated second. I'll honestly admit that I was scared right after I'd said it because I didn't know what she would say. She just looked at me and said, 'Don't you forget your place, boy. Do you really mean to speak to me like that?'"

Aster huffed. "That rotten shrew."

Marin fidgeted, kicking his legs out in front of him. "As if either of us could forget our place."

With that, a tension as thick and heavy as the humidity in the air hung between them. Aster got to his feet and paced across the shed. "I'm sick of it." He threw his hands up. "I just can't take one more day of this, the same degradation, the same sense of hopelessness, day after day. There's got to be something better."

Marin shook his head and leaned up against the wall. "I don't think that's written in the stars for us, brother."

Aster stopped. *I don't think that's written in the stars...* It hit him like a punch to the stomach. "You don't actually believe that do you?"

Marin's brow furrowed. "Believe what?" He hadn't even realized the profoundness of what he said.

"That our life is...preordained," Aster said. "And written in the stars like some sort of story we just live out. That destiny controls everything that happens to us."

Marin ran his hand through his hair. "Well, no. No, I guess I don't, but you know what I—"

"Because I don't." Aster's suddenly confident tone made Marin sit up straighter. "I don't believe that." He moved closer to Marin, and his excited energy must have been palpable because Marin shrank back.

"Marin, if we don't do something to change this situation, it's our own fault. You know? It's got nothing to do with the stars. With firelights burning away in the heavens. It's up to us."

Marin looked rigid. "Come on, Aster."

"Marin, you need to change something," Aster insisted. "Look at how this life is destroying you."

CHAPTER 7

Aster was right, and there was no denying it.

How many nights had Marin lain awake and just wished that there were something else waiting for him in this life? How many times had he hoped that the farm and Ilth would simply disappear, and there'd be some new opportunity where he was admired and respected, and where he was happy? Where a humble orphaned servant boy could make something of himself. Become a knight or a prince, just like in the stories of old.

Aster sat down next to him. "Why do you think she never told us about each other, huh? Why do you think she kept us apart?"

Marin had spent weeks asking himself that exact question. "Uh…"

"Marin, look—why have you never tried to run away?"

What a stupid question! "Because." Marin said. "Well, because there's no assurance the outside world will be any better or more merciful than this farm." He had never actually referred to everything far away from Ilth's farm as "the outside world" aloud before, but it was how he felt. "At least here is safe," he added.

"I know," Aster said. "And that's the same reason I've never run away either. But look—there's two of us now, and we can count on each other. The two of us might be able to get away with some things that only one of us alone couldn't."

Marin's heart skipped. If Aster were actually willing to do this…if he knew Aster would be there alongside him…

"You're being serious?" he said.

"Yes." Aster scooted closer. "Look, I don't think our future is written out in the stars. If I had to compare it to anything, I'd say it's more like a vast ocean, and we have to set sail when the tide is in our favor."

How long had Marin been thinking that same thing? Marin had heard both those metaphors in one of the books he read. Maybe it had been verses or a play about an ancient political revolt. The men behind it could not decide how much they owed to fate and how much to free will. Was life written in the stars, or was it a tide they needed to set sail on and navigate?

There were so many aspects of life that were out of his control— would always be out of his control. But staying on Ilth's farm was different. Aster was right—they had the choice to leave. And now that there were two of them, and they could stick together….

It's not as scary to think about.

"This is our chance," Marin said. "That's what you're saying? You think the tide is in our favor?"

"If we don't take advantage of it now," Aster said, "we'll be stuck here forever. You know, like we're docked here in shallow water. I don't want that."

"Neither do I."

They both stared at each other. Marin couldn't figure out what he wanted to say next.

"Who knows when she's going to find out that we know about each other?" Aster said. "You know it'll happen eventually. And when she does, she'll do something to keep us apart. We'll lose our chance of ever getting out of here if we wait too long."

Marin nodded. "Where would we go? And what would we do with ourselves?"

"I don't know," Aster replied. "That's the great thing about it. We could do anything and everything. We could leave tonight if we wanted. Run away to the city and seek our fortunes there."

Excitement washed over Marin. "You're serious? You would really do this?"

"Why not?"

Marin climbed to his feet, trembling. "All right. All right, we'll do this. But not tonight." He started to pace. "We can't go spoiling our one chance at freedom by being reckless. We need to plan. And we'll need to pack—food, money, clothes."

Aster nodded. "Give me a week and I'll steal what I can from around the house."

"No stealing," Marin said. "You've read the ancient scriptures, haven't you? Stealing's depraved and heaven frowns on it."

He looked behind him at some of the well-worn leatherbound volumes stacked among his collection of books. He hadn't read all of them cover to cover, but he'd read enough. "Ilth threw those scriptures out like they were trash, but...but I don't want to stoop to being the person Ilth is. If we're going to do this, we're going to do it right."

"Aye, but we're entitled to something, aren't we?" Aster said. "After so many years of working for her, at least some of what's in her home has to be considered ours."

Marin couldn't deny that. "You're right." He paused, trying to collect his thoughts. It was all happening so fast. So fast. "You're right," he repeated. "We'll take what we deserve, but no more than what we need. And not a week—we can't take that long. She might start to catch on."

"I can scrounge up some money tomorrow," Aster said. "You just need to pack up some clothes and whatever you want to take with you, and we'll leave at midnight."

Tomorrow night? That soon? Marin stammered. "I..."

"Marin, you don't have doubts, do you?"

How could Marin have doubts when the two of them were in this together? Whatever happened, he wasn't going to be doing it alone. That gave him all the strength he needed. "No...no, I don't."

"Good."

They sat still, soaking in the realization of what they agreed to do. Then came their laughter—Marin first, then Aster.

"Well," Aster said at last. "I, uh...I ought to get to bed. So should you."

"Yes."

Aster stood. "I feel much better now."

Marin climbed to his feet, ready to follow Aster out. "So do I. And maybe—maybe it's wrong of me, but I'm really proud of us."

Aster stopped in the doorway. "Aye, same. No regrets at all."

Marin could hardly believe it. Only another day and they would be gone from this place. "Goodnight, brother," he said.

"Goodnight, brother," Aster said, and he slipped out into the dark.

Then it was just Marin and his nerves. His deep fears that told him this wasn't possible, that they'd never succeed. That they would be caught by Ilth and she'd make their lives even more miserable than they already were.

And if they did succeed? On the chance that they did make a successful getaway? What waited for them in the wide world away from the farm? Would they starve or get hurt? Would they find themselves at the mercy of the wild animals that lived in the woods, or dangerous gangs that patrolled the roads?

"Stop," he whispered to himself. "Stop worrying. You two will be together. By yourself, you might not be cut out for the adventure. But together, you two are unstoppable."

He hoped that was the truth. He hoped. But there was no way of really knowing, was there?

CHAPTER 8

Elspeth stretched and stared up from the depth of the pit.

The goblins would come for them soon. The sky over the pit had taken on a hazy grayness, telling her that sunrise was imminent. Another day.

How long has it been now? She'd lost track of the days, of the weeks.

"Why has nobody come to rescue us?" she whispered.

She glanced over at Carys, asleep on the other side of the pit. Her sister lay curled with her knees tucked close to her chest, her body gently rising and falling with each breath.

Carys. Brave and fierce and fiery. At least, that's how she used to be—her courage had started to wane. Too much time in captivity. Too much fear of their goblin captors.

"You've got to stay brave for both of us," Elspeth said. "Please stay brave, Carys. I need you to stay brave."

Elspeth might have been the crown princess and heiress to the throne, the one possessed with renowned beauty and learned in all the courtly manners, but Carys had always been her strength. Carys, who could wield a sword better than any boy, and who never hesitated to speak her mind, even when it would have made the maidservants gasp, chastise her, and remind her of propriety.

How innocent and different they had been before the goblins took them as prisoners.

Innocent as flowers, we were, Elspeth thought when she remembered it. Innocent, and as beautiful. And as vulnerable—as easily snatched up and carried away as one of the wild irryliann blossoms that grew on the hillside.

That terrible afternoon had come back to her just last night, in one of the vivid dreams she was so prone to. Everything about the dream had been so real, so lifelike. Just as the dreams always were. The warmth of the summer air, scented with all the fragrances of nature. The clear sky, with the sun blazing bright. Only a few clouds drifted languidly across the expanse of blue overhead as their coach bounced up and down across the open field of green below.

"Oh, Elspeth, what a mission that was," Carys had been saying.

They were on their way back from bestowing their blessings on a coven of sorceresses—it was one of their royal duties as princesses of Blunia, and although Elspeth had been doing such missions for years now as part of her royal training, this was the first time Carys, who was only a year younger, had been sent to join her.

"Yes, it was, Carys," Elspeth said, folding her hands gently in her lap. Her tone was encouraging but formal. When they were alone together at their father's palace, they could be sisters, but here in their coach, where they were attended by a maidservant each, it was important to remember their royal station. Carys forgot that sometimes, and Elspeth always had to set an example.

"Will we go again soon?" Carys asked, pushing her brown tresses behind her ears so they didn't hang in her face. No matter how much care the maidservants took in preparing Carys for her courtly duties, she never managed to stay tidy for long. "When's the next one?"

"The work of royalty is never done," Elspeth said. It was a reply she had been taught by one of her royal tutors. "Yes, we will go again.

We will have to ask Father what mission we must do next. It is up to his wisdom." Again, a rehearsed reply. In private, Elspeth had often urged her royal father to let her have say in matters of politics. She could make a difference in the kingdom if he let her, she knew.

"I truly wish you could decide for yourself," Carys said. "I truly do. When you're queen, won't you be able to decide your own missions?"

"Yes, of course," Elspeth said.

When she was queen. Oh, but for all she understood of politics and leadership, there was always more—and there was still so much for her to learn before she became queen. *If* she ever became queen.

"But don't ask senseless questions, Carys," she continued. "You know I won't be queen for many years. I'm still so young, and Father is strong and healthy. He'll rule for many years before I will need to take the throne."

She would be the first woman to inherit the throne of Blunia. Sometimes—though Elspeth would never admit it to anyone, not even to Carys, whom she told everything to—her father didn't treat her the way he should treat his heiress.

Of course, their royal father always dictated certain responsibilities to her, such as the one she and Carys undertook now, and Elspeth always took pride in the work she did. But he never talked to her about politics, or relations with other kingdoms in Monte Prospera, or included her in his councils with his advisers.

Kind and jovial and magnanimous though her father was, it was almost as if he wasn't ready to prepare his little girl to rule a kingdom.

Except Elspeth was not a little girl. She was nearly a woman grown—the crown princess with golden hair and sapphire eyes. *Yes, they all know I'm beautiful,* Elspeth often thought. *But it'll take more than beauty to rule a kingdom.*

At tourneys and jousts, all the brave knights asked to be her champion. She knew it was only another year or two before princes from far-off kingdoms would come asking for her hand in marriage. They would be handsome, no doubt. But she would need more than handsomeness in a groom if he were going to make a suitable king to rule beside her.

"When Father is ready to step down and retire," Elspeth continued, "I'll take on the royal duties of the throne."

"Well, of course, I know that," Carys replied. "You don't always have to be such a know-it-all."

Elspeth smiled. She glanced at their maidservants. Old Nynce was pursing her lips in disapproval. Lady Luce shot dagger eyes at Carys. How long would it take them to learn there was no suppressing Princess Carys of Blunia?

A shout came from outside, and the coach suddenly shook violently. Elspeth's stomach lurched and a shriek escaped her lips. Startled, she reached for Old Nynce's arm. The matronly maidservant instinctively threw one arm around Elspeth, her other hand going to her breast in fear.

Carys slid across the velvet upholstery of the coach's seat and threw back the curtain that covered the window, then leaned her head out. When she turned back, she had a panicked expression such as Elspeth had never seen.

"Goblins!" she shouted. "There are goblins!"

Everything happened so fast after that. The sound of screams and growls filled the air outside, the clang of steel swords striking. The carriage shook, veering back and forth as if the horses were scared or the driver had lost control of the reins.

Goblins! Carys's startled voice echoed in Elspeth's mind. They'd heard rumors of the goblins that lived in the wastelands on the outskirts of the forest, but no goblin had ever been seen in the fields or villages surrounding their father's kingdom. Did Carys even really know what a goblin looked like? They had seen illustrations of them in the history books they read with the royal tutors, though maybe Carys was mistaken.

But Elspeth knew deep down Carys wasn't mistaken.

Elspeth pushed herself close to the window to get a look for herself, and Old Nynce pulled her back. "Don't, your highness," she shouted. "It's too dangerous."

"I—"

Before Elspeth could respond, the carriage lurched. Elspeth flew forward, striking the opposite wall, along with Carys and their maid-servants. The sound of chaos raged outside, though the carriage was suddenly still. They had crashed.

Carys's hand closed around Elspeth's. "Come on, Elspeth! We can't stay here!"

"Carys!"

Elspeth got to her feet. Her sister already had a hand on the latch to the carriage door. "Elspeth, we have to make a run for it."

This is serious—we're in danger, Elspeth thought. She couldn't tell whether it was the crash or her fear that made her lightheaded, that made it seem as if the carriage were spinning.

She looked at their maidservants, both of whom were frozen with fear. Their years of doting on and caring for princesses had not prepared them to deal with this danger.

"Come," Elspeth said to them. "You have to come with us!"

Carys pushed open the door to the coach and Elspeth followed her into the open air. A battle raged in the fields around them. Every one of the knights who had been riding guard alongside their carriage fought a twisted miscreant with green scales. Swords and armor threw darts of sunlight as they moved around. Bodies of injured knights—*or were they dead?*—littered the ground beside equal numbers of conquered goblins. Brownish-red blood streaked the grass, along with discarded swords and spears and shields. Elspeth screamed.

"Protect the princesses!" one of the knights shouted.

But the next thing Elspeth knew, sharp claws gripped her shoulders from behind and threw her down on the grass. A scratchy burlap sack swept over her head, throwing her into darkness, while those same sharp claws wrestled her arms behind her back.

Oh, gods, what's happening?

She screamed. She jerked at her arms, trying to pull free, but the claws were too strong. Pain erupted across her arm as they scratched at her, followed by the warm stickiness of her own blood pouring all over her skin.

That was when everything went dark and she lost consciousness.

Elspeth revived in a haze, her senses waking slightly ahead of her mind. She blinked, letting her eyes adjust to the dark. Her entire body ached with pain. The air held a bitter chill to it, and it smelled of blood and rot and sweat and mold.

She shifted and pushed herself up. Moving sent pain through her body. She drew a deep breath, trying to suppress the agony.

Had she been knocked unconscious because of a blow to the head? Or had she simply passed out from fright? She had no memory of how she came to be in this place of darkness.

She padded around in the dark. Cold stone underneath her led to a cold stone wall nearby. Elspeth climbed to her feet, taking in what shapes she could see in the dark. She was in some kind of pit—and Carys was there, lying nearby in a crumpled pile on the floor.

"Carys!" she shouted, going to her. "Carys!"

Dark splotches covered Carys's dress. Blood? Or just muck? Elspeth dropped to her knees beside her sister. "Carys! Are you all right?"

No. Neither of them would be all right for a long time to come.

Elspeth couldn't even figure out what her intention had been in waking her. *Was I just trying to make sure she wasn't dead? Or was I so scared that I needed her awake beside me, to share in my fear?* Elspeth had been so driven by impulse at the time that she wasn't sure. But now Carys was just as upset as she.

Elspeth and Carys spent the rest of the night crying and holding each other until morning. The slow lightening of dawn revealed their surroundings in more detail—the stone wall of the pit circling around them, the crisscrossed ironwork covering the mouth of their prison, the grimy stairs that led to the floor of the pit from the entry up above.

Before it was fully daybreak, a lumbering foreman of a goblin descended into their captivity pit, a long spear gripped in his claw.

"Well, well, well," he grumbled as he reached the foot of the stairs and approached the girls. "Awake, are ye?"

All the breath went out of Elspeth's chest at the sight of the brute's green-scaled face and hunched form. Yellowish pus oozed out from between his scales.

She choked on the scream caught in her chest. Carys's fingers dug into her arm as she clung to her.

The goblin threw back his head and laughed at their fear. His laughter was joined by others as well. In the gray haze of morning at the top of the pit, a crowd of twisted figures looked down, all of them roaring with cruel guffaws.

Now was the time to be brave. Elspeth drew a deep breath. "I demand you release us," she said, shaking Carys off and climbing to her feet.

Make eye contact with him, she told herself. *You are a princess, and you do not shrink away in fear.*

She stared into his orange eyes. "Do you know who we are?"

The goblin thrust his claw across her face, backhanding her. The force sent her stumbling. She steadied herself, trying to regain her footing. The skin of her cheek burned where the goblin's scaly hide had scratched it. She wouldn't let him see her cry.

"A forthright little wench, you are, aren't you?" the goblin snapped.

"Oh, yes, we know who you are. You're the daughters of King Hector. And you're our prisoners now."

You're our prisoners now.

And prisoners they had been ever since. Elspeth tried to push the memory to the back of her mind as she stared up at the bars over their prison pit. Her body trembled as she let out a stifled breath. She reached out a hand to touch the wall beside her and steady herself. Her fingers landed on cold stone.

Holding her breath, she waited, anxiously expecting the sound of heavy footsteps from above. Nothing yet. Nothing but overwhelming quiet.

"Elspeth?" Carys's voice startled her, and she jumped.

"Carys. Don't scare me like that."

Carys appeared as nothing more than a shadow moving around in the dark. She pushed herself to her knees and crawled closer. "Are the goblins coming?"

"Not yet, I don't think. But they'll be here soon. It's almost morning."

She drew another stifled breath. She couldn't let her fear show— not to Carys, and not to the goblins. She was the future queen of Blunia.

"Elspeth?" Carys whispered. "Somebody will come to rescue us, won't they?"

It was the first time either of them had spoken out loud what Elspeth had been asking herself for weeks.

CHAPTER 9

The green fields glowed beneath the setting sun. Marin leaned on his scythe. It was almost as if the clouds rolling gently across the sky and the cornfields blowing gently in the breeze were saying goodbye to him.

Just think. You never have to see this field again.

The prospect almost made him a little sad. He hated the fields, and his little ramshackle shed, and the barn with the rude two-headed cow. Every day throughout his life, they had beaten him down a little bit more, drained the energy from him, pushed him to the brink of despair.

Still, they were all he had ever known. They were home. They were comfortable in their own terrible way.

And the sunset was beautiful. But there would be other sunsets, and there would be other places to explore that would soon come to feel like home. A warmer home. A better home.

He just had to find the courage to leave it all.

"Only a few more hours," he whispered to himself out loud. He had to say it out loud to make it real. "Only a few more hours and you're moving on to a better life."

At least, he hoped it would be a better life. At least, it would be a life where he might be more than just a lowly servant, a meaningless little nobody.

Those hours passed by quickly. He carried the grain to the mill and the vegetables to the kitchen. By the time he got back to his shed, it was completely dark. He lit the lanterns for light as he readied his pack, then sat, watching through the door of the shed until the lights in the house went out.

The boarded-up windows gave little indication of what was going on in the house, but in the dark of night he could always see the glow around the edges that signified a candle or lamp was burning inside. When those lights were gone, the house was nothing more than a dark shadow up on the hill.

With one last tug to ensure his pack was secure, he extinguished his own lanterns and slipped out into the yard. The song of crickets and frogs filled the air as his shoes pounded up the sloping grass.

He paused on the porch outside the kitchen door to catch his breath and let his heart slow a little. He hadn't realized how nervous and eager he was.

With a jittery hand, he reached forward to undo the latch and ease the kitchen door open.

It took a moment for his eyes to adjust to the darkness inside. The moonlight streaming through the door behind him caught the edges of the silhouetted shapes in the kitchen—the cauldron, the butcher's block, the hearth.

The door to the hallway creaked open. Aster's shadowed face peeked in. "Are you ready?" he whispered.

"I've been ready for this for years," Marin replied.

Aster stepped into the kitchen and closed the door behind him. A pack hung over his left shoulder. "Good."

He sidled across the room toward one of the cabinets. "Let me see what there might be for us to take."

"Aster," Marin whispered. "Remember—we're not stealing anything."

"Just some food," Aster whispered back. "There's no harm in that, is there?" He opened the cabinet door and reached inside. "Whatever we steal, it's the crops you've grown and the bread that I've baked."

Marin swallowed. "Aye."

Aster knelt to examine a lower shelf. "Bring me that candle, won't you?" He turned and gestured toward the mantel above the hearth.

Marin scooted over and grabbed a candle standing in a pewter stick. The coolness of the metal shocked his sweaty palm when he touched it. He gripped tightly, suddenly aware he might drop it and create such a clatter that Ilth would wake up, no doubt about it.

With his spare hand, he grabbed a box of matches nearby.

"Here." He crept over to Aster and set the candle down on the floor, lit it, and shook his hand to extinguish the match.

Aster, down on all fours, turned back to pull the candle closer to the cabinet. "This is where Ilth keeps the ingredients for her potions." He leaned forward again and reached toward the shadowy pile of clutter on the bottom of the cabinet. "I'm not allowed in here."

Not allowed. Marin didn't like the sound of that. Forbidden witchy things usually led nowhere good. "Uh, Aster…"

"Don't say anything," Aster added before Marin could express any reservation. "You know you're curious about what's in here too. Besides, we might find something that'll come in handy when we're out on our own. You want to be prepared, don't you? Or don't you?" Aster picked up the candle and held it inside the cabinet. The glow illuminated rows of bottles, all different shapes and sizes, jars and boxes, and other odd containers. "Would you look at this?" He extended his arm to reach deep into the cabinet to the way back of the shelf, pulling out a small burlap sachet. By the dim flicker of the candle, Marin could make out loopy script on the label tied to the drawstring. "Fairy Dust."

Fairy dust? Marin had read about the substance in his books, but he never thought he would come across it. It was supposed to be very rare, something that only the most experienced of human magicians knew how to manipulate. To think that it was right here in their possession!

Aster undid the twine and opened the pouch. The candlelight shone on fine white powder inside.

"I'm sure something like that cost her a fine price at market," Marin said.

Aster huffed. "Then what's Ilth doing owning it? Stingy old harpy." He held up the pouch, eyeing its size. There wasn't much—the bag was only about the size of his fist—but there was enough to think such an amount would cost a considerable sum if it were truly valuable. "We should still take it with us though," Aster said.

"Do you know how to use fairy dust?"

"Of course not." Aster retied the twine tightly around the mouth of the pouch. "But it might prove useful anyway, right?"

"I guess."

Aster stood, carrying the candle and pouch of fairy dust to the table. Setting them down, he swung off the strap of his pack and opened it up to put the fairy dust inside.

Creak!

The sound came from the hallway just outside the kitchen.

Marin's blood ran cold. He looked at Aster, whose eyes were so wide they shone in the candlelight. Neither of them breathed. The air in the kitchen became unbearably heavy.

The unmistakable sound of footsteps approached—Ilth's hobbling walk moving over the floorboards with aggressive languidness.

Aster tossed the pouch into his pack and stood, kicking his pack under the table and out of sight as he moved. "The cellar. Quick!"

Marin slid across the kitchen in the dark and fumbled in the shadows for the cellar door. It swung open easily. He padded down two or three steps, leaving the door ajar only so much that he could see what was happening in the kitchen.

Ilth appeared in the doorway, looking especially old and bent and haggard. Light from the hall shone behind her. She must have already lit an oil lamp.

"Aster," she barked. Despite the shadows, Marin could still see enough of her expression to recognize the furrowing of her brow she always made when irritated.

"Yes, ma'am?"

Aster set his candle on the table. Something about his attitude was different—he lost his usual pluck in the presence of Ilth. Marin had never seen him be meek like this.

"What are you doing awake at this hour?" Ilth still stood framed in the doorway, but her gaze bore into Aster, threatening, menacing. Even at nearly a foot shorter than either of them, she still carried a domineering presence. Marin suddenly hated himself for being so afraid of her when she was a wretched, feeble old woman.

"I couldn't sleep." Aster gave nothing away. He stayed cool and calm, whereas Marin, hidden in the shadows of the cellar stairs, thought he was going to choke on his own heartbeat.

"Couldn't sleep?"

"No, ma'am." Aster faltered a little, almost as if he were about to lose his nerve—almost, but not quite. "And, uh, I came down to get the kitchen in order. It will make tomorrow's chores easier if everything is ready to go when I get up."

Ilth didn't reply right away. The silence in the room was oppressive, deafening, heavy with fear and uncertainty. Ilth cocked her head as if Aster were something strange and foreign to her that she needed to make sense of. "Getting the kitchen in order, you say?"

"Yes, ma'am." Aster turned away from her, grabbed a nearby rag, and started to wipe down the butcher's block next to him.

"I don't want you moving about the house this late at night, boy. Doing tomorrow's work tonight? Tell me what you're really doing."

Aster turned back to her. "Exactly what I told you, ma'am."

Ilth opened her mouth as if she were going to say something, then paused. After what felt like forever, she spoke. "I would like a fire in my room tonight."

"A fire?" Aster said. "But, ma'am, it's the middle of summer. It's sweltering hot."

"All the same, I would like a fire, boy. I said I wanted a fire, and it is your job to obey, not to advise me."

Aster hesitated.

"Come now," Ilth said. "Get some of the firewood and bring it up to my room. I'll not ask again."

Aster sidled over to the hearth and lifted three or four logs in his arms. He didn't even look toward the cellar, instead casting his eyes down as he obeyed Ilth and hurried out of the room.

Marin held his breath. Would Ilth search the kitchen? How assuredly did she suspect something was amiss? Did she have some way of knowing he was in the cellar?

She traced the room once with her eyes after Aster was gone. With a heavy sigh and a shake of her head, she turned to go, pulling the door closed behind her.

CHAPTER 10

Silence and stillness. Marin could see the outline of objects in the dark kitchen steeped in shadow. He waited only a few minutes before he crept out from the cellar stairs and back out the kitchen door into the open air of the yard.

He started to run and didn't stop until he got to his shed and collapsed onto his bed of hay.

It was all ruined. There was no way they could risk running away again, not after a close call like that. Marin lay in his scratchy bed, staring up at the crisscrossing beams that formed the shed's roof. Never before that night had he paid such close attention to those beams. He had always been so tired at the end of the day that he fell asleep as soon as he had lain down.

But there they were now. He stared at them. He rolled over onto his side, wishing sleep would come. Sleep and forgetfulness of what had just happened. Maybe in the morning, he would wake up and realize it had all been a terrible dream, that Ilth still wasn't aware he and Aster knew each other, and they could go on being brothers without fear of any repercussion.

Daybreak came both too soon and too slowly after a night of tossing and turning. When the first traces of light appeared outside the window to the shed, before the roosters even began to crow, Marin pulled himself to his feet and stretched.

The chores dragged on that morning—milking Prunella and delivering the previous day's vegetables, then tending to the fields and carrying grain to the mill.

By midday, blazing summer sun bore down on him as he was plucking ears of corn off the stalks. Sweat poured down his face while his mind buzzed. The stagnant air of humid summer sent only an occasional gentle breeze across the fields, rustling the cornstalks ever so slightly; besides that, the fields stood so quiet and peaceful that the stillness overwhelmed him. It left too much room for his thoughts and fears.

Ilth knew! She knew! Marin wiped a dribble of perspiration from his brow and tore another ear from the stalk, then dropped it into his basket. *Ilth knew last night, and she knows this morning, and now everything is ruined.*

The one bit of happiness Marin had managed to eke out in this miserable existence—his friendship with Aster and their hopes of escape—was all over.

All he could expect from life was just endless days of drudgery and labor, cruel words from Ilth, and the hopeless reality that he would never amount to anything in the world. He would grow to be an old man who never accomplished anything more than farm chores, and he would probably die without making any impact on the world. *That's just the life that you're meant to live. Nothing you can do to change it.*

"Marin!"

It was Aster's voice. Marin looked up, his heart jumping.

Aster came running through the tall grass in his direction, looking completely carefree despite the audacity of what he was doing.

"Aster!" Marin exclaimed. "What in the world?"

"We have to talk," Aster slowed as he came close, casually rolling up the sleeves of his tunic and looking as if there were nothing unusual about his being out there.

"Aster…" Marin faltered. "Are you—are you out of your mind?"

Aster shook his head. "Don't worry. She has me locked in the cellar. She thinks I'm scouring pots and pans down there."

"How did you get out?"

"There's a loose panel where I could get between the walls and shimmy up and out," Aster said. "It's how the squirrels and mice get into the house in the winter, I think."

"If she catches you out here, she'll whip both of us."

Aster's face rumpled, almost as if he were disappointed by Marin's reply. "Don't worry, she won't. You can't see the cornfield from the house. Unless she comes out into the yard—"

"Which she might!" Marin said.

"And then we can fight her," Aster insisted. "She's a little old woman."

"She's a *witch*! Don't you understand, Aster? We don't know *what* she's capable of doing if she really wanted to."

Aster took Marin by the shoulder and eased him down below the tops of the cornstalks where he would be out of sight. Aster knelt beside him. "Better? Now she can't see us."

"She'll beat us bloody."

"Then just listen and we can get this over with faster," Aster said. "We're trying again tonight."

"No," Marin said. He had to be realistic. "It's too risky."

"Trust me on this," Aster said. He put his hands on Marin's shoulders and looked him in the eye. "Won't you? Believe me, we can make this work."

Marin wanted to believe that—he wanted so badly to believe it.

Aster stood, taking a deep breath. "Don't come to the house this time. I'll sneak out—it'll be easier that way, and it's what we should have done from the start. I'll meet you at the gate at midnight."

"Aster…"

"Marin, I'm not giving up," Aster said. Marin could see the desperation in his expression. His wide eyes held so much hope. Marin recognized what hope was. He felt it himself yesterday. "I'm not staying here," Aster went on. "You said it yourself—you're sick of this place. If we wait too long, she might get even more suspicious, and who knows what she'll do then. She's been eyeing me all morning like she knows something's up."

"That's exactly why we are better off just forgetting the whole plan and letting everything go back to normal." An ear of corn lay in the dirt nearby, one that Marin must have dropped when he was tossing it into the basket. He reached for it, picked it up, and tossed it onto the pile.

"Back to normal, huh?" Aster said. "So, we just remain servants forever?"

"Yes."

"No, Marin, that's not right." Aster sat down next to Marin. A second ago, he had been set on going back to the house. *He's not going to leave unless you agree to this plan.* The stubbornness of him! The stubbornness and the recklessness!

Do you really think I want to remain a servant? Marin wanted to ask, but he couldn't bring himself to say it. He knew the answer. It was why Aster was being so persistent. Aster was doing this because he knew exactly what was going on in Marin's mind.

Marin climbed to his feet and reached for an ear of corn on the stalk. Aster grabbed his arm. "You're worth more than this," Aster said. "You deserve more than spending your whole life tending crops for some withered old hag."

Marin gritted his teeth, trying to hold back tears. His whole life. Tending crops. For some withered old hag. He hated the way that sounded. "But…"

He stopped. He didn't know what to say. *It's like we said the other night,* he thought. *We have to set sail when the tide is in our favor. If not, then we will be stuck here where there's no hope for anything better.*

"We were so close last night," Aster said.

So close! Yes, they had been. If only they had slipped out a little bit earlier and Ilth had not come into the kitchen. She had to sleep at some point. There was no way they would make the same mistakes again.

"Fine," Marin said. And once he said it, that energy started to come back to him. "Yes. Yes, we can do this."

"Good!" Aster's smile lit up his face. "That's the spirit. I knew you had it in you."

"Midnight? At the gate?" Marin asked. They had to wrap up this meeting fast. For all they knew, Ilth might be going into the cellar and finding it empty, no sign of Aster anywhere.

"Yes, at the gate," Aster said.

"I'll be there. Now get back to the house before she figures us out."

"Right. Until tonight."

Aster turned and took off running back through the fields toward the house. Marin watched him go. *Aster. How did you ever convince me?*

Or rather, how could Marin have ever let himself believe that they shouldn't? Thank the gods he had Aster to talk some sense into him.

Marin lifted his basket of corn. "Let's set sail," he said aloud to himself.

The rest of the afternoon moved by at a brisk pace—his chores easier, the heat of the afternoon sun less oppressive. By suppertime, he couldn't bring himself to eat anything. They had a long journey ahead of them, but his stomach felt twisted up in so many knots that he didn't think he'd be able to keep food down if he tried.

He busied himself by doing one last sift through his pack to make sure he had everything. He had his hat and scarf for times when the

61

weather turned cool. Underneath that lay his knife, its blade wrapped up in a scrap of burlap, and his pocket watch and deck of cards tucked beside it.

The knife might do you some good, friend, he thought to himself. *Those cards and the watch are worthless.*

They weren't worthless though. The watch would let him know what time it was—if they ever needed to know for whatever reason. And the cards meant more to him than anything in the world. Those cards were how he had passed the time for years throughout his youth, playing solitary games to entertain himself. In their own way, they had a value far greater than gold. He couldn't bear the thought of Ilth throwing them away or burning them when she realized he was gone.

The last item, one he had tucked away with proud forethought, was a map printed on a piece of crumpled parchment he'd found tucked away in one of Ilth's old books. He used to admire it and dream of exploring the world beyond Ilth's farm but never thought it would happen one day.

This is really happening, he realized. The hairs on his arms stood up with nervousness.

He reached for his pocket watch and flipped open its cover. Midnight—finally.

Pack over his shoulder, he slipped out the door and into the yard. An unseasonable chill had crept into the air, or maybe he just felt tingly from nerves. He snuck up the lawn toward the house. The sound of cornstalks in the night breeze rustled in the distance.

"Marin."

He heard his voice before he saw him. His brother's lean form appeared out of the shadows on the porch and stepped into the silvery gleam of moonlight that lit up the yard. Aster grinned. "This is it. It's happening."

"It's happening," Marin repeated. "Come on."

Marin gestured for Aster to follow, then led the way along the path toward the gate. *We're really doing this, and we're getting away with it.*

Even if Ilth were to look out her bedroom window now and spy them, what could she do? All they would have to do would be to make a run for it. And they were ready to do that. Oh, Marin was as ready as ever to do that!

He looked over his shoulder, back toward the house. No sign of Ilth. No sign of any movement at all. The dilapidated cottage stood on the sloping hill, silhouetted against the velvet sky, still and quiet enough that it might be abandoned if Marin didn't know better.

At the end of the path stood the gated entrance that led out onto the road, the farthest point on the farm Marin had ever been in his life. He reached forward and unlatched the gate.

"Marin?"

It wasn't Aster's voice that had called his name, but it was a familiar one. Both of them turned at once to see a spindly form approaching on four legs.

"Holdfast!" Marin exclaimed, trying still to keep his voice low.

"What are you doing?" the barn dog asked. Moonlight glinted on his large black eyes as they moved from Marin to Aster. His canine face filled with shock. "Is that...Aster?"

Those words hit Marin like a punch to the chest. Holdfast recognized Aster. He called him by name. "You knew?" Marin asked. "You knew about him?"

How is it the old barn dog has known all this time? I thought he was my friend!

"Of course, I knew about him," Holdfast whispered, drawing nearer. Marin took a step closer to Aster, though he didn't know why. He had never known Holdfast to be aggressive.

Holdfast continued. "I've known—I—what are the two of you doing?"

Not that Holdfast really needed to ask. The two of them stood there with packs slung over their shoulders, sneaking across the yard at midnight, headed toward the gate and the road that lay beyond.

"Please," Marin said. "You won't tell Ilth, will you?"

Holdfast stared at him, a kind expression in his eyes, but still Marin found himself gripped with dread. Tension hung in the air so thick that Marin probably could have cut it with his scythe.

"Go," Holdfast said. "Go, get out of here. I've seen nothing, as far as I'm concerned."

Marin heaved in relief. He hadn't realized how scared he had been. He looked over at Aster, whose exasperated expression reflected the same.

Holdfast barked and tossed his head in the direction of the gate. "Best of luck to both of you, my young lads."

Neither of them could muster a word. Marin opened the gate and nodded to Holdfast. "Thank you!"

"Thank you," Aster echoed.

"Go," Holdfast said.

And with that, the two servants turned their backs on Ilth's farm and set off running down the road, ready to put as much distance between themselves and their wicked old mistress as quickly as they possibly could.

Everything familiar yet awful lay behind them now, and a world full of possibilities and unknown dangers was in front of them.

CHAPTER 11

After an hour of walking, Aster started to laugh.

Marin couldn't resist joining him—it was a relief. *We're free,* he thought. *Free! We got away.*

He turned and looked back the way they had come, at the road behind them disappearing into the darkness. Somewhere back there, several miles away, was Ilth's farm. And Ilth was probably still sleeping in her ramshackle old cottage, still hours away from waking up to discover that they were both gone. *Oh, won't she be angry!*

"Goodbye, Ilth!" Marin called back. "We won't miss you!"

"Good riddance, you old sow!" Aster shouted.

Marin paused, letting the moment sink in. "It feels good, doesn't it? To be rid of it?"

Aster moved his pack from his left shoulder to his right. "I knew it would be."

"I mean, just think, we never have to think about that wretched farm again."

"Aye. Never again."

They both exhaled together. "What a beautiful night it is," Aster observed, looking up at the stars.

Marin nodded but didn't say anything. He scanned the sky

overhead to see whether he could pick out any constellations—any of the great heroes of old who were preserved in the stars for generations to admire. He had read about most of them in his books, but he had never felt so connected to them as he did right now.

"And…and all the opportunities of the world are now in front of us," Marin said. "We could actually do something great with our lives."

None of this had ever seemed possible until Aster suggested it. "Those opportunities are ours now," Marin went on. "It's like—it's like this big open sea for us to sail forth in, right? And the tide is in our favor?"

Aster looked over at him. "That's the Marin I knew was in there."

Marin dropped his gaze from the sky. Had it been obvious all along how scared he was, how stilted and wary and afraid to act? "What do you think we'll make of ourselves?" he asked. "Now that we're free men?"

Aster shrugged. "I don't know. We could be anything."

Anything. They could be questing knights or merchant sailors. They could be bestowed a noble title and live in a castle one day! "Aye," Marin agreed, half to Aster and half to himself. "Anything."

They continued the rest of the night, powered by sheer adrenaline, pressing forward into the dark ahead of them. Even when it was three or four hours past midnight, and they had walked for miles, Marin didn't think he would be able to sleep if he tried.

When dawn approached, they slipped off the road into the nearby woods and fumbled their way through the trees until they reached a glen where the soft grass offered them a place to rest. The sky overhead grew hazy with the grayness of dawn.

Exhaustion hit Marin as soon as he lay down. He barely had the energy to roll over and wish goodnight to Aster, who was already sound asleep a few feet away.

However long they slept, it felt like it had been only a second or two. Marin opened his eyes to bright morning sun streaming through the leaves overhead. He rubbed his eyes but didn't stir from his place in the grass.

For the first time in his life, he was waking up in some place that wasn't his shed. It was some place new, some place unfamiliar, some place full of possibilities. He looked around, taking in the sight of the forest where they had spent the night. None of it had been visible in the darkness when they arrived. The clearing lay open and airy, sparsely dotted with trees and bushes. Shafts of light illuminated emerald leaves and leathery bark. The songs of birds and cicadas chorused together in the air.

He reached over for his pack and undid the drawstring, pulling out the scarf and hat he brought. Under that was his pocket watch. He flicked it open to see that it was a little after seven o'clock. Ilth would be awake by now, and angry that her servants were nowhere to be found.

He reached for his map, unfolded it, spread it out on the ground to study it. The continent of Monte Prospera was vast—Ilth's farm sat on the edge of the forest that divided the kingdoms of Grythium and Blunia. Two kingdoms he never thought he would ever have the chance to explore. Now that day had come.

Aster stirred. He lifted his hands, rubbed his eyes, and stretched.

"Good morrow, brother," Marin said, looking up from the map.

"Good morrow," Aster replied. He sat up.

"How did you sleep?"

"It wasn't bad, truthfully," Aster said.

Marin nodded. "I think we were both exhausted. No wonder we slept like the dead."

Marin picked up his dagger and secured it in his belt around his tunic. "Just think," he said, "Ilth is probably realizing we're gone now. She's probably furious."

Aster's eyes lit up. "I just wish I could be there to witness her tantrum." His eyes fell on the map spread out in front of Marin. "What's that?"

"A map I brought," Marin said. He pointed to the woods. "Here's where we are. The kingdom of Grythium is here. And here's the kingdom of Blunia. Think of the fortunes we'll seek for ourselves in either place."

Aster reached for his pack. "And that's not all we've got with us." He undid the drawstrings and withdrew the small burlap pouch of fairy dust. "Don't forget about this."

Marin sighed. "I can't believe you actually took that from Ilth. I thought you said you didn't even know how to use fairy dust."

"Of course I don't." Aster retied the twine tightly around the mouth of the pouch. "But it might prove useful anyway, right?" He tucked it carefully into the pocket at the side of his tunic.

Before Marin could say anything, the sound of movement in the brush rose above the songs of the birds and cicadas. Aster gaped at the sight of something behind Marin. "What's that?"

Marin turned and sprang to his feet. They weren't alone. And what an outlandish group of strangers were out here with them! A procession of people approached through the woods. It was maybe ten or twelve of them, a mix of young men and women, all of them so attractive they looked like they could have been artwork or statuary brought to life, thrust out into the world where ordinary mortals would look meager in comparison. The shimmering white silks they wore—the men in tunics and trousers, the women in long ethereal gowns—caught the sunlight, glinting and gleaming and glowing with every movement.

These are no ordinary people, Marin thought.

They carried something with them. Something huge. At first, Marin couldn't figure out what it was. But as they came close, weaving

68

their way through the trees and ferns, it became clear the something was an enormous gold palanquin, a type of rudimentary carriage carried around by footmen. Marin recognized it because he had read about them in books. The gold posters of each of the palanquin's four sides showed ornate carvings, and its white silk curtains drifted in the morning breeze.

Marin glanced back at Aster. "What is this?" he mouthed.

One of the women stepped forward, the train of her gossamer dress drifting languidly behind her in the breeze. Her gaze moved from Marin to Aster. For as perplexed as Marin felt to see her and the others wandering through the woods, she didn't seem surprised at all. By the gods, it was almost as if she had been *expecting* to find two runaway peasants sleeping deep in the woods. When she smiled, dimples appeared in her rosy cheeks.

"You are well met, young sirs." She brushed her black curls off her shoulders, then held her hands out to them in greeting. "Pray, tell me your names. We wish to know who it is we meet this morning."

Whatever Marin had expected they would encounter when they left Ilth's farm, it had not been this. "Uh…my name is Marin, if it please you, miss." He turned to Aster. "And this is my brother, Aster."

The woman bowed. "Marin and Aster, we are honored."

The others in her group bowed their heads and murmured a chorus of greetings. They reminded Marin of a host of angels.

The woman raised her head. "Will you meet with the prophetess?"

The prophetess? Had Marin heard that correctly? "What?"

The woman lifted her hands, stretching out her arms and holding one open palm out toward Marin and the other out toward Aster. "We," she declared, "are the followers of the great prophetess." She indicated the palanquin. "And the prophetess seeks your company. She has words to give you."

Marin felt his face scrunch with confusion, despite how hard he was trying to be polite. "Words? For us?" He looked over at Aster. His stomach twisted.

Aster shrugged. "Why not?"

If this were an epic or a legend, Marin realized, this would be the part where the young hero gets assigned his quest. The magical being—in this case, the prophetess—would tell the hero what he had to do. Could this really be their big moment?

He had read about prophecy. It was supposed to be that prophets and prophetesses could see the future, could communicate with the gods, could understand the spirit world in a way that other mortals couldn't. Some of the ancient scriptures emphasized that real prophecy was to be trusted—but not all prophecy was reliable.

There was a passage from one of the texts that said anyone gifted with foresight was bound by magic to relay the truth in this regard. They couldn't lie when they relayed the prophecy to others. Still, prophecies were not always reliable because they could be vague or incomplete or misleading.

Would they even like what this prophetess had to say?

"We'll meet her," Marin said. After the words were out of his mouth, he couldn't decide whether he was brave or stupid to agree the way he did.

The woman released their hands and turned back toward her angelic companions. They parted to let her approach, and Marin and Aster followed behind her. When she reached the palanquin, she stood and gestured for Marin and Aster to go ahead of her. Marin tried to swallow the lump in his throat but couldn't. He looked over at Aster behind him and nodded as a way of saying, "Well, let's do this, shall we?"

Then he reached forward with a trembling hand and pulled back the white curtains to step inside.

There was no getting out of it now. Whatever business this mysterious prophetess had with them, they were about to find out.

CHAPTER 12

They passed through the white draperies over the entrance to the palanquin and into a spacious room. Marin paused, taking it all in. White silk curtains framed the four sides of the palatial chamber, which was dressed with opulent gold furniture, soft carpeting, and shimmering crystal lamps.

There was no way all of this could be contained inside the palanquin. It was all too big on the inside for how it appeared on the outside.

Seated at a table in the middle of the room, a woman looked up at them. Raven hair framed her sweet, pretty face, and her arching eyebrows rose when she saw Marin and Aster together. She stood, making the white robes draped over her ample figure dance ethereally.

"Good morrow, my young sirs," she said.

Marin found his voice. "Hello."

"Hello," Aster echoed.

This woman—the prophetess—gestured to two of the gold chairs set out beside her small table. "Please, have a seat."

She crossed to a gold cabinet on the far side of the room. When she moved, it was as if she floated through the air, effortlessly, gracefully. "Shall I get you something to drink? Some wine, perhaps?"

Despite how extraordinary and outlandish all of this was, there was something about the woman that put Marin instantly at ease. She was…warm. Caring. Doting. No, none of those was the right word. Marin couldn't figure it out. No word he had learned from all the books he read could adequately describe her. Something about her manner, even in the mere half minute they had been in her presence, made him feel instantly, inexplicably comfortable.

As if she could read Marin's thoughts, the prophetess said, "You don't need to be nervous." She laughed and smiled as she settled her dainty little hand on a crystal decanter atop the cabinet. "I invited you in here because I'm eager to meet with you. My name is Tsema."

She poured two goblets of wine and returned to the table. Light from the lamps danced on the dark red liquid inside the crystal glasses. The fabric of her dress shimmered like pearls or spiderwebs. She handed the goblets to them. "Please, sit."

With that, she lowered herself into the gold chair where she'd been when they entered. She leaned forward, resting her elbows on the table and cradling her chin in her hands. A kind smile came across her face as she looked at them.

Marin moved toward one of the chairs first, and Aster followed his lead.

Aster found his voice first. "Well," he said. "What do you know about us?"

That wasn't exactly how Marin would have started the conversation. "Aster…"

"I cry mercy, but if she's a prophetess, she's got to know something about us already," Aster said. "Right?"

Marin turned back to Tsema, ready to make an excuse for Aster's candor. She didn't look offended though. "That is true," she said.

"So," Aster ventured again, "what do you know about us?"

Marin reached for the goblet and lifted it to his lips. He had never tasted wine before, but he'd read about it. It seemed like such a dignified thing to drink, something fit for royalty and nobility. It wasn't something he would associate with the likes of him and Aster. But they were servants no longer, or so he had to keep reminding himself. They could be anything they wanted—so why couldn't they be wine drinkers?

Even at seven o'clock in the morning. This was an adventure, after all.

The wine had a pleasant taste, bold and rich, spreading over his tongue and filling him with warmth from his head all the way down to his toes. He took another sip.

Aster hadn't reached for his wine glass just yet. He still stared at Tsema, waiting for an answer to his question.

She laughed again, the sound like windchimes or silver tinkling on glass, winsome and melodic. "Very well. I know that you were once servants to the witch Ilth, and that up until earlier this summer, she kept you ignorant of each other. But now that you have bonded as brothers, you have escaped to seek your fortunes in the great wide world."

The quiet stillness of the room overwhelmed them for a second while Marin registered what she just said.

"Damn," Aster murmured.

Tsema leaned forward in her chair. "And now…I suppose you're hoping I might tell you what those fortunes are."

Marin's heart skipped a beat. *Actually, no, you were the one who requested an audience with us*, he wanted to say. *We didn't express hope for anything from you.*

He hesitated. Saying all of that might come across as rude. And strictly speaking, she wasn't wrong. Marin *did* hope to hear his fortune. "Can you tell us?" he asked.

"I am afraid not."

Marin's spirit sank at her reply.

"Why not?" Aster asked.

73

Tsema straightened up and leaned back in her chair. "Forgive me, Aster, for returning your question with another question, but can you tell me why it is that you are no longer a servant?"

Aster narrowed his eyes. Marin knew exactly what was going through his mind—how could she know so much about who they were and where they'd come from, but she didn't know what had happened to them last night?

"Well," Marin ventured before Aster could speak, "because we ran away."

"And why did you run away?"

She's trying to get at something, Marin thought. She was prodding him with questions to get an admission or a confession of some kind. She wanted some insight to work with if they expected her to tell their fortunes—something more than just knowing they were servants who ran away from a witch's farm.

If Marin expected honesty from the prophetess, he had to show honesty in return. "We got tired of being servants," he said. "And we decided we wanted something better."

Tsema smiled. "Oh. So, you took your fate into your own hands?"

"Aye," Marin agreed.

She nodded. "And that is exactly why. It must continue that way."

Marin raised his wine to his lips and took another sip. Maybe this prophetess just didn't have any way of seeing the future. Just because she rode around in a gold palanquin, followed by a bunch of shimmering disciples, that didn't mean she had any actual power. Did it?

"You don't need to doubt my power, Marin," Tsema said. "I give you my word that I am what I say I am."

Marin nearly choked on his sip of wine. He swallowed and tried to stifle a cough. *How did she know what I was thinking?*

Tsema leaned back in her chair, looking the two of them up and down with her ice-blue eyes that seemed to see straight through them.

74

"The world is in need of willing heroes like the two of you," she said. "That is why I asked for an audience with you. I see a great future ahead of you—if you have the determination to pursue it. There is unrest throughout this land. The kingdoms of Grythium and Blunia could be on the brink of war, led by kings who are bitter enemies. Neither kingdom has a hopeful future. King Donovan of Grythium sentenced his heirs to death many years ago and has descended into madness. King Hector of Blunia not so long ago lost his heiresses to a goblin army, and he has rapidly given up all hope. The land needs heroes."

She said this in a voice that sounded as if she were far away, not entirely present with them there in that opulent chamber, in that palanquin that was so much bigger on the inside than it looked from the outside. Then something about her changed, and she spoke in her sweet, motherly voice again. "Take heed, and know that you have the power to change the world for good."

Marin recoiled. "Us? You think we can make that kind of difference?"

"Why not?" Tsema asked, as simply as if Marin had asked whether birds could fly or fish could swim.

No, Marin wanted to say. He loved the idea that they had a "great future" ahead of them. He had spent his life dreaming about it, wishing for it. Now that they'd escaped Ilth's farm, it seemed more possible than ever.

But Tsema had said it herself—they were a couple of runaway servants. He had to be realistic. They weren't heroes. Was this an assignment, or did she just think all of this sounded like some sort of lofty encouragement? *"Why can't you just tell us what we have to do?"* he wanted to say.

But he couldn't bring himself to say any of that. "Well, because," he replied politely. "Because we're nobodies."

Coward.

"I'm sorry," Tsema said. "But I would hardly say you are nobodies. I would not be telling you about the turmoil in the land if I thought you were." She turned her gaze to Aster, looking at him with the same penetrating stare she gave Marin. "Aster, come closer."

Aster did as he was told, scooting his chair nearer to the table and leaning in toward their hostess. She reached forward and took his hand. "Your companion, Marin, doesn't seem to have much faith in himself," she said. Before he could reply, she continued, "You and Marin must always stick by each other and help each other, for it is from each other that you will draw your strength and courage."

Aster nodded. "Aye."

"Good," she said.

She released his hand, then pointed at him and Marin both. "Be wary of danger, for there are those who will try to thwart your purpose for their own gains. When you encounter trouble, know that you will overcome it with enough determination and effort. And whatever happens, always trust that if you do what is virtuous and noble and honorable, you will be on the right path."

Marin hung on her every word. "Yes, ma'am," he murmured.

Tsema lifted her glass of wine and sipped it. "Understand this— just because you grew up as servants does not mean you cannot accomplish greatness. The world beyond the witch's farm holds many surprises. Why, three days from now, who knows where you might be? Three days from now, you might have a wizard mentor, one who can nurture you and encourage you in a way far different from how the witch degraded you and abused you."

A wizard mentor. Marin liked the thought of that.

"I might even send one to look out for you, now that I think about it," Tsema said. "A wizard would be a great advantage for young adventurers searching for glory and fortune." She drew a deep breath and nodded, rising from her chair. "That is all."

76

Marin couldn't believe it. What a brief meeting and vague prophecies. She had given them something of a mission—to be the heroes that the kingdoms of Grythium and Blunia needed. But how were they supposed to do that?

"My companion will see you out," Tsema said, gesturing toward the woman who led them inside.

Aster laughed. "That's all?"

Marin shot him a look.

"Forgive me, my lady," Aster recovered quickly, trying to suppress an awkward grin, "but that was hardly any kind of prophecy."

Tsema raised her chin. Her expression showed no sign of being insulted. She actually looked kinder and warmer for having heard this from Aster. "If I gave away too much, then you would not know what to do with the information I gave you. I can see the future, but that doesn't mean I know how we get from here to there."

Curiosity burned up inside Marin. Whether he believed in prophecy or not, he wanted to hear more from this woman.

Or do I? What if what she tells you affects your actions, and then that changes the outcome of where you'll end up?

That could happen, Marin knew. He had read stories about kings and warriors who were told by magicians of what would happen to them. These great heroes became so consumed by achieving their great destiny that they ended up falling into ruin because of their brash, foolish choices. They waged wars and tempted their enemies in stupid ways. They defied the gods and found themselves condemned to terrible fates. Marin didn't want to end up like them—but if he knew the future, he might very well make the same stupid choices.

Tsema stepped around the table, putting an arm around each of them. "I will be honest and tell you that I have erred before in giving too much prophecy away, and there have been those who have tried to prevent it from coming true." It was almost as if she could read

Marin's thoughts. She knew what he was thinking. Her voice was too kind and gentle for such a harsh message.

Aster took a breath to say something, but she held up her hand. "The truth, Aster, is that the stars cannot control you. But some things that they tell will happen no matter what you do."

She turned to Marin. "You must take the tide when it is in your favor, but you cannot resist a strong current that insists on carrying you in a certain direction."

She drew them both close to her, pressing her cheek first to Marin's shoulder, then to Aster's. It was a comforting embrace. She radiated warmth and kindness and…and…love. *Love. Motherly love!* Marin had never felt it before, but still…she seemed to truly care about him in a way he couldn't explain.

She let both of them go. "Do you understand?"

"If that's the case," Aster said, "then what's the sense in keeping it a secret from us?"

Marin clapped his hand on Aster's shoulder. "I think what my brother means is that maybe it would help us if you told us everything you knew. If you think it would help us, of course."

"Aye," Aster nodded. "I suppose you could put it that way."

Light from the nearby lamps gleamed in Tsema's eyes. "Oh, my sweet boys," she said. "I would love to tell you everything. But if I did, then there would be nothing great about what you did. You would just be following the directions I give you—and where's the glory in that?"

"I wouldn't mind," Aster said. "By my troth, I wouldn't."

"Patience, Aster," Tsema said. "Follow the advice I gave you, and you two will find your place in the world."

With that, she gave a low bow. "Until we meet again."

When the handmaiden led them out, the morning sun hung higher in the sky, blazing on the emerald leaves and grass where it fell through the branches in shafts of hot light. The disciples waited patiently, some of them seated or reclined on the mossy ground, others leaning up against trees. When Marin and Aster appeared, they righted themselves, standing at the ready.

Marin wasn't used to having so many people give him undivided attention—not to mention displays of respect. All he had known for years had been Ilth and Prunella and Holdfast. And the only one who had actually been nice to him had been Holdfast, even though Holdfast was never attentive and devoted the way these people seemed to be.

These people didn't see them as lowly servants. *Because*, Marin thought, *we are no longer lowly servants. That doesn't have to be who we are anymore. We've left that life behind us!*

"And now we leave you," the handmaiden said.

Marin turned to face her. She stood beside the palanquin, her hands folded in front of her. Now that he looked at it again, he was baffled by how the palanquin appeared so normal from the outside. How could such a modestly sized box hold such an open, airy room inside?

Is this the kind of magic we will come to expect out here in the world?

One of the disciples bent down and grabbed their packs. "Here, my good sirs," he said, offering the satchels out to Marin and Aster. Marin's pack felt lighter when he shouldered it. Was it just that his spirits were higher? Or could the disciples have enchanted their packs so that they weren't such a burden? Anything was possible as far as he was concerned. Nothing was going to surprise him.

"Well, thank you," Aster said.

"Yes," Marin said. "Thank you."

The handmaiden raised her hands and kissed the fingertips of each, then stretched out her arms to touch their foreheads. "Marin. Aster. As you go off into the wide world, know that you have our blessing. May the gods smile upon you."

The group of men and women stepped forward to lift the palanquin from the ground. Their expressions were blank, their voices quiet. It was as if they didn't even recognize that Marin and Aster were there anymore, as if they had passed into some other part of time and space.

Without a word, the group wandered off through the trees, their feet moving with delicate grace over the sticks and leaves on the ground.

"Goodbye," the handmaiden said.

She lifted the hem of her gossamer dress so as not to trip over it, then turned and followed the other members of the sect as they weaved through the trees.

Marin and Aster stood in stunned silence until it was just the two of them alone in the woods again.

Aster sighed. "Well, what do you think of that?"

Marin's mind blazed, but he couldn't find the words. "I don't know. Something tells me this adventure is going to be a lot stranger than either of us ever imagined."

CHAPTER 13

At first, Elspeth believed—nay, she knew, really knew—that some brave hero would come to rescue them. That was how it always was in the epics and ballads and legends. A princess held captive by a terrible monster was always saved by a daring knight or a brave adventurer.

It's destiny that the same should happen to us, she thought. *Why, all of this might be a great blessing in disguise if it means I'm going to be saved by a handsome knight or a prince.*

And then that brave prince would take her home to her father, they would be betrothed, as was tradition, and then she would begin her training to be queen one day, with her husband-to-be beside her.

But now…now Elspeth was giving up hope. After all, what power did hope have when she spent her days cowering in fear, trapped in a captivity pit that goblin guards with spears and clubs patrolled from sun up to sun down?

At night, it was even worse. Though it was a relief when the guard patrol left at twilight, the fears and feelings of despair always gained strength in the coldness and darkness of night. Carys would sometimes ask what they were going to do to escape, and Elspeth never had a good answer for her.

The goblins hadn't hurt them badly. Not yet. Elspeth's arm still ached from where one of the guards twisted it in his claw. She looked down, tracing the bruise with her finger, remembering the fear she felt in the moment. Carys had come to her rescue, being so bold as to shove the goblin away and demand he leave her sister alone. The goblin had struck Carys with the blunt end of his spear in rebuke.

The memory of it sent a chill through Elspeth, causing her to shiver. She leaned back against the cold stone wall and slid her legs forward, her bare feet emerging from where they had been tucked under her shift.

Drawing a deep breath, she looked up at the stars that appeared in the velvety expanse of sky just above the opening of the pit. They shone bright that night, giving her enough light to just barely see her surroundings. Carys lay on the cold stone several feet away, deep in slumber.

There was no valiant hero coming to rescue them. They were going to spend the rest of their lives at the bottom of the pit in the impenetrable center of the goblin fortress.

I am the daughter of King Hector and heiress to the throne of Blunia, she thought.

Heiress to the throne of Blunia. She might have been once. Not anymore.

She heaved, as if she could push all the despair and agony out of her. She didn't want to close her eyes. When she did, she always saw the fierce orange eyes and mangled teeth of the goblin who threatened her three days ago. He had been on guard duty, and he had come to deliver them a cup of water and stale heel of bread. When she accepted the bread from him, his gaze lingered on her a little longer than she was comfortable. "Pretty," he muttered in a gruff whisper.

"Don't you be eyeing the princesses," said the other guard on duty. "They're our captives. Orders are they're to be kept alive and unharmed—for now, at least."

For now, at least. Those had been his words. How long until the goblins decided it was time for captivity to give way to torture? Maybe even execution?

She rested her head back against the wall and closed her eyes, letting exhaustion overtake her, despite the fears running through her mind. For several minutes, she waited in the haziness between consciousness and deep slumber.

Then shapes started to take form in front of her. She saw her father—her father, appearing to her in a dream.

Or maybe it would have been more accurate to say *she* appeared to *him*. After all, he was sitting on his throne at the head of the great hall. And Elspeth was just there. Inexplicably.

A dream. A dream was the only word she could think of to describe it. How else could she have fallen asleep in the goblin pit and then been in her father's throne room only a moment later?

But it wasn't exactly a dream. It was so real. So lifelike.

The compulsion to run up and hug her father wasn't there. Her heart ached at the sight of him, with his face buried in his big hands. He lifted his head and tears gleamed in his eyes. There were wet streaks down his face. Elspeth had never seen him cry before. And here he was—crying for her and her sister.

He missed them. He was scared for them. Elspeth just knew.

"Father," she said. "Won't you send help for us? Can't anyone come to our aid?"

But he didn't hear her voice. He didn't see her. She couldn't move from where she stood, her entire body paralyzed in the spot she was in when she appeared in the throne room.

"Oh, my sweet girls," King Hector murmured. "Oh, my girls." He choked and fresh tears erupted. He dropped his head into his hands again and wept.

Elspeth stared around the great hall. Nobody else was there. Not even a guard. *Father must have sent them all away.* He didn't want anyone to see him cry. He didn't want anyone to know the king was in such a broken state.

This might be the tragedy that would undo him. The thought ripped through Elspeth, making her skin prickle. Losing her and Carys might drive their kingly father into despair. Then what would happen to their subjects? Would he neglect his royal duties?

She had always known her father to be a jovial and exuberant man, whose bellowing laughter and kindly smile endeared him to the lowest of the peasants and made them feel instantly loved.

But she also knew his life had not been without heartache. Part of it had been her mother's death. Sickness took Queen Megdahlia shortly after Carys's birth.

Then there was the kingdom of Grythium. The story went that her father had once been famously good friends and allies with King Donovan, whose land bordered Blunia across the forest to the west. King Donovan and her father had grown up as close as brothers, bound by oaths of friendship, the dearest of companions, and when they inherited their thrones, they had hoped to one day see their kingdoms united by the marriage of Elspeth to Donovan's son.

That had all been when Elspeth was only a babe in a cradle. Something happened between Father and King Donovan, and they now swore themselves the bitterest of enemies. Some rumors even said that King Donovan had gone mad, turned into a tyrant whose subjects feared him.

Elspeth only learned all of this from snatches of gossip she overheard from the maidservants and courtiers. She had spent several fleeting moments of girlhood dreaming about what King Donovan's princely son must have been like. If her father and King Donovan ever made peace with each other...

As a little girl with a mind full of dreams and wishes, she liked the idea of an arranged betrothal to a handsome prince a year older than she and an inheritance of a neighboring kingdom waiting for him when he came of age.

But that would not happen now. Rumors said that King Donovan had his baby son executed.

Now this. Elspeth watched her father cry, and she knew that this was the worst loss he had suffered yet. She might have been frightened—hurt—tormented—but she had to stay strong for him. She had to hold onto hope, to keep up her strength and morale—she had to survive. At least until someone could come rescue her. Then she would return to her father and the royal court, and her subjects.

"Oh, my little girls," King Hector whispered to himself, rubbing the tears from his eyes. "My joys. The lights of my life. How could I lose you?"

"You haven't lost us, Father," Elspeth said. "We're trapped in the goblin fortress, and we're still alive! We want to come home to you as soon as we can!"

He made no indication that he heard her.

"Oh, Father!" she called again, but he held still with his head in his hands.

Something seized up in Elspeth's throat. She struggled to choke back tears. *No,* she told herself. *No, now is not the time for that.*

Oh, what a time this was if a mighty king could weep and a delicate princess could not. But if she started to break down…if she started to break, then how would she ever be able to survive the cruel captivity of the goblins?

Why? What do the goblins want with us?

As if the answer weren't obvious. Elspeth knew the history of Monte Prospera. She had learned it from her royal governesses at a young age. The goblins had been forced into darkness and shadow since the beginning of time, lurking as nocturnal creatures by the light of the moon and scavenging on the carcasses that more capable beasts of prey left behind.

But then came the day the goblins banded together and rose up in rebellion against her grandfather. This had been more than thirty years prior, before she and Carys were even born, back when their father was scarcely more than a boy himself. Prince Hector had been the one to rally the royal army and lead them in the fight against the goblins.

And although her history lessons did not dwell on this any more than giving it a passing mention, the royal army of Grythium had fought by their side. Prince Donovan and Prince Hector even crossed swords with the Great Goblin himself, the closest thing the monstrous clan had to a king or a leader. The vicious creature was twice the size of the other goblins, with claws that could shatter stone and teeth that were nearly as long as a man's arm.

It had been Prince Hector who had pierced the Great Goblin through the middle with his sword and smote his ruin upon the hillside. Then, as the histories told, all the goblins retreated in fear. The Blunian army drove them back into the wastelands far to the south, an awful little corner of the realm where they were allowed to eke out an existence as long as they proved no further threat to the peace and prosperity of Monte Prospera.

But now they threatened the kingdom of Blunia again—they had kidnapped the princesses, the young women who were the king's only children and the heiresses to his throne.

And I know why, Elspeth thought as she watched her father cry. *I know why.*

It was for petty vengeance. For years, the goblins had been denied any of the realm's bounty. While other tribes and clans flourished, the goblins did not. They were denied the fertile fields where the farmers and the serfs planted wheat, and they were denied the seashores where the merchants would return from their journey and set up market.

They were denied the hillsides and the forests, the lakes and the rivers. They were denied it all.

Now they'd have their revenge.

Elspeth watched her father lift his head and brush a tear from his eye. The sorrow in his expression had given way to another emotion. Fear. Fear and worry.

Elspeth understood—of course, she understood! A king had much to think about besides his own well-being. Just as she, a princess, had more to think about than herself. They had their subjects to concern themselves for. A good ruler had a responsibility.

It all occurred to Elspeth at once. King Hector, in his grief, no longer cared. He could no longer bring himself to care for his people.

He no longer had an heiress, because she was locked away in the pits of the goblin fortress.

And this left the kingdom of Blunia in terrible danger.

CHAPTER 14

B y the time night settled, Marin and Aster were deep in the forest. Back on Ilth's farm, and even on the open road, the moon had shone down and set silver linings on every surface under it. Not quite the case when they were deep in the forest. The shadows of trees crisscrossed all around them, black on black on black, and if Marin stumbled over a root or a rock or a patch of ivy one more time, he was going to lose his mind.

This is awful, he kept thinking. *This is absolutely miserable. I hate it. I hate it.*

He couldn't bring himself to express any of that to Aster. How was he supposed to admit that he hated being out here in the woods, far away from the Ilth's farm? Despite how bad it all felt in the moment, at least they were free.

But he was beginning to realize that freedom sometimes meant not being familiar with the path ahead of you, and sometimes not knowing where you're going to spend the night.

"We need to rest at some point," Aster said.

Marin sighed. *Rest.* Rest sounded nice. But twilight had brought on thick cloud cover, and the air grew thick with imminent rain. If they went to sleep on the forest floor the way they did the night before, they would wake up in a puddle of mud before morning.

"I just wish we could find a safe place," he said.

Thunder rumbled in the distance, and flashes of white light lit up the clouds between the overhead tree branches.

"Where are we going to find shelter in the middle of a forest?" Aster said. "Come on. We're just as well off underneath one of these trees."

Maybe Aster was right. Marin felt like the worst adventurer ever. After years of living in a shed, was he really too good for sleeping outside in a rainstorm?

The first drops hit him with a vengeance, followed by more, heavier and faster.

"Oh!" he shouted.

And then, all at once, a summer storm unleashed. Heavy rain drove down on them. The sound of the downpour pounding on the leaves above them filled the night air.

"Well, this is just awful," Aster said.

Lightning flashed again, illuminating something just ahead of them through the trees. Its boxy shape and arched top were unmistakable. It had appeared for only a fleeting heartbeat of a moment, but…

A sound escaped Marin's chest, something between a gasp and a shout. "Did you see that?"

"I'll be damned," Aster said. "It couldn't have been."

Finding new energy, Marin stumbled toward the dark shape he was almost certain had been a house when the lightning illuminated it. There was no way whoever lived there would let them stay outside on a night like this, with the rain falling in heavy torrents and the thunder so bold that the earth shook a little every time it rumbled. Who could possibly turn them away?

Marin approached the door and knocked. A moment passed, but no response came. There wasn't even any sound of movement inside. He pounded again. "Hello?!" he shouted over the torrential rain.

Again, no response.

Marin traced his gaze around the doorframe and across the front of the little cottage. It was hard to tell in the dark, but the wood façade looked mossy. Loose thatch from the roof hung at odd angles. "Maybe it's abandoned," Marin said.

Aster pushed forward. "Who cares—let's just let ourselves in. Come on." He reached for the wooden handle and shook it. The door fell open, revealing an even deeper darkness than the storm-drenched forest.

It took a second for Marin's eyes to adjust to the dark as they slipped inside. He looked around, studying the odd shadows that surrounded them as he padded into the black room. A flash of lightning erupted outside the windows, followed by a roll of thunder. The flash illuminated the cottage long enough for him to see his surroundings and turn his insides to ice.

"Aster…"

Another flash of lightning again showed them a room full of broken furniture and other debris. Puddles of something thick and dark spread across the floor. There wasn't enough time to take in the sights of everything, to recognize every detail, but the fast glimpse of it didn't bode well.

"I have a bad feeling about this place," Aster said.

Marin swallowed. He felt the same way. "At least…at least it's dry."

"Marin—"

"Do we want to sleep outside in the rain?" Marin said. "This place is abandoned. Nobody will bother us here. We'll be safe for the night."

"But it's…well, it's filthy."

"It's no dirtier than a barn," Marin said, taking a few more steps into the center of the room. He felt more confident as long as there wasn't lightning to show him their surroundings. "Have you forgotten your attic so quickly, brother?"

"An attic is one thing; a grim cottage is another." Aster walked around the edge of the room. The sound of heavy raindrops pounded the roof overhead. "You're right though." He sighed. "At least we're out of the rain."

Marin set his pack on the floor. "Should we light a fire?"

Aster shrugged. "I'm just going to go straight to sleep. I'm too tired to make dinner, and there's no sense in our staying up late planning what we'll do tomorrow when we have no idea what tomorrow is going to bring."

"I guess you're right."

Aster made his way through the dark to one of the decrepit wooden beds pushed up against the wall. "I'll take this bed here," he said as he lowered himself onto it.

Not that he wanted to lie down on it, but it was better than the floor. And much better than the muddy ground outside in the forest.

Marin went to the bed beside Aster's and crawled onto it. The lumpy mattress reeked of sweat and mildew.

For a few minutes, Marin stared up at the ceiling. "Goodnight, Aster," he said.

Aster didn't reply. He was already asleep.

A rumbling sound came from outside the cottage. At first, Marin thought it might have been the thunder. But it was growing louder. He pushed himself up on his elbows. It was too dark to see anything.

When the next bolt of lightning illuminated the rain-streaked forest outside the window, there was a group of figures pushing their way through the trees. The flash was so sudden and short-lived that Marin hadn't seen much, but whatever these approaching figures were—well, they were much taller and bigger than humans.

The sudden banging of the door sent his heart racing. The pounding rain outside was suddenly much louder as footsteps came over the threshold, lumbering across the floorboards, fresh mud squelching between their toes. They grumbled and mumbled and snorted loudly.

Marin froze, paralyzed with fear. He drew a deep breath, held it, forced himself to move despite his terror. He slipped off his bed onto the floor. Thank the gods the heavy rain fell so loudly or else he was sure they would hear his heartbeat.

Whatever these creatures were, they seemed to be the inhabitants of the cottage. And they definitely weren't the friendly type—to say the least.

CHAPTER 15

Without taking his eyes off the shadowy figures, Marin crawled over to Aster's bed.

The figures continued grunting to one another, seeming to communicate in a half-formed language Marin didn't recognize. One of them slammed the door shut.

Marin reached up to slip his hand over Aster's mouth, then shook him gently by the arm. Aster jumped under Marin's grip, but he didn't shout.

"Be absolutely quiet," Marin whispered. *Oh, please don't let them hear me.* He glanced across the room. The figures were so preoccupied with their mumbling that they didn't hear him. "We're not alone," Marin whispered. He lowered his hand away from Aster's mouth.

Aster turned his head, and his eyes went so wide that Marin could see the whites even in the dark. "Oh..." He slipped off the bed onto the floor beside Marin. "What do we do?" he whispered.

A sudden blaze erupted in the fireplace, lit by one of the creatures, who then dropped what looked like a piece of flint onto the hearth. The figure drew itself up to its full height, almost seven or eight feet tall.

The light of the fire illuminated the room just enough for them to finally take in the sight of the clan that lived in the cottage. Maybe trolls—or ogres, Marin couldn't determine which. They were all well over seven feet tall, broad of shoulder and heavily muscled. Their matted hair hung past their waists, practically indistinguishable from the tattered animal pelts they wore.

It was then that Marin realized the biggest of the trolls had something over its shoulder. Ambling over to the battered table, the troll dropped its cargo with a heavy thud. Even by the firelight, Marin couldn't tell what it was.

Almost as if prompted by Marin's morbid curiosity, the lightning flashed outside, revealing for a brief moment that the something hauled in by the troll and dumped on the table was a blood-splattered corpse. Whether it was human or not was impossible to tell in the dark.

Marin barely had time to register his terror. In another moment, the trolls were gathered around the table, devouring their kill with unrestrained boorishness. Not even the rain could drown out the sound of their growls and slurps as they ripped the body apart, pulling at the limbs and flesh with their bare hands and bringing it to their gnashing teeth. Every few seconds, the firelight would gleam off flecks of blood and spit as they ate.

As disgusted and horrified as he was, Marin couldn't take his eyes off the scene. He could sense the same tension from Aster right beside him. "What do we do?" Marin whispered.

"Like I have any better idea than you do?" Aster hissed. "We just keep quiet. Until we have a chance to get out of here."

"All right."

The feeding seemed to stretch on forever. When the trolls had finally skeletonized the corpse, having licked every last bit of flesh from it and gnashed at every last organ, the largest of them let out a long, echoing belch.

The other trolls laughed. Another belched, sending them into more laughter.

"Ugh," Marin choked back the vomit in his throat.

The trolls continued to belch one by one, laughing more uproariously as each of them took part. One of the figures reached forward and tore a bone off the skeleton—maybe an arm or a leg, though it was hard to tell in the dim light of the fire. With a piercing cackle, the troll dropped the bone, letting it clatter to the floor, then brought his foot down on it with wild, unrestrained cruelty. The bone cracked as he stomped on it, and this sent the trolls into even more laughter.

This gross moment of bonding gave way to each of the trolls dragging themselves off to the nearby beds. Marin realized one of them was stumbling toward the bed he and Aster crouched under. He raised his arm to push Aster back, holding his breath as the thudding footsteps came closer, closer, closer, then collapsed on the bedframe. It creaked over top of them.

The room slowly quieted, the stomping and grunting giving way to nothing more than snores. Their oversized bodies slowly rose and fell with each breath, but there was no denying they were fast asleep.

In the quiet, with no more sound but the snoring all around them and the pattering rain overhead, Marin realized just how fast and loud his heart was still beating. His entire body, drenched with sweat, suddenly felt very cold.

He looked at Aster. The dread and fear he felt was evident on Aster's face. They had to get out of there—but how soon was too soon?

Do you think it's safe? Marin wanted to ask. But he was afraid to talk. One of the trolls might still be awake. One of them might be a light sleeper and be awakened by the sound of their whispering. But to stick around there longer than they had to? No, Marin wouldn't do it.

His eyes darted from Aster to the view they had looking out from under the bed. Still, no movement aside from the rise and fall of the oversized bodies snoring away on their beds. It felt as if hours had passed since they went to sleep. Marin knew it had probably been only a few minutes.

Aster caught Marin's eye and nodded. Marin didn't need words to understand the meaning: *Go ahead. Let's get out of here.*

Marin drew a deep breath and crawled out from under the bed. Slowly, his hands and knees moving at a cautious pace across the wooden floor, waiting for one of the boards to creak underneath him, he made his way toward the door. Aster trailed behind him.

No part of him wanted to look at the table as they crept past it, but he couldn't help it. The stench of blood hung too heavy in the moist night air. Marin turned to see the ominous black shape of whatever fully devoured thing lay across the table, the faint moonlight glimmering on bloody bones. He looked away.

They were halfway there. The room felt so big. So big. But the door was getting closer.

Creak! One of the boards moved ever so slightly beneath his hand. It sounded thunderously loud in the still room, even over the pounding rain.

Before he realized what had happened, one of the monstrous shapes in the beds rose. Then another.

"Run!" Aster shouted. "Run!"

Marin leaped up. There was no use crawling anymore. He turned to make sure Aster was following his lead, then darted toward the door.

The trolls sprang to their feet one by one, and as an army, they started moving after them. Marin threw open the door and sped out into the dark, wet night. The muddy ground sloshed and splattered with every footstep, the blanket of leaves threatening to make him slip. The rain had relented by now, but everything around them was still heavy with wetness. Tree branches whipped at him as he sprinted past. All he could think about was trying to put as much distance between them and the trolls as they could.

Oh, who would have thought we'd find ourselves in danger so fast? One day out in the world and we're going to die!

He looked over his shoulder. Aster's face bore a look of sheer terror, but he was keeping pace. The trolls were several yards behind them. Not as fast as the boys, they barged through the forest, swiping at tree branches and other foliage as if to tear it out of their way.

But if they caught up, Marin and Aster were done for!

All of a sudden, one of them came crashing through a tangle of vines to their right. Marin and Aster both erupted with terrified shouts. The enormous brute reached forward with one brawny arm and grabbed for Aster. Marin whirled just in time to see Aster fall to the ground, kicking up muck and stormwater as he slipped in the mud.

"Marin!" Aster shouted. "Help!"

There wasn't time to think. The other trolls were approaching fast. Marin could see movement in the shadows behind them, could hear their earthquaking footsteps. The troll that had caught up loomed over Aster and raised his club up above his head. He gave only a malevolent little snort as he swung the club downward. Moved by sheer impulse, Marin stepped forward and raised his hand to block the club. Searing pain shot through his body as the heavy wood struck his open palm. The troll, startled, drew the club back and cast it aside.

Everything around Marin spun, either because of the pain in his hand or because the jolt of the club hitting him had made him dizzy. The next thing he knew, the troll had him by the collar of his tunic and lifted him off the ground.

Marin's stomach lurched. He kicked his legs, trying to break free of the brute's clutches. "Aster!" he called. He couldn't break his stare-off with those big white eyes blazing out of the dark.

We're done for, Marin thought.

Then there came a hideous squelching sound, and the troll threw its head back in a roar of agony. Its grip slackened around Marin, dropping him onto the ground. Marin looked up to see Aster stumbling back away from the troll, holding his hands out in front of him as if completely dazed by what he had just done. Marin noticed the hilt of Aster's dagger jutting out of the troll's side.

An excited shout escaped Marin. "You stabbed him! You got him!"

"I know! I know! *Run!*"

The rest of the trolls were only a few strides away. Marin pushed Aster ahead of him and brought up the rear, the two of them leaping through the overgrowth at their feet and pushing their way through low-hanging branches.

They slogged their way another quarter mile through the forest before they reached the bank of a rushing creek overflowing from the storm. There was no use trying to ford the heavy, coursing flow of water, so Marin turned to run alongside it.

Aster grabbed his sleeve and pulled him in the direction of the creek. "This way!"

"What?" Marin hissed, his voice nearly lost in his heaving breaths. "Why?"

"Well…" Aster stammered. His cheek bore a long scratch from one of the tree branches that whipped him across the face, and his wet hair lay plastered to his scalp. "I don't know," he said at last. "Maybe trolls are like dogs—they'll lose our scent over water. Or something like that."

"What makes you think that?" Marin asked. The sound of the trolls was drawing closer. He still couldn't see them through the darkness.

Aster tugged at Marin's sleeve again, urging him toward the creek. "Do we have any other choice?"

Marin found no argument. He nodded.

Together, the two of them hopped over the bank and went splashing into the shallow waters of the creek. The rushing current bubbled up around their legs, and they took off running in the direction it flowed.

CHAPTER 16

Moving through the water was harder than running on land. Water filled Marin's shoes, making them heavy. For the first few minutes, he worried their splashing as they ran would call attention to them.

The night air seemed suddenly quiet except for their own splashing. No footsteps. No shouts. No growls.

Marin looked over his shoulder. No movement behind them, neither splashing around in the creek nor pushing through overgrowth in the woods.

We've lost them, he thought. *We've lost them, or they've given up. I hope...*

At last, the creek reached a larger river where the forest opened up to a narrow beach. The sand had turned to mud from all the rain. The sky had cleared by now, and moonlight illuminated the surface of the water and glimmered on the wet mud.

As they pushed their way from the stream into the river, Marin ducked into a patch of cattails to avoid the open, making room for Aster to huddle close to him. Aster's breathing was so loud it echoed off the water. They ducked down, letting the water come up to their chests. Marin studied the forest behind them, trying to detect any movement as he steadied his own breathing. "Are...are they...following us?"

Aster heaved beside him. "I...don't think so." He sighed. "We... we lost them."

Marin slowly stood again, raising himself to his full height, the river rippling around his waist now. He raised his hand out of the water and stared at it. The throbbing pain returned, nearly as bad as it was when the troll first struck him. His adrenaline must have suppressed the pain as they ran.

An ugly black bruise had already formed across his palm, and the line where the wood had broken his skin was washed with blood. Little pools rose up from the scrape as the river water slipped away.

"Are you hurt?" Aster asked.

Marin looked down to see Aster's gaze fixed on his hand. "Oh. No. I'm fine."

"You intercepted that club. You saved my life."

"It's nothing. Nothing you wouldn't do for me."

Marin could hardly believe what had just happened. "Something tells me the world is a lot more dangerous than we realized," he said at last.

"Aye," Aster said. "Do you suppose so?"

Marin recognized the sarcasm in Aster's voice and couldn't help laughing despite everything. No matter how bad things got, no matter what they were up against, it was good to know they were by each other's side.

"I think so," he said. "But we'll get through it."

Aster nodded at Marin's hand. "Aye, when we stick together like this."

"Aye."

Tsema's handmaiden had asked the gods to smile upon them—but so far, on their first day out in the world, they'd had a terrible brush with danger. They had almost died.

They sat in quiet for a moment, watching the darkness of the

100

forest just to make sure there was nothing following them. No trolls or any other predators or stalkers of any kind. Everything stood still except for the rushing creek flowing into the river.

Aster spoke. "Are you...are you regretting we ran away?"

"No. Are you?"

"No."

Neither of them even had to think about it. They trudged out of the cattails and up onto the bank, the likeliest place for them to make camp that night. Even if it started to rain again, they were already soaking wet.

This is the life of adventure we were looking for, Marin thought.

"Ilth's farm might have been safe," he reflected out loud, "but that's all it was. I would rather face whatever waits out here in the wide world than be stuck there forever."

They might have lain awake for a few minutes staring up at the stars and talking, but Marin hardly remembered any of it come morning. Exhaustion clouded his mind so much that he barely remembered lying down to sleep in the muddy sand. Sleep overtook him and that was the last he knew.

When he blinked his eyes open next, the faint light of dawn hung on the horizon, illuminating the little beach where they had made camp. Last night's raindrops glistened on the leaves of the trees skirting the beach, and the river itself was a foggy turquoise color. Mist streaked the gray and pink sky.

Marin lay still for a moment, watching the gentle morning breeze move the cattails where he and Aster hid the night before. Seagulls squawked in the distance. Despite the terror that had driven them there, this beach felt peaceful, safe.

He stretched and sat up, looking around to see Aster reclined against the back of a large rock, watching the sunrise.

Aster noticed Marin. "Good morrow."

Marin reached up to rub his eyes. "How did you sleep?"

"Not well. It took me a while to quiet my mind."

A pang of guilt struck Marin. He'd been able to fall asleep so easily. "We have a big day ahead of us," he said, then added hopefully, "Mayhaps we'll find ourselves fulfilling that great destiny the prophetess mentioned." He sat up and looked around for his pack but it wasn't beside him. Panic rose up in his chest. "My pack!"

Had he left it back in the troll's shack? Or had he dropped it when they were escaping through the woods? He couldn't remember. Everything from last night had happened so fast.

Aster nodded. "I realized that when I woke up. I lost mine too."

That left them with nothing. Not even food.

"Did you lose everything?" Marin asked.

Aster shrugged, then patted the pocket of his tunic. "Unless Ilth's fairy dust ends up being useful..."

Marin clenched his teeth. How could they be so reckless to lose everything? Here they were, lost and hungry, his hand throbbing in pain. Nothing to aid them except a pouch of fairy dust that they didn't even know how to use.

It won't do you any good to have regrets, he told himself. "What a shame," he said out loud.

They walked along the river's edge, the sand still soft and slightly muddy beneath their shoes. Marin hadn't expected that seeking their fortunes would feel so aimless. At least they were out of danger. For the moment.

"Aster," Marin began, "do you..."

But he never got a chance to ask the question. He stepped onto a patch of ground with no weight or solidity beneath it—suddenly, he was up to his waist in soft, wet sand. The surface of the ground rippled like water.

"Marin!" Aster shouted.

Marin kicked his legs beneath the surface of the sand, but there was nothing solid there. Suction pulled at him from below. "Aster!" He looked up to catch Aster's terrified expression, eyes wide at the sight of Marin sinking so quickly. "Aster, it's quicksand!"

"Don't struggle." Aster edged slightly closer, holding his hand out to Marin. The sand rippled at his feet. Aster looked down, shifting his feet around, unable to tell where the solid sand ended and the quicksand began. One false step and he would be in there with Marin—and then who would there be to save them?

"Don't struggle," Aster said. "You'll only sink faster."

Arms flailing, Marin tried to lunge forward and grab at the solid ground, sink his fingers into the dirt. The quicksand was up to his shoulders now. He couldn't tread as easily as he would've been able to in water. "I can't pull myself out. It's…" He gasped for breath. "It's… it's too thick. I can't tread."

Aster dashed to the water's edge and grabbed a thick piece of driftwood that lay nearby. He dropped to his knees and held it out to Marin. "Here! Take this!"

Marin grabbed at the driftwood, but its wet surface slipped from his fingertips, eluding his grip. He reached again, grasped at it, again to no avail.

Sludgy wet sand slopped around him. It was an inch higher now. Marin had to crane his neck to keep his chin above the surface.

Aster hurled the stick aside and sprinted toward a nearby log that lay at the edge of the beach. With two heaves, then a third, he forced it as close as he could toward Marin without letting it sink down into the sand.

"Aster, what are you doing?" Marin said, tilting his head back to keep his mouth above the surface of the sand.

"Just trust me!" Aster crawled along the log to get as close to Marin as he could. He reached out his arm. "Here, take my hand!"

"No, I'll pull you in."

"Just take my hand!"

Marin flailed his arm in Aster's direction. Their hands joined, wet sand sliding between their fingers. Aster heaved, partly out of exhaustion and partly from relief. "I've got you!"

But Marin could still feel the pull of the quicksand—it was stronger than Aster. The surface was up around his lips now, cold and grainy and wet. Aster kept his tight hold around Marin's hand, but he was no match against the steady sinking. *If he doesn't let go, I'm going to drag him down with me.* Marin tried to tug his hand away, but Aster's grip tightened.

The sand rose up around Marin's chin and swallowed his head.

Darkness closed around him as he lapsed under the surface of the sand, deep and deeper, the feeling of Aster's weight plunging after him.

CHAPTER 17

O f all the perils waiting in the great wide world, quicksand had never seemed a likely one.

Before Marin could register what was happening, he came crashing down with a sickening wet, sloppy thud on muddy ground. Aster came crashing down beside him. A mix of mud and clay splattered around them as they landed.

They were alive. And unhurt, as far as Marin could tell, though the fear and the fall had taken the wind out of him. He lay panting, trying to catch his breath as he stared up at the darkness they had come from. He looked over at Aster, splayed out in the mud, still clutching Marin's hand.

"Whoa," was all Marin could muster.

Aster had wet sand streaked across his shocked face. His eyes gaped. "What just happened?"

"I'm not quite sure." Marin sat up, taking in the sight of where they had landed. Tiny oil lanterns flickered from mounts on the sloping dirt walls that arched over their heads. Though the light was dim, it was enough to see they were in some kind of tunnel stretching out in front of them and behind them. No, not a tunnel. It was more like a… an animal's burrow. But tall and wide, large enough for them to walk upright alongside each other.

"I have a feeling we're underground," Marin said.

Aster got to his feet. "I have a feeling you're right, brother." He nodded at one of the tree roots poking its way out of the dirt walls.

"Now the question is...how do we get out?"

Aster turned his head, looking back and forth. "I don't know."

Marin followed Aster's gaze. No direction seemed better than the other.

"I guess it doesn't matter which way we go," he said. Something about feeling as if his choice didn't matter upset him. To think they escaped Ilth's farm, took control of their own fates, earned their freedom, only to find themselves out in the world where choice didn't matter.

He ran his hands over his ragged clothes to wipe as much wet sand off him as he could. Aster did the same. "I have to admit I hate this," Aster said.

Marin nodded. "As do I," he said. *I do hope he's talking about being wet and sandy,* Marin thought. *Not about the whole adventure.* "But we'll get through this," he added, as if that might soften the sense of cynicism they shared. "Let's go find a way out of here."

They set off walking. There were only two ways the tunnel could go—it would either take them deeper into the earth, or it would take them back up to the surface. Marin tried to swallow his pessimism. "I guess we're no worse off down here than we were up above ground. Either way, we're sure to be led somewhere."

Aster pushed his hair out of his eyes with a muddy hand. "Yes, but I liked it much better when we had daylight and open air." He sighed. "It's too cramped down here for me."

Marin lifted his hand, his eyes going wide. "Shh." A faint sound came from down around a bend in the tunnel. Distant, muffled, but it definitely sounded like—

"Do you hear voices?" Marin asked.

Aster stopped. Once they listened for them, the voices were more distinct. Aster lifted his arm and indicated the way down the tunnel. "Up there!"

They slowed their pace and made their way across the muddy ground with as much care as they could, the voices getting louder as they approached. Three voices, though it wasn't until they got close to the bend in the tunnel that they could make out what they were saying.

"Simply unbearable," a gruff voice said. "We've got to do something about it. It's a threat to all of us."

"But who's going to face it?" another voice said, this one higher, slightly nasally. "It won't be I."

"Certainly, you can't expect me to do it?"

They peered around the corner to see three small figures standing around in the shadows of the tunnel. Flickering torchlight illuminated them partially, revealing distinct features from their silhouettes. An overgrown mole stood on its hind legs and gestured with one of its claws at what must have been a gnome, or so Marin assumed based on its bushy beard and pointed cap.

"You are the only one of us with hands, I'm afraid," the mole said to the gnome. Its voice was the second they had heard, the shrill, nasally one. "The better to grip a weapon with, if I'm being honest."

"How about you do it?" the gnome replied to the mole. "You're blind. You won't even see your death coming."

The third figure—who looked like a dog or fox covered every inch over in thick, clotting mud—lifted one of his forepaws. "I see nobody is volunteering me," he said, globs of mud dripping off him as he shook his head. "Not that I want to go, but I don't want anyone to think me incapable."

Marin stepped back around the bend, indicating for Aster to follow him. "Sounds like they're in some sort of trouble."

Aster nodded. "Maybe we should go back the other way."

If only. The thought of avoiding trouble was tempting. "Maybe they know the way out of here," Marin said. "Maybe they can help us." He paused, thinking. "And maybe *we* can help *them*. If they're truly in trouble, I mean."

It was the right thing to do. It was what Tsema had told them to do. *When you encounter trouble, know that you will overcome it with enough determination and effort,* she had said. *And whatever happens, always trust that if you do what is virtuous and noble and honorable, you will be on the right path.*

Or being virtuous and honorable could get them landed in danger—that was always possible.

"What if they turn out to be enemies?" Aster said.

Marin bit his lip, unable to think of a reply. After their close call with the trolls the night before, he had very little interest in taking risks. These creatures were so small and looked so harmless, but there were likely more of them. Far more than the three he and Aster faced here.

Then again, if these people were in trouble…

If these people were in trouble, they had to help them. It was the right thing to do.

"What d'you think?" Aster asked at last.

"We should approach them," Marin said. "And find out what this danger is."

Aster nodded, but didn't move. Marin realized he was going to have to take the lead here. "I guess I should go first, huh?" he said.

"Well, I was just thinking—since it's your idea and all."

Marin smirked. "Very well. Come on."

He stepped past Aster and crept around the bend in the tunnel again to the small alcove where the trio argued.

"If none of us goes, then all of us might perish," the gnome was saying.

Marin took a deep breath and stepped out of hiding. "Excuse us."

The three creatures paused in their chatter and looked up. Marin felt a flutter in his stomach. Their expressions were difficult to read.

For a fleeting moment, he regretted their decision to approach. It might've been easier not to choose heroism.

"Well," the muddog said, "who would've guessed—we've got guests!"

The mole stared at them with unseeing eyes. "What is it?"

The gnome stroked his beard and came forward. Though he was twice the size of the mole, he still stood no taller than Marin's knee. "It's two...boys," he said. "Humans?"

"Yes," Marin replied. He looked over at Aster, realizing that maybe the less they said about themselves, the better. "Yes, we're humans."

"A pleasure to meet you, good sirs," the gnome said. He swiped his pointed cap off his hand and fell into a low bow. The muddog gave a bark and lowered himself down to the ground.

"Pray, how did you come to these underground dominions?" the mole asked, gazing just past them as he spoke. *He's blind*, Marin realized. He crouched down to bring himself closer to the little councilmembers.

"We hit a patch of quicksand and got sucked down," Aster said. "We're trying to find our way out."

"What were you all talking about just now?" Marin asked. "Are you in some kind of trouble?"

The gnome straightened his cap as he put it back onto his head. "Well, there's a terrible beast that has infiltrated these tunnels," he said. "I'm afraid it's a threat to all who live here." With that, the gnome indicated the two others. "We three are each a delegate of the populations that live in this underground territory—gnomes, moles, and muddogs."

The mole lifted his snout up in the air, almost snobbish in his demeanor. "Not normally quite so unified are we."

The muddog raised his head. "What our dear friend the mole means is that we normally keep to ourselves." His big yellow eyes peered up out of a face of sloppy brown glop. "But something has to be done about this creature. We're all afeared."

A beast, Marin thought. The hairs on the back of his neck prickled. "Has…it hurt anyone?" The words were hard to form in his mouth, difficult for him to express. He stood, drawing himself back up to his full height.

"Well, no," the gnome said, staring up at Marin. He scrunched his nose as if the question offended him. "But it's only a matter of time."

Aster put his arm around Marin's shoulder. "If we help you," he gestured between himself and Marin, "will you show us the way out? How to get back above ground?"

The gnome's eyes narrowed. "You're lost down here."

"Yes," Marin stated simply. "We are. And we need to find our way back out. If we agree to accept this mission, will you help us?"

The gnome glanced at the other two. "You're saying you'll do it? You're saying you do accept this mission?"

Marin realized Aster was waiting for agreement from him. Why did doing the right thing feel so daunting? He never had to make these kinds of difficult choices back when he was just a servant. "We will," Marin said. "We'll do it."

The mole moved forward. "How do we know you're worthy of this challenge?"

"Are you volunteering, Dimitri?" the muddog asked.

"I did not say I was," the mole replied. "But why should we trust they can do it?"

The gnome turned to the mole. "What choice do we have?"

"None," the muddog said.

Silence and tension mingled in the air, enveloping all of them— mole and gnome and muddog and boys.

This is your chance, Marin told himself. *Remember that—this is your chance. These are people who are counting on you.* This was their chance to be heroes. This was their chance to make something of themselves. The whole reason they ran away from Ilth's farm in the first place.

"Good sirs," the gnome turned from his fellow delegates to face Marin and Aster. "My name is Loff. I represent the gnomes who live in these tunnels. We thank you for your bravery."

These words were a formal acceptance of Marin and Aster's offer. A little pretentious, but maybe this must be how the culture down here underground worked. Maybe that was how all culture worked when you weren't a put-upon farm boy.

"The monster was last seen down this way," Loff continued. "Come along. I'll show you."

He pushed past them and waddled down the hall on stubby legs. Marin and Aster followed. As they went, Marin looked over his shoulder at the other delegates who were watching them go. *We won't let you down*, he wanted to say, but he resisted the urge. There was an important distinction between being confident and being an idiot.

The tunnel pressed on, becoming darker and darker, the torches and lamps on the walls getting fewer and farther between. The only sound was that of their footsteps shuffling through the dirt and the gnome's heavy breathing. Occasionally, he would mutter to himself under his breath, but Marin didn't want to ask what he was saying.

Loff eventually came to a stop at a bend in the tunnel. Three mounted torches cast a circle of orange light around them. The gnome raised his arm to gesture into the inky expanse of black beyond the torchlight. He looked off in the direction he indicated with his arm, even reached over with his other arm to adjust the cuff of his sleeve, but his muddy boots remained planted where they were on the tunnel floor. He had no inclination to step into the darkness himself.

"I…uh, I wish we could offer you some weapons," he said as Marin and Aster approached.

"We'll manage," Marin said, instinctively reaching for the place on his belt where his knife should have been. It wasn't until the words were out of his mouth that he realized how unsure he sounded. He glanced down at the scrape on the palm of his hand, the bitter reminder of his first attempt at fending off an enemy. He hadn't done a great job. Two days ago, he might have been rushing headlong into this opportunity—it was a chance to prove himself. But after their brush with danger in the den of trolls last night, not to mention the frightening experience in the quicksand…

Maybe he had been right all of those years on Ilth's farm. Maybe boring and safe might have suited him better than perilous adventure.

Aster took his arm. "Come on, Marin." He stepped forward and pulled one of the torches down off the muddy wall. "I hope nobody will mind?" he asked the gnome in a tone of voice that suggested he couldn't care less. Without waiting for a response, he handed the torch to Marin and grabbed another one for himself. The third torch remained on the wall, a solitary beacon in the dark tunnel.

"Good luck," Loff muttered. "May the gods deliver you."

"Thank you," Marin said. The gods deliver them! If the gods had any regard for them, they would not have delivered them down into a tunnel beneath the earth. The gods seemed to be wreaking havoc for them, as far as Marin could tell.

Marin and Aster set off into the dark. For several minutes, they padded their way around overwhelming shadow, their torches illuminating only a little way ahead of them. It might have been less than a hundred steps, but it felt like a lot longer than that.

When they came to a bend in the tunnel, they turned and continued on in a different direction, moving around aimlessly without anything to suggest they weren't utterly alone in the tunnel. For a monster that was supposed to be so fearful to all the inhabitants of the underground realm, this creature didn't seem to pose much of a threat.

"I wonder…what happens if we never find the monster?" Marin said.

"Then I guess we never find him," Aster said. He didn't sound disappointed by the thought. "But in that case, we might never find our way out of here either."

Marin had a sudden sinking feeling in his stomach. He and Aster might be trapped to wander the tunnels underneath the earth for years!

The sound of footsteps in the dark up ahead made him jump. Sudden dread swept through him, his heart hammering. He glanced at Aster, whose eyes were wide. Marin lifted his torch, but its meager light illuminated nothing but empty tunnel and blackness beyond.

Then, heavy breathing. A low growl.

Marin's heart raced, but neither he nor Aster dared move. They stood frozen in place.

Whatever it was up in the darkness took a deep breath, then roared. Aster grabbed Marin's arm and dragged him backward, turning and sprinting. "Run," he hissed.

"But—!"

Whatever argument Marin planned to make, he quickly forgot it. For a moment, it sounded as if heavy footsteps were following them, the sound of slobbery huffing and puffing making Marin think of powerful jaws that would attack them. Then he slowed and stopped.

All was quiet.

"Did...did it go the other way?" he heaved.

Aster looked back in the direction they'd run from. "I...I think so."

Marin swallowed the lump in his throat. "I can't believe we just ran from danger," he said. "We'll never get out of here unless we bring ourselves to face—to face—well, to face whatever that thing is."

Aster nodded. He swiped his arm at a tree root protruding from the ceiling of the tunnel. "They're really going to hold us hostage down here unless we fight that monster. They're not going to show us the way out."

Marin held his torch out to assess the tunnel. "Well, we did agree.

This is a mission we accepted."

Such an observation hardly enthused Aster. "Maybe we'll find a way out of here before we encounter the monster again."

Marin shook his head. "Aye, how opportune that would be! But then we wouldn't make good on what we agreed to do. It would look dishonorable."

Aster hesitated. "That it would."

"We need to stick to our word," Marin added.

After all, escaping this underground territory—particularly if they had no reason to be down there in the first place—without facing down a monster wouldn't necessarily be so dishonorable. Yet what would happen when it was a princess captured by a dragon? Or a city under siege by an army of the undead? These were the sorts of things that happened in the great wide world, at least according to the ballads and epics. If he and Aster wanted to amount to anything, they had to be ready for such challenges.

A thunderous roar erupted from the darkness ahead of them, a sound so sudden and startling that Marin was dragged out of his thoughts and nearly out of his own skin. He jumped, grabbing Aster's arm to steady himself, his heart clamoring in his chest.

Aster held his torch aloft. "What was that?"

Trying to hold his voice steady, trying to sound as brave as he could, Marin replied, "Something tells me it's the monster."

Neither of them turned to run. Instead, Marin's feet moved forward before he could fully process the thought, and Aster followed. The roar came again, closer this time. They were headed in the right direction. Not necessarily a happy thought, but it was progress at least.

Torchlight revealed the tunnel ahead of them as they proceeded, an orange glow catching on the sleekness of the muddy walls. When they reached a bend in the tunnel, Marin paused.

Roooooarrr!

The vicious cry came from around the bend. A tree root dangling from the dirt overhead trembled, and several drops of mud came plopping down on top of them.

They were only a few feet from this monster, whatever it was.

Marin took a step back. With his breath caught in his throat, he glanced over at Aster. "There's no turning back now," Marin murmured. "We have to go through with this."

Aster didn't reply beyond a nod, his brow furrowed. This was the moment.

Torches held high, they dashed around the corner to see whatever creature it was that terrorized these underground tunnels and its inhabitants.

Fear had overwhelmed Marin up until that point, or so he thought. It was nothing compared to what he felt then. Seeing the beast right there in front of him made him seize up. It was the size of a hound, moving around on all fours, its entire body covered with a patchwork of matted gray fur and glittering scales.

With another roar, the creature raised itself up on its hind legs, bringing itself to a height nearly as tall as they were. It beat its large forepaws on the dirt wall in front of it. Behind it, a spiked tail lashed back and forth as its upturned head continued to scream. *Rooooaaaarrr!*

The monster dropped down on all fours and spun itself in a circle twice, then thrice. Another roar erupted from its snout. Now that its head was lowered, Marin could see flames flash in its eyes. With a low growl, the creature turned and charged at the opposite wall of the tunnel, raising its forepaws up to beat at the mud.

Marin caught Aster's eye. "You ready?"

"Ready as I'll ever be."

With a deep breath, Marin dashed forward, Aster close behind him. "Hey!"

The beast looked up as they charged toward it. It wasn't until he

115

saw those fiery eyes that Marin became aware of how unprepared he was. He wasn't sure exactly what he would do once he confronted it, whether he would just chase it down or try to actually attack it with fire.

But as soon as the creature took notice of them, it scurried as far as it could into the alcove, lowering itself to the ground with a pathetic whimper. The fire in its eyes dimmed as it tucked its head close to its forepaws, resting on the ground in front of it.

Marin stopped. He raised one arm to grab Aster by the sleeve of his tunic.

It's scared! Marin recognized that fear. In all the years he lived on Ilth's farm, Marin had developed something of a sense of animal emotions. There were ways of reading squirrels and foxes and birds if you paid close enough attention. But there was no mistaking how this creature felt right now.

"It's...it's terrified," he whispered to Aster.

He lowered his torch. The beast went back against the wall, flattening itself to the ground and sobbing. Its body heaved up and down with each cry. Large tears splashed from its eyes into the mud.

"Aye, I think you're right," Aster said.

A moment passed, neither of them sure of what to do.

Aster took a deep breath. "It...it's more afraid of us than we are of it."

Marin stepped forward. Something about the creature's face and form looked soft, unmatured.

"Aster...I think it's just a baby."

A great brute of a baby, something that would grow up to be horribly large, but a baby, nevertheless. Marin approached the creature with his hand outstretched. "Hey," he cooed. "Hey, it's all right now."

The monster lifted its head and looked up at him with pouty black eyes glistening with tears. Its face was twisted up in fear and sadness.

Somehow, Marin understood. "Are you lost?"

At that, the monster cocked its head. It might not have understood the words, but it seemed to comprehend that Marin and Aster weren't going to hurt it.

Aster approached and stood next to Marin. "Aw. Poor thing."

"I don't think he means to hurt anyone down here," Marin said. "I think…I think he found his way into this tunnel and got lost. Sort of like we did." There was no way this monster belonged down here in the underground. He thought he recognized it as a nulquin. He had only seen a roughly drawn illustration of a nulquin before, but this creature resembled what he'd seen. Once it grew a little bigger, it would have little room to move around. This was a creature that was meant to bound around in the open air.

"Come on," Marin said to the beast. "We won't hurt you."

He took a step back and patted his thigh to indicate for the monster to follow. A moment passed. The nulquin cub remained crouched, its fear still palpable.

"Come on," Aster echoed. "This way."

The nulquin quivered as it raised itself up off the ground and approached them.

"That's it," Marin said. "Good. Good, come on."

Aster took a few steps back and Marin followed. The nulquin continued ambling after them. And when they turned the corner and pressed on down the tunnel, so did the beast.

"It's following us," Aster whispered to Marin.

"I know. Let's hope it remains friendly."

He picked up pace as they pressed on back through the shadowed tunnel, he and Aster taking a few steps at a time to coax the nulquin after them. Its pace quickened eventually.

He's very eager, Marin realized. *He trusts us.*

But what were they going to do if they couldn't find their way back to the council where they had started? And what were the delegates going to think if he and Aster showed up with the monster trailing behind him when the expectation was that they would slay the beast?

Marin took a deep breath, letting his adrenaline subside. He clapped his hands, beckoning the nulquin on. The way its massive paws pounded on the dirt floor made the tunnel shake. No wonder all the inhabitants of this territory, small as they were, lived in fear of this creature!

"I won't lie," Marin whispered to Aster. "Even I'm a little scared of it." He watched the light gleam off the spittle dribbling from the nulquin's snout.

"I hope they believe us when we tell them it's harmless," Aster said. "This could end very badly."

That thought didn't bring Marin much confidence, but he couldn't deny it either. Control the situation they could try to do, but there were consequences to befriending this creature that were beyond his power.

Still—it was just a baby, and they had an ethical duty to protect it.

They kept their voices soothing and gentle, their clapping of hands and snapping of fingers enthusiastic, as they lured the nulquin back the way they'd come, trying to retrace their steps as best they could.

"Wait, Marin," Aster said suddenly. "Do you hear that?"

Marin held his breath. There was no mistaking it—birds chirping. "Come on," he said.

In their excitement, both of them forgot about the nulquin and ran in the direction of the sound. The nulquin trotted behind them as they turned around a bend in the tunnel. Up ahead, a shaft of light shone down across a slope leading up to a hole gaping into the world above.

The appearance of light after so long in darkness, stumbling around by only meager torchlight, was blinding and startling. The shining white shaft poured through the opening, washing the muddy walls with a warm glow. Marin recognized blue sky and green foliage beyond the hole.

"Eeeeehhhhh!" The nulquin gave an excited howl and bounded forward, its paws kicking up splotches of mud. It went up the slope of the burrow hole onto the soft grass that waited outside. Only then did it turn around to look at Marin and Aster, its eyes wide and its snout stretched into an eager smile.

"I think it wants us to follow," Aster said.

"Aye. I think so too."

Neither of them moved forward. "I...I don't think we should leave just yet," Marin said. "I think we should stay. To say something to the council before we leave. We owe them that much. To tell them that their territory is safe again."

"I was thinking the same thing," Aster replied.

But the thought gave Marin a slight pang of disappointment. He had already started to think of the nulquin affectionately. Almost like a pet. Or another companion.

The nulquin continued to stare at them. Its tail wagged eagerly.

"Go on," Marin urged. "We can't leave just yet. Go on."

The nulquin bowed low, nearly touching its chin to the ground, obviously an expression of gratitude. It raised itself back up and bounded off, disappearing into the brightness of the day outside the burrow hole.

Marin gave a low chuckle, one that hardly masked how bittersweet the moment felt. "I guess it really was nothing to be afraid of. It was sort of cute, in its own way."

"I don't know about you, but I thought it was pretty scary."

"You know what I meant."

Aster laughed. "Aye. I do."

What a strange world this is, Marin couldn't help thinking. Nothing he had read in his books prepared him for this. Nothing was as he expected it to be. What seemed safe turned out to be dangerous, and what seemed dangerous turned out to be safe. At least they had made good on what they agreed to do and completed the mission. That was what mattered.

At first, the delegates seemed excited when Marin and Aster returned. Loff the gnome even shouted, "Oh, praise be!" when he saw them unhurt. He grabbed at his cap and swung it around over his head.

Dimitri the mole immediately declared, "They've slain it!" He clapped his forepaws together, though his gaze was slightly askew, not directly looking the way Marin and Aster were coming.

"Well, we haven't exactly slain it," Marin said, before he and Aster delved into the whole story of what had happened. They made special effort to emphasize that the baby nulquin didn't like being down in the tunnels and now that it was back up above ground, it would not be wandering back down.

"It wasn't a ferocious beast," Aster concluded. "It was just a hatchling. A cub."

"It was lost, and we helped it find its way," Marin said. The thought occurred to him that the nulquin's circumstances weren't much different from his and Aster's—cast down into the underground world by accident, lost, scared. If he and Aster had fangs and fur, they could just as easily have been perceived as a threat by these little people underground.

"Rest assured though," Marin concluded, "your tunnels are safe now."

The muddog cleared his throat, something between a bark and growl. "Well, that's good enough for me." He looked at the other two as if to gauge their agreement. When neither of them responded, he addressed the gnome. "Loff, will you be so kind as to help them find their way back up to the world above?"

Marin looked back down the tunnel whence they'd come. Pools of orange light dotted the darkness as far as he could see. "Thank you most kindly, but I think we'll be all right from here." He looked at Aster, who nodded. "We…uh, we just wanted to come tell you. Seemed like the right thing to do, I mean. So that you didn't think we abandoned you." Why did talking formally have to be so awkward? They had just completed a valiant mission, so why was he stumbling over his words?

Loff stepped forward, smoothing the wrinkles of his burlap tunic as he did. "And we thank you for it." He reached a knobby white hand from inside his pocket and pulled out some small trinket clasped between his stumpy fingers. "Here. Take this!"

Marin couldn't make out what the small token was in the gnome's hand. "What is it?"

"It is a ring," Loff declared, blinking expectantly, holding the ring up closer to Marin. His short arms reached no higher than Marin's waist. "A magic ring, I might add."

Marin could see it now. Simple brass, unadorned, battered—sized for a human. It caught the torchlight on its uneven edges. Marin reached down to accept the gift from the gnome. The piece bore surprisingly heavy weight despite its small size. Marin held it out for Aster to see as well.

Aster took the ring in his hand and eyed it. "Magic, you said? In what way?"

Loff chuckled, making the hairs of his graying beard shake. "That's a secret I can't tell." He must have recognized perplexed looks on their faces because he quickly added, "No, not because I'm forbidden to tell you. It's just because I don't know."

Aster handed the ring back to Marin. "Then how do you know it's magic?"

Loff smirked. "Oh, we gnomes know these things. Don't ever doubt what a gnome knows."

Don't ever doubt what a gnome knows, Marin thought. Clever adage. Had he read that before in a book? There was so much about the

121

world that he and Aster still had to learn. Which beings were wise, and which ones were ignorant. Which beings were to be trusted, and which ones were malicious. It was all so hard to guess without much experience beyond farm chores.

Loff arched one of his bushy eyebrows. "If we could give you greater rewards, we would," he said. "Why, I'd bestow upon you the lost royal relics of the Kingdom of Grythium, and then you'd be able to declare yourself the rightful ruler of the land. You certainly deserve it, as far as I'm concerned, young sirs."

Marin tried his best to follow what the gnome said. *The lost relics of Grythium…and then you'd be able to declare yourself the rightful ruler of the land?*

"Lost royal relics?" Aster asked, just as surprised to hear this as Marin was.

"Heh!" Loff chuckled. "They're not hidden here in these underground tunnels, that's all I know. But if you do manage to find them, ah, well, I think the realm could benefit from your heroism. This ring is the greatest token of our appreciation I can offer."

"Thank you," Marin said. He couldn't help wondering whether it might be worthwhile trying to find the lost relics, if the realm did indeed need such heroism. Tsema had hinted at such a thing, hadn't she? That the realm needed heroes?

"If you figure out how that ring works, use it wisely," Loff added.

Marin slipped it onto his finger. It fit as if it had been made for him. "You can trust we'll do that," he said, staring at his hand. Between the wound across his palm and the ring on his finger, the hand looked like a testament to the adventures they'd had so far since leaving Ilth's farm.

Awkward silence. Marin and Aster exchanged glances. "Well," Marin said with a clearing of his throat. "We thank you. And now we'll be on our way."

CHAPTER 18

Prophecies, a clan of trolls, underground monsters—all in only three days' time. Now that they had survived it, Marin thought their mission to make something of themselves in the world was turning out remarkably. Could some of it have gone better? Of course, Marin would not have denied that. They had hardly proven themselves much of a match against a clan of trolls, but they managed to rescue a defenseless nulquin cub and restore order to the underground realm. That had to count for something, didn't it?

Besides, the prophetess had assured them they were meant to do great things. Now all they had to do was discover what those great things were.

It didn't take long for them to find a direction once they were back above ground. The tunnel had led out into an open expanse of field where overgrown grass lulled gently back and forth in the morning breeze. It must have still been an hour or two away from high noon, as the sun was not yet at its full height in the sky.

They found the road easily enough. It wasn't paved, but its width stretched large enough to accommodate a carriage. *That must mean it leads somewhere,* Marin thought. *Somewhere reputable. Anywhere is better than being lost out here in the middle of nowhere.*

They started walking, and their conversation turned to hopeful expectations of what might await them when they reached the next city or village. Marin tried to remember the map he always looked at many times late at night in his shed while he dreamed of seeing more of the world. Its yellowing parchment had shown that Ilth's farm lay deep in the valley between the forests that separated the kingdoms of Grythium and Blunia.

Grythium and Blunia. Tsema had mentioned the kingdoms were at odds with each other, and that neither kingdom had an heir. What political turmoil something like that must cause! Marin couldn't resist wondering what that meant for two vagabonds seeking their fortunes—would that make it easier or harder?

"Maybe we'll find jobs there," Marin said, trying to be hopeful. "Or apprentice ourselves to some tradesmen. Find an honest way to make money."

"Don't we want to have a few more adventures first?" Aster said. "See more of the world before we commit ourselves to one place?"

"We can do all of that once we've saved some money," Marin said. He looked down at the ring on his finger. "We're not going to make it far with a magic ring and a pouch of fairy dust, for all the good they might do us."

Aster shrugged. "True."

They stopped briefly to rinse the mud off themselves in a brook that ran alongside the road, then continued on. Not knowing what lay ahead had a certain excitement to it, but Marin would have liked to have had that map. He could still picture the cartographer's drawings of forests and mountains. Memory was all he had now though.

But maybe—just maybe—they were on the right track finally. If they could make their way to Grythium or Blunia, they might find themselves closer to achieving the destiny Tsema foresaw for them.

"How far to the nearest city, you think?" Marin said.

"I don't know any more than you do," Aster replied. "But look— isn't that a crossroad sign up ahead?"

Aster nodded and Marin followed his gaze. The road sloped up a hill to where a rickety signpost stood amid unkempt grass, its weatherworn arrows pointing north, south, east, and west. Several feathertoads resting on the sign took off and flew away as they approached.

It wasn't until Marin and Aster got closer that they saw the man sleeping at the foot of the sign, reclined in what looked like an uncomfortable position. His head lay against the pole so that his scraggle-bearded chin rested on his chest, his pointed cap drawn over his eyes to shield them from the sun.

Their approaching footsteps must have awakened him because when they were two or three feet away, he lifted his head and pulled the brim of his hat out of his face. His eyes went wide and he sat up.

Marin raised his hands to show they meant no harm. "Good morning! Good morning, sir! We didn't mean to startle you."

The man scrambled to his feet and lifted himself to his full height, which was not much higher than Marin's chest. Despite his stature, the man had an arrogant expression suggesting his demeanor more than made up for his small size. His pasty gray-white skin and pointed ears made Marin think he might've been one of the morgglors, small elfish people from the far north.

"Good day, good day," the man said. He cocked one of his bushy eyebrows and stroked the matted gray hairs of his beard. "Good day, young sirs."

Marin admired the gold brocade on the man's tunic, the jewels stitched into the fabric that glimmered in the sun. It was all a little too much finery for someone who was standing unattended by the roadside without footmen or valets. Stolen? Or was he traveling in disguise? Something was amiss. The little man's hands trembled as he ran them over his thighs to smooth out the wrinkles in his velvet trousers.

125

You're being prejudiced, Marin thought to himself. *You've read too many folktales.*

Marin cleared his throat. "Can you tell us how far it is to the nearest city?"

"To the city?" the man said. He shuffled his feet. "Well, of course, of course, it's only another five miles by this road here." He indicated the direction that Marin and Aster had been walking. "But it's not safe." He shook his head. "No, not safe at all. This is a dangerous road."

"Dangerous?" Marin said. "In what way?"

The man laughed, revealing a mouth of gold-capped teeth. "Not to fear, my young sirs. Not to fear." Marin didn't like the sound of that laugh—it was a villainous laugh, one that suggested he and Aster really *did* have much to fear.

Don't be stupid, Marin told himself. *It's just your nerves.* Or was it? There was no telling whom they should trust or what they should expect. They had thought the shack in the forest was abandoned, but it turned out to be a den of trolls. They thought the monster in the underground tunnel was dangerous, but it had merely been a cub.

After the ordeals they had been through, there was no easy way to trust anyone or anything. Maybe he was cynical. Maybe this foul little man might actually be someone they could trust.

"My name is Gnarnus." The man took a step toward them. He reeked of sweat covered up with too much perfume. "I know another way into the city, one that is safer." He grinned. It was an expression a wolf would make before eating a defenseless rabbit or squirrel. "Will you follow me?"

Before Marin could respond, Aster piped up. "My friend asked you a question." Aster's tone was direct but not impolite. "In what way is this road dangerous?"

Gnarnus avoided the question again. "I daresay you're not from these parts, are you, sir? Where do you come from?"

"We…" Marin hesitated.

There's no harm in telling him the truth, as long as we don't tell him too much, he thought. Besides, it was easier than trying to come up with a convincing lie on the spot. *We're still runaways though. Or fugitives. Whatever would be the right word for us.*

"We are visitors from the countryside, yes," he said. "Not city people. We're from the other side of the forest." Marin swallowed, paused, feeling comfortable that he had shared enough and didn't need to give away anymore. "Is this the kingdom of Grythium? Are we approaching the royal city?"

Gnarnus nodded, his beard flopping. "Yes, yes, it is. Come along, young sirs, I urge you. Trust me. Travel no farther down this here road." He laughed again, and again the sound of it gave Marin an unsettled feeling. "I will show you another route. It's longer, but it will be safer for you. We'll take a path through the forest."

"The forest?" Aster said.

"You don't know how dangerous it is for you to walk out in the open along the road like this," Gnarnus said. "Come along. Do I need to wait all day for you to come to your senses? Come along."

Gnarnus barely stepped off the road when the sound of approaching hoofbeats met their ears. He looked up with alarm. "Hide!" he barked. "Hurry! This way!"

He waved his arms to rush them off the road and down the grassy slope of the hill. Marin didn't have to think—Aster grabbed his arm and dragged him in the direction Gnarnus indicated. The dewy grass nearly sent them sliding as they stumbled into an overgrowth of bushes and ducked behind a large oak on the edge of the forest. Marin pressed himself up against the broad trunk and peered around to watch an ornamented coach pass by, drawn by white horses. An exquisitely dressed driver sat up front, holding the reins with white-gloved hands, and two footmen in violet capes rode on the back. If any of them took notice of the three figures hiding in the foliage on the edge of the forest, they gave no indication whatsoever.

The hoofbeats grew softer as the carriage progressed farther down the road, disappearing into the distance. Gnarnus, crouched close to the ground, looked up at Marin and Aster. "There ain't much traffic headed into the city today. You're lucky. You might've been caught long before you met me if there'd been more carriages or riders out and about. Then what kind of trouble would you be in?"

"Why is this road so dangerous?" Marin asked.

Something changed in the man's face. Where there had once been a suspicious sneakiness, there was suddenly unmistakable malice. "Ha! Wouldn't you like to know?"

A glint of light caught Marin's eye, and he looked down to realize it came from a dagger Gnarnus drew from his belt.

"Whoa!" Marin shouted.

"Ha!" Gnarnus cried, lifting the blade up and brandishing it in front of him, first toward Marin, then toward Aster, then back and forth, back and forth. "And now you think I'm your friend, do you? This road is dangerous, yes. At least for the likes of you. And I'm one of the dangers. Now you're my prisoners."

Aster took a step back, his arms raised. Gnarnus closed in on him, knife out in front of him. "Afraid, are you?"

Marin wouldn't stand for this. After what they'd been through over the past few days, the morgglor hardly seemed a formidable threat. "Leave him alone!"

He stepped forward and delivered a swift kick to the back of the little man's legs, sending him hurtling forward and dropping the blade. In a flash, Aster grabbed the blade while Marin wrestled his arms behind him.

"Hold still, you knave!" Marin shouted.

Any trace of villainy quickly dissolved from Gnarnus's expression.

His eyes went wide and his lip trembled. "Please! I prithee, don't hurt me!" Large tears rolled down his face and into his beard.

"You coward!" Aster exclaimed.

Marin would have laughed if he didn't feel so embarrassed on the man's behalf—especially when he thought about how brazen Gnarnus had been when the knife was in his hands. "What's this all about?" Marin asked. "Why would you attack us?"

"I prithee, I am sorry, my good sirs! I am sorry."

"We don't want apologies," Marin said. "We want an explanation."

Aster offered out the dagger and Marin took it. But when he looked back down at Gnarnus, he couldn't bring himself to muster a threat. "Look at him. He's terrified."

"Your good heart is going to get you in trouble one of these days," Aster said.

Marin laughed. "Mayhaps."

Aster had a point. This venomous little bully had been all too willing to attack them for seemingly no reason at all. If they let him go, there was no guarantee he wouldn't try the same thing again.

"Mayhaps this isn't the right time for sympathy," Marin said. "But it is time for an explanation. What do you say, Gnarnus?"

"And you'll have it," Gnarnus replied. "An explanation, I mean."

Gnarnus heaved three or four deep sighs to control his tears. Marin let go of his arms, and their would-be attacker rolled out onto the grass. When he caught his breath, he sat up and looked from Marin to Aster and back to Marin again. He brushed the tears out of his eyes and wiped his hands on his breeches.

"When I said this road was dangerous, I was being truthful," Gnarnus said as he climbed to his feet.

"Obviously," Aster interjected.

"Aster, let him talk. Go on, Gnarnus."

Gnarnus nodded, a very portrait of politeness. "There is a royal decree from the palace of King Donovan that any two young men seen in these parts who look like they might be seventeen years of age—be they peasant or noblemen, knights or tricksters—they should be brought to the king, alive or dead." He shrugged. "There's even a reward."

As if that excused his attack.

"That's why you tried to kill us, is it?" Aster asked.

"Aster, calm down," Marin said. He loved Aster for his loyalty and defensiveness, but this was bordering on aggression. "Answer his question, Gnarnus."

The morgglor started to choke up again. "I prithee—"

"I've already given you my word that we won't hurt you. You don't need to doubt us." Marin looked at Aster to make sure he agreed with this, then back to the morgglor. "But I do demand answers. Why is there a reward out for our lives?"

"Well, it's not exactly *your* lives—"

"You know what I mean."

A strange expression crossed Gnarnus's face. Incredulity? Or just surprise? "Do you not know the rumor?" he said. "Has the kingdom's greatest gossip really not reached wherever you live? Where are you two from anyway? I thought everyone in the province knew. Why, it's the reason King Donovan and King Hector are sworn enemies."

Aster shook his head. "This means nothing to us." His tone had softened, but Marin could still detect a hint of suspicion.

The morgglor looked baffled. "It means nothing to you that King Donovan and King Hector, once the best of kingly friends and allies, turned their backs on one another and swore themselves enemies?"

"We grew up in the countryside, far away from either king's dominion," Aster said. "And where that is...well, it's none of your business."

"Aye, fair enough, fair enough, my good sir," Gnarnus said. "But you should know..." He walked over to a nearby log and seated himself, as if he were trying to get comfortable for the story he was about to tell. "Well, you should know that seventeen years before now, King Donovan of this land of Grythium was the best of friends with King Hector of Blunia."

He paused as if expecting some sort of reaction. Aster had already made it very clear they didn't know anything about King Donovan or King Hector. Ilth's farm lay outside any of the royal provinces, and she never gave any indication that she troubled herself with politics or showed any loyalty to any liege or lord.

"It was a happy alliance between the two kingdoms," Gnarnus continued. "A happy alliance such as history has never known before. The kings loved each other as brothers. But there came a day when Donovan was told a prophecy. It foretold that one day, Hector's child would rule his kingdom. Why, King Donovan suddenly believed his son and heir was a bastard sired by his best friend, that his best friend was guilty of adultery with his beloved wife. He flew into a rage."

Gnarnus paused, looking at the two of them to make sure they were following what he said.

"Go on," Marin urged.

Gnarnus lowered his voice, almost as if he were nervous he might be overheard. As if there were anybody nearby. "They say King Donovan went mad. He condemned his wife to execution for treason and declared Hector his enemy. Then commanded that his son, as well as his sister's son, be killed, ending the chance of the prophecy coming true."

"Why his sister's son?" Aster asked.

"Why, you don't know much, do you?" Gnarnus said. "A man's nephew by his sister is his next heir after his own son. A man's nephew by his sister is a dear bond—a man might not know whether his son is truly his own, but he always knows he shares blood with his sister's son. That's what would have made it all the worse a betrayal."

The thought sent a shiver down Marin's spine. Was the ruler of this kingdom actually a crazed tyrant capable of ordering the execution of babies? His son and his nephew at that!

"King Donovan would have done anything to maintain power," Gnarnus said. "It did not matter that his best friend and closest ally swore he had committed no such wrong. It didn't matter how his wife and his sister screamed for him to have sense, to show mercy."

Gnarnus continued. "Under King Donovan's orders, a servant carried the two babies into the forest and slew them. But still, even this unspeakable deed was not enough to allay the king's fears. Prophecy is prophecy, after all. And those who try to escape it sometimes find themselves trapped by it anyway."

Marin caught Aster's eye. Prophecy again. Was everyone in this kingdom convinced that prophecy was real, that it always came true, that the events of the future are already preordained and can't be changed?

"How could the prophecy come true if those boys were killed?" Marin asked.

Gnarnus shrugged. "There's no guessing. But still, King Donovan remained convinced that King Hector's bastards would find their way back to him. Ghosts, mayhaps? Or the undead? It's a frightening thought, don't you think? Well, anyway, his majesty maintained a commandment that any two unknown boys or young men alike in years as his son and nephew would be—that is, ten years ago, any boys about seven years old, or five years ago, any boys that might be twelve years old, or—"

"We get it," Aster said. "We're peasants but we're not stupid."

Gnarnus sneered. "Good, glad to hear it. And if you're not stupid, you get why it would be unwise for the two of you to cross through the city."

"But we can't turn back," Marin said. "We're on a mission. We have to move forward."

Gnarnus picked his teeth, seemingly apathetic.

"Can't you help us?" Aster asked.

The morgglor exaggerated his look of surprise. "Me?"

"Yes, you," Aster said. "Who else?"

Gnarnus stood up from his seat on the fallen log. "Well, I suppose I do owe you for sparing me life."

Marin tucked the knife carefully into his belt. "You owe us nothing," Marin said. "We would not have your blood on our hands."

Gnarnus bowed. "You are too…uh, *magnanimous*, my good sir." He said it as if this were the first time he had used such a big word. It wasn't clear whether his tone was genuine or sarcastic. Marin didn't like that.

"If you're willing," Marin said, "to help navigate us safely through the city, and help us avoid those who would do us harm, then we would be most grateful." Listening to himself, even he was impressed by how authoritative he managed to sound. Not bad for a ragged young farm boy.

A chuckle escaped Gnarnus. "Right you are, good sir. I think I have an idea."

CHAPTER 19

"Royally appointed." That's how Gnarnus described how he wanted Marin and Aster to look. Marin had never heard the expression before, but it sounded as if it meant they were supposed to look like they were chosen for some kind of important business, the type of important business Marin knew nothing about and probably would not be able to imitate if anyone were to start asking him questions. Royal business. Just what sort of things did one royal communicate to another? Trade? Alliances? Fending off dragons? Marin was pretty sure Gnarnus himself didn't even know.

Still, Gnarnus had agreed to help them. Marin wasn't going to forget he tried to attack them, but at least Gnarnus hadn't done anything aggressive in the quarter hour it took them to walk through the forest to his den.

At least, his "den" was what he called it. As far as Marin and Aster were concerned, it was a cave.

Hoarded treasure filled the space, standing in piles nearly up to their waist. Flickering light from oil lamps danced when it hit the heaps of gold and gemstones. Gnarnus had lit the lamps with flint handled by clumsy fingers, almost as if he were still nervous Marin and Aster might try to attack him again. For such a roguish fellow, not to mention outspoken, he was more cowardly than anything else.

Aster traced eyes around the cave, taking in all the sights. "Where did you get all this?"

"Far be it from me to reveal the secrets of how I acquired my hoard of treasure."

Aster gave Marin a knowing look. "That means he stole it."

"What of it?" Gnarnus said.

But Marin wasn't listening to the banter. He studied the brocaded tunic Gnarnus had pulled from one of his oaken treasure chests. He traced his fingers over the gold inlay along the collar and sleeves, then shucked off his own ratty tunic to put this royal one on. The cold air of the cave prickled his bare skin. He dropped the mud-stained burlap on the floor and pulled the brocaded velvet around him as quickly as he could.

"You'll clean up like a proper gentleman, I should say," Gnarnus said, holding out a wet rag for Marin to scrub some of the dirt off his face. "Once you're dressed the part, I mean." Gnarnus turned and shuffled off to another trunk of fabrics to rifle through.

"Would you look at you, Marin," Aster said.

Marin laughed. "It doesn't feel right." He dropped the rag and started to button the tunic with nervous, clumsy fingers.

Gnarnus reappeared from where he'd been half-buried, digging through fabrics in one of the trunks. "*Hmmph!*" he muttered. He sauntered over to hand Marin a satin doublet and a pair of velvet breeches. "These too," he said. "Put these on." He wrinkled his nose, almost as if he were jealous of how Marin looked in all the finery.

Marin accepted the breeches with a nod and set them on a small block of marble beside him. He finished buttoning the doublet over his tunic, then reached down to undo the rope drawstring that held his woolen trousers up. He hesitated.

"Don't be embarrassed, boy," Gnarnus said, returning to his chest of royal clothes. "We're all men here."

Marin rolled his eyes and dropped the woolen trousers. He didn't care so much about Aster seeing him without clothes—they were practically brothers after all. But it felt violating to have a stranger see him so vulnerable. He reached for the velvet breeches and stepped into them.

"What do you mean 'It doesn't feel right'?" Aster asked. "You look admirable."

Marin gave a nervous smile, reaching down to do the laces on the breeches. "This…this isn't me." *No amount of finery is going to make me a prince,* he thought.

If the prophetess had told him, with all the foresight she had, that he would be wearing velvet and silk and gold brocade, dressed like a prince ready for court, he would have expected such clothes to empower him. If he looked the part, then he could play the part, right?

But alas, he still knew he was nothing more than a peasant. No costumes could change that.

Aster removed his own rags and began to dress in the finery Gnarnus brought him: a satin blouse with brocaded waistcoat, along with velvet breeches, all of it just as nice as the garments Marin wore. Aster picked through the pocket of his woolen trousers before discarding them, taking out the pouch of fairy dust and tucking it into the pocket of his waistcoat. He buttoned the pocket closed and gave it a pat to ensure the pouch was secure there.

Smart, Marin thought. *We might end up needing that fairy dust at some point. Who knows where this adventure is taking us?*

Aster held out his arms and looked down at his attire. His expression brightened. Marin had to admit that Aster looked good. Passable for royalty without a doubt.

And if Marin were being honest, there was no doubting that he himself looked the same way. But still…

"Don't you feel weird?" Marin asked.

Aster put a hand on Marin's shoulder. "You look like royalty. Come on, brother, act like royalty and nobody will know the difference."

Gnarnus returned from rummaging in his trunks one more time. In each hand, he clutched a cape and a feathered cap. "Here. This should be the finishing touch."

"Thank you," Marin said, accepting the final accoutrement.

"Aye," Aster said. "Thank you."

Marin turned to a silver looking glass propped up against the wall of the cave. His reflection was dim by the flickering lamplight, but it was clear enough for him to get a good idea of how he looked.

The sight overwhelmed him. In his wildest dreams, he had never actually pictured himself dressed this way. There was no denying he looked like somebody of great importance, just as Aster said. A witch's servant boy no longer!

You could reject all of this, he thought. *Tell Gnarnus you don't want to go along with his stupid plan. You can never pass for royalty. You and Aster can turn back and run away from Grythium and go seek your fortunes elsewhere.*

But who was to say that the next place they went to would be any less risky? Or that they would have an opportunity there like they did here—to cross through the city dressed like royalty, maybe even hobnob with the kingdom's elite noblemen? Such a prospect could take them anywhere! This was the greatness he had always dreamed about and never thought possible. And it was happening because he was brave enough to put on this royal attire and enter the royal city.

We have to take the tide when it's in our favor.

He slid the feathered cap over his head to hide his dirty hair. *Act like royalty and nobody will know the difference.*

"If only it were that simple," he said.

CHAPTER 20

"A throne without an heir is an easy thing to seize," Captain Blets said. The goblin commander drummed his slime-dribbled fingers on the stone table, looking out at his army of underlings.

Elspeth wasn't supposed to hear him say that. She wasn't supposed to see any of this. She gritted her teeth as the images flashed before her eyes. There she was, standing witness to the goblin battle council just as she had borne witness to her father's grief after she and Carys were taken captive.

Flickering torchlight revealed a cavernous room where the goblins gathered around a crude stone table. Muck and grime covered the walls around them. Rusty abandoned weapons and cracked bones littered the floor.

It all should have made Elspeth go limp with fear. In any other circumstance, she had a feeling she might have. But not this time. It was just a vision. Just a vision.

This second vision had come less than a week after Elspeth's first, the one of her father. *Vision?* That was what she kept thinking of it as. *But is that the right word?* Elspeth refused to think of them as dreams. They were too real. Too vivid. Everything always appeared lifelike, perceivable to all her senses, although she usually found herself a little dizzy or lightheaded when they were happening. She reached her hand out and touched the stone wall to steady herself.

Grumbles and mumbles of agreement went through the gathering of goblins in response to what Captain Blets said. Firelight glittered in their orange eyes.

"Seize the throne," one of them shouted. "Seize the throne." He grabbed for the club by his side and lifted it up, then pounded it on the stone table. The crack of wood on stone echoed in the chamber. The other goblins cackled.

"When King Hector grows old and weak," Blets went on, splaying his gray-green fingers out to demand attention from those around him, "and there is no little prince or princess to ascend the throne, then we'll make our attack and claim this land as ours." His voice rasped, a guttural sound coming from deep within his throat. Elspeth hated the sound of it. "And the kingdom of Grythium as well," Blets added, frothy spittle spewing from his lips. "They have no heir either!"

More grumbles and mumbles followed. Several of the goblins pounded their claws on the stone table while others shook their weapons. Blets cocked his eye and stuck out his lower lip at the response. "That means victory," he said. "Victory."

"Victory?" It was the minion Gluck who spoke. "Uh…victory. Victory?" He reached up and scratched his head with one of his claws.

Captain Blets sneered. "It means we win."

Again, a chorus of cheers and guffaws broke out. Long, sinewy arms rose, clapping and waving, throwing spidery shadows this way and that while other goblins clapped their weapons on the floor and table in celebration. The cacophonous noise filled the chamber, echoing off the stone walls.

Elspeth shrank back. *Have courage*, she told herself. *They can't see you. They can't hurt you. You aren't even really here.*

She could tell herself that. But it was hard to believe it. She didn't like being this close to such an unruly scene. The anger and malice made her skin prickle. And what they were talking about—yes, they had taken her and Carys so they could conquer her father's kingdom!

As the images faded away, Elspeth slowly woke, groaning. Her eyes fluttered, though she could see nothing in the overwhelming darkness, and the cold of the stone floor seeped through her dress.

She sat up, trying to catch her breath. Her heart pounded in her ears, but all was unbearable silence otherwise.

No, not complete silence. Carys breathed gently nearby, sound asleep. Elspeth turned, blinking, letting her eyes adjust to the light. Her sister's shadowy form lay stretched across the stone floor.

Despite her exhaustion and her fear, her body trembled with anger. These goblins had kidnapped her and Carys out of something much bigger than a simple princess hostage situation. That was the sort of thing that monsters did in fairy tales. This was bigger. This was a political move. They were doing this to create anarchy in the kingdom of Blunia.

Elspeth ran a hand over her face, realizing she was damp with sweat. *How dare they?* She was her father's heiress. She would be queen after her father stepped down from the throne. His people were her people. And the goblins intended harm on all of them...

Not that there was much she could do when she was a captive.

What was she supposed to do with what she saw in these visions? They weren't mere dreams, after all—they weren't. She instinctively knew these visions were real, in the same way she recognized a dream as being a dream in the moments after waking up and recognizing her surroundings.

This had happened before. Not just the time when she had envisioned her grieving father—even before that, it had happened when she was a very little girl. *I almost forgot*, she thought. But now that she had two visions since her captivity in the goblin fortress, the memory rushed back to her.

She had been seven or eight years old. She dreamed she was out in the forest that surrounded the royal palace to the west, and she witnessed a mother doe encouraging her fawns as they took their first steps. Even years later, she could remember the warmth of the sun coming through the leaves and shining on her face, the scent of wildflowers and moss, the way the breeze dallied with her soft blonde tresses.

The fawns teetered as they took their first steps, clumsily putting one leg in front of the other. They had the strength—if only they had the confidence. The mother doe stepped toward them, nudged them along.

What a gentle and peaceful vision that had been compared with the ones she had in captivity—her father's grief and the goblin's battle plans.

Elspeth climbed up from the floor and paced the pit in the dark. Her body still ached from a beating one of the goblin overseers had given her with a wooden rod, but she didn't have the peace to sleep anymore. Her mind raced. The goblins wanted to claim the throne from her father! Now that she, the rightful heiress, was lost.

And they just might, she thought. *There's no way we're going to escape this awful place.* And nobody was coming to rescue them.

Maybe the goblins would even seize Grythium as well. Grythiums's heir was dead, and King Donovan was said to have gone mad.

She looked up at the stars overhead. When she was a little girl, her nurse used to say that the stars were where fortunes and destinies were spelled out. Elspeth always wanted to believe that as a little girl, but she knew better now. The ancient scriptures kept in the royal shrine said people had free will to create their own lives, even if that will defied what the gods had in mind when they created a person.

I'm sure the gods didn't intend this, Elspeth thought. *What good could possibly come from this? From being captured by goblins?*

She had been asking herself that for weeks. It was hard to tell how long they had been in captivity at this point.

This was her life now.

Unless...

Unless maybe her fairy tale would come true.

Elspeth hadn't wished for her life to be like a fairy tale in a very long time. If she were going to be queen one day, she had to put aside silly fantasies and girlish indulgences. Being rescued by a handsome prince sounded wonderful when it happened in epics and ballads, but the whole idea was very backward and demeaning when she actually thought about it. A queen doesn't get rescued—a queen is in charge of her own fate.

Is my hero out there somewhere? Elspeth thought to herself on the nights when she couldn't sleep. She stared at the stars overhead. *Are you sending my hero to rescue me, stars? Is that why you've ordained that my sister and I should be captured by goblins and held prisoner?*

It was so stupid. Thinking that bad things happened for good reasons!

Still, when she closed her eyes, there he was—a handsome knight in shining armor, riding a white horse, raising his shimmering sword above his head. He would rescue her from whatever danger she was in, and then together they would reign as king and queen of Blunia.

Maybe it would even be a long-lost heir of Grythium, a handsome prince the gods had miraculously spared from King Donovan's fury.

It was wonderful to imagine, but she never actually had any visions of handsome princes or gallant knights. She saw visions of her grieving father and goblin war councils—but never any vision of hope.

"I need to do something myself," she told herself. "But...what? I don't know what I can do."

More visions would come later. Infrequent but occasional, the nights when she would see her father mourning or the goblins plotting their war reminded her that there was a world outside of the dark, cold pit where she and Carys were kept hidden away...

The dark, cold pit where the princesses of Blunia were forgotten...

Where they might eventually die.

CHAPTER 21

Dressed in all their finery, Marin and Aster followed Gnarnus back from his cave to the roadway and into the city. Past the gates, the streets buzzed with activity as peasants and nobles alike went about their business. Marin had never seen so much splendor and excitement in all his life. Shopkeepers and bakers shouted from their windows. A busker strummed a lute and sang on a nearby street corner. Two ladies in red kirtles laughed and waved as he and Aster walked by.

"Would you look at this place?" Marin said.

"Aye," Aster replied. "To think that all of this has just been here our whole lives while we've been slaving away on Ilth's farm."

Ilth's farm was starting to seem more and more like a distant memory every time they talked about it. Would she be coming after them? Tracking them down? The thought gnawed at Marin, but he couldn't seriously picture a haggard old crone like Ilth doing much to track them through the valleys and forests. No, not at all.

For all the years they had lived on Ilth's farm and all the misery they endured, it was now behind them. Even the most painful memories of it had no power to hurt them anymore. Now they were on a busy street where countless opportunities awaited, particularly for boys who were dressed the way they were, in satin and velvet, with capes and doublets and feathered caps.

Even though all of the finery was just for show.

Even though their royal personas were fake.

Marin looked up ahead at the royal palace in the distance. The white-gray stone of its curtain wall shimmered in the afternoon sun, as did those of its lofty towers that disappeared into the clouds above them. *That's it*, he thought. *The royal palace. Is this really happening?*

"Ahh, watch where yer goin'!"

Gnarnus's voice awakened Marin from his thoughts just in time to see a passing horse rear up to avoid trampling their companion.

"Watch where you're going, morgglor," the rider shouted.

The horse landed its forelegs in a puddle of muck and grime, sending fat globs spewing all over Gnarnus. Several nearby villagers laughed. Gnarnus's cheeks burned crimson under his beard, and he gritted his teeth.

Without a word, the horseman tugged at his steed's reins and cantered off. Marin stared after him. How did people get to be so arrogant? Did they really think that being born to power and privilege made them better than others? How was it that somebody so rich could be so uncivilized?

"Foul!" Gnarnus wiped the mud from his chest with his hairy hand, casting a malevolent glare in the direction of the villagers who laughed at him. "No courtesy whatsoever," he muttered to himself. He raised his voice to shout to the crowd. "Oh, is it because I'm a morgglor, is it? Laugh all you want then!" He lowered his voice again, grumbling, "We're the lowest of the low, even to the peasants."

Marin looked around at the crowd. As much as he hated to admit it, the people did seem to be looking at Gnarnus with expressions of unfettered disdain. Then again, Gnarnus wasn't the most pleasant person. He raised both his fists at the crowd, making obscene finger gestures with each hand and thrusting his pelvis at them. Marin winced.

They pressed on through the city, and the crowd got larger the closer they got to the castle—men and women dressed in finery as exquisite as what Marin and Aster wore, knights in armor that shimmered, finely decorated white horses, groomed dogs escorting eager children. It became difficult to push their way through the crowd because people were packed so closely together. The buzz of their voices and hoofbeats hung in the air.

"I suppose this crowd will make it easier for us to make our way around inconspicuously," Aster said. "The bigger the crowd, the less likely we are to stand out in it."

"Yes, but have you noticed who our guide is?" Marin replied. "I'd bet our last coin he gets us into trouble."

Aster nodded. "I don't think you're wrong about that."

Gnarnus looked up at them over his shoulder, his nose twitching over his scraggly beard. "You know, I can hear you. I might be small, but I'm not deaf."

He pressed forward through the crowd. "I'll tell you, boys, you're lucky to have the likes of me to guide you," he said, though he seemed to be talking more to himself than to Marin and Aster. "Why, you'd be as good as dead without my smarts to get you through the city."

"Hold!" The voice rose above the drone of the crowd, commanding their attention. A nobleman on horseback galloped in front of them, splashing mud across Gnarnus's tunic.

Gnarnus jumped back, shouting. Something about being nearly trampled twice within the same square of the city, splashed with mud so casually, must have set him off. Before Marin knew it, the little man was waving his fist up at the nobleman.

"Watch where you be going, you rag devil! You could have trampled me. Have you no respect?"

The nobleman tugged at the reins of his horse and looked down at Gnarnus. "You watch your tongue, morgglor. You forget yourself." He raised his leather-gloved hands to straighten his hat, balancing himself.

Practically frothing at the mouth with fury now, Gnarnus looked back at Marin and Aster. A dollop of mud dribbled down his nose. "I forget myself, he says." He said it as if he expected Marin and Aster to sympathize with him.

Marin suddenly felt the weight of eyes all around the crowd bearing down on him and Aster, noblemen and peasants alike looking at the two of them, but still their escort raged.

"Do you know who I am?" Gnarnus demanded of the nobleman.

"Please," Marin hissed, trying to keep his voice low, trying to keep the attention on them to a minimum. They were trying to make their way around the city inconspicuously. The last thing they needed was to call attention to themselves like this!

"No respect for a morgglor at all, none of you." By now, Gnarnus was shouting at the crowd as if he expected his fury would instill fear or respect or some other emotion into them. He circled around, waving his fist at the bystanders. "Well, do you know who these boys are? They're royal ambassadors, and if you know what's good for them, you'll show their footman some respect."

What? Marin couldn't believe what he was actually hearing. Gnarnus was actually trying to tell this entire crowd that they were royal ambassadors. Aye, they were dressed as royal ambassadors, but what if people started asking questions?

The nobleman swung a leg around and climbed down off his horse. It wasn't until he was on the ground that Marin realized how tall the man was. Tall and imposing. The darkness of his eyes penetrated deep into Marin. He turned back and looked at the others who traveled with him, a crowd of other men on horses, all dressed just as finely as he was.

"Royal ambassadors, you say?" the nobleman asked.

This situation was escalating quickly. Marin had to stop it. "I pray thee, forgive our servant." He stepped forward. "He is bold and loose with his tongue."

"And simple too," Aster added.

The reproachful looks from all the nobles gave Marin an unbearable feeling in his stomach. Despite the royal garb he and Aster wore, he suddenly felt very vulnerable. He swallowed, as if that could suppress all his negativity, and put on the haughtiest voice he could to say, "May the gods give you good day, sir." He tried to look the nobleman in the eye, but it was too much. He felt his entire body shake. "We'll be going now."

"Not so fast." The voice came from another man in the crowd. Stepping forward, a guard in glittering armor made a low bow to Marin and Aster. Three other guards followed him. "What business brings royal ambassadors to the kingdom of Grythium? What kingdom did you say you were from?"

"Uh..." Marin searched his head for something that sounded plausible, but every reasonable thought eluded him. Nothing came to mind. "We are a smaller kingdom...far on the other side of Monte Prospera."

"And the name of this kingdom?"

Think, Marin, he told himself. *Say something. Anything!* "Uh..."

"Begonia." Aster's voice was as cool and calm as Marin had ever heard it, despite how ridiculous his reply was.

"Begonia?" Marin mouthed at him.

The guard raised his chin. "Begonia?"

"You've heard of it?" Again, Aster's confidence didn't waver.

Whatever the guard thought, he gave no indication of it. His face remained stoic. "It would be my honor to escort you to the palace if you do indeed have royal business with King Donovan."

There's no backing out of this now, Marin thought. *Let's hope you're ready to move forward with this charade.* He gave a sweeping bow, as if overdoing the courteous act might charm them. "Gods bless you, good sir!"

He drew himself back up and raised his chin, hoping he looked believably arrogant, at least a little bit. It should have been easy enough to imitate the expressions of the twenty noblemen looking at him. "We will follow you."

None of their faces softened.

"On we go then," one of the guards said. "Follow us."

As they moved through the city, Marin moved close to Aster. "Begonia?"

"Could you think of anything better?"

Marin looked up at the guards ahead of him to make sure nobody was listening to their conversation. He hoped the hubbub of the streets around them were enough to drown out any whispers he exchanged with Aster. "How are we going to figure our way out of this one?" Marin asked.

Aster swallowed. "I don't know. We ought to think quickly."

CHAPTER 22

"You are welcome, good sirs, to the kingdom of Grythium."

King Donovan had an undeniable regality about him, tall, dark of hair and beard. He smiled at Marin and Aster, his black eyes catching the light of the flickering candles overhead in the gilded candelabras.

But it wasn't just the king's eyes that caught the light. Everything in the throne room glittered. It was the most extravagant place Marin could ever imagine. Ornate tapestries hung over the polished marble walls. A crowd of finely dressed lords and ladies stood attendant on either side of the brocaded carpet leading up to the dais where Donovan sat in his gold throne.

The king extended a hand in front of him, and even the purple silk of his sleeves shimmered. "Pray, tell me where you are from and on what errand you visit us during this most prosperous time of year."

Marin noticed the enormous ring on the finger of the king's outstretched hand. One of his books had once talked about how you were supposed to kiss the ring of royalty—it was a customary show of respect.

Am I worthy? he couldn't help asking himself, even though the answer should have been obvious—of course he wasn't. He was a runaway servant dressed up in stolen clothes and trying to imitate manners that he read about in books. He was about as far from worthy as a person could be!

He stepped forward and laid a gentle kiss on the glittering gemstone. The hard surface was cold against his lips. As he drew his head up, he made eye contact with the king. For the first time, it struck him how sad his majesty looked. Marin had been so impressed by the opulent throne and royal robes that he hadn't noticed there was grief in King Donovan's pale expression.

Aster followed Marin's lead and kissed the ring as well.

If King Donovan had any suspicions regarding two boys their age, he didn't show any of it. Maybe Gnarnus's plan was actually working. Or maybe the rumors about the king's wrath were all overblown hearsay.

Even so, this was a man who sent a servant away to kill a baby—two babies! History was full of tyrants and despots and mad kings. King Donovan wouldn't be the first. Taking desperate measure to secure his lineage was just an unpleasant responsibility of holding the throne. Staying vigilant for two young men he believed to be his enemy's bastard sons on a mission to usurp his kingdom—that was enough to make any ruler take a forceful form of leadership. Could such tyranny be justified?

No, Marin thought. *He's an enemy. Don't lose sight of that. He would kill you just as readily as he killed those babies.*

"Now," Donovan said. "To what do I owe the pleasure of your esteemed visit?"

Marin struggled to find his voice. If this tyrant found out he and Aster were imposters...

"We—well, you see, your majesty—"

King Donovan forced a smile. "Come, my boy, don't be shy. You are most welcome here."

"May the gods bless you, your majesty," Marin said.

Silence. Welcome though they might have been, they had no business to discuss. Marin didn't even know what important royal business would entail. Why on earth would an envoy from one kingdom visit the king of another? What message would he be relaying?

Aster cleared his throat. "Uh…well, your majesty…" He obviously had no ideas either.

Donovan turned to one of his attendant servants, a slight man in purple-and-silver livery. "From what kingdom did you say they came?"

Aster spoke up before the servant could respond. "Begonia, your majesty."

Donovan turned back to them. "I am afraid I have not heard of it." When he spoke, his sharp cheekbones rose so high they practically covered his eyes.

Begonia. Think, Marin! Come on.

"Yes, well…" Marin shrugged, aware of how undignified the gesture was, how unbecoming of a royal ambassador. He couldn't come up with anything better.

"It's far from here," Aster said.

"Yes," Marin said. "But…but we hope that your kingdom and ours will be able to form an alliance. It is a shame that a prominent kingdom like Grythium should stand alone, unallied with any of its neighbors."

Something about what he said must have upset the king. Donovan's face sank. Marin didn't think it would have been possible for Donovan to look more forlorn, but he did.

"Sometimes, you are better alone," King Donovan said. He lifted his head and looked past Marin and Aster, talking almost to himself. "We once considered the kingdom of Blunia to be a friend. But no longer."

King Donovan returned his gaze to Marin and Aster. For a moment, Marin thought he saw suspicion in the king's expression as he looked at the two of them. *Oh, no...*

"So much was lost when we parted ways with Blunia," his majesty continued. "Yes, so much. I had a son once. And a nephew. The two of them might have stood in front of me now just as the two of you do."

Awkward tension came over the room like a heavy wet blanket. Marin was sure Aster could feel it too. He turned to his brother for just a second before looking back up at the king.

Whatever mood had overcome King Donovan, he quickly snapped out of it. His majesty clapped his wide hands on his knees, some light returning to his expression. "Forgive me."

"There is nothing to forgive, your majesty," Marin said.

King Donovan nodded. "Tell me of your kingdom then. How may Grythium be of service to...you have not told me the name of your royal family."

"No, we haven't," Aster piped up. There was a confidence to his voice, almost as if he suddenly had an idea for what direction they could take this whole charade in.

Then came a terrible sound from behind them.

"Oh, cease this madness!"

As soon as he heard it, Marin's blood went cold. The voice was not powerful, but it was shrill. And familiar.

Everyone in the throne room turned to stare at the figure who had just entered through the elaborately carved mahogany doors at the far end of the hall. Several gasps erupted and murmurs went through the crowd, ladies drawing close to their lords, knights reaching for their swords, as the haggard old crone with her tall walking staff came ambling into the hall and started her way down the carpet leading to the royal dais. She moved with such assuredness, as if there were nothing unwelcome about her unkempt rat's nest of gray hair or her billowing black robes that dragged behind her.

"Your majesty," Ilth said. She leered up at King Donovan with a malevolent gleam in her eye as she approached.

Donovan rose from his throne, his expression hard to read. Was it apprehension? Distrust? Maybe even a little revulsion? He raised a hand to his guard, indicating for them not to attack. At least, not yet.

"And what brings the witch Ilth all the way to the royal court of Grythium today?" the king asked. He raised an eyebrow. He recognized Ilth. But what was going on in the king's mind beyond simple recognition, there was no way of telling.

Ilth wasted not a moment. She wrinkled her nose and raised one of her clawlike hands. "I have come to claim what is mine and put a stop to the ridiculous folly your majesty is subjected to." With that, she pointed a bony finger at Marin and Aster. "These here who stand before you are no royal ambassadors. They are my servants on my farm, escaped only earlier this week."

The crushing burden of a hundred staring eyes from all the nobles and courtiers bore down on them. Marin's heart raced. His entire body shook with fear. There was no way they could run from this, no way they could talk their way out of it. There was nothing at all they could do.

He grabbed Aster's arm. "Oh, if only we were anywhere but here," he whispered.

A flash of light erupted around them. Marin went momentarily blind and deaf, unaware of anything except the feeling of Aster's arm still within his grip. If he hadn't already been breathless from the fear of Ilth's arrival and the way she outed them in front of the entire court, his breath would have been knocked out of him now.

He blinked as his senses slowly returned to him. No longer did they stand in the middle of the opulent throne room, surrounded by dozens of important people dressed in finery. A woodland grove spread around them, lush green leaves crisscrossing overhead beneath a murky gray sky. A tepid dampness hung in the air, relieved only by a gentle wind that swept past them, gently shaking the leaves overhead.

Marin let go of Aster's arm, feeling his jaw drop open as he took in the sight of their new surroundings.

"What just happened?" Aster said.

"I don't know," Marin replied. Then he remembered what he'd said: *If only we were anywhere but here.*

"I think..." he said cautiously. "I think we're...well, I think we're anywhere but there."

CHAPTER 23

I t took a few minutes for the shock to wear off.

Marin sighed. To think that they were almost captured by Ilth—or worse, caught lying to the king, which was surely an imprisonable offense—and suddenly here they were, transported someplace far away.

"That was some good luck right there if we ever had it," he said, sitting down on a nearby boulder. He clapped his hands on his knees and looked around. Trees and greenery and open sky through the crisscrossing branches overhead. Never did he ever think he would be so happy to be lost deep in the middle of a forest.

Aster crossed his arms. "I don't think it was luck, Marin."

"Well, no. No, of course not." Marin shifted in his seat. "But what was it?"

"Magic?"

Marin nodded. They didn't know anything about magic, nothing beyond the halfhearted potions and curses that Ilth had always dabbled in while they were growing up. But she'd never been really all that good at magic.

Though magic did seem the most likely reason for this. How else were they supposed to explain disappearing from one place and suddenly reappearing in another? "Aye," Marin agreed. "Aye, it was magic."

Neither of them said anything, leaving quiet enough to recognize the sound of birds chirping close by. Marin reached up and straightened his feathered cap.

"But *how* is the question," Aster said. "So, it was magic, aye. But how did magic just whisk us away?"

It was a question both of them had been thinking. "I don't know," Marin said, getting back to his feet. "I wish I knew. I want to know how we might be able to recreate it again if we ever needed it."

After the way things have been going the past few days, he thought to himself, *after all these brushes with danger and the wild surprises we've faced, we will probably be needing it again. We'll probably be needing it again badly*. He bit his lower lip, unable to bring himself to say that to Aster.

"You don't think the prophetess could be looking out for us, do you?" Aster said.

"I doubt it. She told us that we were meant for great things, but she didn't sound like she was going to magically make them happen. She made it sound like it was up to us."

As far as Marin could tell, the forest stretched out around them in all directions. A low-hanging haze shrouded much of it. The scent of pine and moss was stronger here than it had been in the forest before they arrived in Grythium, or maybe it just seemed that way now. There didn't appear to be much indication they would make their way out of the forest easily, no matter which direction they went.

"I guess we're back to a fresh start then," Marin said, trying to look on the bright side.

"Aye, except now we know that Ilth is hunting us." Aster fiddled with the ties of his cape. "And we have a king as our enemy now. I have a feeling that seeking our fortunes will be a little harder with all of that against us." With those words, he shucked off the cape and draped it over one arm.

"What a shame, too," Marin said. "I felt as if we were finally starting to get somewhere." He moved forward out of the clearing and into the woods. Aster followed.

"I can't tell whether you're being serious or not," Aster said.

"Why would I not be serious?"

Aster scoffed. "We were completely faking it. I mean, you even said it yourself that you felt so uncomfortable in those royal clothes." He held up his arm with the cape draped over it.

"Because I knew we didn't deserve them." Marin pulled the velvet cap from his head and dropped it to the ground as he said it. There was no use in being dressed like royalty out here in the woods. "But maybe we could have done something to deserve them," he said. "We could have proven ourselves worthy."

"We would have needed to make a much more impressive show in front of the king," Aster said. "We sounded like idiots."

"Aye," Marin said. Every uncomfortable moment in that throne room still hovered in Marin's mind. "But the next time I stand before a king, I hope I have reason to impress him," he said. "I hope I'm able to be myself and be honest, and have him say to me, 'Good job, my lord.'"

"Well, if that happens, I hope I'm right there with you."

Marin paused. "You will be," he said. "You better not leave me."

Aster nodded. "Don't worry. I won't."

"Aye. Then I won't worry." Marin knelt down and tightened the buckles on his boots. "Come on, we've got to find some direction for our quest again."

Finding themselves without any direction again, Marin couldn't help wondering whether this was another torturous prank by the gods. As soon as he and Aster were getting somewhere, achieving something, then the divine forces took it away and set them up against a new obstacle.

Marin smelled the smoke before they actually saw the hut itself. Someone had a fire burning. He and Aster followed the scent into a glen where there stood a hut so weathered and overgrown with plants that it looked as if it might have been a natural formation of the forest itself. Moss gleamed on the wooden logs that formed its walls, and the thatched roof was dotted with flowers and herbs seeming to grow from among the straw. The only sign of human life was glittering smoke that piped from a small clay chimney.

"Who do you suppose lives here?" Marin asked. "Friend or foe?"

"We won't know until we approach." Aster looked at Marin and shrugged, almost as if he could read Marin's mind. "It won't be the first nasty scrape we've gotten into."

"No," Marin agreed. "But if we can avoid any more nasty scrapes, I won't be unhappy."

CHAPTER 24

No sooner had he said that than a gnarled old face appeared at the window. Deep wrinkles creased the pale skin, and the only things whiter than the man's milky complexion were his snowy beard and mustache, both of which hung long and unkempt, almost as if they might have been centuries old, grown over the course of an immortal lifespan.

The man raised his bushy white eyebrows. "Ah...guests." He peered at them and blinked a pair of dark eyes magnified by large square spectacles.

He didn't even sound surprised.

He knew. He knew we were approaching. Marin took a step forward. "Were you expecting us?"

The face disappeared from the window, a gnarled hand reaching up to close the shutter, and in another moment, the old man appeared at the doorway. There was something ethereal, almost otherworldly in the way the old man moved. "No." He chuckled. It was warm and jovial, the kind of laugh that suggested Marin and Aster didn't have anything to fear. "No, my boy, I did not know you were coming. But it is not often that travelers make their way this far into the woods."

The elder stepped over the threshold. Again, he moved with

astonishing gracefulness for one who looked so old. It was as if there were some sort of magic animating him. That, of course, was not an entirely implausible explanation.

Marin cleared his throat. "May I ask, sir, what country is this?"

"You are in the woods just beyond the kingdom of Blunia, my good lad." The old man gestured with one of his hands at the forest surrounding his cottage, waving the sleeve of his long robe as if it were a flag or a banner.

Marin glanced over at Aster. "Blunia?"

"As in, the land ruled by King Hector?" Aster asked, recalling the details they had been told by Gnarnus.

The old man nodded. "Aye." His mouth twitched with the hint of a smile.

"Wouldn't you figure?" Marin said, half to himself, half to Aster.

"So...would we be in danger?" Aster took a few steps toward the old man's hut. "My friend and I? Is there any reason for us to be concerned?"

Marin was glad to hear Aster ask it. He remembered the cold stare from King Donovan, the way his own stomach had practically twisted into a knot when he thought the king might kill him and Aster simply for being two boys about seventeen years of age. They needed to know if they were walking into that kind of danger again.

"Danger?" The old man arched his shaggy white eyebrows.

"We've just come from the kingdom of Grythium," Marin said. "The kingdom of Grythium, where we were...well..."

Aster shrugged. He wasn't sure how to explain it either. He didn't want to admit that there was a bounty on their heads, not until they knew whether this old man was friend or foe. Gnarnus had been willing to do them dirty until they overtook him and practically forced him to help them.

"We were what you might call *persona non grata*," Marin ventured.

It was an expression he had read before in one of his books, but it was not something he was used to saying in speech. Still, he understood enough to know it adequately conveyed that he and Aster were two unwelcome people in the land of Grythium. "Something about a prophecy."

The old man—who Marin was starting to understand must have been some kind of wizard—nodded. "I see." He didn't sound surprised. He didn't seem overly concerned by the thought that Marin and Aster were outlaws who might be at the center of some prophecy. *Oh, to be a wizard who has been through so much that he's unfazed by outlaws and prophecies,* Marin thought. This must have been the wizard mentor Tsema had said they would encounter. They must have been on the right track.

"We're not from around here," Aster said. "We're…we're adventurers, seeking our fortune wherever we can find it."

The wizard lifted his head and nodded. He moved forward, the oversized robes he wore shimmering as he moved. The fabric looked like roughly spun wool overlaid with spiderwebs and snailskin. At first, it appeared black, and then when the light hit it, it might have been blue or purple or green.

"Well, then," the wizard said, "if you are adventurers seeking glory and honor, you might have come to the right place." He placed an arm around each of them and clapped them on the back. Ancient though he might have looked, his arms still had surprising strength. "The daughters of King Hector are in danger, and the kingdom has fallen into despair since they've been gone. It might be a worthy task of the likes of you to rescue them."

Princesses? In danger? A kingdom in despair? Marin remembered Tsema mentioning something about the king of Blunia and his captured daughters. Now he had a feeling he knew where this was going—if what was playing out here was anything like the ballads and stories, at

161

least. "Speak more plainly, sir, if you can."

After he said it, he immediately regretted it. Had that been too bold?

The old man smiled. "I dare say that any young man who will see the princesses home safely will receive a handsome reward from the king."

Aster stepped away from the old man, not rudely. "We need you to explain a little more. What sort of danger are the princesses in?"

"Please." The old man stepped toward his front door, gesturing for them. "Won't you come in? It will be more comfortable that way." His hand shook slightly as he indicated the shadowed interior of the hut. With his other hand, he lifted the hem of his robe so as not to trip over it and began to head inside.

Marin hesitated. "Thank you, but…"

"I have no interest in hurting you if that's what you're afraid of," the old man said, grinning. "I'm too old to trouble myself with that sort of thing, and besides, I've always wanted to use my magic for good if I can."

"I would hope so," Aster said.

"But if I can make you two a kettle of coffee, we might be able to discuss your mission," the wizard said.

Mission? Marin couldn't deny it sounded as if he and Aster were already assigned to this task. And if that were the case…well, there wasn't any sense in resisting the call to action, was there? Even reluctant heroes always had to heed the call to adventure eventually. "Very well," Marin said. "We accept."

The wizard proceeded into his hut. "Come this way then," he called over his shoulder.

Marin and Aster followed him through the stooped doorway into a cozy little den. Sunlight streamed in through the windows and candles flickered around them. Smoke from the fireplace hung in the air.

"Sit down," the wizard said. "Make yourselves comfortable."

He gestured toward a circle of rickety chairs made from wood and twine that sat around a stump presumably used as a table, so littered was it with small trinkets and treasures, candles set in old bottles dribbled with wax, parchment and scrolls, and even a thick tome of leather and vellum marked with letters Marin didn't recognize.

He and Aster lowered themselves into the chairs, taking in the sights around them. Shelves stood stacked with books and animal skulls. A looking glass hanging on the wall bore no reflection but simply some endless expanse of swirling mist beyond its surface. In the corner, a collection of wooden staffs and walking sticks leaned up against one another.

"A nice home you have here," Marin said.

"That's kind of you." The wizard moved around in the shadows behind them, then emerged into the light with a battered kettle and two mugs.

"Would you like cream for your coffee?" the wizard asked. "I am afraid we haven't any sugar."

"No, thank you," Marin said as he accepted the cup. "Black is fine."

Aster took the other cup from the wizard's outstretched hand. "I'll have cream," he said. "Why isn't there any sugar?"

The wizard raised an eyebrow. "It has been outlawed. Ever since the goblins seized control of these lands."

"Goblins?" Marin asked.

"They are the ones who hold the king's daughters hostage," the wizard said. He set a clay milk pot on the table for Aster, then lowered himself into the third chair.

Aster reached for the milk pot and poured some cream into his coffee. "Start from the beginning, won't you?" He set the milk pot back down.

The wizard sighed and surveyed the two of them. Marin couldn't help getting the impression the old man was trying to evaluate them before going into detail about the story, trying to determine whether they were worth his effort.

"Tell me your names, my boys," the wizard said.

"My name is Marin, may it please you, sir."

"Aye. And I am Aster. May it please."

The wizard nodded. "And my name is Udifeus. Now we know one another."

He chuckled and took a sip from his own mug of coffee, then folded his hands on the table. Marin took notice of the wizard's long, gnarled fingers with dirty fingernails. Normally, the clawlike hands would have scared him. But if Udifeus planned to hurt them, he would have done so by now.

"It was many weeks ago," Udifeus began. "Many weeks ago that the goblins came for the princesses in the middle of broad daylight, out in an open field while they traveled with their father's guard. Elspeth and Carys. Two fair maidens, their father's pride and joy. No one has seen them since then. But the goblins have held these lands under their tyranny. Even the king himself fears them."

"What do they do?" Aster asked.

"I beg pardon?" Udifeus asked with a cock of his head.

"If everyone throughout the kingdom fears them…well, they must do something to inspire that kind of fear."

Udifeus laughed. "My dear boy, goblins don't need to do anything. Just the thought that they might do something, anything, is enough to make grown men tremble. They are vicious, cutthroat, merciless crea-tures. They could take the peasants as slaves, slaughter livestock in the night, burn the villages to the ground—"

"But they don't," Aster said.

"No," Udifeus agreed. He stared at the two of them with those

164

dark eyes of his. His brass-rimmed spectacles enlarged his eyes to three times their natural size, giving him the appearance of an owl. "But," Udifeus continued, "they do have the princesses held prisoner. And as long as those princesses are in captivity, there will be no joy for this kingdom."

No joy for this kingdom. The way the wizard said it sent a chill down Marin's spine. "What do you mean by that?"

"Life has gotten worse throughout the kingdom of Blunia since the princesses were captured." Udifeus lifted his mug and sipped his coffee. "The king has become reclusive, and the common folk live in fear."

Marin turned to Aster. "This might be our new mission."

"Are you serious?" Aster replied.

"I...I am," Marin said. "If there are princesses in danger, somebody needs to rescue them. Why shouldn't it be us?"

Udifeus stood, smoothing out the wrinkles in his robe. "My good young sirs, be warned: I think you underestimate how dangerous a goblin clan is."

Marin could tell Udifeus was baiting them. The old man himself had been the one to first insinuate this was a task fit for adventurers such as they! Why should he question them now? Marin set down his mug. "Maybe we do." He could hear determination in his own voice. "Maybe I do underestimate the goblins. But something brought us here. I don't know what exactly, but we were in danger...you see, we were in danger in the kingdom of Grythium."

He hesitated. How much were they actually able to tell Udifeus? Was it safe to admit that King Donovan might want them dead?

"I think," Aster said before Marin could say anything, "we can tell him everything." He nodded at Udifeus.

"Tell me what?" Udifeus asked. "What do you need to tell me?"

Marin gulped. Sweat was forming on the palms of his hands. He set them on the table to stop them from shaking with nerves. "You see, sir," he began, "we were servants of a witch up until three days ago. We, uh…well, we decided to run away. But it turns out that two boys about our age are not welcome in the kingdom of Grythium."

He told Udifeus everything. The old wizard already knew about the prophecy, how King Donovan went mad and ordered the death of his heirs—of course. Gnarnus had said everyone through the land knew the story. Marin explained how he and Aster passed themselves off as royalty before Ilth showed up and exposed them as runaway servants.

"Then, suddenly, out of nowhere, we were transported to these woods in the blink of an eye. It was some kind of magic that did it, I'm sure. But we don't know how."

Udifeus did not look surprised. He raised one of his white eyebrows. "Well, it's the ring you wear on your finger."

"What?"

"You were not told how it works?" Udifeus asked.

Shocked, Marin lifted his right hand and looked at the brass ring the gnome had given him. "No, we weren't told. How does it work?"

"I recognized the ring the moment I saw it on your finger," Udifeus said. He lifted a knobby hand and gestured for Marin to give him a closer look. Marin slipped off the ring and handed it over. "They're very rare, and many of them are lost," Udifeus explained, straightening his glasses and raising the ring up close, twirling it so he could see it from all angles. "They were forged by a sect of soothsayers many centuries ago, I believe."

"Does it grant wishes?" Marin said.

"No." Udifeus chuckled as he lowered his hand. "But they can put you on the right path if you ask them to. Their magic works only when you are in great need, in the most desperate of situations, when all other hope has seemingly abandoned you. The way you were in King Donovan's court, I suppose. You must say, 'If only…' and follow it up with how you can be helped in your moment of need. If your request is worthy, and is vital to fulfilling your destiny, then aid will come to you."

Marin shook his head. *Destiny. Did everyone obsess about destiny and what the gods intended?*

Maybe it wasn't such a bad idea though. Maybe the ring transported them because their destiny was to rescue the princesses. Had he himself not just told Udifeus, "*Something has brought us here,*" as if they were meant to fulfill this mission they were now faced with?

"Well," he said. "It sounds as if this ring just happened to be magic enough to get us out of a bad situation, and now it turns out we have princesses to rescue."

Udifeus drummed his fingers on the table. "If it's what's meant to be," he said. "If it's what the gods intend."

The wizard's tone suggested he was baiting them again. Marin ignored the remark and handed the ring to Aster. "Maybe you should wear it for a little while," he said. "If it's as powerful as we think, I don't like the idea that either one of us holds onto it for too long. We should trade it back and forth."

Aster took the ring and slipped it on his finger. "Right." He pushed his chair in and stepped away from the table. He looked so courtly in the royal attire Gnarnus had given them, even out here in a derelict cottage in the middle of the woods. If only Marin could look half as royal as that!

"And now I think it's time we get started," Marin said, swallowing his doubts. "We've got some goblins to defeat and some princesses to rescue. Are you feeling up to the challenge, Aster?"

Aster nodded. "I am, brother. I am ready."

CHAPTER 25

"What foolishness was this?" King Donovan roared.

Still fuming from the sudden appearance of Ilth and the news she brought, as well as the sudden disappearance of the deceitful boys who had the audacity to lie to him, he glowered around his throne room at each of the guards, an angry red color rising to his cheeks. "What gods-forsaken fool thought it would be prudent to bring these boys to court without so much as questioning them first? The kingdom of Begonia? Is my palace staffed by simpletons and guarded by idiots?"

Sir Briceus, the captain of the guard, stepped forward. Only the keenest of eyes would have been able to tell how much he quaked in fear beneath his armor. He kept his movements steady, but Donovan could tell the guard was not his usual fearless self.

"The boys did look the part, your majesty," Briceus said. His voice bore a pitiful note of apology. Still, he maintained his courtly composure well. "And their countenance, the way they carried themselves…"

Ilth's shrill voice rose from the side of the great hall. "They are servants!" she shouted. She shook her fist and clapped her walking stick on the marble floor. Evidently, she had no fear or hesitation, even here in the royal court where she was most unwelcome. King Donovan would have to see to it that she was properly handled in due time.

"They had an air of royalty about them, and that's no mistake," Sir Briceus said. Whether he was defending himself against the king or witch, it wasn't exactly clear. He looked from one to the other as he continued. "Can I help it if we were deceived? Even you, your majesty—you yourself seemed to believe their bid."

King Donovan kept his composure. "I will not have my competence questioned because my guards were foolish enough to bring servants before the court and pass them off as royal ambassadors." He looked from Sir Briceus to the others standing in a line before them—Sir Perot, Sir Garit, Sir Botolf, Sir Druet, and Sir Ilbert. All of them dressed in armor when they should have been dressed in jester's motley.

Sir Druet spoke up. "What of the morgglor, your majesty?" He nodded to indicate the escort who had accompanied the two imposters. Gnarnus still stood there in the throne room, though he'd kept quiet up until that moment, likely with the hopes he would go unnoticed and escape whatever punishment he deserved.

"Your majesty, if you please," Gnarnus said, spreading his arms out innocently and offering a sheepish grin. Gold-capped teeth stuck out from among his scraggly beard and mustache. "I am simply a victim here too."

"In what way?" the king asked, straining to keep his voice steady. His hands clenched.

"Well, the boys…they threatened me," Gnarnus said. He uttered a weak laugh and straightened his vest, as if that might make him more presentable in front of the king. "They said they would kill me if I did not aid them." He must have seen nothing but malice on the face of the king, so he quickly turned to Sir Briceus, an expression of pathetic desperation coming over his face. "I…I had no choice but to lend them some of the finery from my hoard of treasure," he said, frantic for someone to take his side. "You know that no self-respecting morgglor would relinquish his hoarded treasure, particularly not to a servant."

"A poor excuse, if I must say so," King Donovan observed, raising a hand. "Take him away. Let's see whether a few days in a prison cell will make him more amicable to tell the truth, and we'll get a better explanation about all of this."

Sir Ilbert and Sir Garit stepped forward and each grabbed him by an arm, lifting him right off the floor. Gnarnus's eyes bugged out of his little head. "No! No! Unhand me! Let me go!" He shook and fought to no avail—his puny body stood no chance against the tight hold of the king's guards. Still, the wretched little man resisted all the way out the arched doorway of the throne room as Ilbert and Garit carried him away. As the sounds of his screams faded, leaving the throne room in an awkward silence, King Donovan collapsed onto his throne. He buried his angry expression into one hand.

Ilth hobbled forward, the train of her black robe trailing behind her. "If I may, your majesty…"

Donovan looked up. "What is it, Ilth?" His tone gave no indication of graciousness or leniency. No wise person would cross him in that moment or there would be trouble.

Ilth raised her chin, suddenly haughty. "I demand the service of your royal hunting party."

"Demand?" Donovan said, no trace of amusement in his voice. "A witch makes demands of a king?" He lifted his head, almost as if he wanted the light from the chandeliers overhead to sparkle on his golden crown and remind the witch who was in charge.

"A king may rule the land, but a magic user rules the elements," Ilth said. "I will always have the upper hand in this world, your majesty."

King Donovan sneered. "I do not believe your reputation for magic has been highly regarded these last few years, Ilth. Aren't you practically retired from witchery?"

Ilth scoffed. "Can I help it if practicing witchcraft is much work for no reward?" With every word she spoke, Ilth grew haughtier and more aggressive. "I've earned my right to do nothing. And I have servants to work my land for me and keep my farm and household running. Or *had* servants, I should rather say. Which is why you must lend me your hunting party and your royal guard."

"My royal guard is not at your disposal, least of all for a couple of farmhands," King Donovan said. "However you wish to track your runaway servants down, witch, you may do so, but you will receive no assistance from the crown."

Ilth stepped closer. "I believe it is in your best interest, your majesty." She kept her voice conspicuously low.

"I'll hear no more of this," Donovan said. He raised a hand and pointed to Ilth. "Guards, see the witch out."

Sir Briceus and Sir Botolf stepped forward to seize the old woman, each of them taking one of her bony arms. She wrestled in their grip. "Have you forgotten the prophecy?" she called out to the king.

Those words were enough. "Stop!" Donovan called, raising a hand and getting to his feet. The guards obeyed his command and let go of the old crone. She stepped away from them, straightening her robe and cloak, almost as if she were deliberately ignoring the king's penetrating gaze bearing down on her.

"No, I have not," Donovan said in answer to her question. "I have not forgotten." He spoke through clenched teeth, his breath caught in his throat.

Ilth grinned. "Of course not. How could you forget?"

King Donovan became aware of the valets and courtiers who remained in the throne room. He looked around. "Out! Everyone, out! I must talk with the witch alone. Sir Lionel! Sir Robard! You two will guard the entry."

There was a great shuffling as everyone obeyed the king's command.

171

Lords held their hands out to escort their ladies. A few murmuring voices carried across the room, but most of the small crowd remained silent save for quick footsteps over the marble floor. When the last of the crowd passed through the archway into the hall beyond, Sir Lionel and Sir Robard pulled the mahogany doors closed with a thunderous bang that echoed across the now empty throne room.

Now it was just the two of them, king and witch, standing there in heavy silence. Donovan took a deep breath. "If you have a point to make, Ilth, I command you to make it."

Ilth cackled. "Oh, your majesty." She was not so easily ordered around, not even by a king. She pursed her lips and stayed silent as she strode across the throne room, punctuating each of her steps with a strike of her walking stick against the marble.

King Donovan opened his mouth to speak, but his voice caught in his throat. He couldn't think of anything to say, not even to give a command.

Raising her wrinkled face, her beady eyes going wide, Ilth took a deep breath. "I can't imagine how you felt when you heard the prophecy."

Sweat started to form in beads on King Donovan's temples.

"How *did* you feel?" Ilth asked. "Angry? Fearful? You must have." She paused. "It's not lightly that a man declares his queenly wife a whore. It is not without reason that he severs ties with his closest friend and ally—"

Blood flushed in the king's cheeks. "I am warning you, Ilth!"

"Nor sends his son and nephew away to die," the witch said. "Tell me, your majesty, when you gave those infants to your guard and told him to take them into the forest and slay them, did you really think he would follow your command?"

Donovan couldn't believe what he was hearing. Even moments before, when he heard the witch mention the prophecy, he had not actually thought this possible. It was just his senseless fear returning to him after all these years, or so he told himself. "You can't mean this." His voice boiled with anger.

"You did!" Ilth broke with laughter. "You actually intended for your guard to put his sword through those babies." Her laughter subsided and she shook her head, almost as if she pitied him. "Your crown and your dignity mean more to you than I would have ever thought. To kill your own son—"

"Not my son!" Donovan shouted, his voice shaking. "The bastard son of King Hector." Had any guard been eavesdropping at the doors to the throne room, the guard would not have been able to tell whether the king was trying to convince the witch or himself.

Donovan lowered his voice and repeated, "A bastard. Nothing more."

"Your wife's son, at the very least, and a child whom you regarded as your own until you heard your fortune told," Ilth continued. "Regardless, a child. Sent away to be killed."

She took a few steps closer to the king's dais. "I can't decide whether it's bold or not. On one hand, it takes some grit to kill a baby. On the other hand, it's rather cowardly, to harm something so defenseless. But whatever it is, make no mistake, your guard defied your orders."

King Donovan gritted his teeth and shook with rage. "No!"

"You must have known he did," Ilth said. "Or feared he did, at the very least." She narrowed her eyes. "Why else would there be a royal decree that if anyone saw two unknown boys about the age of your son and nephew, then they were to be arrested at once?"

She paused, taking in the sight of the king's expression—it was a mix of fear and fury, all because of her. The king was nothing but wet clay in her hands, so easily manipulated! And he still believed that the boys were sired by King Hector! *What a fool*, she thought.

But after all these years, here was Ilth's chance to torment him.

"You feared that your guard would disobey you and show mercy, and that those boys were still alive."

"That was nearly seventeen years ago," the king said.

"And nearly seventeen years have passed, and those boys grew up," Ilth said. "They grew up as my servants. Your guard brought them to me and begged me to keep them safe, and to keep them a secret. I could have them as servants as long as they grew up never knowing their heritage, and as long as nobody in all the lands of Grythium and Blunia knew they were alive."

For a furious, heart-racing moment, Donovan forgot all about Ilth. He stood alone with his anger. His fingers seized at the sleeves of his royal robe as if he might tear the fabric off him and stand there naked in his crazed state. "I have been betrayed!"

"But not by me," Ilth said. "I did my part." She grinned, her voice softening as she spoke, cautiously trying to calm the king's anger she had just provoked before he ordered her execution. "Those boys grew up never knowing anything about who they are or where they came from. They didn't even know about each other, so far as I'm aware, until recently. Something about their friendship must have emboldened them to run away, I'm afraid, which is how we've arrived where we are now."

"You let them escape!" The king whirled on his heel and stormed back to his throne, collapsing with a huff. "You reckless old sow," he muttered under his breath.

"I'm reckless?" Ilth stepped forward, resentful of the insult, suddenly brazen. "Who sent a guard to do his villainy? You could have taken a sword to those babies yourself if you wanted to." She leaned on her walking stick, trying to catch Donovan's eye. "But you entrusted them to a palace guard, never suspecting his tender and merciful heart."

Donovan shook his head. "I have spent the last seventeen years fearing this. After everything I did to thwart the prophecy."

Ilth cackled. "You cannot thwart fate, your majesty. What's meant to be will be."

Only then did Donovan look at her. "Hold your tongue, Ilth. It has already caused enough trouble."

"Very well, I will." Her tone was a little too casual as she backed away from him and turned to go. "But before I do," she said, calling over her shoulder, "maybe you want to know what else I know." This would really infuriate the king—oh, this would be his undoing!

Donavan stopped breathing. Her vague, teasing statement caught his attention. "What?" he growled. "What do you know? Tell me."

"Back then, your servant left me with something else," Ilth called over her shoulder, still facing the exit to the great hall as she spoke. She paused. "A key."

"No!"

"Oh, yes." She turned back and looked him up and down, hobbling back to the dais as she did. "It shouldn't surprise me that a man who would kill his own son and nephew would lock away the sacred heirlooms of his royal house…"

"Where is the key now?"

"I kept it hidden at the bottom of a pouch of sugar that I disguised by labeling it as fairy dust," she snapped. "I suppose the boys discovered it in my cabinet of magical ingredients and they stole it."

King Donovan gripped the arms of his throne with such anger it was a wonder the gold didn't melt in his hands. "Do you mean to tell me that Hector's bastard sons are still alive and at large, and they have in their possession the key to the vault where the royal heirlooms of Grythium are locked away? My crown and my sword? Is that what you are telling me?"

"That is exactly what I am telling you," Ilth said. She leaned in close to him. "Do you still wish to deny me your royal guard and your best hunting party so that I may find my servants? Is that really such a petty mission for them?"

Donovan stood frozen, his mind racing with everything he had just learned. His eyes flicked from Ilth to the arched doorway. A trickle of sweat made its way from his forehead, along his temple, and down his neck. "Guards!" he shouted out to the hall. "Your king summons you."

"A wise decision," Ilth murmured under her breath.

The guards came running in and each went down on one knee to hear the king's command—that they must search the land far and wide to bring him those imposters who had just escaped. Bring them back dead or alive.

"We must find those boys, those bastards, wherever they have gone," Donovan said to Ilth when his guards had filed out, "and put an end to this prophecy once and for all."

CHAPTER 26

Elspeth knew something was amiss from the way Captain Blets approached the foreman Bogwump, his walk decisive and his expression crueler than it even normally was. Even from deep below in the captivity pit, she could make out the ferocity of his blazing eyes.

Her stomach twisted into a knot. She swallowed, ignoring how dry her throat was. The captain of the goblin army didn't pay visits to the patrol guard during the day for no reason—at least, not in all the time since she and Carys had been in captivity. If only she could get close enough to eavesdrop.

She lunged forward, creeping through the shadows cast by the sinking afternoon sun. Carys lifted her head, her eyes going wide at Elspeth's sudden movement.

Elspeth held up a hand. "Wait here." Whispering sent burning pain down her dry throat. Dizziness briefly overtook her as she moved, though she couldn't tell whether it was from hunger or exhaustion or heat. One misery seemed indistinguishable from another.

"Elspeth," Carys hissed, moving after her.

Elspeth paused at the foot of the stairs, sinking down to her knees, staring intently up at the opening of the pit. On the other side of the crisscrossed iron bars forming the gate over the pit's opening, Blets and

Bogwump stood face to face, grunting at each other, flicks of spittle flying from their jaws as they conversed. Elspeth couldn't make out their
words, but she knew it was about something important.

Something about the energy in the goblin fortress had changed in
the past couple of hours. She could sense it the same way she could
smell smoke when there was fire.

She turned back to Carys. Her sister's brow furrowed with worry,
her eyes wide.

"Something's happened," Elspeth said.

"How do you know?" For the first time since they'd been captured, Carys's nerve seemed to come back to her. She was ready for a
fight—that much was clear. But it wasn't the time for them to attempt
any kind of revolt against the goblins. Not then, not ever. It was too
dangerous. They had to be calm and cautious and cunning if they
planned to survive this until help came.

"Shh." Elspeth raised a finger. "Stay here. I'm going to find out
what's going on."

Carys drew breath to say something, to protest in some way, then
paused. She nodded and took a step back, not saying anything. It made
Elspeth tremble. *She trusts me so much*, Elspeth realized. *I can't ruin this.*

She pressed herself as close to the wall as she could, keeping to the
shadows, and crept up the stairs encircling the pit. As she drew close
to the top, she dropped down to her hands and knees, trying to keep
as low as she possibly could so Blets and Bogwump couldn't see her.

"...Caught them right there in the middle of the corridor,"
Captain Blets grunted, his eyes fixed on Bogwump and completely
oblivious that Elspeth lurked in the shadows only feet away. "Brazen
little wretches. Must've been doing some kind of magic. They just appeared out of nowhere."

Bogwump made a sound, something between a bellowing sigh and
a belch. "Where they now?"

"Ah, we be taking them to the dungeon," Captain Blets said. He nodded his head at Bogwump in a show of deference. "They'll be in your charge now. Two boys."

They, Elspeth thought, hanging on every word of this conversation. *They. Who's they?*

A toothy grin spread across Bogwump's face, revealing razor teeth behind his blistered lips. "It would be an honor." He clapped his spear on the stone floor, then stopped as if a thought had crept into his brutish mind. He tilted his head. "Do we know why, Cap'n? Why was they here?"

Blets sneered, shaking his head. "They won't talk. But wait 'til you see the finery they wear. Must be royalty."

"Ah. You think what I think."

Royalty, Elspeth realized. *That must mean—*

Before she could finish the thought, Captain Blets was speaking it aloud. "If they think they's coming to rescue the princesses…" He trailed off and started to laugh, a cruel, sinister, ugly sound that came out of his mouth and nose at the same time. "Well, if they think they's coming to rescue the princesses, then show them no mercy, Bogwump. Make them suffer."

As he said that, Captain Blets turned his gaze toward the pit. Elspeth didn't have time to shrink back into the shadows. His orange eyes fixed on her. "Ah. The little wretch is eavesdropping, I see."

Elspeth's heart sank into her stomach. She leaped up, placing one hand against the stone wall beside her to steady herself, and fled down the stairs.

Iron clanked behind her, the sound of Captain Blets and Bogwump opening the grate that covered the pit, followed by their pounding footsteps descending the stairs.

"Elspeth!" Carys emerged out of the darkness, rushing toward her. *Carys*, Elspeth thought. *No—they can hurt me, but they can't hurt my sister.*

Not that Carys would suffer to stand by while Blets and Bogwump committed any violence. Carys's pluck had returned with a vengeance, and Elspeth didn't think Carys would rest until she'd had a chance to at least prove herself against these enemies.

"Carys, stay back," Elspeth shouted. She raised a hand. *Please, please, now is not the time for recklessness*, Elspeth thought. *Let me handle this.* She stopped on the stairs and turned back toward the goblins as they descended.

She raised her chin, trying to look as imperial and as commanding as she could. She was King Hector's heiress. She was her sister's protector. She was not intimidated by goblins. No, not if help had indeed come for her finally. After weeks of waiting.

"I knew someone would come to rescue us," she said. She reached up and pushed her hair back behind her ears. "Captive princesses are always rescued." Two boys—dressed royally, princes potentially. At last! Even if the goblins had captured these boys, too, at least Elspeth and Carys were no longer alone.

Captain Blets laughed, his eyes blazing, his serpentine tongue flicking over his jagged teeth. "Pretty little fool," he grunted, ambling down the stairs. He raised a twisted hand and grabbed Elspeth's chin. "Nobody's rescuing you." He started to laugh. "It's time to do what we should have done long ago."

Elspeth's insides froze. *Time to do what we should have done long ago.* She didn't like the sound of that. The goblin's sharp fingernails dug into her skin. She let out a whimper.

Blets looked over his shoulder. "Bogwump, go summon the mances. Send them to me."

Bogwump's eyes went wide, though Elspeth couldn't tell whether it was out of fear or surprise. Maybe both.

"The mances, Cap'n?"

The mances? Elspeth thought. Goblin mances? Goblins knew crude ways of magic, but it was still powerful enough to be feared. At least, so the legends told.

Captain Blets sending for mances…that could only mean…

"Do not question me," Captain Blets sneered at Bogwump. "It's time we undertake some magic to keep these prisoners a secret. And when we're done, nobody will ever know who the princesses of Blunia are."

CHAPTER 27

The Forsaken Delves of the Goblin Fortress held many cells, but it was the one at the far end of the dungeon's sprawling hallways—the darkest and wettest and coldest of all—where they locked Marin and Aster away as prisoners.

The barred window provided only the meagerest view of the outside world. Not that there was much to look at. Only a barren wasteland stretched to the foot of the rocky hillside to the north.

As another dawn broke, Marin sat with his back against the cold stone wall and watched the sun crest the horizon. Mist hung in the air, shrouding the thorny trees like a spider's prey trapped in a web. Another day.

Marin reached for the rusty pike he'd been using to mark the days and scratched another tally on the wall. That made two weeks. When he found the pike among the debris on the dungeon floor their first night there, he never expected to be tracking days for two weeks.

This is your new life, he thought.

It was worse than Ilth's farm. What he wouldn't give to be back there again. At least on Ilth's farm, he had been outside. There'd been food.

His biggest fear had always been running away from Ilth's farm and finding himself in a situation that was worse than servitude to her. And now that had come to pass…

Marin stretched his legs out in front of him, shuffling around the damp straw that was supposed to serve as his bedding. He hadn't been able to sleep much in recent days. The exhaustion crept over him, slowly at first, wearing down his muscles and joints.

Behind him, Aster stirred in his sleep and drew his arm across his face.

"Good morrow," Marin said.

Aster didn't open his eyes. "Is it actually morning?"

"Almost. They'll be coming for us soon, I imagine."

Marin couldn't believe he actually had expected this mission to be easy, one where they would outwit all the goblins in a single afternoon and return back to the kingdom of Blunia with the princesses at their sides—triumphant, victorious, heroic. Instead, here they were, prisoners with no hope of escape.

With a huff, Aster pushed himself up off the floor. The shoulders of his tunic still bore bloody lashes from where a goblin foreman had struck him with a whip yesterday. Or maybe it had been the day before that. All the days were starting to blend together now. Marin glanced over at his tallies on the stone wall. The rust scratches stood out, red and angry.

"How many days has it been?" Aster asked, almost as if he could read Marin's thoughts.

"Two weeks," Marin said. Not that he was sure his tally was accurate. He might have missed a few days. On some days, it just didn't seem like it mattered much.

Aster stood and stepped over to Marin's tallies on the wall. He ran his fingers over them, counting one by one, almost as if he were hopeful that Marin overestimated how much time they'd been in captivity. The light from the window hadn't grown very bright yet, but there was enough light to clearly see the red tallies scratched onto the stone.

Aster closed his eyes. "If only we were anywhere but here."

They waited a moment.

"Still doesn't work," Marin observed bitterly.

"It worked back when we were in Grythium," Aster said, staring at the ring on his finger. "Why doesn't it work here?"

Marin remembered what Udifeus had told them. "Maybe we're right where we're supposed to be." It wasn't a happy thought—but one that still gave him a little bit of hope.

Aster shook his head. "I doubt it. Remember how the prophetess told us we had a great future ahead of us? What kind of great future is this? Is this the destiny she was talking about—being prisoners in a goblin fortress?"

This coming from Aster—Aster, who insisted that destiny wasn't real. Aster, who insisted that they take their lives into their own hands and run away from their life of servitude on Ilth's farm. Now he was questioning why they were here in this terrible goblin fortress.

"We're supposed to be here to rescue the princesses, remember?" Marin said.

"Some great job we're doing at that. We haven't even seen them in the weeks that we've been trapped here."

That same thought had been weighing on Marin's mind the past couple of days. He hadn't given up hope just yet, but he was close. "Something makes me wonder...well, maybe this was some sort of trick," he said. He hated the thought of it. Udifeus had been so kind to them, so helpful. But he practically sent them on a hopeless mission.

Aster gritted his teeth. "I bet King Donovan is pretty damn happy about it."

Marin went to the window and looked out, watching the heavy mist roll over the valley. "We'll find a way out of here eventually."

"You keep saying that, but..." Aster gestured toward the tallies on the wall. "All the while, we're doing nothing worth celebrating." He gritted his teeth in frustration. "Just labor as if—as if they're trying to torture us."

Marin shrugged. "Goblins don't strike me as the most creative bunch." He hesitated. "Don't be like this, Aster—don't start giving up." He didn't think he'd be able to handle it if Aster lost hope.

Aster swallowed. "I hate them so much."

A voice at the door to the cell caught them both by surprise. "Ah, and who is it you be hating this morning?"

Two orange eyes peered through the bars at the cell entry. The goblin guard had snuck up on them. He leaned in close to the bars and the details of his brutish face emerged from the dark.

"Nobody," Aster said.

"You best be watching your tongue," the goblin said, lifting a burly arm to shake the spear he carried by his side. "You don't want to give us reason to flay you. I'd be happy to do the honors meself."

Marin stepped forward. "You'll have no such honors."

The goblin wrinkled his bulbous snout. "Or maybe we be giving you over to the tigers. They'll tear you bit by bit."

This was a daily threat. Marin was used to it by now. How many times had the goblins threatened to throw them to the tigers if they didn't do as they were told? The tigers—one white and one orange— lived in a pit in the center of the fortress. Marin wouldn't give the goblins the satisfaction of acting scared. "What is our chore today?" he asked, barely containing his disdain through clenched teeth as he spoke in feigned respect. "What does the goblin army command?"

The goblin jerked the barred door to the cell open, letting it clang against the stone wall. With a growl, the goblin raised his spear up and pressed it against Marin's chest. The point of the stone blade felt sharp even through Marin's tunic. "That's better," the goblin commended his obedience. "You're learning manners, I see. Well then, come on.

185

We don't got all day."

Marin and Aster followed the goblin down the long corridor that led out of the dungeon. It was another day of hard labor for them ahead.

To think they sought out this place by choice! They actually thought they were suited for this mission that knights and warriors were afraid to undertake.

Even now, weeks later, Marin vividly remembered the first time they set eyes on the stone structure built deep in the wasted valley beyond the forest. The mass of black rocks and rusted iron sent a shiver down his spine. "That's it," he whispered to Aster from their hiding place at the top of the hill. "That's the goblin fortress."

"It looks exactly how I imagined it would," Aster replied.

"And something tells me these goblins will prove to be just as bad as we expect them to be," Marin said. Little did he know at the time how the goblins would be worse than he ever could have imagined—more vicious and forceful and cruel.

"Look," Aster said. "There are two down there."

Aster pointed down into the valley toward one goblin lumbering along the perimeter of the fortress wall and another approaching from the other direction. Short, stocky creatures covered in green scales that dripped with slime, they wore rudimentary armor of beaten metal and boiled leather. Both carried spears as long as they were tall, topped by heads of pointed steel.

Marin and Aster held their breath together as they watched. When the goblins encountered each other, whatever exchange they had between them quickly descended into angry violence. They crossed spears in a fight that lasted less than a minute before the larger one whirled his spear overhead and thrust its sharp point through the other's skull. The point went straight through like an arrow into an apple. Whatever sound it made was too far away for Marin to actually hear it, but the sight of blood splattering was enough to make his stomach turn.

The defeated goblin's body went limp and crumpled to the ground, sending up a cloud of dust as it landed. The other goblin ripped his spear back out, sending another spray of blood all around him, then continued on his march around the outside of the fortress as if the confrontation had been only a minor inconvenience.

"What in the cursed underworld!" Aster murmured in a quavering voice.

Marin swallowed the lump in his throat. "Oh, my gods."

For a second, neither of them could speak. They watched the killer goblin disappear around the corner of the fortress wall, leaving the corpse behind in a spreading pool of its own black blood.

"Well," Aster said, looking over at Marin, "are we doing this or not?"

Marin climbed to his feet. "Let's do it," he said weakly.

They descended the hill. As they passed the goblin they had just watched be killed, Marin stopped to stare at its corpse. The black blood pooling on the rocky ground gleamed in the dim, misty light. The gaping hole left by the spear separated the goblin's head, leaving an angry opening where the goblin's right eye had once been. The sight of it sent a shiver through Marin, but he couldn't look away. *Those goblins started fighting without a second thought,* Marin told himself. *That one killed this one without any show of remorse. That's what we're up against when we go into this place.*

"Don't think too much about it," Aster whispered as if he could hear Marin's thoughts.

"You're right," Marin said. And they pressed on.

When they reached the arching gate leading into the fortress, the two of them pressed themselves up against the wall so as not to be seen. This was as close as they dared get lest they attract unwanted attention.

Aster leaned in next to Marin. "Do you have it?"

"Aye."

Marin reached into the pocket of his doublet and pulled out the tiny silver phial Udifeus gave them. The sound of liquid sloshed inside as he shook it. "There's not much."

"He said an hour, right?"

Marin nodded. An hour. An hour of invisibility. "We should at least be able to infiltrate the fortress at that rate. We might not be able to free the princesses that quickly, but at least we can find where they are and figure out what we should do from there."

It had seemed like such a good plan. But an hour of invisibility had not been enough time. And when the spell wore off, they found themselves at the mercy of the goblins.

Here they were, weeks later, and still no sign of the princesses, and still no idea how they would ever escape. Held captive by the goblins, kept in squalor, made to toil every day, but never had they seen the lost daughters of King Hector. For all they knew, the girls were dead. Their bones were lying in a heap in the filthy courtyard. Maybe they had been tortured to death the same way Marin and Aster were. If they had been subjected to the same kind of daily abuse? *There's no way two delicate princesses could hold up to this kind of abuse*, Marin told himself. *Aster and I are barely surviving!*

How terrible it was going to be to have to take this news back to the subjects of the Blunia—that was if Marin and Aster ever did escape, and there was no guaranteeing they would.

Marin and Aster reported for duty in the great antechamber of the fortress, a cavernous hall surrounding one of the many deep pits full of rocks and muck and who knew what else.

"You'll be carrying rocks up from the pit today," the goblin foreman told them, saliva dribbling off the sharp end of his underbiting teeth. "A hundred stairs to climb, up and down," he went on. "And a hundred boulders to be carried. There be no supper for you till it's done."

Why? What's the point? Marin wanted to shout. His muscles and joints already ached from their task the day before and the day before that. *There's no sense in hauling boulders up from a pit just to pile them here in this antechamber! They only want us to suffer!*

Several goblins gathered to watch them work. The clan of scaly brutes, clad in boiled leather and rusted chainmail, lumbered around the perimeter of the pit. Marin hated the sound of their chanting and guffawing and growling almost as much as he hated the smell of their sickening body odor. Not that he ever dared to show his disgust—not if he didn't want to find himself pierced all the way through by one of the pikes or spears the goblins carried.

Up and down the stairs, Marin and Aster went, lugging stones that weighed nearly as much as either one of them did. From the bottom of the stairs, the height seemed to stretch on forever.

By mid-afternoon, Marin's face burned from the suffocating heat, his sweat-drenched hair and clothes clinging to him, his hands and forearms rubbed raw from clinging to the cumbersome rocks.

Aster looked just as bad. What was worse, he looked dejected. Marin always counted on Aster's fierce spirit, but it waned every day they were in captivity.

Is this actually going to be the day they break us? Marin wondered. *What will happen to us if we give up? If we reach our limits and just can't go on…*

His thoughts were interrupted as his foot caught on a crack in one of the steps and he stumbled forward. The rock he held toppled out of his arms onto the stone stairs, giving a clattering sound that echoed around them in the pit. Marin tried to catch himself, but his arms weren't quick enough, and he collapsed onto the stone on his hands and knees, then slid several steps down. Pain shot through him as the stone stairs tore his skin.

"Marin!" Aster called out.

Before Aster could rush to help him, a whip cracked in the air. Marin lifted himself up off the stairs to see one of the goblins descending toward them. It was Bogwump, the foreman. "Come on, wretch! Get up."

Marin's palms and knees burned. Faint splotches of blood spread across his raw skin. "Give me a moment," he wheezed. "Please! Just a moment." His heart pounded. He tried to push himself back up to his feet, but dizziness overtook him. The stairs seemed to tilt and sway, sending him topping back down onto his hands and knees.

"I told you to get up! Or it'll be to the tigers for you!"

Bogwump stopped on the stair just above Marin, raising his whip over his head. His orange eyes twitched with fury and he bit his lower lip. His fist hovered there in the air, gripping the handle of the whip. The whip's tail swung back and forth. Marin held his breath and closed his eyes, anticipating the strike.

The sound of stone clattered against stone. Marin opened his eyes again and looked behind him on the stairs. Aster had dropped his rock and was approaching. "He said give him a moment."

Bogwump flicked his stare from Marin to Aster. Torchlight from the sconces around the staircase glittered in his eyes. "You stay out of this!" Bogwump bared his fangs at Aster.

"Aster," Marin hissed, still unable to catch his breath. "Don't."

With his fist still gripping the handle of his whip overhead, Bogwump stooped down and, with his free hand, grabbed at Marin's collar. "Get up. Now." Bogwump jerked him to his feet. "Or I'll show you the real meaning of pain!" With that, Bogwump threw back his head and cackled, spit spewing and tongue wagging.

Marin's legs shook under him, but he managed to maintain his balance. What bothered him more than the dizziness and the pain was the sound of the goblin's malicious chuckle. It was awful—so awful! Cruelty was their sport. Maliciousness was their idea of fun. Inflicting pain was playtime.

Bogwump clapped his hand on Marin's shoulder, his overgrown nails digging into flesh. "You know, you're tougher than you look. I never would have expected you to last this long. How long is it going to be? How long until you start to give up?"

Now the taunting starts, Marin thought. This didn't happen every day, but it happened often enough. When he or Aster would show signs of weakness, the goblins would take it upon themselves to taunt and jeer at them. It was as if they were trying to get inside their heads and wear them down mentally as much as they did physically. It was like dealing with Ilth all over again.

"That's what you want, isn't it?" Marin said. His voice wavered as he said it. "You want us to give up, don't you?" He had never talked back before, but he wanted the goblins to know his will was stronger than their cruelty. He wasn't weak. He wasn't breakable—at least, not by them.

"Somebody's feeling brave today, isn't he?" Bogwump sneered. "What's gotten into you?"

Aster stood frozen on the stairs behind Marin, unsure of what to do.

Bogwump grinned. "You never did tell us why you came here. Did the king think you two would be able to rescue his daughters? The sweet, beautiful princesses?"

Marin's entire body quaked with rage. "Where are they?" He wanted an answer. He just wanted an answer.

Bogwump spat. Hot, phlegmy saliva struck Marin's face and dripped down his chin. He balled his hands into fists, fighting back the urge to swing at the goblin. If he did, he knew he would be flayed for it.

"You'll never find 'em," Bogwump boasted. "And your time is limited. We'll see how much longer you last. Maybe it's time to take your rations away."

Marin couldn't hold back anymore. There might have been one way to save the princesses—and Aster. And Marin was just desperate enough to try it.

"Is that what you want?" Marin shouted. "You want to torture someone?"

Aster exhaled sharply at the sound of Marin's retort, but Marin avoided turning around to look at him. *Stay strong*, Marin told himself. *Show these goblins they aren't going to break you.*

"Fine! You have me," Marin continued. "Torture me. If the princesses are still alive, you'll let them go. Let Aster take them safely home, and I'll stay here—"

The whip cracked overhead. "Be quiet," Bogwump demanded.

Marin held his breath.

"Noble, are you?" Bogwump sneered. "You think that's gonna be enough." He wrinkled his nose. "You disgust me."

Two goblins dressed in guard armor and carrying spears were coming down the stairs. Bogwump turned to them as they approached. He jerked his head to indicate Marin. "Seize him. Remove his shirt. It's time for sound lashing."

Aster lunged forward. "Keep off him!"

But before Aster could get too close, one of the guards raised his spear, thrusting its jagged tip toward Aster's chest. Aster stopped, not daring to get too close.

"I'll deal with you next," Bogwump barked at Aster. "If you stay quiet, maybe I'll be sparing your friend's life."

Marin looked up and met Aster's gaze. "Aster."

"And you be quiet, too!" With that, Bogwump grabbed Marin and shoved him toward the two guards. "Hold him!"

No sooner had the guard lowered his spear and stepped down one of the enormous stairs to take Marin by the shoulder than Aster lunged forward. "No!" he shouted.

Marin whirled around just as Aster lunged up the stairs and shoved one of the guards away. Bogwump cracked his whip, sending it across Aster's torso and arm, knocking him backward. Where the whip struck Aster, his tunic split open and drops of blood spewed across the landing. Three or four warm droplets sprayed Marin's face.

"Stop this!" Bogwump shouted, snapping his whip again. This time, the lash struck Aster's side, slicing open the small pouch of fairy dust stashed in his doublet pocket. Fine white dust went flying.

A collective gasp went out among the three goblins, and they drew away from Aster in sudden fear. Only then did Marin realize some of the fairy dust had landed on one of the guards, and where it had touched his scales, he now started to sizzle and smoke.

"No!" Bogwump cried. "No! No, it cannot be!"

The goblin who'd been touched by fairy dust howled, dropping to his knees. He dropped his spear and clutched his sizzling wound. "Sugar! The boy has sugar!"

Marin stumbled away from the goblins. He could hardly believe what he was seeing. Smoke spread out in a cloud around the afflicted goblin. "Aster," Marin whispered, unsure of what else to say.

Aster was already removing the sack from his pocket, staring at it in amazement and catching the white grains in his hand as they spilled out. "It's Ilth's fairy dust," he said. "It must be..."

"Stay away from the boy!" Bogwump shouted. He raised his whip as if to scare Marin and Aster back. "Stay away from them!"

"It's sugar," Marin exclaimed. He reached toward Aster and grabbed a handful from the split in the pouch. With a thrust of his arm, he scattered the fine white grains across the stairs, just as he would have scattered seeds back in Ilth's fields.

Terrified cries from the goblins chorused together as the brutes stepped back, all of a sudden seeming far less menacing than they did before. When the sugar hit them, they screamed in agony. Smoke erupted from burn marks on their scales.

Aster tore the sack open wider, taking out a handful of sugar and following Marin's lead by tossing it at the goblins.

Putrid gray smoke filled the air around them, quickly growing so thick that Marin had to take a step forward to see what was happening to their aggressors. The goblins shrank, growing punier and more pathetic as their skin burned away. The sizzling sounds from their disintegrating bodies soon grew so loud it drowned out their screams.

But it wasn't just the goblins themselves burning. Smoke erupted even from the places where the sugar grains hit the walls and floors, the once firm stone now suddenly vaporizing.

Marin drew a breath to shout but started coughing from the smoke. "This whole place is going to burn away!" he wheezed.

Pop! Pop! Entire stones forming the floor erupted like giant boils, sending up bursts of putrid gray smoke. Bogwump and the goblin guards had withered away like mushrooms left to fry in a pan of oil, and now it was impossible to tell one from the other, so shapeless and melted together were they. Their shrunken forms stumbled back and fell against the wall, causing that to disintegrate as well. Steam billowed out from the cracks between the stones.

"We've got to get out of here!" Aster shouted.

Marin nodded. "Aye! Come on!"

They hurried up the stairs toward the opening of the pit, just as a crowd of goblins, no doubt summoned by the sound of the screams, appeared at the top, all their swords and spears drawn.

But it was too late. The smoke was too heavy at this point, and as it surrounded the goblins, they felt its burning effects.

Screams and smoke, smoke and screams—it was all Marin could see and hear by that point. Gasping for air, he fumbled to grab Aster's arm, to hold him tight lest the two of them be separated in all the madness.

"Aster!" he shouted.

"I'm right here! I'm right here!"

The shouts and screams rose to a deafening chorus, then started to die away, softening until the only sound was that of sizzling smoke. When that had quieted, and the dust around them thinned, Marin raised his arms to wave the smoke away as best he could. He gave several heavy coughs to clear his lungs.

He and Aster now stood in the midst of smoking ruins that had once been the goblin fortress. Marin could hardly process it. "What just happened?"

Aster stared at the empty pouch in his hand. "I think…I think the sugar dissolved them."

He peeled away the fabric and a few remaining grains of sugar fell out onto the ground. Something solid and heavy remained at the bottom of the pouch—something red that caught what little light made its way through the clearing smoke. Aster held it up. "It's a key!"

The key was so ornate it could have passed for some piece of jewelry or treasure, but it was undeniably a key carved from glittering red phoenix bone. "It was at the bottom of the bag," he said.

Marin reached forward and touched the shimmering discovery in Aster's hand. "Something tells me we should hold onto that."

Aster nodded. "Aye." His voice had a hazy quality to it, as if he were still in disbelief, still dazed, still trying to process what had just happened. He pocketed the key. "Aye, that would be wise, I agree."

Before Marin could respond, movement appeared in the smoke behind Aster. It took only a moment for Marin to realize what it was. "Aster, look! The tigers!"

Aster whirled around. The tigers! The enormous beasts the goblins kept in captivity, always threatening to set on Marin and Aster if they didn't comply. Here they were, prowling free! The monstrous beasts Marin and Aster had spent weeks fearing, now suddenly freed by the same disaster that killed the goblins. Marin felt his skin crawl. His eyes went straight to their enormous claws—those claws that could easily tear him and Aster apart.

The white one walked in the lead, followed closely behind by the orange one, both ambling across the burnt grass.

But for some reason, neither beast looked as menacing as it should have. They looked…smaller, daintier than tigers should have been. Their walk was almost graceful, not threatening or predatory.

They were shrinking—their forms growing slighter, more lithe and delicate with each passing step. They hardly looked like tigers at all except for the furs draped over them.

"Well," Marin gasped. "I'll be damned."

The furs themselves melted away just as the rest of the goblin fortress had done. Where the great beasts had once stood were now crouched two slender feminine forms dressed in tattered silks. The first was fair-skinned, her hair the color of honey and her dress white, stained though it was; the other was ruddy with chestnut hair in a dress the color of burnished copper.

The blonde looked up and her eyes met Marin's. Marin had never seen eyes so blue. They pierced right through him, making him feel all warm and nervous inside. The girl's face spread into a smile, and she worked her mouth as if she had forgotten how to use it. "Th-th-thank y-you."

Marin rushed forward and sank down to his knees, offering out a hand to the girl to help her to her feet. It wasn't until his hand was extended that he became suddenly self-conscious of how dirty and scarred his hands were. They weren't fit to touch her pure, sweet, gentle ones. Wouldn't she be disgusted?

Before he could draw his hands away, the girl reached forward and took them in hers. She didn't seem disgusted in the least. Her touch was warm and sent a shiver through him. He felt his cheeks burn.

"Thank you," the girl repeated. "You've freed us."

Aster was at the brunette's side, helping her to her feet. She placed a delicate hand on his shoulder and laughed sweetly, a sound like windchimes dancing in the gentlest of breezes.

Marin looked from one girl to the other. "Are you...?"

But he didn't even have to ask. There was nobody else the girls could be.

They had found the lost princesses of Blunia.

CHAPTER 28

"Look! It's the princesses! They've returned."

"Who are those young men with them?"

"Have they defeated the goblins?"

"They must have."

Marin caught the words from the crowd among all the fanfare and rejoicing as he, Aster, Elspeth, and Carys drew close to the royal palace of Blunia. The cobbled streets were thronged with peasants and commonfolk of all ages who shouted and waved. Hundreds of eyes fixed on Marin as he rode, making him suddenly aware of how dirty and ragged he must have looked, how undeserving he was of the horse he mounted or the princess sharing the saddle with him, one of her delicate arms wrapped affectionately around his neck while she waved to the crowd with the other.

This is all too much for me, he thought as he forced a smile on his face and, following Princess Elspeth's example, waved to the crowd. *Oh, they all adore me, but that's only because they think I'm a hero.*

Marin wasn't a hero. Not by a long shot. He and Aster had simply been in the right place at the right time, holding the right bag of common table sugar, and it could have just as easily have been any other young man. Maybe even one who was handsome and strong and trained in courtly manners, not some rough farmhand who only knew about the world through reading books.

Aye, he and Aster had set out for the goblin fortress with the plan to destroy the goblins. But he had pictured a daring victory on his part. When the time came, he would be brave, and he would prove himself heroic by brandishing a sword against a gang of goblins all at once, then hoisting the princess into his arms and carrying her to safety.

Instead, all they had done was spend a couple of weeks in captivity and then toss a few handfuls of sugar. It wasn't the test of heroism he would ever think to brag about. The princesses must be embarrassed that they were rescued in such a way—if it could even be described as a rescue.

He caught Aster's eye while they rode. Aster raised an eyebrow and shrugged his shoulder, as if to say, "We might as well enjoy all of this, mightn't we?"

Marin sighed and looked around the crowd again as his horse pressed forward. Elspeth leaned back, her slender body pressing against his. His stomach quivered. He and Elspeth had ridden like this for the past two days, and he should have been comfortable with it by now.

Should have been. But wasn't.

At first, he had found himself out of breath and gripped with nervousness every time Elspeth so much as looked at him. She was the type of princess that bards would have written songs about and knights would have gone to war to defend. She wasn't the type of princess who would ever fall in love with a ragged farm boy.

And yet Elspeth took a liking to him almost instantly.

"What may I call you, my good sir?" she had asked as they made their way out of the smoldering wasteland where the goblin fortress had burned away. She didn't address him as "my good sir" in a mocking way—her tone suggested she really, truly admired him.

"Uh, Marin."

"My lord Sir Marin," she said, her smile glowing.

"Marin is enough, your highness."

"I pray thee, call me Elspeth. There's no need for formalities, Marin. After all, you did just rescue me. All of Blunia is in your debt."

Imagine that, Marin thought. *All of Blunia being in debt to a farmhand.*

Carys took Aster's hand. "And your name, good sir?"

"Aster."

"Aster," Carys repeated. She looked at Elspeth. "What should we say to Sir Aster and Sir Marin?"

Elspeth rolled her eyes. "Oh, in the name of the gods, Carys, they've asked us not to call them *Sir.* We must respect that." Elspeth looked from Marin to Aster. "Forgive my sister. She is still training in courtly graces, and...well, she falters sometimes."

"She means I would have been better training as a squire than a princess," Carys said. "You can say it, Elspeth." And the two girls laughed.

They made their way up the side of the ravine leading out of the valley and into the forest beyond. After weeks in a putrid, gray, cold stronghold, the open air felt so sweet to breathe in, and Marin relished the warmth of the sun on his face and the sight of the bright green of the trees perched on the top of the hill.

Elspeth and Carys made their way over the rocks with surprising ease for maidens who must have grown up stitching needlepoint and playing the harp, or whatever princesses did, Marin thought. Once or twice, Elspeth faltered, acting as if she needed Marin's assistance to climb over a boulder or get up a steep part of the hill. *She must think it unladylike to have an easy time out in the wilderness,* Marin thought. *How silly royalty must be, so concerned with pretense and conditions.*

They reached the top of the hill to find two gray stallions waiting for them, standing content in the grass and peering at Marin and Aster with large black eyes.

"Oh," Marin almost laughed at the sight of the horses. "And who are these?"

He took a slow step forward, holding out his hand as if he might startle the horses if he dared to draw too close too quickly. One of the horses bowed.

"Greetings and good morrow, my good lads," the horse said.

"Good morrow," Marin replied, hearing the awkwardness in his own voice. He looked at Elspeth to see whether she noticed. Then he added, deepening his voice ever so slightly to show authority, "Am I right in thinking you're waiting at the top of this hill to greet us?"

The other horse neighed and reared up on his legs. "Forsooth," he said. "Yes, we're waiting for you. Do you think saddled horses just wander around waiting for heroes to find them?"

The first horse turned his head and bellowed at the second. "Enough with the mockery. It's not becoming for a royal steed." He looked back at the boys and the princesses. "Yes, my young lord. We are waiting here for you. We've been conjured, you might say."

"Conjured?" Aster exclaimed.

"Yes. By the wizard Udifeus."

Udifeus. Why, he already knew they'd defeated the goblins! "Word travels fast," Marin says.

"Magicians have their ways," the first horse replied. "And we are here now to carry you to Blunia."

Neither Marin nor Aster had ever ridden a horse before, but neither of them wanted to admit it in front of Elspeth and Carys. Something told Marin the princesses could tell, but they were too polite to say anything as they watched the boys struggle to gain their footing in the stirrups and hoist themselves up into the saddle. Marin then helped Elspeth up to ride with him, and Aster did the same with Carys.

That was how they journeyed for two days, crossing through

forests and fields, over hill and through dale until they came to the main road leading into the royal city. "I might dismount the horse and walk beside it while you ride," Marin said to Elspeth. "At least once we start to get close to your father's palace." The hairs on the back of his neck stood up every time he thought about how her body was pressed close to his.

"Why would you do that?" she asked. He couldn't get over how large and blue her eyes were. With her sitting in the saddle in front of him, her face was only inches from his.

"Well, wouldn't it be scandalous to have you seated this close to me?"

She laughed. "Don't be silly, my lord." She placed a hand on his cheek, causing Marin's stomach to tingle. "It would be an honor, and I want all the kingdom to know who it was who rescued me and brought me home."

Marin could feel blush burning his face. He swallowed, trying not to show how embarrassed he was.

"Besides," Elspeth said, "I am the crown princess of Blunia and heiress to my father's throne. I am in line to be queen one day, and if I say you are a hero, then nobody may question it."

"Oh," Marin replied.

Night fell after their first day of riding, bringing a wave of exhaustion over all four of them. The light of the moon and stars proved too meager for them to travel safely by, and the air grew chilly. "Shouldn't we stop to make camp and build a fire?" Aster suggested. "And get some rest?"

Marin realized his own stubbornness to keep riding through the night was a disservice to all of them. The mossy floor of the forest was no place for princesses to sleep, but the only other option was to keep them awake all night long, sitting up in a saddle when their father's palace was still miles away.

"We're not delicate flowers," Carys said to Marin as if she could read his thoughts. "We survived for weeks back there in a prison pit."

"I think it's adorable that they want to take care of us," Elspeth said. "Really, Marin, it's very sweet of you. Both of you are valiant gentlemen."

Marin opened his mouth to protest. "I—"

"But my sister's right. You don't need to worry about pampering us. Let's make camp here and ride the rest of the way tomorrow."

After tying the horses to one of the trees, Aster set about building a fire with a bit of flint while Marin collected a pile of fallen leaves to make a bed for the girls. In less than an hour, they had a blaze burning, and they were sitting around, laughing and telling stories as if the four of them had known one another for years.

Marin lay awake later, staring up at the stars. He knew he should have been tired enough to fall asleep right away. But something kept him awake—some wild energy deep inside his soul that wouldn't settle.

Is our destiny really written out in those stars up there? He wondered as he traced his gaze around the sky. *Aster and I really were in just the right place at the right time. Anyone could have rescued Elspeth and Carys. But…but if destiny is real…then what's the point of anything?* What was the point of anything he had done before this and anything he would do after this?

Movement in the dark drew his attention away from the stars. By the light of the fading embers, he could see Elspeth's shadowy form standing over him.

"Elspeth."

"I hope it's not a bother to you, Marin. I'm cold."

It took a moment for Marin to realize what she was suggesting. His entire body froze up with nervousness. "Oh," he murmured. "Oh, well, in that case…well, if it's just to keep warm, why don't you lie down here by me."

"Yes, it's just to keep warm."

She knelt down and crawled close to him. He could smell the sweet scent of her skin. Reluctantly, he wrapped one arm around her and held her. "Is…is that better?"

"Yes."

She pressed her head against his chest, then placed an arm across his abdomen. At first, Marin couldn't breathe. But after several minutes of lying there, a sense of comfort overtook him. It was as if he *wanted* Elspeth to be close to him. He wanted to pull her even closer and never let her go.

"You know," Elspeth murmured, her head still resting on his chest. "I spent weeks wishing to be rescued. I knew a handsome prince or knight would come save me."

"Oh." Marin's heart thumped. "I'm sorry."

"Why would you be sorry?"

"I just…well, if you were expecting a handsome prince."

"No." She stifled a laugh. "You misunderstand me, Marin. You *are* my handsome prince."

Silence. Marin didn't know how to respond to that.

"And," she added. "It will be expected now that you'll marry me."

"What?" Marin's stomach twisted. Marry? To this princess, with her unparalleled beauty and her easy confidence? "Is that really expected?"

"Don't act so scared," she said. "It's quite customary. When a handsome adventurer rescues a princess, he takes her hand in marriage. Isn't that what you want?"

Of course, Marin thought. How could he say no to such a prospect? And did she actually call him handsome? Him? Handsome?

But still…

"I admit that I'm nervous about it, too," Elspeth said. "An arranged marriage, I mean."

Marin didn't know whether that made him feel better or worse.

Quiet followed. "You are?" he asked.

"Marin, I'm my father's heiress. Do you understand what that means?"

"You're going to inherit his kingdom one day."

"Yes," she shifted, drawing herself closer to him. "I'm going to be queen. I have a duty to the throne. Whoever marries me is going to have to be a partner in ruling my kingdom."

"And you don't want a king who is going to try to downplay your sovereignty." It wasn't a question. He understood what she meant.

"You speak very well for…well, for a…"

"For a commoner? It's all right. You can tell me that."

"How did you learn? About sovereignty and politics, I mean."

Marin sighed. "Reading, I suppose. It's the only way I knew about the world before Aster and I escaped from Ilth's farm." They had told the girls about their years of servitude while they sat around the fire earlier. At least, they had told them about it in the most matter-of-fact way. They hadn't delved into the emotional burden of it all. How Marin was mostly ignorant of how the world worked, save for what he read about in ballads and epics.

"Reading is the same way I learned that princesses are supposed to be rescued by gallant knights," he added. "Which is why…" He hesitated. Did he dare say it? If he said it, then he was admitting his own insufficiency. "Which is why I wouldn't mind if you decided you couldn't marry me." He paused. "You have no reason to love me. I just did what anyone else would do."

Elspeth lifted her head and leaned close. "Not what anyone else would do," she said. "Nobody else did it. And even though it makes me nervous and makes me scared, and even though I'm questioning whether it's right, considering all my duties as a princess—I'm so grateful, Marin."

"You are?"

Her breath was warm on his cheek. Nervousness had left him completely, replaced now with a sense of comfort he never wanted to end. It took him a second to find his voice. "Can I...?"

"Yes. You can."

His lips touched hers. His first kiss washed over him like a warm rain. When they pulled apart, she leaned in and kissed him again. When they were done, she put her head back on his chest and snuggled close to him, their bodies warming each other in the cold night. After all, they were only lying together to keep warm.

Marin drifted off to sleep feeling as if everything were right in the world.

The hazy gray of dawn had just started to appear around the tree branches overhead when Marin woke. Elspeth stirred beside him. She lifted herself up.

"What's wrong?" he whispered.

She hesitated. "I'm going to...well, I'm going to lie a little farther away. Just so we aren't so close when Aster and Carys wake up." She must have sensed Marin's self-consciousness, because she quickly added, "Just for propriety's sake. I don't want my sister asking questions." She leaned in and kissed him. "Thank you for keeping me warm last night."

How had this all happened so fast? Marin tried to fall back asleep after Elspeth crawled away, but his spirit felt as if it wriggled around inside skin that had suddenly become too small for him. He swung from feeling excited to feeling nervous to feeling excited again as he watched the sky grow lighter overhead.

By the time morning arrived and the others awoke, Marin's joy from the night before had given way to doubt again. Had the princess really kissed him and talked of marriage? *She's grateful you rescued her, no doubt about that. But how soon until she realizes you aren't anything special? She might be duty-bound to marry whoever rescues her, but you aren't worthy.*

You're not. You're not worthy of marrying the princess of Blunia, no matter what tradition dictates.

Yet as they rode the rest of the morning, Elspeth sitting sidesaddle with one arm around Marin's shoulder, Marin couldn't resist thinking that maybe—just maybe—it wasn't because she was trying to hold on for balance while riding. Maybe she really wanted to be close to him.

He glanced over at Aster, who looked completely at ease with Carys pressed close to him in the saddle. What Marin wouldn't give to have the self-assurance Aster always seemed to exude.

Even when they rode through the streets of Blunia and heard the people cheering, Marin couldn't help thinking about how none of these commoners would really be impressed with him if they knew he was really lower than they were—he and Aster weren't even villagers or city folk or merchants or tradesmen. They were mere servants, the lowest of the low, raised in rough-spun garments and trained in farm chores. Would these people be cheering if they knew the boys who rescued the princesses had spent their lives chopping firewood and tending kitchen fires for a witch?

The royal palace of Blunia rose up before them as they drew close, the sunlight glittering off the pale gray stonework that formed its curtain wall and the polished oak of its gate. Marin heaved a deep breath—it was just as beautiful as King Donovan's palace in Grythium. Here they were at another royal court. *Let's hope it goes better this time*, he thought.

The gates swung open, and two guards stepped out. The coat of arms on their jade-colored livery showed a bird with its wings outstretched over a sun with ornate sunbeams encircling it.

"Sir Anselet!" Elspeth shouted. "Sir Gifford!"

The guards swept into low bows, their movements so synchronized they gave off the appearance of trained acrobats. "My ladies," one of them murmured.

Elspeth offered her hand out, suddenly possessed by courtly

manners. Marin no longer recognized the carefree girl he knew out in the woods.

"My good sirs," Elspeth said to the guards, "may I present Prince Marin and Prince Aster."

Prince? Marin knew he'd heard her correctly, but it still sounded so wrong. Or did it? After all, they *had* rescued the princesses, hadn't they? And Elspeth did seem to respect him, didn't she? Even so...

If they deserved such a title—and maybe, just maybe, they did—why did he still feel so nervous? At any minute, somebody would see through the façade and realize he was a fake, just a servant posing as a prince. Just as he had felt back in Grythium when Ilth exposed them before the court.

"Your highness." The guard whom Elspeth addressed as Sir Anselet nodded to her. He took Elspeth's hand and kissed it. "His majesty, your father, has been told of your rescue. He's eager to see you."

Carys climbed down from the saddle she shared with Aster. "Father? He's waiting for us?"

Elspeth held a hand up as if to tell Carys to calm herself. She kept her poise, chin slightly raised. A winsome grin was the only thing that stopped her from looking haughty. "Sir, we wish to be taken to our father, the king."

"At once, your highness." Sir Anselet stood.

Realizing they were about to be led inside the palace, Marin swung one leg over the saddle and dropped down to the ground, a little too clumsily for someone trying to pass for royal birth. "Oof," he grunted, making all of it worse.

Elspeth dropped down beside him. "Oh, my prince. Are you all right?" She held out a hand.

Marin looked up at Sir Anselet and Sir Gifford, his face burning. Neither guard seemed critical of his fall—on the contrary, they both looked down on him with concern.

208

"I'm fine," Marin said.

He took Elspeth's hand and let her help him to his feet. "I…uh… it's just been a while since I dismounted a horse. I mean…this is not my usual steed, and…I…"

"No need to apologize, Marin," Carys chimed in as she offered a hand to Aster and helped him down from his horse. He dropped to the ground in one smooth motion, landing on both feet.

A slight boy, several years younger than they were, approached from around the side of the curtain wall. Dressed in riding pants and a loose-fitting tunic, he looked like a squire. "Shall I care for your horses for you, your highness?" he asked Marin.

"Uh. Yes." Marin nodded. "Thank you, sir."

"I am no sir," the boy laughed, taking the rein of Marin's horse in one hand and the rein of Aster's in the other. Without another word, he led the steeds away.

"Come, your highnesses," Sir Anselet said. "His majesty awaits."

He turned and passed through the enormous oak doors into a grand hall within. Glittering stonework shimmered under the light of elaborate chandeliers. Tapestries stitched with spun gold and encrusted with gemstones adorned the walls. The scent of lavender and rosemary hung in the air.

"Uh…Elspeth," Marin whispered. "Do you mean we're going to the royal court *right now*?"

Elspeth, still demonstrating her courtly manners, nodded her head gently. "Yes, my lord. Our father, his majesty, will want to meet you and Aster." Then, in a lower voice so that the guards could not hear, she whispered, "Don't be nervous. You're doing fine."

"I fell off the horse and landed on my face," Marin whispered back. "How is that 'doing fine'?"

A smile cracked Elspeth's face. "I thought it was charming."

Marin looked down at his ragged clothing. The finery that Gnarnus had dressed him and Aster in back in Grythium had been worn away during their days in captivity. The goblins themselves had ripped away much of the ornamentation—the ornate buckles, the gemstones set in the fabric, the fine jewelry—and throughout the hard labor, the velvet and satin grew shabby and stained until it was hardly recognizable as fine fabric. It might as well have been the burlap or rough-spun wool they had been given when working on Ilth's farm.

"Shouldn't we...you know, put on more appropriate attire first?" He glanced at Aster, hoping he would protest as well. Aster simply shrugged.

"No need for that," Carys said. "Father won't mind. You look more like adventurers this way. He will be quite impressed, I'm sure."

Sir Anselet paused and looked back at the four of them. "Should I wait, your highnesses?"

Elspeth laughed. "No, not at all, Sir Anselet. Prince Marin simply wants to make a good impression upon his majesty." She looked at Marin as she continued, "But we mustn't keep his majesty waiting. My sister and I want to see him. Lead on."

Who was Marin to stop Elspeth and Carys from seeing their father right away, no matter how embarrassed he might have been about the clothes he was wearing as he walked into the royal court?

Even if you were dressed in the best attire money could buy, do you really think you would feel better about standing in front of a king and asking for his daughter's hand in marriage? Marin thought. There was no way of knowing for sure. Maybe he would still be uncomfortable. But fine clothes wouldn't hurt.

Each corridor was grander than the one before it, and when they finally passed through the archway into the throne room, the glittering splendor overwhelmed Marin. At first, he thought he would have to shield his eyes from the shimmering lights that bounced off the silver lining the walls from end to end. A gold-brocaded stretch of green carpet led from the archway up to the marble dais where a man sat waiting on a shining wood throne.

"Girls!" the king shouted, standing. "Elspeth! Carys!" He threw his arms open wide, beckoning for his daughters.

"Father!"

The princesses dashed along the stretch of green carpet as fast as they could run in their long skirts. Any worries Marin had about the royal court being a stuffy, stilted, overly dignified place vanished in a flash. This wasn't a greeting between a king and princesses—this was a father greeting his daughters. It was a show of love as the girls jumped up onto the dais and fell into his open arms.

King Hector laughed. "My precious girls! Oh, my precious little girls!" He lowered his face to bury them in kisses.

Marin looked up at Sir Anselet. "Go on," the guard encouraged. "The king wanted an audience with you, too."

A formal introduction from the guard must have been too much to hope for. Marin and Aster walked down the carpet toward the throne together. How lucky they were the king had not been holding court this afternoon. The throne room was empty save for the king and the guards. The vast openness of the grand hall made Marin feel small, but it was better than having hundreds of eyes watching them as they met the king.

"I thought I'd never see you again," King Hector said as he pulled the girls in close for another hug. "Oh, my babies."

Marin didn't want to interrupt the joyful reunion. He paused, lifted a hand and rested it on Aster's shoulder. They would wait until the king addressed him.

His majesty turned his gaze toward them. Only now did Marin fully take in the sight of King Hector. He was a big man, tall and wide across the shoulders, though slender through his waist, which was cinched neatly with a satin sash around his velvet robe. His flaxen hair and beard were flecked with trace hints of silver, and despite the creases in his skin that showed his age, his blue eyes blazed with the energy of a much younger man. Any nervousness possessing Marin up until that point suddenly left him when he saw the king's expression. Everything about King Hector radiated warmth and kindness.

"My lords," Hector addressed Marin and Aster. "You are the ones who have brought my daughters safely home."

Marin couldn't resist smiling—the king's respect was so flattering. "We're not lords, I'm afraid, your majesty. We're as common as they come." He paused. "But...well..."

King Hector laughed. "Speak up, my boy, speak up." He stepped down from the dais and approached Marin. "Common, you say? No. No, you're not common." He closed in on them and put one arm around Marin and the other around Aster, just as he had around his own daughters. It was an act of love that almost made Marin melt. Was this what it was like to feel a parent's affection?

"You have rescued my daughters," the king continued, leading Marin and Aster up to the dais. "And for that, I am forever in your debt. Whatever you ask of me, you'll have."

"That's very generous of you, your majesty," Aster said. "There's nothing we could ask for."

Elspeth flashed an encouraging look at Marin. He knew what she insinuated. "Your majesty," he addressed the king. But he couldn't bring himself to say anything more. Even if he had feelings for Elspeth—even if she showed feelings in return—even if royal tradition dictated that a princess be betrothed to her rescuer—

He couldn't ask to marry the princess. He couldn't.

"Your majesty," he said again, "I can't ask for more than I deserve. It...it's not my place to make requests of a king."

King Hector laughed. "Nonsense." He patted Marin's shoulder, then drew back and took a seat on his throne. He rested his hands on his knees and leaned forward. "What can I give you, my boy? Gold?

Titles? Land?"

Aster laughed. "We would most gratefully accept."

"Then you should have it." King Hector clasped his hands together, beaming a smile at them.

Elspeth cleared her throat. Her father's attention suddenly on her, she smiled, batted her eyes twice, and nodded her head ever so gently in Marin's direction.

The king got the message. "And what about my daughters?"

"They are very beautiful and very kind, your majesty," Marin said.

"And you are very modest, my lord," Elspeth said.

Marin smiled at her. "Your highness. It would be impossible not to fall in love with you." *It's expected*, he told himself. *When a hero rescues a princess, he's supposed to marry her.*

As if he actually believed himself to be a hero!

Marin crossed the dais and put a hand on Aster's shoulder. "My brother and I would consider ourselves lucky if you would...well..."

King Hector cleared his throat. "If you wish to wed my daughters, you need only ask. You see, *I* would consider *myself* lucky to gain sons such as you."

When he said that, something glinted in his eye. Was it a tear?

"Such a pair of princes I once wished I would see marry my girls," he said, as if this betrothal brought up a painful memory. "And such they might have stood before me now, young men in their prime, handsome, charming." He stared at Marin and Aster, his gaze heavy but his face remaining stoic.

What does he mean? Marin thought. *He can't mean the son and nephew of King Donovan, can he?* The story went that King Hector and King Donovan had once been the best of friends. How could they not have wished to see their kingdoms united by the marriage of Donovan's son to Hector's daughter?

And if that were to happen, Marin mused, wouldn't that mean

Hector's child would indeed rule Donovan's kingdom? If Hector's child married Donovan's? Nobody seemed to interpret the prophecy that way.

Besides, that was before Donovan went mad and had his son killed.

Hector rose to his feet and approached his daughters. "Elspeth, Carys, what do you say?"

Elspeth's face lit up. "It would be our privilege, Father."

Carys nodded. "Yes, Father."

King Hector clapped his hands. "A royal betrothal it is! But not here. Not like this." He surveyed the four of them. "You're weary. You need rest." He laughed, then added gently as he looked Marin and Aster up and down, "And bathing, and clean clothes."

Marin and Aster couldn't resist chuckling at that as well.

"And good food," King Hector added. For the first time since his daughters and the boys entered the room, his majesty turned his attention on the guards standing at the entry to the hall. "Send for my valets. We will have a royal ball tonight."

Sir Anselet nodded and disappeared out the entry from the throne room into the hall beyond.

"Nothing extravagant," King Hector said to the four of them. "Only a feast and a few hundred bottles of wine, and music and dancing. I'll discuss the preparations with the palace staff. For now..." He looked back up at Sir Gifford, who still stood by the door. "Sir Gifford. Show these two young men to comfortable guest quarters."

The king paused and looked at Marin and Aster. He lowered his voice. "My good young sirs, your names, I pray thee?"

Marin flushed. Here he was, practically engaged to the king's daughter and the king didn't even know his name yet. "My name is Marin, may it please your majesty."

"Aster, your majesty."

King Hector smiled. "See to it that a valet takes care of every need

214

Prince Marin and Prince Aster should have. See to it that the royal tailor can fit them in new clothes—something appropriate for the celebration tonight, and for royal court in the days ahead."

Royal court? Marin thought. This was all moving so fast!

And faster still it continued. The next few hours rushed by in a way Marin had never before experienced. Each minute led to another that was grander and more overwhelming than the one before. Sir Gifford led him and Aster out of the throne room and through more illustrious hallways to a royal bathhouse where a team of valets had filled two marble tubs with steaming water. They discarded their ragged clothes and were given time to soak away the filth and muck from their adventures. Afterward, they were presented with fine clothing even nicer than the royal attire Gnarnus had given them.

"It still doesn't feel quite right," Marin said as he studied himself in the looking glass that hung in their private chamber. The beautiful furnishings of the room glowed with hazy warmth from the light of candles shining on so much gold. Two beds flanked the room, dressed with satin sheets and velvet duvets over downy mattresses. Marin couldn't wait to sleep soundly later that night—after the ball, of course. He ran his hands over the gemstones stitched into the broad collar of his doublet.

"I think you'll get used to it in time," Aster said. "If you let yourself."

Marin realized they'd had this same conversation before. Back when they were dressed in royal attire the first time—back in Gnarnus's hideout. That seemed like so long ago now.

But this was slightly different. Back when Gnarnus dressed them, they were disguising themselves as royalty. This time, it was a king's own palace staff that dressed them. They were actually being perceived as royalty. It should have felt real. They were now engaged to princesses—unofficially, of course, but it was only a matter of hours before King Hector announced the betrothal before all the important

215

people in the kingdom.

You're still a little nobody, Marin thought. *Whether it's a renegade morgglor who's dressing you, or whether it's the king himself. They can dress you up all they want, but they can't turn you into a prince.*

"Would you stop?" Aster said with a laugh as Marin fiddled with his collar. "You look great. Come now, you look like royalty. We both do."

Marin turned away from the mirror and faced his brother. "You always believe in me, don't you?" He really didn't deserve to have a companion like Aster. How would he have made it this far without this brother of his?

Aster nodded. "Yes. I do. You just need to believe in yourself."

CHAPTER 29

Marin peered through the velvet curtain, drinking in the sight of the opulent ballroom the way a parched man would chug water for the first time in days. It was all too much, so much that he thought it might make him sick. Hundreds of lords and ladies gathered on the expanse of marble floor, each of them looking more elegant, more attractive, and more important than the one standing next to them. The gemstones that adorned their royal attire shimmered in the torchlight like an expansive sky of multicolored stars. Their chattering voices rose up above the sound of the harpists and flutists playing their instruments.

In only a few minutes, we're going to be introduced to these people.

He traced his gaze along the wall on the opposite side of the hall, hoping he might see Aster peering out from the matching set of curtains that covered the other alcove, where Aster presently waited with Carys. Just an encouraging glance from his brother might be enough to get him through this.

"I'm so nervous." Marin turned back to Elspeth and let the heavy velvet drape close behind him, shutting out the rest of the banquet and all its guests. "I know I shouldn't admit that."

For now, he and Elspeth were alone. The gold furnishings in the cozy alcove didn't provide much comfort to sit on, but at least he and Elspeth had privacy. Elspeth stepped close to him. Her pale blue gown, dotted with diamonds, gave her a mystical, ethereal quality in the low-burning lights of the alcove. "You've no reason to be nervous."

Marin huffed. He wiped the sweat from his palms on the sides of his velvet breeches. "I know. No reason to be nervous. It's only the highest lords of the kingdom I'm being introduced to."

"You'll be fine." Her hands closed on his shoulders and she turned him to face her. *She feels so comfortable now*, Marin thought. *How was I ever nervous around her before?* Her touch and her smile and her voice— they might have been the touch and smile and voice of a princess, but they were also the touch and smile and voice of a dear friend. Familiar. Warm.

"Listen to me," she continued. "They will all be so impressed with you. I know it."

She raised herself on her tiptoes to kiss his cheek. A shiver went through him. He might have been used to her smile and her touch, but something as intimate as a kiss still turned him stupid. *What are you going to do when it's time to engage in love acts that are even more intimate?* As much as he wanted to hold her and never let her go, he still couldn't accept the idea that he deserved her, that at any minute, she would come to her senses and realize he was just a lowly servant after all.

And would she have really kissed him like that if the entire royal court were watching? What would King Hector think if he knew Marin had cuddled his daughter in the dark out in the forest, had placed his hands on the soft curves of her body? Would the king think less of Marin, even if Marin had done what he did with the notion of keeping both of them warm on a cold night?

What would the rest of the royal court say? There had to be other noblemen who wanted Princess Elspeth for a wife. Other noblemen who were probably wealthier and more handsome and more refined in their manners than Marin could ever hope to be. Was everyone going to think Marin didn't deserve the king's blessing to marry the princess?

"Come on," Elspeth whispered. She took Marin's hand and led him back to the edge of the curtain. "We need to be ready when the fanfare plays. That will be our cue to go out."

They waited. Despite the faint buzz of sound from the ballroom on the other side of the curtain, the quietness of the alcove overwhelmed Marin. He never realized quietness could be so heavy and uncomfortable. He looked down at Elspeth's hand clasped around his. *She probably feels your palm sweating.*

"I wish Aster were here," Main whispered.

Elspeth smiled. "You think so highly of him."

Marin immediately regretted what he had said. It was so tactless. Here he was with his betrothed beloved, and he had just wished for his brother's company to comfort him. Not even his real brother even—just a fellow servant he thought of as his brother. "I…I'm sorry," he said.

"About what?" Her eyes were so blue. They glowed even in the dim light of the alcove.

"It's the happiest day of my life. Our engagement is about to be announced." Marin sighed, unsure of how else to put it. "But I don't feel comfortable here. I admit that." He averted his eyes, unable to say the next part to her face. "It must be so offensive to you how I'm completely unfit for court, isn't it?"

"That's why you need Aster here with you." It wasn't a question. Her voice bore no judgment or disappointment.

Marin gripped Elspeth's hand more tightly, grateful that she didn't seem upset. "Aster…well, he…he was the first person who really treated me like I meant something. Who acted like I wasn't just some nobody." It surprised him how comfortable he felt admitting this to Elspeth. "When I was growing up on the farm, it was as if…it was as if

I could have disappeared and it wouldn't have mattered."

"I'm glad."

"Huh?" He looked at her to see she was smiling.

"I'm glad Aster could see in you what that old witch didn't." She reached up and pushed a strand of his hair back behind his ear, then straightened his cap for him. "If only you could see yourself the way he sees you—the way *I* see you. If you could, you wouldn't have doubts like you do now."

A nervous laugh escaped Marin. He rolled his eyes. He hadn't been searching for this kind of affirmation. It made him even more uncomfortable. "Oh, Elspeth," he said. "Thank you—really, thank you, but—I know it's stupid—"

Before he could fumble over his words anymore, she held up a hand. "Whatever happened when you were growing up on that witch's farm, it's in the past now. You fought off a goblin army and rescued a princess, and you're about to be announced as my betrothed."

Marin shrugged. "Right place, right time."

"No." Her tone was sweet but firm. "Marin, you didn't have to come rescue me and my sister. You could have turned around and left, but you didn't. You could have found fame or fortune or glory somewhere else."

Something about that struck him. "Fame and fortune..." he repeated, the words sounding funny in his mouth.

"You didn't ask it of my father," she continued. "You didn't ask for anything. Why did you rescue us if it were not for fortune or glory, or the hand of a beautiful princess in marriage?"

"Because it was the right thing to do."

Everything about his memory of that day in the wizard's cottage, when he and Aster first decided they would set off for the goblin fortress to rescue the princesses, seemed so long ago and vague. Why had they decided to take on the mission? Was it to gain fame and fortune?

Was it because they just knew it was the virtuous thing to do? Or were they just so excited by the prospect of adventure that they accepted the mission without questioning it?

And what is with this "right place, right time" excuse? You're sounding as if you actually believe in fate, Marin, he admonished himself. *You're standing here in this palace, with this princess, because you took on a quest that nobody else would.*

"I…"

Before he could say anything else, the sound of trumpets came from the ballroom. By the time the fanfare ended, the musicians had ceased their playing and the chorus of voices from the guests went quiet.

Elspeth lifted Marin's hand and kissed it. She batted her eyes. This was it. They were about to step out among the royal guests.

The voice of the royal herald came next. "Announcing, their royal highnesses, Princess Elspeth and Princess Carys, and their honored guests, Prince Marin and Prince Aster."

The curtain in front of Marin and Elspeth parted just as thunderous applause broke out. The bright lights of the ballroom took Marin by surprise after the dimness of the alcove. He stood frozen, momentarily transfixed by all of it.

When he looked beside him at Elspeth, he forgot everything just as quickly as he had let it overwhelm him. Nothing mattered when she was right there to give him strength—the beautiful princess who loved him as he was, no matter what was in his past. The girl who recognized his worth.

He offered her his arm, and she gently looped her hand through. She took the first step, and he let his stride fall into pace with hers. They emerged onto the marble floor and approached the crowd. The faces watching them were kindly, admiring, respectful—they had none of the cold judgment or stern disapproval he had been expecting.

They see me as Elspeth sees me, he realized, *and as King Hector sees me.*

They see me as...

A prince? Whatever it was, however they perceived him, it was not as a lowly servant. Elspeth was right—that part of him was in the past. It was in the past if he were willing to leave it in the past...

Across the ballroom, Aster and Carys stepped out from behind the curtain of the opposite alcove, walking at an even pace alongside each other. Aster looked so dignified and confident in the brocaded doublet and velvet breeches—if only Marin could look half so much the part of a prince! At Aster's side, Carys looked as magnificent as Elspeth, the gold stitching on her burgundy gown shining like fire.

The four of them met in the center of the ballroom. Elspeth and Carys curtsied to each other, both of them dipping low, the wide skirts of their gowns pooling around them. Following the example the girls set, Marin and Aster bowed to each other. It felt strange and unnecessary, but what formality wasn't? It would get more comfortable in time, wouldn't it? Marin felt painfully aware of the fact that everyone was watching them.

After the curtsies and bows, the royal four turned and made their way to the front of the hall. King Hector awaited them, robed and bejeweled, crowned, attended by four valets on each side. When they got close enough, Marin noticed the mistiness in the king's eyes. But then his majesty blinked away whatever tear was there, gaining his composure, and smiled as he looked at each of his daughters, then each of his future sons.

This is my future father, Marin realized. He'd never had a parent before this. And King Hector...his majesty already felt so caring, so warm, so ready to accept Marin and Aster as his own. It gave Marin a funny feeling—he wasn't sure he was ready to accept a father's love any more than he was ready to accept a wife's.

Marin and Elspeth turned to face the crowd, placing themselves slightly to the king's right. Aster and Carys stood slightly to the king's left.

Hector cleared his throat, raised his hands, palm upward in a gesture of gratitude to the guests who had gathered on such short notice for such an important occasion—the homecoming of the lost princesses.

The homecoming of the lost princesses and, of course, a crucial announcement.

"My dear subjects." The king's booming voice echoed around the cavernous ballroom, even with so many people gathered around him. King Hector might have been gentle and affectionate, but he knew how to command attention, Marin had to admit. "It is my honor tonight to welcome my daughters home."

Applause and cheers followed.

"And," the king continued, looking from Marin to Aster, "to host their noble rescuers." He gave each boy a nod of approval. "May I present to my people Prince Marin and Prince Aster."

More cheers and applause.

They're cheering for us, Marin thought. *For me and Aster. They are cheering for us.*

The king raised his hand for quiet. "But tonight, I am not just bringing them into my home as my guests. I am welcoming them into my royal house as my sons and heirs."

The king paused and Marin held his breath. He stared around the crowd, trying to read the expressions of the courtiers and nobles who were watching him. Did they accept him as a prince, as the betrothed of their beloved crown princess? There was no indication they didn't.

"They have asked for my daughters' hands in marriage," King Hector said. "Prince Marin to Princess Elspeth, and Prince Aster to Princess Carys." He drew a deep breath. "And it is my great honor to give my consent."

A third round of applause and cheer erupted. Marin tried to remain stoic, but the joy overtook him. He smiled, unable to suppress it.

For once, his heart pounded in an excited way, not a nervous one.

King Hector gestured to a nearby servant who stood at the ready with five goblets on a gold platter.

"Tonight, let us celebrate," Hector said. "A toast."

The servant rushed forward, offering the tray out in front of him with an eagerness that suggested this was his first time participating in such a lavish affair and he was desperate to prove himself to the king. *Good for him*, Marin thought. *I can relate.* At least Marin wasn't the only one being thrust into a glorious situation he hardly felt prepared for. If only he could show the same unapologetic readiness this servant did.

Marin reached out and accepted the goblet from the tray when the servant offered it to him. "Thank you," he said. The servant's eyes went wide, almost as if he weren't expecting to be thanked by the royalty he served. Marin choked back a laugh, not wanting to offend. He took another goblet and handed it to Elspeth.

The king raised his goblet. "To Marin and Aster. And to a long and glorious future for the kingdom of Blunia."

CHAPTER 30

"No sign of them, your majesty."

King Donovan looked the huntsman up and down. A tall man, thick with ropey muscle, the huntsman carried a reputation for being the greatest in all the land. Why else would Donovan have sent for him, demanded that this free agent join his own royal hunting party? So many legends had been told about this aloof huntsman who trekked the Grythium forest that it was difficult to tell fact from fiction. If all of it were to be believed, the huntsman knew how to track any beast through the woods, and he could creep upon any creature without being heard. When his blade came out from its sheath, no quarry stood a chance against him.

Was it any wonder that the king's own knights feared this man? This stranger known only as "the huntsman," as if his name were long forgotten, if it were ever known at all. Some even believed the huntsmen would kill a human venturing through the woods if the sport were not exciting enough for him that day.

And that was what made the huntsman a perfect choice for finding those boys.

"No sign?" the king said. "Whatsoever?"

"I'm afraid not, your majesty."

The king struggled to swallow his anger. He would never admit he was intimidated by the huntsman, but something about this stranger's stark features—exaggerated now by the glaring shadows in the lantern-lit tent—suggested something murderous. What was to stop the huntsman from fulfilling his need to hunt something by knifing the king himself, then slipping out of the tent and escaping into the night before the king's own hunting party knew what happened?

Anyone else would have suffered the king's wrath—but not the huntsman.

Even so, Donovan had not followed his own hunting party out here into the deepest part of the woods so he could be there as their mission failed, as they spent days trying to find two teenage boys in the wilderness surrounding Grythium and never finding any sign of them.

Donovan had not spent three nights, now his fourth night, sleeping in a hunting tent instead of his royal quarters in the palace so that he could go on living in fear.

He had not sought the help of the legendary huntsman and even granted audience to this huntsman in the privacy of his own tent just to be delivered such bad news.

No sign of the boys.

"You are supposed to be the best huntsman in the kingdom. No deer nor boar nor eagle is said to be safe from you. And yet these boys—"

"Have vanished from your lands," the huntsman said. "Or so it would seem."

Vanished from your lands. Donovan's stomach lurched. Did the huntsman choose those words deliberately? Could he have some way of knowing that, yes, the boys had quite literally vanished into thin air? And there was no way of knowing whether they were near or far, or when they would return to Grythium.

But as long as those boys lived, they were a threat.

Donovan steadied his voice as he asked, "How far have you ventured?" No indication of fury in his voice. No indication of fear.

"All through the woods, your majesty." The huntsman's voice remained steady as well. No way of telling how he felt about Donovan. Was it any wonder he made such a good hunter with such self-control? "Unless," the huntsman said, "you would have me venture into Blunia…"

"No!"

The king had not meant to lose his temper, but the reaction had been compulsive. He froze, realizing the risk he took in shouting at the huntsman. *He could kill you*, Donovan thought. *You arrogant fool.*

Donovan took a step back. He heaved a deep breath, composed himself, and went to the makeshift table where he had spread a map of the forest earlier that afternoon when consulting with one of his own knights. He didn't need to look at the map again—he just needed to sit down.

"No," he repeated. "You'll not trespass into their lands." He maintained a calm tone. "We keep our tenuous peace with Blunia, now most of all."

"As you say, your majesty."

"Then you are dismissed," Donovan said. "Continue your hunt tomorrow at first light."

"Yes, your majesty."

The huntsman bowed. The gesture bore no mockery to it, which annoyed Donovan even more. If this huntsman had no respect for him, it would be easier to hate him. But the huntsman never wavered in his respect.

Yet still he failed the king! He could not track down those bastards! After days! Weeks!

The huntsman rose from his bow and, without another word, left through the tent flaps into the dark night outside. A flash of the star-studded night sky, crisscrossed with the shadows of trees, appeared between the tent flaps when the huntsman opened them.

There was also another figure standing out there. Donovan recognized her immediately despite the darkness covering her.

How long had she been out there? Had she been listening to his entire conversation with the huntsman?

"Witch," he growled. "Get in here."

She emerged through the flap, a cruel expression on her little wrinkled face. She was even uglier than the king realized she was when she first arrived in his throne room weeks ago. How those beady black eyes and that twisted little mouth annoyed him! How he loathed her snide demeanor and the unsettling way she always seemed to be plotting against him behind a show of mocking obeisance.

She leaned on a gnarled wooden walking stick as she hobbled into the tent. "Yes, your majesty?"

What an audacious way to greet him! *Yes, your majesty?* She had been waiting outside his tent as if she knew he would want an audience with her. She knew what he wanted. And she had to know how angry he was, angry that she had been of no help up until this point. No help whatsoever. She had shown up in his throne room, dropped the revelation of who the boys were, then used none of her witchcraft to be advantageous at all in tracking them down.

Donovan rose to his feet. "What have you to say for yourself? There is no sign of these boys anywhere. They vanished from my throne room, and now they are nowhere to be seen. Even this huntsman who is said to be the best in the land—who is said to be able to track and kill any quarry—is unable to find them."

Ilth smacked her lips. "And how may I be of service to his majesty in this regard?"

King Donovan tightened his hands into fists at his side. "What else are witches good for?" he snarled. "You know how all of this will play out—you have the gift of prophecy. Tell me what I must do. How can I find those boys and stop them?"

Ilth cackled. How Donovan hated the sound of her laughter! "Prophecy is a tricky thing, your majesty," she said. "It cannot be commanded and controlled at will. Some matters can be foreseen, and others cannot."

"Of course, you would say that." He sank back down into his chair.

Ilth switched her walking stick from one claw-like hand to the other and approached him. "His majesty is troubled."

"Why would I not be troubled?" Donovan said. "I sit so precariously on my throne without an heir. Do you know how easy it will be for Hector to take my kingdom when I get old and weak? For those boys to take my kingdom? When I get old and frail, who is to inherit my throne?"

He felt his face burn as the blood rose up into his cheeks, flushed with anger.

Ilth hesitated a moment. "I do not have an answer for that, your majesty."

King Donovan stood again. His blood boiling, he began to pace the tent. "I wouldn't expect you to have an answer, witch. But these are things a king must think of. Who is to inherit my kingdom when I have no heir and a prophecy says a bastard will take my throne?"

Ilth's eyes shifted, hanging on his every word.

"Whom can I even trust?" Donovan continued, desperation making him uncharacteristically honest. "Maybe a knight, maybe a lord, maybe a member of my council. Maybe I will find another queen who can produce a legitimate heir."

Another queen. How he had loved his Raella! Before she betrayed him. Before she gave birth to King Hector's bastard. Before he had to execute her to preserve his own dignity.

But there was still time to find love again. Any woman would be honored to marry the king and bear him children. He might not love her the way he had once loved Raella, but she would serve her purpose if it came to that.

And with those bastard boys on the loose, maybe it was time to consider naming an heir if he could not produce one.

"Understand this," Donovan said, raising a finger at the witch. "I am not getting any younger, and as long as those boys are free and capable, there is still a chance that they will sit my throne one day. I will not have my dignity cast aside and my legacy erased by the bastards begat by my slattern wife and the man whom I thought my dearest friend."

Ilth smirked. His anger never scared her. "Nor will such circumstances come to pass, your majesty," she said. "Trust in me. I will see to that." She loved that he still believed the boys were Hector's bastards—he never even questioned that they might truly be the rightful heirs of Grythium. His foolishness made him so much easier to manipulate. To think that she once thought to use the boys as leverage against him if she ever got the chance—now they might be more valuable to her if she actually helped the king kill them. Then think about what sway she would have over the king when he didn't have an heir!

Donovan scoffed. "How can I trust a word you say when you cannot even foretell the future the way you should?"

He said it with full knowledge that such an insult would offend her. Ilth's beady eyes flared at him. He took satisfaction in watching her sneer, her long nose wrinkling with disapproval.

"I think this conversation is over, your majesty," she replied.

"Very well."

Ilth bowed. Unlike the huntsman's respectful gesture, hers was indeed marked by mockery. Everything she did goaded the king. "Goodnight, your majesty," she said in a cold voice, barely able to suppress a cackle.

He didn't reply. He sat back in his chair and watched her disappear through the tent flaps.

CHAPTER 31

Marin and Aster couldn't stop laughing as they made their way from the ballroom back to their guest suite.

"Shh!" Marin held a finger to his lips, but he couldn't contain himself any better than Aster could. It was unprincely behavior. Marin's head swam from too much wine and his spirit felt light from all the emotions of the evening. He could still taste Elspeth's kiss on his lips from when she bade him goodnight and departed for her own private quarters.

Oh, it was the sweetest kiss she had given him yet. Their first kiss as a formally betrothed couple! He could have let himself get lost in those enormous blue eyes of hers. It took all his self-control not to follow her back to her own chamber—just to spend more time together, of course. He wouldn't dare consummate their union before they were sworn in front of the gods as husband and wife.

After saying goodnight to Elspeth, Marin had reunited with Aster in the corridor just outside the ballroom and neither of them had the composure to form a full sentence. Aster, having just said goodnight to Carys, brimmed with the same excitement. They fell into each other, hugging each other, then raced back to their room, taking several stumbles and bumping into several walls. Marin thought of the adage

"Love makes fools of us all" and it suddenly made sense.

It wasn't until they had closed the door to their chamber that Marin was able to think of something to say.

"Can you believe it? Seriously, Aster, can you believe it! We've had a stroke of good luck, no doubt about it."

"We have!"

Marin flopped backward onto his bed. The downy mattress caught him. He could smell the fragrant oils that had been used to launder the bed linens. All of this finery—it really was meant for them, wasn't it? He reached his arm up and ran it across the front of his doublet. Elspeth's hand had been there only an hour ago, clinging to him. Elspeth! A girl he didn't deserve, and somehow she was his!

"I'm still scared that all of this is a dream," he said. He lifted his head. Aster sat on the bed across from him.

"It's certainly not a dream, brother."

Marin sat up. Aster grinned at him. "A princess for each of us to call our bride," Marin said. "A kingdom to inherit." He looked Aster dead in the eye and punctuated each word as if Aster might not fully appreciate what he was saying. "And to think that only weeks ago we were slaving away on Ilth's farm! Who would have ever believed it?"

Aster reached up and undid the laces of his doublet. "Could you imagine if we stayed on that farm forever? We had no way of knowing what was waiting for us out here." He shucked off his doublet, removed his cap, and tossed them onto the chair beside his bed.

"No," Marin agreed. "No, we didn't, did we?" He slid his cap off, then stood and started to remove his own court attire. "And if we had been too afraid to sneak into the goblin fortress."

Aster reached for the pair of silk pajamas that lay folded at the foot of his bed. "Exactly. Remember, I told you—the tide was in our favor, and we had to set sail."

That was right. *I had just resolved myself to life as a servant forever*, Marin thought. *I thought it was safe. I thought it was my place in the world—that there was nothing better.*

"You were right," Marin said. "We had to set sail." He reached for his own pajamas. "I mean, I always wished and hoped and prayed that something like this would happen, that we were meant for bigger things, but…but, I don't know, I never thought it was possible. How did we get so lucky?"

As soon as he heard himself say the word, he realized the irony. Lucky. He had just said the same thing a minute ago—he had exclaimed to Aster they'd had a stroke of good luck.

But was this really good luck?

Or did all of this happen because they went after it? Elspeth said it herself—they could have stayed far away from the goblin fortress and never made it their mission.

"Lucky, yes," Aster said, turning down the duvet and climbing into his bed. "But don't sell yourself short on how hard you've worked."

"And you!" Marin sat on the edge of his bed and looked at his friend, his companion, his brother. "I couldn't have done this if it weren't for you, Aster."

Aster smiled. "I know. And I couldn't have done it without you. We're a duo."

There was a moment of comfortable quiet. They'd been through so much. Here they were, having achieved the great destiny they had dreamed of for so long.

"Where is it going to go from here?" Marin asked. "It's only going to get better, isn't it?"

"I hope so."

Marin flopped down on his bed. "And Elspeth," he said. "She makes me feel like I've never felt before."

Aster laughed. "Is it love or lust, brother?"

"Oh, I don't know. Can't it be both?" Marin rolled over so he could face Aster. "All I know is that I want to be with her *always*. Do you know what kind of self-control it took for me to come back to our room here tonight? Not to betray the hospitality of her father's house, and go with her to her bed before our wedding vows?"

Aster nodded. "I know exactly what you mean."

"Because you feel the same way about Carys." It wasn't a question. Marin smirked. They had set out to seek their fortunes—who would have ever thought they would discover romance along the way? "Tell me how much you love her," Marin goaded. "Come on, brag a little."

"She's…she's a dream come true."

Marin nodded. "So is Elspeth. Sweeter than honey, and warmer than sunlight." He sat up, only vaguely aware that this was shamelessly boastful. *I'm allowed to be boastful tonight*, he thought. *It's all the wine and dancing that's made me excited, and besides, I'm a servant who's suddenly found himself proclaimed a prince. I'm allowed to be boastful!*

"She's more beautiful than all the precious gemstones waiting to be mined from the earth," Marin continued.

"That's a mighty big claim for any woman to live up to."

Marin nodded. "But if any woman can live up to it, she can. And she's her father's heiress. She's going to be queen one day. Won't she make a good queen, as kind and smart and brave as she is?"

"And you'll make a good king."

The thought hit Marin like a punch to the face. Even though he'd heard Elspeth talk about her duty to be her father's heiress, he had never actually pictured himself on the throne, ruling beside her. "Aster…"

"What?" Aster laughed. "I mean, you will. You will make a good king. Don't you think so?"

"I didn't even think of that," Marin murmured.

All the energy had left the room. The mood felt suddenly heavy. All the joy and excitement the two of them had felt just a few minutes ago felt impossible to get back.

"Don't start to have your doubts now," Aster said. "You're marrying the crown princess. The king wouldn't give you his blessing if he didn't think you were right for it."

Marin hadn't expected the conversation to take this serious turn. Now that it had, he couldn't shake off the oppressive weight of anxiety that had dropped on him.

You're such an idiot, he thought. Wouldn't anyone in all the world dream of being king? It was an honor. It was also a responsibility. It sounded great when it was just a dream—but when the truth loomed over him that one day the whole kingdom would be his to care for, it was a much more intimidating thought.

"I'm...I'm not anything special."

Aster shrugged. "You should let the people decide that. You heard all of them cheer for you tonight. People respect you and admire you... if you would only let them."

They did cheer for us tonight, Marin thought. *For me and for Aster and for Elspeth and Carys.* Still, just because he and Aster had saved the princesses, that didn't mean they were fit to rule. Being a hero was different from being a ruler. Winning a crown was one thing, and wearing it was quite another. Being king would mean creating just laws and protecting his subjects.

"Do you remember what Tsema said to us?" Marin said. "About how there was so much unrest throughout the land? Maybe we have the chance to make things better. Maybe we have the chance to make this land a better place."

"Here's what I know," Aster said. "You've been making things better everywhere we've been since we left Ilth's farm. You were the one who insisted we help the undergroundlings—and who ultimately realized the nulquin was just a baby who meant no harm."

"Aye, but—"

"You were the one who showed mercy to Gnarnus, even though

236

he tried to attack us," Aster went on. "Then you were the one who decided we needed to go rescue the princesses from the goblins. And you ultimately stood up to the goblin foreman and brought about their downfall."

"You were right there with me the whole time," Marin said. "Give yourself some praise."

"Oh, I'm giving myself plenty of praise," Aster said. "But what I'm saying to you is you're a leader even if you don't realize it."

You're a leader even if you don't realize it. Hearing those words from Aster meant everything. It never failed to overwhelm him to think that other people actually saw him as something other than a servant.

"Just because we brought the princesses home safely, that doesn't mean we're heroes," he said.

"I would let the subjects of this kingdom decide that," Aster said. "Elspeth seems to think you're special. Her father could have given her away in marriage to anyone. But he chose you, and she doesn't seem too upset about it."

No, Marin thought. *She doesn't.* "I just…"

But words failed him. Marin pushed himself up on his elbow and reached for the knob on the oil lamp burning on the table. "Let's, uh… we should talk about this tomorrow. For tonight, let's just be happy about what we have now."

"We can do that."

Marin turned the knob, drawing the wick down into the lamp and extinguishing the flame. He lay back on the pillow, pulling the duvet up to his chin.

"Goodnight, brother," Aster whispered from across the room.

"Goodnight."

CHAPTER 32

A hush fell through the royal court when the visitor made his appearance the next day. At first, Marin couldn't tell whether this being was human or something else entirely. Based on the way others reacted, it was safe to assume nobody else knew what to make of it either—that this visitor was the strangest and most unexpected thing to grace the royal court of Blunia before.

"Who is it?" one lord whispered.

"Is it a *who*, or is it a *what?*" another whispered back.

Marin could hear these and other hushed conversations from where he stood at the front of the hall close to the king's dais. Hector had been presiding over court, hearing petitions from noblemen and commoners alike. It had been a valuable lesson for Marin, being able to observe firsthand what kings did all day. He leaned close to Aster. "Are you seeing what I'm seeing?"

But Aster didn't have to answer. Marin hadn't been looking for a response. He just felt uncomfortable standing there in dumb silence as the man walked down the length of carpet leading to the dais. Impressively tall, at least two feet taller than any other man at court, the being moved with formidable confidence. Every part of his gnarled body looked as if it were some element of nature, as if he had crawled forth from the earth's surface only that morning. Tree bark patched his mud-spattered skin, and grass and leaves grew from his hair. The clothes he wore resembled moss, hanging from his large form in lush green masses.

King Hector stood. "You are welcome, Terro, god of the earth."

Terro, god of the earth? So the king recognized this being. This deity, to be precise! Marin kept his gaze fixed on Hector, trying to read his expression. Something about the king's tone sounded wary, uncertain, nervous. Marin tried to catch the eye of Elspeth, who sat on a smaller chair beside her father's throne, Carys on the other side. Neither princess took her eyes off her father.

"To what do we owe the pleasure of your visit to our royal court?" Hector continued, his voice formal and polite.

Terro lumbered forward. Each of his steps spanned what an average man would need two or three strides to accomplish. The god of the earth planted his enormous clay feet just a few steps away from the dais and raised his chin, staring down at his majesty. *That's how tall he is*, Marin realized. *This man looks down on a man as big as King Hector, who is standing on a dais.*

"King Hector." The god of the earth's voice boomed—it was what Marin imagined an earthquake or an avalanche would sound like. "My daughters have been greatly insulted."

His daughters? Insulted? What was the meaning of this? Terro said it in such a way that it was as if he expected everyone to know his daughters by the mere mention of them. Marin thought he knew the doctrines of the old pagan ways, at least passably well, from all the myths he read growing up, but he couldn't remember anything about the nature god's daughters.

King Hector looked just as confused. "Your…your daughters?"

"Yes!" Terror thundered again, stomping his foot. Flecks of dirt and clay went flying. The floor shook. "My beautiful daughters!"

This had gone from strange to terrifying in less than a minute. Marin hadn't expected his first day at court to be quite like this! Up until now, every petition the king had heard had been about land disputes or other petty matters. Now an ancient pagan god had shown up to the surprise of everyone present—this definitely didn't happen every day!—and was upset about some insult somebody made to his daughters. The uncontrolled anger made Marin's muscles seize up.

He'd read stories about the ancient gods followed by those who practiced the old ways. The ballads and myths always depicted the gods as being driven by raw emotion. They were angry, vengeful even. The newer traditions might have followed gods that were merciful and that encouraged the balance of good and evil, that preached redemption. But not the old ways. The gods of the old ways knew no constraints on their power, and they saw mortals as petty beings to be used for their amusement.

Terro was one of those gods of the old ways.

But King Hector would get this under control. That's what kings did. He would find a way to appease the gods if they were angry.

"My daughters," Terro continued. "My daughters, whom the mortals mine from their homes deep beneath the surface of the world. My beautiful daughters who are cut and polished to be made into jewelry and trinkets and ornaments. The diamonds and emeralds and rubies and sapphires. Is it not enough that you should take them from me to marvel at their beauty and use them to decorate your world?"

With those words, he raised a lanky, branchlike arm and gestured around him at the opulence of the room. Marin suddenly felt all too aware of the glittering gemstones and jewels that ornamented the throne and the chandeliers and sconces and tables. The jewelry worn by the courtiers. The designs embedded on the wall. There were gemstones everywhere. *These are his daughters?* Marin thought.

"And that boy," Terro shouted, "dared insult them!"

He pointed his crooked finger directly at Marin. "He dared to declare that Princess Elspeth—a mere mortal—was more beautiful than they."

A murmur swept through the crowd of courtiers. Gasps and whispers filled the air. Marin suddenly felt all the weight of their stares on him, and not in the admiring way they had looked at him the night before. This felt awkward, frightening.

Marin couldn't breathe. "What? I didn't—"

He remembered his words to Aster the night before: *More beautiful than all the precious gemstones waiting to be mined from the earth!* He had said that. Even Aster had pointed out how boastful it was last night. Marin glanced at Aster to see whether he remembered, but Aster's face was twisted in an expression of confusion.

King Hector cleared his throat. "Forgive him, your excellency." His voice trembled. "I am sure the boy meant no offense."

"His meaning is nothing to me," Terro declared. His eyes, dark as iron ore when he stepped into the throne room, now glowed like pools of magma. "How dare he make such a boast? To declare a mortal girl more beautiful than the daughters of the earth?"

Terro took a step forward, drawing closer to the dais, as if he wanted to get a better look at Elspeth, to see for himself this girl who had been declared more beautiful than all the gemstones of the earth. Marin's heart pounded. He scanned the throne room, trying to see whether a sword or other weapon lay within reach if Terro tried to hurt Elspeth. *I don't care if he's a god*, Marin thought. *I won't let him touch her.*

Marin strode forward, stepping up onto the dais. A few courtiers gasped at Marin's audacity. Even King Hector himself looked shocked. Now that he was face to face with the god of the earth, Marin couldn't actually bring himself to say anything. He dropped to one knee beside Elspeth's chair and put an arm protectively around her.

Terro ignored Marin and continued to address King Hector. "My own daughters adorned the clock in your hall just outside his chamber when he made this bold claim." With two hulking steps on his tree-trunk legs, he turned to face all the courtiers in the hall. "I will not stand for such vanity from you mortals. Hear me—I come to demand this wrong be righted."

Under Marin's protective arm, Elspeth trembled. She held her breath, trying to maintain her composure. *Nobody is going to hurt her*, Marin thought. *I won't let them. Her father won't let them.*

The only people in the world whom Marin cared about were in this room right now. Aster. Elspeth. Carys. King Hector. His found family—the ones who showed him love and warmth and belonging after a lifetime of wishing for that.

King Hector took a step down off his dais, as if he were trying to humble himself, put himself on the same level as this god. Now that he stood on the floor, Terro towered over him even more.

"And how can I offer reconciliation, your excellency?" Hector asked, polite but not timid.

Terro did not hesitate. "I demand her life for this insult. You will repent of your sin and offer her as a sacrifice to the earth."

"No!" The shout escaped Marin's mouth before he could control himself. He jumped to his feet, one arm still protectively clutching Elspeth's shoulder.

Terro fixed his volcanic eyes on Marin for a fleeting second but said nothing. Marin refused to look away. He would show this god that he wasn't afraid. He wouldn't let this god hurt Elspeth—or Aster or Carys or King Hector or anyone in Blunia for that matter—simply because of something stupid he said.

"In one week's time, the equinox will be upon us," Terro boomed, addressing Hector. "Your daughter must be taken to the edge of the city and bound to the pillars outside the gates at dawn. I will send the vraotyr from deep within the tunnels of the underworld to claim her. See to it that she is dressed in her finest and pampered to look as beautiful as her betrothed prince claims her to be, so that she may serve as the fitting sacrifice I demand."

Marin froze. The vraotyr was a fearsome creature that lurked deep beneath the earth's surface. Nobody had seen it for centuries, according to the ballads. All the first kings of Monte Prospera had joined their armies to fight the creature. Grythium had wounded the vraotyr—not mortally, but enough to weaken it—and it had retreated down into the caves that were said to lead to the center of the earth. The mortals had then made a pact with the gods to keep the vraotyr at bay so it would never emerge again to take innocent lives.

No drawings of it existed, but accounts handed down from the ancient world described it as serpentine, covered in scales as thick as granite, large enough to encircle an entire forest when it touched its head to its tail. Each of its fangs was as long as a tree was tall.

Terro continued. "She must be pure, a virgin, unknown to this boy or any other, and she must be adorned with no jewelry bearing any of my daughters, lest another comparison be made between their beauty."

Marin couldn't continue looking at Terro, or at anyone else in the hall. He looked down, fixing his gaze on the top of Elspeth's head as she buried her face into his side. This was it—the cruel twist of fate he had always feared. He had escaped Ilth's farm, found the happiness he never even dreamed he deserved, and now a spiteful demigod would take it all away from him because of Marin's own foolishness?

"If this is not done as I say," Terro said, "the vraotyr will destroy your kingdom and all the people in it."

King Hector took a step forward. "Your excellency, I beg you—"

"Begging will gain you nothing, Hector. I have no interest in mercy. Only justice."

Marin glanced up to see Terro thrusting his arm out toward him and Elspeth, pointing his gnarled finger at them. "And the justice I demand is your daughter's life. Do as I say, or your kingdom will suffer for it."

With that, the god of the earth departed.

CHAPTER 33

"Well, this is some fine trouble you've caused, your highness." Sir Valgeth sat across the council table from Marin, crossing his arms in a display of arrogant contemptuousness. He raised one bushy eyebrow in an expression that made Marin feel fresh shame all over again. Every single person in the council chamber stared at him—at least, that's what it felt like.

Princess Elspeth cast a fiery look at the guard. "You will speak to my betrothed with more respect, Sir Valgeth." Under the table, her hands curled into fists in her lap. Only Marin could see that though—Marin and Carys, who sat on Elspeth's other side. To everyone else in the room, Elspeth remained composed.

It was only a small group of them gathered in the king's private counseling quarters. King Hector had called the meeting immediately after Terro left the great hall. "I must adjourn court for the day," he declared, maintaining an air of graciousness that Marin could hardly believe he was seeing. "My people, excuse me. I will continue hearing your petitions tomorrow. But this urgent matter demands my attention."

I guess a king must be magnanimous like that, Marin thought. *King Hector cares about his subjects as if they are his family.* But now his majesty's own daughter was in danger. Because of Marin.

Neither the nobles nor the peasants made any commotion as they filed out of the great hall. Something about the stunned silence made the reality of what just happened weigh heavily on Marin. These people were in danger as well—or at least, they could be. If King Hector didn't do as Terro commanded, the entire kingdom faced a ghastly demise, the kind that legends would speak of for centuries. The once great kingdom of Blunia, destroyed by the vraotyr. Its people killed, its buildings knocked to the ground, and all set ablaze with fire.

"Your majesty," Marin said the moment the hall was empty, approaching King Hector. The overwhelming emptiness of the cavernous room caused his words to reverberate off the stone walls, almost as if to serve as a reminder of his own foolishness. His words were what caused all of this. Did he actually dare open his mouth again to ask forgiveness of his father-to-be?

"Marin," Hector said. "Please, my boy. I know this is as upsetting for you as it is for me. Wait a moment. We'll call a formal council and then there will be a chance to talk."

"I just—uh—I'm sorry."

"I know, Marin." The king's voice remained calm. In a way, that almost hurt Marin even more. If Hector had roared at him in anger or broken down and wept, it would have been different. Instead, he remained focused on his kingly duties—call a council, develop a plan.

Hector called for four knights—Sir Valgeth, Sir Anselet, Sir Gifford, and Sir Teres—as well as three royal councilors—Lord Downhelm, Lord Evenmore, and Lord Pridefallow.

"And my sons will join us as well," he said, nodding to Marin and Aster. *His sons*. That stung, Marin had to admit. He had hardly been Hector's son for a full day before he caused all this ruin.

"I will join you, Father," Elspeth said, stepping down from the dais and trailing after her father before he could leave the hall.

King Hector turned. "No. No, my sweet girl, that is thoughtful of you, but a king's council is no place for princesses." He looked from Elspeth to Carys, who stood just behind her. Both girls wore expressions that Marin could only have described as determined.

"It is my own life you will be discussing, Father," Elspeth said. "Besides, I am your heiress as long as I am alive, isn't that true? Matters of politics are just as much my concern as they are my husband-to-be's." Elspeth looked over her shoulder at Carys. "My sister and I will be part of this council." It was not a request—it was a command.

King Hector had been unable to argue. Marin never thought he would get over Elspeth's forwardness, her unapologetic confidence. She handled all of it with such grace that nobody could ever question her. She would make a great queen someday.

They followed the knights along a series of corridors and into the private council chambers, where another surprise awaited them.

"Who are you?" Sir Anselet exclaimed when he stepped into the chamber. "And what are you doing here?"

Marin passed through the doorway and couldn't believe his eyes. Udifeus sat at the gleaming oak council table, his eyes luminous behind his spectacles, the billowing sleeves of his robe blanketing the table as he leaned forward on his elbows.

"Udifeus!" Marin exclaimed.

"What ho, my boys," the wizard exclaimed, standing. "I understand you've found yourselves in quite a bit of trouble again."

So many questions swam into Marin's head that he couldn't process them all at once. "But…how…?"

"Well, I'll be damned," Aster muttered.

King Hector stepped around the side of the council table, approaching Udifeus. "You know this man?" he asked Marin and Aster, indicating their old friend.

"You might say I am their wizard mentor," Udifeus said, as if that were a perfectly normal answer. "All heroes must have one, you know."

Sir Valgeth sneered at that but kept his peace.

"How did you get here?" Marin asked.

Udifeus waved his hand, wiggling his fingers, as if to indicate some sort of force swirling around his head that the others couldn't see. "We users of magic have a sense of when there's trouble," he said. "Isn't that right, your highness?" He fixed his gaze on Elspeth.

"I…" Elspeth faltered. "I'm sorry, what?" Her voice remained polite, though her face twisted with confusion.

"Oh, nothing, my dear." Udifeus winked. He looked at Marin and Aster. "Consider this a fairy godfatherly sort of appearance. I'm sorry to just show up like this, uninvited and unannounced. But you can't have a proper council without input from your wizard mentor, can you?"

Marin honestly found himself surprised that King Hector let Udifeus stay. If an ancient old madman in flowing robes seemingly appeared out of thin air and insisted on providing advice in any other situation, Marin wasn't so sure that he himself would welcome it. But this situation was different. This situation was desperate.

Besides, he trusted Udifeus. For the most part. At least, he didn't have any reason not to.

All through the meeting, Marin felt as if everyone in the council looked at him with the same contempt that Sir Valgeth had just expressed. Even if Elspeth had silenced the knight's criticism, it didn't change the fact that pretty much everyone present hated him.

"Your majesty, I beg your forgiveness," Marin said, addressing the entire council as much as he was addressing Hector himself. "Had I known—"

But King Hector raised a hand. "It is not my forgiveness that needs granting, Marin." He sighed. "My boy, there is nothing to forgive as far as I am concerned. But what the gods demand, they must have. You rescued my daughter and brought her back to me. And now it seems fate takes her from me again within a day."

Fate. It wasn't fate that was taking Elspeth away. It was Marin's own foolishness. It was now up to him to set things right.

Marin looked around the table, first from King Hector himself, then to each of the knights and the counselors. "There must be a way to undo this god's command. Or to defeat the vraotyr."

Sir Valgeth scoffed. "There is none. To think that a mortal man can defeat the vraotyr."

The other knights said nothing. The counselors busied themselves with scrolls and parchment spread out on the table, suddenly eager to read whatever these pages said. None of them contradicted what the knight said or offered their own insight.

"You see," King Hector said, "even my bravest knight knows it is useless to go up against such a creature."

Bravest knight, Marin thought. *How am I supposed to think of him as brave when he's not even going to try?*

Udifeus, who had remained standing quietly in the corner, raised a hand. "Forgive me, your majesty, but there may be one way."

The muscles in Marin's shoulders unknotted themselves. He turned to Udifeus, the idea of some hope suddenly making him feel lighter. "What?"

None of the knights or counselors said anything. They stared at Udifeus, still unsure of what to make of him.

King Hector extended an arm. "Come forward, wizard."

Udifeus obeyed. He approached the table with an air of humility unnecessary for the one person in the room who claimed to know a way of defeating such a formidable enemy as the vraotyr.

"Your majesty," Udifeus said, "I believe there may be a way that a champion of men may beat a champion of the gods." He stopped beside Hector and placed his hands on the table, addressing everyone present. "But it is not a feat accomplished lightly." Those shining eyes of his, magnified behind his spectacles, fixed themselves on Marin. "Still, if a man's motive is pure and his mission is just, he will rise above what adversities the gods put before him."

"Speak plainly, wizard," Sir Valgeth demanded.

If Sir Valgeth's aggressiveness offended Udifeus, the wizard didn't show it. Instead, he cleared his throat and looked back at Hector. "Do you remember the sword of Grythium?"

The way he asked the question was unassuming enough—straightforward, candid, innocent, matter-of-factly, with none of the vague mystique that magic users had a notorious reputation for talking in. But still, everyone in the room became suddenly uncomfortable. Counselors and guards and even the king himself looked surprised. The air practically crackled with fiery tension.

"Yes," Hector replied, "but…"

Before he could finish the question, Aster piped up. "Sorry, the what?"

If King Hector minded being interrupted by Aster, he didn't show it. "The sword of Grythium," he said. Everyone else in the room seemed to know what he was talking about. "It belonged to King Donovan, once my friend and blood brother. It was an heirloom of his kingdom."

King Donovan. Marin had almost forgotten about him, and the close call he and Aster had only a few weeks ago in the royal palace of Grythium. That seemed so long ago!

Once King Hector's friend.

"Legend says," Udifeus explained, "that when the sword of Grythium was wielded by a good man for a good cause, it could not be defeated in combat." He turned to Marin. "Marin?"

"Yes?"

"Do you love Elspeth?" Udifeus asked.

"I do." Marin didn't even hesitate. What sort of question was that? Of course, he loved her!

"And are you obliged to protect both her and the people of the kingdom?" Udifeus continued.

"The people of the kingdom are..." Marin faltered. "I have a duty to protect them, or I will when Elspeth and I are bound by marriage." He looked to King Hector. "His majesty will be my father, and I will be his heir."

Elspeth lifted her hand from her lap and clasped it over Marin's on the table. "And we cannot put them in danger," she said. "No, not even to protect me." Marin hated how sad those blue eyes of hers looked now. What he wouldn't give to see her radiant smile again.

Udifeus nodded. "But if there were a way to protect the princess and protect the people of the kingdom, would you do it?"

"Well, yes," Marin said. "But..."

Udifeus clapped one hand on the table and lifted his other hand to point at Marin, a look of triumph crossing his face. "Then you must wield the sword against the vraotyr," he said. "If you are the man you present yourself to be—fair and honest and brave—then I think you will be able to stand against the vengeance of a jealous undergod and come out triumphant." The wizard looked around at the other members of the council. None of them responded. None of them seemed to believe what he said.

"Where is this sword?" Marin said hesitantly.

"It was hidden away," King Hector said. "Many years ago. When Donovan and I broke our alliance." He looked pained by the memory, as if the betrayal still hurt.

King Donovan thought King Hector lay with his wife and his sister, Marin remembered. Now that he knew King Hector, he realized how absurd a delusion that was. His majesty would never do such a thing.

Udifeus raised both of his hands in the air in front of him, palms facing each other and bony fingers slightly bent. A glowing cloud of smoke appeared in the air before him. Several gasps rose up around the room.

"When King Donovan heard the prophecy that Hector's heir would rule his kingdom," Udifeus said, staring at the smoke as it swirled, "he hid away the three sacred relics of the throne."

Maybe Marin was just getting immersed in the display of magic, but he could have sworn the torchlights dimmed, making the glowing smoke appear even more prominent. Three forms took shape within the mist—first, a sword, its hilt ornately carved. Then a shimmering crown studded with sapphires. Last, a flowing cape trimmed with spun gold. Something about their appearance made Marin's skin prickle, as if something deep within him understood their importance at the first sight of them.

Udifeus described them as they appeared. "The sword, which could never be defeated in battle, and the crown, which could only be worn by the rightful king, and the mantle, which could be worn only by the rightful queen."

All three objects dissipated as quickly as they appeared, leaving only smoke behind. Marin blinked, unsure whether he had actually seen the shapes or not. The torchlights blazed bright again.

"If you're going to defeat the vraotyr, you'll have to retrieve the relics of Donovan's royal family," Udifeus said.

Marin looked around the room. Nobody showed any indication of enthusiasm for what Udifeus had just said. "This is not a mission we can avoid," Marin murmured. "Someone must undertake it, your majesty."

Sir Valgeth laughed. "And I suppose you think you're the one to do it."

Marin stared across the table at the knight and had to bite his tongue not to snap at him. *It looks as if I'm the only one willing to do so*, he wanted to say. *If you think you're so brave and valiant, why aren't you stepping up and doing it yourself?*

Not that he could ever get away with snapping at a knight like that. Instead, he addressed the entire council.

"I will go and seek out the sword. To save my princess. I will do this."

Even that would not silence Sir Valgeth's scorn. "You are not fit for it," he said, standing. "Who knows what dangers will present themselves on such a mission? Do you think King Donovan hid such sacred heirlooms where they could easily be found?"

Marin's whole body trembled, but he tried to keep his voice steady. "Maybe I am not fit, but I will do it anyway." Now was not the time to seem weak, not the time to seem like a second-rate hero. "I see nobody else stepping forward." He looked around at the rest of the council. "Who will go with me?"

None of the counselors or knights responded. The councilors made themselves busy, shuffling through the parchment and scrolls spread out in front of them. The knights took keen interest in studying cracks on the floor.

Only Aster spoke up. "I will."

Aster. Marin's fear went away. Who knew what this mission entailed, but at least he would do it with Aster by his side. Aster, who had given him the courage from the very beginning. Aster, who had been by his side through all of it.

Marin smiled and stood. "Of course, you will, brother."

Following Marin's lead, Aster stood. He pushed his chair back and came around the table. "If this is going to be your peril, then it'll be mine as well."

Silence followed. Nobody responded.

It's just the two of us, Marin said. *The two of us doing what must be done to save Elspeth's life—and the fate of the entire kingdom.*

252

"I see that my brother and I will do what no other man in this kingdom is brave enough to do," Marin said, emphasizing each word to the knights and nobles around the table. "Very well." He looked at King Hector. "We will set forth at dawn, your majesty."

CHAPTER 34

It was another hunter King Donovan sought out this time. The man stood alone on the greensward, looking over the forest below the hill.

"Who is it who approaches?" he asked. He didn't turn around. Donovan became aware of the rustling he made as he pushed his way through the overgrowth of foliage at his feet. He tried to keep to the paths where the grass and ferns and brambles were worn down, but the deeper he came into the wilderness, the thicker the undergrowth became.

Donovan stepped out onto the soft grass of the forest clearing. "I am your king." Nobody else came with him. He slipped away from the hunting party that morning without so much as a word to anyone, not wanting them to follow or even know where he went. No guards, no knights, not even a footman or a valet to assist him. He would speak with this hunter alone.

Sir Hardegan of the Forest, as the hunter was known. He turned around. His green tunic and cloak matched the leaves around him so seamlessly that he could have easily disappeared into the wilderness if he wanted. His brown stockings hugged his thickly muscled legs. "Your majesty," he said, bowing. "I must say I am surprised to encounter you out this far in the woods. Alone."

"Yes, well," Donovan said. He swallowed. "I must say I never expected to be seeking Sir Hardegan of the Forest. But if the rumors are true, I may have need of your assistance."

Sir Hardegan nodded. A scar cut across his face, an angry red mark traveling diagonally from forehead to chin. "What does the king want with a lowly woodland hunter."

"The people in the village——"

"They gossip."

Donovan paused. Nobody spoke to him brazenly or curtly. But out here in the wilderness, away from courts and castles, he did not have the power. When he consulted with legendary hunters, the wild men who roamed the forests and made their life by killing and dominating, civil laws didn't matter. These masters of the hunt had the power. And the king needed this huntsman's assistance.

"You say they lie, but I believe what they tell me," Donovan replied.

"Why?"

Why? Why? The boldness. It wasn't this hunter's skills that Donovan needed anyway. It was simply a weapon—an object. This hunter should be grateful Donovan didn't bring his guards to kill him so Donovan could take the weapon for himself.

Donovan raised his chin. "Who are you to question your king?"

Sir Hardegan blinked. His expression wasn't cruel. He might have abided by the law of the forest, but he wasn't interested in hurting simply for the sake of hurting. *Or so you like to think*, Donovan told himself. *These foresters are not to be trusted. They kill for sport.* Donovan's royal status didn't matter out here. "You must understand I hold great power in the societies of men," he said. "And I expect the same courtesy out here in the wild."

"Ah," Sir Hardegan said. "You expect the same courtesy. But you don't get it. Not from me, and not from any of the other wilders. Do you?"

"No."

"It's the law of the forest that matters out here," Sir Hardegan reminded him.

Yes, I know, King Donovan wanted to retort. He held his tongue. There was nobody nearby to protect him.

When the king didn't reply, Sir Hardegan continued. "So, tell me how it is that I can be of service? You have an entire hunting party at your command. You've scoured the forests and lands surrounding your kingdom for weeks now. Most ungracefully, I might add."

"You have something I think might be of assistance to me," Donovan said. *If the gossip is true...*

"Do I?"

"The people in the village say your bow never misses," Donovan said. "No matter what you shoot it at, it will always strike its intended quarry."

Sir Hardegan reached an arm behind his cloak. In one swift, fluid motion, he withdrew a bow, its arc formed of polished wood that gleamed in the afternoon sunlight making its way through the trees overhead. "This?" Sir Hardegan asked. He held it out, his gloved hands gently gripping its curved form.

He doesn't deny it.

"Yes," Donovan said. "Is that it? I've heard the stories about it. Whether you're hunting deer or wolf or stag or boar, you always catch what you want."

Sir Hardegan's lips drew into a rigid line across his face. "King Donovan does not travel all the way to the outer provinces seeking a lowly common huntsman simply because he needs to kill a deer," he said.

"No, he does not." The way Sir Hardegan said what he said made King Donovan's skin prickle. *How does he know?*

As if Sir Hardegan could read Donovan's mind, he said, "I told you—the people of the village gossip."

King Donovan averted his eyes from Sir Hardegan, walked past him and approached the summit overlooking the forest beyond. He stared out at the vast expanse of trees and who knew what else. *Those boys are out there somewhere*, he thought.

"I'm sure the people of the village do gossip," he said. "Tell me. What are they saying about their king?"

Sir Hardegan laughed. It wasn't an unkind laugh, but King Donovan still didn't like the sound of it.

"They say the king is in a tirade and has been for weeks," Sir Hardegan said. "They say he is mad. They say that he set out from the castle with a hundred knights and his best hunting party. That he travels in the company of the witch Ilth. That he is seeking two boys about seventeen years of age."

Donovan's blood turned to fire and his face burned. Sir Hardegan made it sound as if he were hunting down children for sport, as if it were some cruel or fearful act. "Not just any ordinary two boys!" he turned to face the hunter. "Those boys are—"

"Are what? A threat to your rule?"

Donovan clenched his teeth. Yes, those boys *were* a threat to his rule. Those boys were prophesied to usurp his throne. "Who are you to speak so boldly to your king?" he said.

"A man who has what you need." Sir Hardegan reached over his shoulder and drew an arrow from the quiver he wore on his back. He held the arrow out for King Donovan to see it, then fitted it into his bow as he spoke. "This enchanted bow was given to me by a witch just like the one you travel with. It never misses its target."

So, the gossip is indeed true, Donovan thought. *I knew it.*

Sir Hardegan raised the bow as if ready to shoot the arrow into the woods, then looked sideways at the king. He lowered the bow, keeping the arrow still tightly strung. "If you are so cruel as to release it for the purpose I think you wish to, it is yours." He extended his arms, offering for Donovan to take the bow from him and shoot it.

Cruel. That was the word Hardegan had used.

"I need no judgment from a common huntsman," Donovan replied. He hesitated. "How does it work?"

"As any ordinary bow would," Sir Hardegan said, his eyes tracing from Donovan to the point of the arrow where it crossed with the bow's arch. "Put the arrow in the quiver and pull it tight. Then you whisper to it what you want to shoot, and let it fly. It will not stop until it has struck the heart of your quarry."

Donovan stepped forward. "Give it to me."

Sir Hardegan handed the bow and arrow over. Donovan raised the bow, aiming the arrow out over the forest below. His fingers trembled, holding the string taut. All he had to do was let go. Let go and be done with it.

"It was a dull autumn," Sir Hardegan said, "when that witch passed through our village and gave the bow to me."

Donovan couldn't bring himself to loose the arrow. Not yet.

"My wife had just died and left me to raise our son myself," Sir Hardegan continued. All warmth had left his voice. "Raising a child is difficult work. I had trouble being a hunter and a father at the same time. There are not enough hours to do a day's labor and care for someone who needs you so much as a child does."

Why is he telling me this? Donovan focused on the pointed arrowhead. He gripped the bow tighter.

"What a blessing this was, or so I thought," Sir Hardegan said. "What a blessing that this witch would give me a bow like this. I could kill enough to feed the whole village without even trying. 'Shoot it, and it is yours,' the witch told me."

Sir Hardegan took a step closer to King Donovan. "I did as I was told. What a fool I was to trust a witch."

258

Donovan knew where this story was going.

"Instead of striking a deer or a bear, the arrow struck my son who was playing with some friends deep in the woods," Sir Hardegan said. "I thought this arrow would make my life easier by targeting the beasts of the woods. Instead, it took away the only joy in my life."

He paused. "But the witch was not entirely dishonest. Since then, I have not had to worry about being a father. All I have had to worry about is the hunt."

A bead of sweat rolled down Donovan's temple. "I...I am very sorry for your loss."

Sir Hardegan ignored the sympathy. "You wish to kill those boys. They are a threat to your duty." It wasn't a question.

Donovan lowered the bow. "Our situations are not the same."

"No," Sir Hardegan said. "They're not the same. Not exactly."

"By what right does a commoner judge his king?"

Sir Hardegan didn't reply. He nodded toward the bow in Donovan's hands. "The bow is yours, your majesty. To do with as you see fit."

You're damn right it is, Donovan thought.

In one swift, merciless, unrepentant move, he raised the bow again and tightened the string, aiming it high over the forest. He leaned his face close to the arrow. "Kill the bastard sons of King Hector," he whispered.

He held his breath and released his fingers from the string. But instead of sailing through the air and into the forest below, as he expected it to do, the arrow simply fell dully into the grass.

"What is the meaning of this?" he shouted.

He stooped and grabbed the arrow from where it had fallen. Any hesitation he once had now gone, replaced by frustration and anger, he fitted the arrow back into the bow.

"Kill the bastard sons of King Hector," he whispered and released.

The arrow dropped to the grass. Donovan stared at it.

"Perhaps such quarry doesn't exist, your majesty."

"Be silent!" Donovan stomped on the arrow, letting it crunch beneath his boot. *No such quarry? No such quarry? What is that supposed to mean?* He had seen the boys with his own eyes, heard from Ilth exactly who they were. How could the bow simply fail to kill them?

He thrust the bow back at Sir Hardegan. "Take your stupid bow. I have no use for it."

Sir Hardegan took the bow but didn't say anything. Donovan glared at him. "I don't know what game you're playing," he said. "I was a fool to believe stories about a magic bow and arrow. An utter fool!"

With a swish of his cape, he stormed off into the woods, making his way back to camp, feeling even more desperate than before.

CHAPTER 35

At least it was a small group that gathered to see them off on their quest. Marin had to be grateful for that, at the very least. He liked the privacy and intimacy of it. He wanted the chance to say goodbye to those whom he cared about before he and Aster set out. The last thing he wanted was to have half the kingdom gathered outside the palace.

"Where will we even know where to start?" Marin asked Udifeus as the old wizard escorted him and Aster from their sleeping chambers out to the courtyard. He hadn't expected to see Udifeus that morning when he and Aster stepped out of their room, but there he was, waiting for them as if he were a loyal dog. *Maybe he's been guarding our room all night*, Marin thought, disliking the notion. It was nice to have a wizard mentor, but he didn't like the idea that he needed to be guarded.

"Seek the Wise Man of the Desert," Udifeus told him. For somebody with a tendency to limp along with a walking stick and a long cape trailing behind him, Udifeus managed to keep a brisk pace with them as they powered their way along the corridors from their room to the entry hall. It was almost as if there were some aspects of his ancientness that were put on for show—and in that case, Marin wouldn't begrudge him that. Magic users had to put on some degree of performance, had to rely on spectacle in some sense, he figured.

"The wise man in the desert?" Aster said.

"*Of* the desert, my dear boy, not *in*. It's an important distinction—he's much more than an ordinary man in an ordinary desert, as you'll see for yourself. The Wise Man *of* the Desert." The way he emphasized the words told Marin that such a name should be spelled out with capital letters to indicate the Wise Man's legendary status.

"He is very elusive," Udifeus continued, "but if you find him, he will tell you what you need to know."

Will he? Marin thought, but he didn't express the doubt aloud. How did they have any way of expecting what lay ahead of them? And just when everything seemed as if it were going right. Just when he had found what he thought was a happy ending to all of their adventures! Here was more danger—and even worse this time. He didn't feel ready to leave the comfort of King Hector's palace or the side of his beloved Elspeth.

But it didn't really matter what he felt ready for, did it? Life had a way of happening whether he wanted it or not. They had to set sail. Sometimes the tide wasn't going to be in their favor.

"Where will we know how to find him?" he asked Udifeus. "This Wise Man of the Desert." The three of them emerged onto the landing overlooking the grand staircase into the palace foyer.

"Travel to the east," Udifeus said as they descended the stairs. "When you reach the great sandscape…" He paused. Marin had never heard Udifeus speechless before. "Uh…well, nobody has gone that far before, so I can't quite tell you what comes next."

Marin glanced at Aster, who exchanged an apprehensive look with him. It would be nice to have more guidance than simply to be told to wander around the desert and hope for the best.

"But if you find the Wise Man," Udifeus continued, "he has an ancient book in which is written all the secrets of the world. He can look into it and find where you must go to find the sword's hiding place."

A book containing all the secrets of the world, Marin reflected.

"I suppose it's out of the question for us to find an ordinary mortal who knows where the relics are hidden," Aster said.

It wasn't a rude observation. Marin had to admit it was a good point. Why did they have to undertake one outlandish, fantastical mission before they undertook another?

Udifeus shook his head. "I'm afraid the only one who would know might be Sir Bedivere the Ironclad. He was the knight who was sent away to hide the relics."

"What happened to him?" Marin asked.

"I don't know for sure, but I assume—that is, some rumors have always said—that he's the same man who was sent away to kill Donovan's son and nephew. After he had slain the boys, he was supposed to lock away the royal relics of Grythium."

"But nobody knows where he is now?" Aster asked.

"He was never seen nor heard from again," Udifeus said. "Mayhaps the gods punished him for carrying out King Donovan's heinous command."

That's possible, Marin thought. He knew all too well now how vengeful the gods could be. If they saw Sir Bedivere as entangled in King Donovan's sins, maybe the knight came to a grotesque end. Maybe he was suffering in the underworld for it.

But if that were the case, why should the knight who carried out the execution be punished, but the king who gave the order be allowed to remain on the throne? That hardly seemed like divine justice.

The front gate of the palace already stood open. Marin lifted the hood of his riding cloak over his head as they stepped out onto the terrace. The sun had just crested the horizon, but the morning air still had some of night's chill to it.

"Ah, my sons." King Hector's voice came from behind them.

They turned to see his majesty coming out the castle gate, escorted by two of his footmen, Elspeth, Carys, and a group of their handmaidens. King Hector wore a simple satin robe cinched tightly at the waist with a belt of gold rings. No crown rested on his head, his flaxen hair standing up in places. Even in the most understated of royal attire, he still commanded a presence.

"Good morrow," Marin said. He lost all sense of formality and rushed forward to greet Elspeth. She fell into him, wrapping her slender arms around him and holding tight. Marin leaned down and kissed her. He should have been embarrassed to show this much affection for her in front of her father, but he didn't care. He might never see her again. He might fail and condemn her to death. All he wanted was to hold her in his arms, to feel the warmth of her lips against his.

They parted and Marin sighed. He looked over at Aster and Carys. The two stood with their hands clasped together, their fingers entwined, down by their waists.

"Leaving so early?" King Hector said. His tone sounded forced, as if he were trying too hard to be the same warm, jovial man he always was. As he came closer, Marin could see dark circles under his eyes. *He didn't sleep at all last night.*

"Day has broken," Marin said, giving a nod of his head toward the sunrise just visible over the city walls. It seemed surreal to think that he, Elspeth, Aster, and Carys had arrived at this very spot only two days before. This was where they dismounted their horses and the guards had told them they would have an audience with the king. That seemed so long ago.

"We won't waste any more time," Marin said. "Daybreak must be a sign to leave." *Leave.* He hated the thought of leaving. This was home.

"Has the kitchen staff provided you with breakfast?" King Hector asked.

"They were most generous," Aster said. It was not exactly a lie.

264

In truth, neither of them had wanted to trouble any of the palace staff more than they had to. They had requested bread and cheese and fruit for their packs, and although the royal chef had sent word that he would be happy to make them a final meal, neither Marin nor Aster had much of a stomach for it. Instead, a valet had delivered the provisions they asked for, wrapped up in muslin, while they were still dressing themselves that morning.

King Hector put a hand on each of their shoulders. "My sons. Oh, my sons. I cannot thank you enough. You prove yourselves worthy of my daughters once again with this deed. My kingdom is lucky to have you."

Marin didn't know how to respond. This man was thanking them? This man, who opened up his palace, who welcomed them into his family—this man who called them his sons when nobody else ever before had done that?

Maybe what he said was true. They were worthy. The kingdom was lucky to have them.

Marin had to choke back a rush of emotion. Two days before, when he dismounted his horse in that very spot, he had been terrified to stand in front of the king because he thought he wasn't worthy. He was just a lowly servant! And now, he could hardly imagine himself feeling intimidated by this man who had given him the blessing to marry Elspeth, this man who had shown him the fatherly love he had never known.

"Thank you, your majesty."

"Please...call me Father, won't you, Marin?"

How badly had Marin spent his whole life wanting a father or mother? He looked up at the king's twinkling blue eyes. "Father," he agreed.

The king embraced him, then Aster.

Marin stood in front of Elspeth, unsure of what to say or do. One goodbye kiss was not enough. All the goodbye kisses in the world were not enough. He reached out and took her hands.

"Hurry back, my prince," she said. She reached up and pushed his hood off his head, then ran her fingers through his hair. The gesture made him go warm all over his body. He just wanted to get lost in her touch.

"Your horse, your highness." A stableboy stood beside them. Marin hadn't even heard him approach. He recognized him. It was the same youth who had led their horses away when they arrived in Blunia. Both his horse and Aster's had been saddled with fine leather to replace the roughshod ones they previously had.

Marin nodded at the boy. "Thank you."

The stableboy handed the reins to Marin and took a step back. Now it really was time to depart. They had their packs, their horses were saddled and ready, and their goodbyes had been said. Marin released Elspeth's hands, unsure of what else there was to say, and hoisted himself up on the horse.

Elspeth gave the horse a pat on the snout. "You'll take care of my prince, won't you?" she whispered. She smirked at Marin. "Your horse says he'll take good care of you."

Marin couldn't resist smiling.

She tucked her hand into her sash and pulled out a white handkerchief. "Here," she said, handing it to him. "Every knight who rides must carry a token of his lady's favor. It's a silly tradition, I know."

He took the handkerchief and held it close to his face. The scent of rose and citrus hung on it. That smell would remind him of her when they were apart. He bit his tongue. He wasn't going to cry. Not here.

"You're wonderful," she said, those large eyes of hers beaming.

Aster accepted the reins to his horse from the stableboy. He paused before mounting, almost as if he were considering something he wanted to say to Carys. "You know...you know you may come with us. You rode this horse better than I did when we were coming to Blunia. You might be able to help us on our quest."

Carys leaned in and kissed him. "I'll miss you. But I must stay with my sister. I cannot leave her side at this time, even to be with you." She looked over at Elspeth. "My sister has no choice but to stay here. Terro's wrath would be terrible if she tried to leave the kingdom."

King Hector stepped closer. "Yes," he said. "Besides, it is not right for princesses to go questing. What would my people think?"

"Well, they might think you have some sense, Father," Carys said. "They might respect you for knowing that princesses aren't condemned to sit at home and exist as if they were decoration." She moved closer to Elspeth and took her sister's hand. "We're not joining our men on their quest, but that's not because of some ancient code of patronizing chauvinism. This is just how it has to be."

It was hard to tell whether King Hector really accepted what his daughter said or whether he simply nodded out of fatherly devotion to assuage his child. Marin smiled at Aster as if to say, *These are some strong wives-to-be we have here.*

"Well," Aster said. "Let's be on our way?"

"Yes," Marin said.

Then there were hoofbeats and the whipping of the wild wind through their hair, and the city of Blunia rushed past them in a blur of colors, and they were off—Marin and Aster, together against the great wide world all over again.

CHAPTER 36

The desert spread out around them, a vast wasteland of orange sand set beneath a cloudless sky. Marin had never known such unbearable heat before—smothering, oppressive, painful. His skin burned. Sweat drenched his tunic and breeches.

Where was this Wise Man of the Desert, and how would they ever know if they were getting close to finding him? They had encountered nothing but endless sand. No plants or buildings or even an animal. Marin traced his eyes around the sky, wishing there were some indication of what time it was, but there was no sun. The sky blazed white endlessly. No morning or afternoon or evening. Before they arrived in the desert, they had ridden for two days through the wilderness surrounding Blunia. The days had been broken up by night, when they made camp and ate and slept.

As soon as their horses set foot on the sand, it just became one infinite day. One *hot* infinite day.

"This is awful," Aster muttered, wiping the sweat from his brow.

Marin couldn't disagree. This oppressive heat, this hopeless searching, all of it truly was awful. *There has to be a better way of fulfilling this quest*, he kept thinking.

But then—

"Aster! Aster, look!"

Was it a mirage? It was almost too good to be true. But there was a being in the distance, a floating form hovering in the air above the unbroken stretch of sand. The heat rising from the ground made him ripple and swirl.

As they got closer, he became more tangible. His features took form, solidifying out of the rippling mirage into something solid and real. Withered limbs emerged out of heavy robes that draped over his stooped form in numerous billows and folds despite the oppressive heat. He sat so comfortably and cozily in an overstuffed armchair hovering in the air that it was impossible to tell where his robes ended and the upholstery began.

The enormous book spread out in front of him took up his whole lap. The man bent over the pages, peering down at them through square spectacles that rested on a large, hooked nose.

Although the man's shape resembled a human's, there was something otherworldly about him too. A cerulean-colored beard and mustache covered his lemon-yellow skin. His fingers splayed out nearly a foot in length—the pointer finger and thumb of one hand held his spectacles in place while the pointer finger of his other hand ran along the text on the page as he read.

He took no notice of Marin and Aster even when their horses stood right in front of him.

"Do we say something?" Marin asked.

"I…uh, I guess," Aster said.

Marin cleared his throat. "Excuse us, sir…"

The man looked up from the book. A smile spread across his face, sending wrinkles and creases through his glowing skin. When the man's lips parted, Marin saw teeth capped with silver.

"Ah. I was wondering when I would be seeing the two of you."

"You know who we are?" Aster asked.

The man nodded. "Of course, I do." He swept his hand across the open pages of the book. "It's all written down in here. Here in my book, my boy. I have already read it."

Marin swung his leg over and jumped down from his horse. Standing still, he agonized once more at how hot the air felt. He wiped his sweaty palms across the front of his tunic, which was already drenched. He knew he must have looked like a terrible sight, but now wasn't the time to worry about appearances.

You're a prince, he told himself. *You're a prince on a mission, even if you don't look like it. Act the part, and nobody will question you.*

How ironic that only a few days ago he had complained to Aster about how even the finest royal attire couldn't make him feel like a prince. Now he stood here in a sweat-stained tunic of simple linen, his vest and cloak removed and cast aside many miles behind him—but he couldn't waver in his determination. He just couldn't.

"Do you mean that's the Book of Records right there?" Marin asked, keeping a polite tone. "We have heard of it, my brother and I."

Aster climbed down from his horse. Several beads of sweat dripped from his hair onto his face.

"We have come to seek your help," Marin continued. "If that book tells you everything, then it must be able to tell you where we can find the lost sword of Grythium."

The man stared at him. "The sword of Grythium," he said. "Yes, I read about where it was hidden. That was many years ago." He straightened his spectacles. "But tell me—why should I tell you the secrets that are written here in my Book of Records? Anyone could seek me out. What makes you so fit?"

"Uh…" Marin couldn't think of a proper response. What *did* make them so fit for knowing what was contained in the Book of Records? After all, if this enchanted book contained everything that ever happened in the world, then it would have to be a great privilege to know its contents.

Before Marin could answer, Aster spoke. "Anyone could seek you out, but few do."

The old man stroked his beard. "Hmmm?"

"We came to you seeking knowledge," Aster said. "Not everyone is so forward to do something like that. Knowledge should be available to those who seek it, no questions asked."

Marin couldn't deny how grateful he was that Aster always had something to say in any given situation. Indeed, there were times it got them in trouble. But this was a time when Aster's bluntness was a gift.

"My brother is right," Marin said. "Unless...unless you have a duty to say no to us." He paused. "Do you?"

"I do not."

"Then please," Marin said. "I pray thee...tell us where we can find the sword." He didn't want to sound desperate, but it was impossible to swallow his fear. His wife-to-be's life depended on it. Did he dare tell the Wise Man this was his reason? Was that a worthy reason? She was not just his betrothed—she was the future queen of Blunia.

And he and Aster didn't have forever to complete this quest. If they had been wandering around here in the desert for days to no avail...

"I am impressed." The wise man's voice shook him out of any anxiety he felt.

"Why?" Marin asked.

"Not everyone would claim a right to know what is written in my Book of Records," he said. "Some people would stammer or go silent, thinking that they are unworthy." He paused, looking at both of them. "You are not some people."

"We're not," Aster agreed.

Silence hung in the air, as oppressive as the dry desert heat.

The sage raised one of his bushy eyebrows. "The sword of Grythium—and the crown and the mantle—are locked away in a vault high up on the highest peak of the Blood Mountains." He hesitated a moment. There was something else. This pause gave Marin a bad feeling. "But," he continued, "the vault is locked, you know."

"Locked?" Marin tried to hide his dismay, to mask it with bravery and resilience, but his voice betrayed him. They had come so far! And now in the same minute they learn about the vault's location, they learn that it is locked.

"So where is the key?" he asked.

The old man turned his gaze back down to his book, turning the page as he did. "I do not believe that was a secret that was ever revealed, so I'm not sure whether it would be in my Book of Records." He looked back up at them. "You see, the key to the vault...well, I believe it was sent away to be thrown into the sea..."

Marin loosened the collar of his tunic. He had a feeling it wasn't merely the desert heat that was making him feel so worked up. His heart pounded. They were close—so close to figuring out the truth of all of this.

"But...?" He could sense there was a twist coming.

"When you say, 'sent away...'" Aster said. "What do you mean?"

"The same man who gave the order for the vault in the Blood Mountains to be locked up also ordered for the key to be thrown into the ocean where it would never be found," the old man said. "The man who tried to thwart fate."

Marin was certain he knew whom the Wise Man referred to. "King Donovan?" he asked. King Donovan hid the relics so that King Hector could never come into possession of them.

"Yes."

"Wait," Aster said. "You said he ordered the key to be thrown away. Just because the key was supposed to be thrown away, that doesn't mean that it was. Who was supposed to throw the key away?"

Marin could already tell where this was going. Udifeus said the same man who was supposed to kill Donovan's son and nephew was the same man who was ordered to hide the relics.

"Why, Sir Bedivere the Ironclad." The Wise Man's voice was so calm, so straightforward. Marin recognized the name. Udifeus had mentioned it only days before.

"But there's a chance," Aster said, "that this order wasn't carried out. Sir Bedivere defied the order. This key *wasn't* actually thrown away in the ocean."

Marin looked over at Aster. Was he thinking the same thing Marin was? Aster met Marin's eye and gave a slight nod, placing his hand across the pocket of his tunic, closing it around something he had held there.

The Wise Man ignored whatever silent exchange Marin and Aster shared. He looked back down at his book. "I would have to go back and check the records to see. Sometimes, things that are done in secret don't get recorded the way they should."

"How do we find the Blood Mountains?" Marin said.

The Wise Man raised one of his bony arms that emerged from the heavy piles of fabric forming his sleeve. He gestured to the sands around them. "First, you must find your way out of the desert. And that is not something I can do for you. I can give you facts, but I cannot give you guidance."

He grinned again. Marin wasn't sure he liked this old sage. He had no doubts about the man's honesty—after all, he had no reason to lie to them—but he didn't like the enigmatic way he revealed the truths he did.

"But if you must know," the Wise Man said, "it lies in that direction." He pointed his finger to his right, toward an endless expanse of desert that looked exactly the same as any other endless expanse of desert in any other direction. "Simply head straight and you will come to it eventually. Mayhaps."

Mayhaps. What did this old man mean by *mayhaps*? Marin swallowed. He had heard enough about prophecies over the last few weeks—even the last few days—that he now found himself frustrated to hear what *mayhaps* would come to pass.

"But don't you want to know why the Blood Mountains have their name?" the Wise Man said.

"Why?" Aster asked.

"From far away, the mountains appear to have a fearsome red color, something ominous and formidable to even those with great courage," the man explained. "When you get closer, you'll find them to be beautiful. They lose their angry glow. They have lush trees and rocky hills and sparkling waterfalls. But they are still dangerous—very, very dangerous. Innocent blood is always spilled when the mountains are traversed."

"Well, doesn't that sound nice?" Aster said.

"Three tests you'll face as you go up the mountain," the Wise Man said. "You'll need to pass all three if you ultimately wish to reach the top."

Three tests. Marin didn't like the sound of that. Why couldn't they just casually hike up the mountain and unlock the vault? Why did there have to be tests?

"I don't suppose you can tell us what those tests are?" Marin asked.

"I am afraid I cannot."

Marin nodded. He exchanged a look with Aster, who shrugged.

"Right then," Marin said. "I thank you for sharing your knowledge with us." He hoped he sounded polite.

"You are most welcome, my boy," the Wise Man said. "Good luck to you."

Without another word, he dropped his head, staring back at the expansive pages on his lap and continuing to read.

Marin reached his hand up to push his sweat-drenched hair from his forehead. "We should get going," he said to Aster.

"Aye."

They mounted their horses and had just turned to ride away when the old man's voice rose again. "By the way, do you know who you two are?" He didn't even look up from his book.

Marin gripped the rein, tension going through his whole body. He didn't like the way the Wise Man said that. As if there were some secret about the two of them, about their identity. Some identity beyond runaway servants who rose to royal status.

"What do you mean?" he asked.

The Wise Man's tone remained exactly the same. "Do you know who you two are?"

For once, even Aster was speechless. "Uh..." he glanced over at Marin.

He wants us to ask, Marin thought. *But we're not going to.*

"We know who we are," Marin said to the old man. "We know very well." And that was the truth. He looked over at Aster for reassurance. "Who we might have been once...well, I'm not sure whether that matters at this point."

The Wise Man continued to stare at the pages of his book. He kept silent, not saying anything else. Was he angry they didn't press him for the truth? But Marin meant what he said—he and Aster knew who they were. If they had a different identity that neither of them knew about...

Marin pushed up the sleeves of his tunic. "Come on," he whispered to Aster. He tugged at the reins of his horse and rode in the direction where the Wise Man told them the Blood Mountains would be. Aster's horse neighed and followed behind him.

They rode for a few minutes in complete silence. The unending day's blood-boiling heat continued to torture them, but Marin had a little more hope now that he knew they were headed in the right direction and they knew what to look for.

He glanced over his shoulder to make sure the Wise Man was no longer in sight. He looked at Aster.

"You know what he was going to tell us," Aster said. It wasn't a question.

"I have a feeling," Marin said. "Not that it matters."

"Doesn't it though?"

Marin shrugged. He didn't have all the answers—he knew that. But in that moment, he didn't care to hear what he was almost sure the Wise Man of the Desert was going to reveal to him. That he and Aster were the heirs of that wicked King Donovan. That they were sent away to be murdered as babies.

"I don't think it matters," he said, "whether you were born as a prince or raised as a servant. It's not about what's written in any Book of Records any more than what's written in the stars. I'm starting to think, Aster, that you're right. What matters is what we do with the tide when it is in our favor."

Aster nodded, "Right, but—"

"No *but*," Marin said.

He couldn't believe Aster was letting him actually start believing in prophecy and destiny and preordained fates, not after they had proven all of that wrong. If they hadn't taken their lives into their own hands, the two of them would still be living on Ilth's farm, or wandering around the woods on the outskirts of Blunia, or wasting away the days until his beloved Elspeth was to be sacrificed because no knight in the kingdom would be her champion.

And if Sir Bedivere the Ironclad had actually obeyed King Donovan and carried out the gruesome command...

Still, there were things Marin couldn't explain. He looked over at Aster's hand gripping the horse's rein, at the brass ring around his finger, remembering the power it had to transport them away from King

Donovan's court in the direst of circumstances. That was still a power he couldn't explain.

"If we're long-lost princes," he said, "well, what of it? It doesn't matter too much, does it? It doesn't benefit us at all. What matters is what we're making of ourselves right now."

Aster nodded. "So, we're off to the Blood Mountains, then?"

"Aye."

"Marin?"

"I'm glad I'm with you on this."

"As am I, my brother. As am I."

CHAPTER 37

"What's that up ahead?" Aster said.

Marin squinted. "I don't know. But there's definitely something there."

Something. Anything to break up the maddening expanse of desolation that stretched around them in the desert. Since they left the Wise Man, they had seen nothing but sand. Sand led to more sand, which led to more sand, which led to more sand. Even if they now knew they had to find the Blood Mountains, it didn't seem to make any difference. The desert went on and on with no end in sight. Everything seemed the same.

Are we lost, or do we need to keep going farther? Marin thought several times.

Even the hour of the day stayed the same. Without the sun to change positions in the sky or nightfall to bring relief from the blinding white heat overhead, there was no way to tell the passage of time. Had they been riding for a full day? Maybe even two or three?

"Should we stop to rest at all?" Aster asked once.

"We could," Marin said. "But I don't think I could get much sleep in this, no matter how tired I am. Could you?"

"I don't think so."

This must have been how the desert killed those who dared to trek across it. It drove them crazy. It exhausted them until they couldn't go on any farther and simply gave up.

We're getting close to that point now, Marin thought. *We might not last much longer.*

But shapes up ahead of them in the sand, even if they didn't know what those shapes were—it brought hope. It meant there was something else out there in the desert. It might even mean *someone* else out there. Someone who might be able to help.

"What do you say we approach?" Aster said.

"Aye," Marin replied. Talking proved difficult. The dryness of his mouth hurt. He didn't want to drink any more water than he had to. There was no way of knowing when they would be able to refill their waterskins.

Trees took shape as they got closer, appearing out of the clouds of sand, dark shapes against the orange-red monotony. Marin held his hand over his eyes to shield them from the white blaze of the sky. These weren't the normal, healthy trees he and Aster would have found in a forest back in Grythium or Blunia. These trees were black, almost as if they had been burnt to charcoal by the heat, and they stood leafless with their branches stretched out in all directions. Among the patch of trees, tents made from animal hides stood, blocking off some hubbub just beyond—a disturbing cacophony of sounds rang in the air around the camp, steel against steel, cruel laughter, and the roar of an animal in pain.

"On second thought," Aster said, "we could just ride on by."

"No," Marin whispered. *There's definitely trouble happening here, but that's not a reason to run away.* "We should help."

"Marin," Aster said.

"We should," Marin said.

"I know we should," Aster groaned. "Why do you always have to be so virtuous?"

They reached the trees on the outskirts of the strange camp. Marin dismounted and tied his horse to one of the branches. Aster dismounted beside him, his feet hitting the sand with a gentle thud, but Marin didn't look over, his gaze instead fixed on the scene ahead. Shadows moved on the sand beyond the tents, and occasionally, a sword or another weapon appeared above the tops of the tents as someone swung it overhead.

"This is definitely trouble we've found here," Marin said. But his curiosity had the better of him at this point. It didn't make sense to turn around and not find out what was happening.

He gave the rope a hard tug to ensure his horse was tightly tied. "Ready?" he asked Aster.

"Ready as I'll ever be."

Marin's stomach knotted itself up. After so many adventures, why was he still so nervous in situations like this? Months ago, on Ilth's farm, where he dreamed of a life of adventure, he always thought he would get braver and braver with each escapade until at last nothing fazed him at all. Not so.

You could just turn around, he thought. *Nobody would think less of you for it, least of all Aster. There's no need to put yourself in danger.*

The animalistic screech came again. Somebody was being hurt. There was no way they could turn around and act as if they had never encountered this. Not when somebody was being harmed.

He and Aster crept around the side of one of the tents, slowly approaching the corner where they could peek around and see who or what was making this ruckus.

A group of humanoid creatures—scrawny, spindly, their skin seemingly made of sand—gathered around a mass of fur they had tied up to a tree. The beast thrashed, trying to free itself from the bindings.

But these twisted little beings—sand gremlins, they must have been, also known as sandmen, according to what Marin once read—had tied the creature up tight. Swords, clubs, spears, and maces swung through the air, landing on the creature's furry back with sickening *bump, bump, bump* sounds. The creature howled with each strike.

Marin couldn't believe what he was seeing. And he thought the unrelenting cruelty they suffered back in the goblin fortress was bad!

"What in the cursed underworld," he murmured.

"That's awful," Aster said.

Marin didn't want to stare, but he didn't want to look away either, not daring to move or speak, hardly even able to breathe.

He found his voice. "We have to fight them."

"Right," Aster said. "How?"

"I think we should be enough to take on these people, whoever or whatever they are." They had learned a thing or two throughout their adventures about their own strength. Marin's sword hung at his belt—the royal armorer had made it for him, but he hardly had time to learn how to really swing it. There had only been one lesson with King Hector's swordmaster the afternoon after they agreed to undertake the quest. Even though the lesson had gone on for hours, it hadn't been enough. How was he ever going to face the vraotyr if he didn't even know how to swing a sword in a common fight against a pack of sandmen?

"Aye," Aster agreed.

Marin hesitated. "The only thing is…"

"Is what?" Aster winked at him. "Don't tell me the valiant prince of Blunia is doubting himself now."

"No," Marin said.

"Good," Aster said. "I'll create a diversion."

With that, Aster drew his sword. Holding it close to his side, he crept around the side of one row of tents, moving over the sand with surprising stealth. Marin held his breath. He peeked back out at the sandmen and the abuse they were inflicting on their captive. They shouted something between their cackles and guffaws, something in a language Marin didn't recognize. The captured beast let out a moan, a pitiful sob that made Marin's soul hurt. As ferocious as this animal looked, it was clearly in pain.

Then came Aster's voice, loud and unwavering. "Hey!"

Marin still couldn't see Aster, but he could tell just by the tone of his voice that he probably had his sword drawn, an intimidating look on his face.

"What do you all think you're doing?" Aster shouted.

The sandmen stopped their torture and looked over in the direction where Aster's voice had come from. One of them started to shout in their chattering language. Whatever it was the sandman said, it sounded threatening.

Aster stepped into Marin's view, holding his sword out in front of him. "Why don't you pick on somebody your own size?" he shouted.

More chattering, angrier this time. The sandmen approached, surrounding him.

"All right, fair enough," Aster said. He spun around, holding his sword out at each of the sandmen—the ones in front of him, behind him, to his left, to his right. They were on all sides.

What now? Marin thought. He hadn't thought this far ahead. Neither of them had.

With his eyes locked on the scene in front of him, not even letting himself look away for a moment, Marin reached down and grabbed the handle of his sword. He took a deep breath.

The next thing he knew, before he could overthink it or allow himself to give way to fear, Marin was running forward, swinging his sword overhead.

It wasn't much of a battle. For a minute or two, the sandmen tried fighting back as Marin and Aster came at their pack from both sides. The sound of steel on steel rang all around them as swords met, but the brief training Marin and Aster had undertaken with King Hector's staff was enough to make them formidable opponents to the crude sandmen. Soon enough, the spindly foes retreated, leaving dust hanging in the air and footsteps in the sand as the only sign they were ever there.

Aster huffed, something between a sigh and halfhearted laugh. "Well, that was easier than I expected."

Marin shrugged. "I guess some monsters are more cowardly than we would expect. All fangs and fakery but no real fierceness to speak of."

"That was poetic," Aster said.

"I'm feeling a little poetic lately, I think," Marin admitted. "There's been a lot to observe. We're going to have a story worth telling when all of this is over, and I want to make sure I'm able to do it justice."

Before Aster could respond to that, a sound erupted from behind them, something crossed between a growl and a cry. The captive!

They wheeled around. The animal, whatever it was, which the sandmen had taunted mercilessly only minutes before, wrestled with its tethers, trying to get itself free.

"We've got to help it," Aster said.

"How do we get it to hold still?" Marin asked.

"I don't know," Aster said. "Come on. Let's see what we can do."

They moved closer. Marin didn't like the violent way the animal thrashed around, but when it noticed them approaching, it calmed down, relinquishing its fight against its bonds. It blinked a pair of pleading eyes at the two of them.

"I pray thee," it heaved in a pitiful voice. "I pray thee—don't hurt me."

It was scared. Scared. A monstrous animal like this one was scared.

But why wouldn't it be scared? The sandmen had been mercilessly torturing it.

"Of course, we won't hurt you," Marin said. "We're trying to help you."

He had to cut the cords, but he couldn't make any sudden moves that would scare this creature more. The beast trembled, making its orange fur shake. The enormous black eyes watched Marin from out of a patch of green scales across its face.

Marin lifted his sword and held it out in front of him, as if to demonstrate he wasn't going to use it against the creature. The tension on the beast's face slackened, relaxed. With a few quick slices, Marin cut the tethers away, sending the creature tumbling onto the ground.

In a flash of movement, the oddly shaped creature scrambled to its feet. Now that it was on the ground and standing upright, it didn't look as big—not much larger than a hound, though its masses of orange fuzz growing out from all angles gave it a little more mass than its scaly face alone did.

"Thank you, sirs!" the beast shouted. "Let the gods bless you!"

With those words, it reared itself up on its hind legs, standing upright like a human, and made a low, sweeping bow. When it lifted its head, it smiled at them, revealing gleaming white teeth. "Thank you, thank you, thank you!"

"You're very welcome," Marin said, trying to hold back a laugh. Something about the creature's exuberant energy humored him despite how weary and stressed he was. The sheer unrestrained joy seemed contagious.

"Terrible creatures," the animal said, shaking its head. "Terrible creatures! Frik so afraid."

"Frik?" Marin said. "Is that your name?"

"Ah, yesss! Yessir!" He made another low bow, rose up, then bowed once to Marin and once to Aster. "Frik's me name."

Marin returned the bow as a show of courtesy. It didn't seem formal enough of an occasion for a bow, but he wanted to return the creature's obeisance with something of the same. "Frik, my name is Marin, and this is Aster."

"Marin!" Frik repeated. "Aster! How cans me ever thank you?" He blinked his large black eyes, and Marin got the impression Frik had an animalistic loyalty, a sort of pack mentality that bonded him to them.

"That's very kind of you," Aster said. "But I don't think any thanks is necessary."

"We only did what anyone else would do," Marin said. "Or what you would do for us."

Frik shook his head. "But me's must be thanking you. You's done Frik a kindness. I am in your debt always."

"I—oh, wait!" The thought came to Marin suddenly. "Do you know the way out of this desert? Do you know how to find the Blood Mountains?"

An expression of delight crossed Frik's large face. "Out of the desert? The Blood Mountains?"

If only I could find anything that made me this kind of happy, Marin thought. *He's overjoyed at the thought of helping us. I guess I could learn something from Frik about serving others.*

"Yes, I's knows the way," Frik said. "Follow me!"

Marin and Aster hardly had a chance to mount their horses before Frik took off. His form became a sudden blur of orange and green as he whizzed off into the desert ahead of them.

"C'mon," Marin shouted, half to his horse and half to Aster. "After him!"

"Let's go," Aster shouted.

Marin tugged at the reins. Wind whipped past him as his horse sped off in the direction Frik went. If it weren't for the cloud of sand Frik kicked up around him as he sped through the desert, they might have lost his trail.

Don't go so fast, Marin thought, trying to will Frik to slow down.

Didn't this creature understand their horses couldn't run through the sand as fast as he could?

But just as Marin started to get nervous that Frik would outrun the horses, leaving him and Aster stranded in the desert again, the Blood Mountains appeared in the distance, materializing out of the haze, miragelike, just as the Wise Man and the sandmen camp had done, one moment there and the next moment gone, then finally there again.

That's it! Marin's heart hammered at the sight of it. "The Blood Mountains!" he shouted. "We've made it! We've made it!"

"Yes!" Aster cheered, throwing his fist into the air. "Yes!"

Finally, after hours or maybe even days of wandering in the desert, their quest had meaning again. They were getting somewhere.

Red crags jutted up out of the sand on the horizon. They grew larger and larger as Marin and Aster rode closer. The wind rushed through Marin's hair. It was getting cooler. The desert heat was disappearing behind them.

Their horses pushed on until the desert sand gave way to grassland at the foot of the mountains. Frik waited for them, leaning up against a rock in the shade of a tree, his whole body rising up and down as he heaved to catch his breath.

Marin slowed his horse and looked up at the rising slope of shimmering red stone. "Would you look at that?"

"Impressive," Aster murmured.

The blazing whiteness of the sky dissipated as soon as their horses stepped onto the grass, giving way to blue skies streaked with clouds. The sun had begun its afternoon descent, lowering itself just beyond the peak of the mountains. The blood-colored rocks glowed under its rays.

Marin swung one leg around and jumped off his horse, landing in the soft grass. What a relief it was to be out of the stifling desert heat, to be back in a place where the grass was green and the sky was blue.

Frik's voice snapped him back to reality. "You's not venturing up the mountain, is you?"

Something about the way Frik said that gave Marin a sinking feeling in his stomach. "Well, yes," he said.

"We have to," Aster added.

Frik's black eyes doubled in size. He lowered his snout, looking again pitiful in his expression. "Oh, no, sirs! No!" Frik padded forward on all four paws, then reared up to grab Marin by the hem of his tunic. "You mustn't!" Frik dropped down onto fours again and rushed over to Aster. "You mustn't!"

"Why not?" Aster said.

"It's full of bad things. Baaaaad things, so they says." Frik choked as if he were trying to hold back tears. "Despair things. Nobodies goes up there." He whimpered.

Marin went down on one knee. "Hey," he cooed, trying to calm Frik. "Hey, it's all right." He shuffled forward in the grass, putting one hand on Frik's back. "We appreciate your warning," he said. "We do."

Frik's eyes misted up. His snout wrinkled with a sniff. It was almost touching how concerned he was for them. Marin still wasn't used to having others concerned for his well-being.

But Elspeth is waiting for you, he thought.

"My brother and I must go up the mountain," Marin said. "You see…there are people who are counting on us. Do you understand? People are counting on us to—well, to do something up on the mountain."

Frik shook his head. "Not for long. You will no longer be, so they can't count on you."

Aster coughed. "No longer be? You mean…we might die?"

Frik looked up at him and gulped. "Or worse."

Marin stood. They didn't have time to waste comforting Frik or dealing with his ominous forebodings. They had a quest to complete.

287

"That's just a risk we have to take," he said.

Frik nodded to show he understood, drew himself up on his hind legs, and made another sweeping bow. "Then best of luck to you, sirs." His voice trembled as he spoke. "And gods bless you again."

"Gods bless you, Frik," Aster replied.

Frik gazed at them, his eyes full of pity. "Should yous needs me— I's always willing to come to help."

"That's very kind of you," Marin said. "We'll remember that."

He stared at Frik, wondering how much stock he should actually put in this creature's fear for them. After all, the Wise Man had mentioned they would face three challenges. What would those challenges entail? They would just have to find out.

With nothing left to say, Marin and Aster turned and began their trek up the mountain.

The poor creature might be right though, Marin thought. *We don't know what we're going to face on this mountain. We might never come back down.*

CHAPTER 38

The surface of the truth pond gleamed, flat and shining like polished jade, in the clearing. White spots danced on its surface where sunlight shone on it. The trees formed a perfect circle around it, almost as if the forest itself revered the pond, keeping a respectful distance away. Or else the forest was afraid—the truth, after all, could sometimes be a fearful thing.

What a foolish notion, King Donovan thought. *Why should anyone be afraid of the truth?*

He held his breath as he approached, stepping out of the forest undergrowth and into the peaceful clearing. A clump of bushes grew around the pond to one side, but the side closest to King Donovan had nothing but rocks piled around its edge.

"That's it," King Donovan said. He looked over his shoulder at his lone companion. He'd left his horses and all his knights and attendants a half mile away, choosing to go ahead on foot. He'd given only his steward Clovis permission to come. He didn't like the idea of bringing anyone along with him, but as anxiety tightened its grip on him more with each passing day, he started liking the idea of going anywhere alone less and less.

He could have brought the witch along, but he almost disliked that idea as much as he disliked the idea of going alone. Ilth served her purpose, but he didn't enjoy her company.

But Clovis was simple. He could offer assistance without being overbearing.

"Aye, sir," Clovis said. "That's it. The truth pond."

Donovan exhaled sharply. "So, it does exist."

Up until the moment he saw the truth pond, he had his doubts. It always sounded like something out of a myth or a fairy tale. People told stories about it, but few people ventured so far into the forest to seek it out. According to the stories, most people who looked into it didn't like what they saw.

Those people are fools, King Donovan thought.

Almost as if he could hear the king's thoughts, Clovis piped up. "Just because you've found the truth pond, your majesty…well, that doesn't mean you need to look into it." Clovis had no way of knowing what it was King Donovan wished to know, but all of those within the king's inner circle knew that something had been troubling him for the past few weeks. Even Donovan himself was aware he had done a terrible job of hiding it.

"Sometimes," Clovis said, trying to get the words out before King Donovan got too close, "it's better not to know."

King Donovan paused. What an utter idiot this Clovis was. *Why did I have to bring the idiot steward*, he thought. He gritted his teeth, trying to swallow his irritation, and turned away from the pond to look at Clovis. "When you look at me, what do you see?"

Clovis blinked, confusion marked on his stupid face. "I see…I see a king, your majesty."

"Exactly." To emphasize the point, Donovan raised his chin up, making himself even taller than his already impressive height. He placed his hands on his hips, gripping the studded leather belt that cinched his satin tunic. "And should secrets be kept from a king?"

"No, your majesty." Clovis's voice was meek, timid.

"No, no, not at all," Donovan said. "I am the king, and I should think I deserve to know everything that happens within my kingdom."

But the steward had a point, and Donovan couldn't deny it. The wisdom of the ancient scriptures taught that the truth could make a person's life easier from the burden of lies and misunderstanding. But right now, Donovan wasn't so sure he believed that.

Still, if he didn't know…the questions would drive him insane…

He had to know the truth.

He turned back and stepped closer to the truth pond.

Clovis's voice piped up again. "We are no longer in your kingdom, your majesty."

"What?" King Donovan called over his shoulder.

"You…you said you deserve to know everything that happens within your kingdom," Clovis said. "But we're no longer in your kingdom. We're in the woods just on the outskirts of—"

"And all the lands surrounding my kingdom then!" Donovan barked over his shoulder. "If foreign affairs affect my kingdom, I deserve to know them. Why do you argue?"

Clovis said nothing.

"Those boys elude me," Donovan said. "And I will not be made a fool of. I want to know where they are. If this pond can show the truth, it will show me where they are hiding."

"Yes, your majesty."

Donovan sighed. But that wasn't the entirety of the reason he sought out the truth pond. If only it were! If only he could look into the pond and command it to show him where those boys were—

It won't be any use to have that idiotic steward hovering nearby when you look into the pond, he thought. *Who knows what it will show? Who knows what the steward will see?*

Donovan regretted ever bringing Clovis with him.

"Stand back," he commanded. "I'll approach the pond by myself. It's not for you to see."

"Yes, your majesty."

"And stay silent."

"Yes, your majesty."

Clovis took a step back into the overgrowth lining the edge of the clearing.

Donovan stepped up to the pond and knelt down. Its surface gleamed. He had never seen water so smooth before, not a ripple to disturb it. He might have even mistaken it for glass if it weren't for the lily pads and its blossoms.

"Who approaches?" a voice called out.

Donovan jumped. "Who said that?"

"Down here!"

He looked down and noticed a large bullfrog perched on a rock at the edge of the pond. Its green hide bore all kinds of bumps and warts, its back as rough and uneven as the surface of the pond was smooth. Bulbous black eyes stared up at Donovan.

Of course, there was a talking frog. Why did there always have to be a damned talking frog?

"I am King Donovan of Grythium."

The frog croaked. "What do you seek from the truth pond? What is it you wish to see?"

Donovan had not expected to be interrogated when he visited the pond. He didn't like it. After all, he was king—who was he to be bullied by a frog?

Still, there was nothing to be gained from arrogance now. If he wanted the truth, he had to submit to powers greater than himself. And this frog guarded the pond.

"All my knights and all my hunters have been tracking two boys across the land for weeks," Donovan said. "There has been no sign of them. We cannot find them. I wish to know where they are."

The frog blinked its bulbous eyes. "Ask the pond, and you will see."

The king leaned over, looking into the shining blue-green depth of the pond. His reflection stared back up at him. He drew a deep breath. "I demand to see the bastard sons of King Hector."

Nothing happened. No change happened whatsoever.

"I demand to see the bastard sons of King Hector," Donovan repeated.

The water remained the same. Nothing happened. Just as Sir Hardegan's enchanted bow had failed to shoot and kill those boys, this pond failed to reveal them to him. Donovan's head throbbed.

The frog's voice interrupted his fearful agony. "If the pond shows you nothing, then—"

"I don't care what it means," Donovan snapped, tearing his eyes from the pond and staring at the frog.

But he knew what it meant. *The bastard sons of King Hector do not exist. He has no bastard sons.*

The frog cocked its head at him and blinked. "You already know what it means, I suppose."

"Silence before I throw you into the pond and drown you myself," Donovan shouted, slapping the surface of the pond, sending ripples across the water. "Silence, I say!"

He leaped to his feet and stared furiously at the frog.

Those two baby boys…my wife's son…my sister's son…

My wife! My sister!

A chill went through him and he choked back the tears rushing to his eyes. No, there had to be something wrong with this pond's enchantment. There had to be a reason it wouldn't show him King Hector's bastards who planned to usurp his throne!

The wretched little frog made no reply. It gave a simple *ribbit*, but no words were spoken. How much would the little amphibious monster deserve to be smashed right there with one of the rocks! How much did Donovan want to do it?

He stomped away, his whole body shaking. Clovis sat just beyond the edge of the clearing, resting up against a tree, picking petals off a flower with the placidity of the contentedly stupid. The steward jumped to his feet as Donovan approached. "Did you learn what you needed to know, my lord?"

"Call off the hunt. It's over," Donovan said. "We're returning to the castle."

"Is something wrong, your majesty?"

Donavan stopped in his tracks and raised a pointed finger. "Ask me that again and I'll have your head," he said. "We are returning to the castle. The hunt is over."

Knowing better than to disobey, Clovis ran on ahead to alert the others of the king's order, and King Donovan continued walking back alone.

He had found out the truth, and he refused to believe what it told him.

CHAPTER 39

For the first time since returning home from the goblin fortress, Elspeth had another one of her dreams. She saw Marin and Aster making their way across the desert, both of them riding their horses in the direction of the Blood Mountains. She'd been able to taste the acrid desert air, feel the burn of the sand-flecked wind as it grazed across her face, soak in the heat of the blazing sky across her face.

But even if she called out to Marin—her Marin, her beloved prince—she doubted whether he would actually be able to hear her.

She sat up in bed and threw the satin duvet off her bed, then slipped across the room to her window. The night air here was cooler than it had been in the desert. Refreshing. She liked the way it felt. It wasn't until she threw back the curtains and looked out at the star-flecked expanse of sky that she realized a thin layer of sweat gleamed on her skin.

"Oh, Marin," she whispered to herself.

The city beneath her window appeared as nothing more than dark shadows. No movement. No sounds. As far as she could tell, every subject of her father's kingdom was asleep.

How can they sleep? How can they find rest and respite while their dear princes are off on a dangerous mission? When Prince Marin and Prince Aster could be riding into mortal peril right at this very moment! Or tomorrow. Or the next day.

She crossed her arms, hugging herself, running her fingers along the soft silk of her nightgown. Marin and Aster were in danger, but so was she. In *more* danger than they were, actually. If they failed on their quest, then her life would be forfeit.

Somehow that thought didn't bother her as much as it should have. Except that she would have duties as queen one day. She had an obligation to her subjects.

A light wind swept through the window, sending goosebumps along her skin. She stepped back and pulled the curtains closed.

When she turned around, she wasn't alone.

Two women stood across from her, their figures only vaguely visible in the dimness of her sleeping chamber. One was short, her body thick with a maternal softness. The other was tall, thin, broad through the shoulders.

"Oh!" The sound escaped Elspeth's throat, but she didn't feel herself make it.

"Good evening, your highness," the shorter one said. "Be not afraid."

"I'm not," Elspeth said.

"Pardon our intrusion," said the other. "But we must meet with you. May we have some light?"

Light. Yes, light would be nice.

"Of course." Elspeth went to her vanity where a candelabra sat. Before she could strike a match to light any of the wicks, a faint glow from behind her threw her shadow across the wall. She looked over her shoulder and saw that the tall figure already held a glowing candle with both hands. Its white light blazed bright, illuminating the entire chamber.

"We came prepared," the woman said.

"It is a pleasure to make your acquaintance, Princess Elspeth," said the shorter woman. She had a face that made Elspeth instantly feel at ease. Elspeth had to suppress an urge to run forward and hug the woman, to bury herself in the woman's arms, to be held tight against the woman's bosom, to be comforted and assured that nothing in the world could hurt her. Nothing in the world could hurt Marin.

"Who are you?" she asked.

"You stand in the presence of the Prophetess Tsema," the tall woman said. "She has something important to discuss with you."

"My dear princess," Tsema said, drawing forward. The train of her flowing white robe trailed behind her like water. "What disturbs your slumber?"

"I...I had a dream. A very realistic dream. Lifelike." Did she dare tell this woman she had these kinds of dreams? That these weren't dreams at all, that they were visions?

"Is that all?" the prophetess said, seating herself on the stool beside Elspeth's vanity. "Come. She indicated the floor beside her. "Come close, dear."

Elspeth obeyed, going close to the woman and kneeling beside her. "I have to admit I'm a little surprised to see you here.

The prophetess nodded. She understood what Elspeth said. "Tell me of your dream."

"I saw Marin. Marin, my beloved prince. He and his brother, Aster, are on a great quest. To save me."

"To save you?" the prophetess said. "A headstrong, mighty princess like you?"

This woman understands! Elspeth sighed. "Not everyone sees me that way. Princesses aren't supposed to be headstrong and formidable. We're supposed to be damsels in distress, waiting for our knights or our princes to come rescue us. That's the way it's always been."

"But you're going to be queen one day." It wasn't a question.

"Yes," Elspeth said. "That's what's special about Marin. He understands. I will rule by his side. And my sister will rule by Aster's."

297

Tsema nodded, taking in all of this. Something about her expression suggested she already knew what Elspeth told her. Elspeth was saying it out loud more for her own sake than for the sake of the prophetess.

"Terro, the god of the earth, has called for me to be sacrificed," she admitted. She didn't know why she felt ashamed to say it out loud. "My life is supposed to be forfeit. I'm supposed to be given over to the vraotyr to atone for Marin's boast that I was more beautiful than all the gemstones beneath the earth's surface. And now I have to sit here in my father's castle and wait for my prince to rescue me."

Elspeth sighed and stood. "It's insufferable. I should not be resigned to this fate, to be denied any control or authority just because I'm a woman. I'm a princess, and I'm going to be queen one day." She faltered, realizing what she said. "I'm going to be queen one day if…if…"

Tsema smiled. "If what?"

Elspeth went to the window, looking out again at the town below her. How could everyone be sleeping so peacefully? "If I'm not doomed to this evil fate."

"Is it fate?" Tsema asked. "Is it written in the stars, or does it lie in you?"

"How can it lie in me?" Elspeth turned away from the window, back toward Tsema. She looked into the woman's enormous blue eyes sparkling in the candlelight. "How can I have control over my destiny if I'm shut up here in this tower—an object, something to be controlled by men? That's not what I am. That's not *who* I am. Marin agreed. I am to be queen, and rule alongside my king. It will be a partnership between us. My father's kingdom will be mine, not my husband's."

"But now…"

"Now I have no choice but to stay here while my prince goes off and fulfills his quest to rescue me," said Elspeth. "And I'm to stay here as ransom. Or else the gods inflict their wrath on my father's kingdom."

Tsema stood. "Just because you stay here, according to the demands of the gods, this does not mean you are completely helpless. Have you heard of dreamsight?"

"Dreamsight?" Elspeth had never heard of it before, but she had a feeling she already understood what it meant.

"It is a gift that very few of us have," Tsema said. "But it is strong in you. You are just now learning to use it." She stepped closer to her handmaiden, who pulled a small crystal amulet from within the folds of her gossamer robe.

"My child," Tsema said, circling Elspeth's head with the amulet, "trust your heart and trust your mind. You are not without influence. Your prince will encounter three tests on his journey. He'll need assistance."

She reached down, took Elspeth's hand, and placed the crystal in her palm. "Be the queen you are meant to be."

And with those words, Tsema and her handmaiden vanished, as if they were never there to begin with. Sparkling shards of light danced in the air where they once stood before fading away, leaving the room in darkness.

Elspeth stared around, her breath caught in her throat. Even in that moment, she wondered whether it was a dream, even after she crawled back into her bed and lay beneath the covers, drifting off into whatever sleep she could.

When she woke up, sunlight shone around the edges of the curtains pulled across the window. Elspeth stretched, rolling over beneath her satin duvet. Something heavy rested in her hand.

She pulled her hand out from under the duvet and opened her fist. The crystal amulet sat in her palm, its silver chain winding down around her wrist. She'd been holding onto it all night while she slept.

I had another dream, she suddenly thought. She remembered! After the prophetess Tsema had paid her a visit and given her the amulet, she went back to sleep, and had another dream.

No, not a dream. A vision.

She'd seen Marin and Aster cross the desert and arrive at the foot of the Blood Mountains, led by a furry creature called Frik. She almost had the sense she'd been there with Marin and Aster in person.

Could I have really been there?

She stared at the amulet in her palm. A memory flooded back to her of what the wizard Udifeus had said to her. He suggested she was a magician. Could he have seen something in her, just as this prophetess did?

Elspeth climbed out of bed and reached for the robe hanging on a nearby dressing screen. Modesty be damned. Here she was, leaving her private chamber in nothing but her nightgown and robe, her hair down, her feet bare. If any servants saw her in the corridor, they would be aghast.

"Who cares?" she said out loud to herself as she walked. "I don't have time to waste on such formalities. Am I a princess or not?"

She arrived at the entrance to Carys's private chamber and slipped through the oaken door without knocking. Carys was already awake, sitting at the windowsill, staring out at the forest beyond. Her chestnut hair fell in loose waves over the shoulders of the purple kirtle she wore.

She looked up when Elspeth entered. "Good morrow."

"I need to talk to you," Elspeth said. "And I'm not sure whether you're going to believe this."

Elspeth told her everything. She told her about her sleepless night, about the visit from the prophetess and her handmaiden, about the vision she had of Marin and Aster in the desert. When she finished, Carys stared at her with a mystified expression as if Elspeth had found a way to turn sand into stardust.

"Elspeth, what does this mean?" Carys said. "This...this was magic at work here."

"I think so too."

"This crystal," Carys went on, "do you think it makes your visions stronger? Or gives you control over what happens in them?"

"I don't know. Whatever this crystal is—however I'm seeing these things—I don't have any explanation for it. But I don't think it's all coincidence. And I don't think these are all silly dreams. This is real. I know it is."

Carys fiddled her thumbs, as if she were trying to decide whether to ask the question on her mind. "Do you think you'll dream of them again tonight?"

Elspeth stood and paced the room. "I don't know. Maybe? But— but I think that this is the way the prophetess has given me to play a part in everything. I told her that I don't want to be some damsel in distress. I refuse to be."

Carys stood. Her hands were at the laces of her kirtle before she was even on her feet. "Come on. Help me change out of this dress, and then you'll have to go get changed yourself."

"Why?" Even as she asked the question, Elspeth complied. She reached out and took the laces, fumbled with the fabric, helping Carys undress.

"Because I'm going to put on fencing clothes. And so should you. You can't practice sword fighting in your nightgown."

"Sword fighting?" Elspeth laughed. "That's not what I meant—I want to control my own fate, but I don't have to wield a sword."

"But I will. I'll wield one, and I will need you to be my training partner."

"I don't understand. What's this about?"

"Because I'm going to have to play a part in all of this, too. Eventually." Carys let the kirtle fall to the floor. She went to her dressing screen where she had a pair of leggings and a tunic stashed away for just such emergencies as this one was. "I can't travel through space and

301

time in my dreams, Elspeth. So, I might as well prepare in other ways."

In a quarter hour, Carys and Elspeth ran into the courtyard outside the kitchen, both of them dressed in leggings and tunics, hastily stuffing pieces of unbuttered toast in their mouths for a quick breakfast. They spent the morning clanging swords together, steel ringing against steel as they kicked up dust from the ground. The servants left them alone. Even their father did not call on them for any royal duties.

Carys knew about sword fighting. She had secretly practiced it ever since she was a little girl, and by the time she was ten years old, she could best any stable boy or squire.

That was when their father learned about her skill. "My daughter wants to be a little warrior, does she?" he said with a smile. "Well, then, I will have to bring in a proper trainer for you. No sense in having you simply play around if this is truly what you want to do."

No amount of training had prepared Carys for fending off the goblins when their army had come for her and Elspeth. It had been a devastating defeat, and Carys didn't even have to confess to Elspeth that her pride and confidence suffered from it.

This was the first time in many weeks she had been able to practice with a sword, but none of the time off had dulled her ability. Elspeth kept up as best she could.

"You're a worthy training partner, sister," Carys said when they finished. Her face gleamed with sweat and her hair billowed around her. Her expression had lost none of its liveliness—still as full of energy as she was at the start of the morning.

"I do my best," Elspeth said. She put her sword back in its sheath and sat down on one of the stone benches nearby. "I have to keep up with my sister if she's to be the swordstress she aspires to be." *Swordstress* sounded like the wrong word, but it was all that came to mind. "What's the word for a woman who wields a sword? It's not a swordstress, is it? Knighttress? Fightress?"

"I don't think they have a proper word for women who fight," Carys said. "It just goes to show you how unfair this world is."

"When I inherit the throne, we will have an army of women as well as men," Elspeth said. "I'll put them in your charge."

Later that night, Elspeth—exhausted from fighting by the end of the day—took her supper in her private chamber. She asked her maids to draw her a warm bath so she could soothe her muscles and scrub the dust of the courtyard from her skin. Afterward, she put on her nightgown and crawled into bed, falling into a deep slumber a half-breath after her head touched the pillow. In her hand, she clutched the crystal the prophetess had given her.

The next morning, she awoke with dreams still vivid in her memory.

CHAPTER 40

There wasn't much Marin liked about the Blood Mountains, but he had to admit the sunrises were beautiful. The sun always appeared over the distant summits in a blaze of red and orange. It served as a reminder they made it to another day—he and Aster made progress little by little.

We're alive, he thought, watching the clouds glow fiery against the purple sky. *Another day behind us. Another day ahead of us.*

And one day fewer to accomplish this mission. With each new day, their time drew shorter. They didn't have forever to reach the top of the mountain and retrieve the sword. And that meant Elspeth was still in danger.

In the haze just before dawn, he stretched and crept away from the grassy patch where he and Aster slept the night before. They'd been following a creek up the mountain, a babbling stream of blue-black water that bounced and splashed over rocks in its path. It didn't just provide them with a steady direction upward—it was a source of water, something they could drink and something they could use to wash the dust of the trail off their skin and clothes.

Marin would never forget how glorious it had been when he and Aster first saw it, shortly after they first set foot on the Blood Mountains, when the gleaming red rocks they'd seen from across the desert mor-phed into a sloping green hillside dotted with trees and bushes, and the sound of rushing water met their ears. Even days later, the water was still a source of comfort to them.

They had left their horses at the foot of the mountain—unsuited for the rocky terrain such as their steeds would have been—and hiked for two days and two nights. On the morning of this third day, Marin felt hopeful.

Something is going to happen today, he told himself. *I know it. I know we're making progress.*

Marin counted in his head while he splashed cool water on his face to wash the dust and dirt away: They had wandered the desert for a day, spent two days hiking, so that left three days to reach the top of the mountain. The Wise Man of the Desert had said they would encounter three tests.

Three tests. He didn't like the prospect of it.

"Good morrow." Aster's voice startled him, and he jumped.

"Oh! Good morrow."

"Sorry. Didn't mean to scare you."

"No," Marin laughed. "It's all right." He got to his feet, wiping his wet hands on his trousers. "I was just thinking. About how much farther we have to go. And, you know, the three tests the Wise Man of the Desert said we would have to face."

"I've been thinking about those too. I wonder why we haven't seen anything so far."

"Maybe we have to get farther up the mountain," Marin said. "Closer to the vault, I mean."

But another day of hiking passed and they encountered nothing. They traversed the rough terrain with little incident besides a trip over an exposed tree root or the need to slip between two large boulders blocking their way.

By the time the sun dipped behind the trees again, Marin started to worry. *Another day come and gone*, he thought. *No challenges. Do we need to be worried we're on the wrong path?*

"I think maybe we press on for another hour and then we try to make camp for the night," he said. "It's going to be dark soon." They'd found it was easier to build a fire when there was at least a little bit of daylight left.

"Aye, and my feet are sore," Aster said. "Yours?"

"They've been worse. But I'm hungry."

Aster slipped his pack off from around his back and undid the ties. He looked into it. "We don't have much bread left."

"I know." Marin had been aware of it when they had stopped for lunch. "Only half a loaf for both of us. But it'll be enough for dinner tonight. Come tomorrow morning, we'll have to find something else."

"What else are we to find on this gods-forsaken mountain?" Aster said. "I haven't seen any trees with fruit or nuts. There are no animals we can hunt."

"I know."

"This isn't good, Marin."

"I know."

Marin paused. Rarely did anything interrupt the quiet stillness of the mountainside. Now something came from up ahead. Footsteps. Many footsteps, running, jumping, pounding the ground. And voices. High-pitched childish voices.

Am I hearing what I think I'm hearing?

He narrowed his eyes, trying to read Aster's expression. "What is that?"

"I don't know," Aster said. "It almost sounds as if it's children."

Just what Marin had suspected. But there couldn't have been children this far up the mountain, could there? Nobody actually lived up here, did they?

They rounded an enormous boulder standing along their route through the trees and found themselves approaching a derelict old structure. If it weren't for the shadows moving in the windows, Marin would've assumed the shack was abandoned. Crumbling bricks and stonework met with rough, weather-bleached wood.

The rickety door burst open with a resounding *slam* and a group of small children came running through it, bounding in their direction with unbridled excitement.

Eagerness showed on their young faces, a stark contrast to their dirty, threadbare clothes and unkempt hair, which would've suggested there was not much joy in their lives. They ran full speed out the door and several paces down the dirt path leading up to the house. They stopped at the edge of the rocky terrain to stare at Marin and Aster.

There were three of them at first, but these three were joined by another two who came running out the door and rushed over. It was difficult to tell which were boys and which were girls, their hair was so long and unruly and their bodies so emaciated.

"Hello," one of them said. The child looked up at Marin and Aster with large eyes almost too big for his head.

"Good evening," Marin greeted, bowing low to the youth. He remembered his manners. His clothes might have been nearly as tattered and torn as those the children wore, but it wouldn't do to forget he was a prince, at least by betrothal. He had a duty to King Hector, to Elspeth. That duty included caring for everyone they met on their journey.

"Pray, little ones, tell us who you are," he continued. "We are strangers in these parts."

"You're welcome to stay with us," one of the children said. She was taller than the others, though not by much. "It'll be dark soon. You won't want to sleep outside along the road, will you?"

Aster smiled. "Oh. That's awfully kind of you to invite us. But we must be invited by your mother and father before we can make

307

ourselves guests in your house."

"We have no mother and father," the smallest of the children said. "None of us does."

The way he said it sent a tingle down Marin's spine. Orphans. Living alone, up here in the mountains, in this decrepit house.

"You're all by yourselves?" he asked.

"Oh, yes," the tall girl replied. She folded her hands in front of her, demonstrating perfect manners that belied lack of parenting. She nodded. "That's why we were sent up here to live in this house together. Because none of us has mothers or fathers, and this is the only place there is for us in the world."

"Do you have any food?" one of the children asked. He toddled forward, holding cupped hands out in front of him.

Marin looked over at Aster. The response caught in his throat for only a moment, but he could tell that Aster shared his thought. *We have to give them something to eat.*

"Yes," Marin said. "Yes, but not much. You're welcome to whatever we have though."

Aster reached into the pack and pulled out the half-loaf of bread meant to be their dinner that night. He held it out to the children, and at once they clamored around him, each of them reaching to take it with eager hands.

"Thank you," the tall girl said. "Thank you ever so much!"

"We haven't eaten in three days," said the smallest boy.

They tore the bread apart and divided it among themselves, each of them taking a piece and stuffing it hungrily into their mouths. They chomped and chewed and gasped as if it were difficult for them to eat and breathe at the same time because they were so eager to devour the bread.

"I pray thee," the tall girl said, sending crumbs flying as she tried to talk with her mouth full. "Won't you stay here with us? It will be better than sleeping out here on the cold ground."

Marin nodded. "That would be most kind of you."

Two children reached forward and took his hand in theirs. He noticed scars and welts on the backs of their fingers. Their nails were overgrown and caked with mud. "Come with us," one of them said.

"Aye, c'mon," said the other.

Marin followed. They moved with a quick, eager pace for ones who were starving. *Oh, the energy of little children*, he thought.

The little boy with enormous sad eyes took Aster's hand and dragged him after the others. The children led Marin and Aster past a picket fence overgrown with briars bearing no roses, across an overgrown lawn and into the decrepit little cottage.

The door, sitting loose on its hinges, opened up into one large, open room—filthy but not cluttered. Indeed, there weren't any possessions to clutter the place. No toys, no comfort items, nothing spare or splendid at all.

Marin took in the sight as best he could by the dim light. Cobwebs stretched across corners and ceiling beams. Dust and grime coated everything, and patches of mold cropped up on the walls and windowsills. The only furniture in the room were several crudely built cots that stood without mattresses, and a table with no dishes or cutlery set out on it.

Two other children crouched in a corner when their fellows brought Marin and Aster inside. At the sight of visitors, the two jumped up and bounded over. "Who's this?" one of them called.

"These are our new friends," the littlest one said, except he pronounced it *fwiends*. Marin's heart melted.

"My name is Marin," he said. "And this is my brother, Aster."

Brother, he thought. This was the first time he had said it out loud in a while. *Or cousin? Cousin might indeed be more accurate.*

He wouldn't worry about that right now. At this moment, there were little ones who demanded his attention. Besides, whether he and Aster were cousins by blood didn't change the fact that Aster was his brother—always would be. And by the law of the land, they would be brothers when Marin married Elspeth and Aster married Carys.

"Look," said the tall girl, holding up the torn-up piece of bread—or what remained of it at least. "They brought us bread!" She thrust the crusty heel of the loaf toward the two little ones and let them break off pieces for themselves.

Marin caught Aster's eye. Despite the rumbling in their stomachs, they could think of no better use for the food.

After the children finished devouring the bread, Marin and Aster spent the night singing with them and telling stories. Aster showed them how to build a fire so they could keep warm, and by the light of the fire, Marin performed shadow puppets on the wall that made the littlest one actually squeal with delight. He clasped his hands together to cast the shape of a large dog on the wall, then barked and howled for several minutes straight for the amusement of all. Even Aster laughed as if he had forgotten the dire stress of everything else that awaited them outside that derelict little orphanage. The only thing that mattered, at least for the night, was caring for these little ones who had nobody else.

Elspeth would want you to do this, Marin thought. *As a prince, you have a duty to care for everyone you meet. You represent the throne.*

After the children fell asleep in their cots, Marin and Aster lay down on the floor of the cottage and got what little rest they could. They were awake again at first light, and after lining up each of the children to give them one last hug and encouraging word, they continued on their journey up the mountainside.

What a blessing that night was, Marin thought. *That might not have been something I expected along our journey, but I'm glad it happened.*

"How do you feel?" Aster asked, almost as if he could read

Marin's mind.

Marin thought for a second. "Good."

"So do I."

They continued for three or four paces. Aster started to laugh. "But I *am* hungry," he said. "I'm glad we were able to feed them. But I do wish we had some food left for ourselves." He reached his hand around and slapped his pack. They both stopped.

It sounded full.

"Aster…" Marin hesitated, not sure whether to believe the sound.

Aster slung the pack off his shoulder and tugged the drawstrings open. His face lit up.

"Marin!" he exclaimed, his voice rising. "It's full. My pack is full!"

"What?"

Aster handed the pack over to him so he could look inside. Three loaves of bread filled the pack, along with bunches of grapes and carrots. The cloth wrapping was full again, suggesting it held a full chunk of cheese inside it.

Food, Marin thought. *Food!*

He reached inside and grabbed one of the loaves of bread, tearing it apart and handing half of it to Aster. They both paused on their feet, forgetting about everything else around them, while they scarfed the bread down, savoring its fluffy inside and crusty outside. It was even warm!

"Has anything ever tasted better?" Aster laughed.

Marin smacked his lips, trying to chew and swallow what was too large of a bite he had taken. "But I don't understand," he said with his mouth full. "We gave them the only food we had last night."

"I have no idea how this happened," Aster said.

Neither of them had questioned it in the heat of the moment. They had been so hungry they just started eating on sheer impulse. But now confusion set in.

"It has to be some kind of magic," Marin said.

"Do you think it's because I wished for it?" Aster held up his hand and indicated the bronze ring. "You heard me. I said, *I do wish we had some food left for ourselves*. Or something like that."

Marin shook his head. "That's not how it worked before though," he said. "You have to say, *If only*. Not, *I wish*."

"Then how do we explain this?"

"I don't think we can," Marin said. "We ought to go back. To share it with the orphans. We have more than enough now."

"Aye," Aster said.

But when they retraced their steps, weaving their way back the way they came, the ramshackle cottage was nowhere to be found—all that remained was a clearing in the trees where it once stood.

"I think...I think maybe what we just witnessed was a miracle," Marin said. "We gave the last of our food to those in need. And we're being rewarded for it."

"You really think it works that way?" Aster said. "That miracles exist?"

"I don't know what I believe, Aster." Marin hadn't expected to have this conversation, but it came spilling out of him anyway. "I'm not sure whether fate or destiny is real. Or witchcraft, or prophecy, or demigods, or vraotyrs. None of this makes any sense."

"No. No, it doesn't, does it?"

Marin sat down on a nearby log and reached for Aster's pack, helping himself to some fruit. While they had plenty of food, it made sense to enjoy as much of it as they needed. Another long day of hiking waited ahead of them.

"But," Marin said, "I do get the feeling that things are falling into place the way they should be, don't you? I feel as if we're part of this big, grand adventure and everything is just...I don't know...working out the way it's supposed to."

Aster didn't reply.

Marin took a bite of an apple. "When you read a legend or ballad, you always get the sense that it's always going to turn out all right in the end. That the hero will win and the villain will be defeated, and that virtue will be rewarded, and that everything will be at peace when the story concludes."

"Aye."

"Real life isn't always like that. Or at least, it never had been for me or you. But don't you get the sense that all of this," Marin gestured vaguely, suggesting not just their surroundings but everything that had been happening to them for days and weeks, "is all headed in the right direction? That everything is going to work out the way it's supposed to?"

An image flashed across Marin's mind of the Wise Man of the Desert, the Great Book of Records spread out across his lap. Was it possible that this was all some great story they were just living out? How much control did they actually have over destiny?

No, he thought, *those records were determined by choices we made. That's exactly why the Wise Man couldn't tell us everything we needed to know, isn't it?*

He tossed the apple core into the nearby foliage and stood. "Sorry, I'm just rambling now."

Aster nodded. "Marin, I don't know any more than you do. But there's one thing I do know—our mission isn't over yet."

CHAPTER 41

The dreams were more vivid this time. The cave, the giant—and another princess. A princess just like Elspeth herself.

When she woke up, a little breathless with a sheen of sweat on her brow, morning sunlight streamed in through the parted curtains, glittering on the marble floor of her chamber. Another day had come. Another day until her doom awaited her. Another day closer to when Marin's quest had to be fulfilled.

There's no reason to have doubt, she told herself. Marin would be back to rescue her. He would. She was certain of that, especially with the progress he and Aster were making on their trek up the Blood Mountains and the way they overcame the tests.

The tests. Last night had been the second. The first had been the orphanage, and the second...

Elspeth sat up, kicking the covers away and setting her bare feet on the floor. She paused, trying to remember. It had all been so vivid while it happened, but now that she awoke, some of it faded from her memory. They had passed the second test though—that was all that mattered, and that much she remembered.

"I...I helped them," she whispered to herself.

She couldn't explain it. None of it made any sense. She couldn't remember much, but she did remember the way the giant looked into her eyes. She stared him down, and for a moment, she had the power to hypnotize him. At least long enough for the other princess—the one whom the giant held captive—and her prince to be reunited.

Elspeth stood and paced her room. She had appeared to Marin and Aster, not just witnessing them the way she had with her dream-sight previously. She'd made contact with them, talked to them, joined them on their mission for the day. The only explanation she could think of was that the power of her dreamsight was getting stronger. She reached up and touched the crystal around her neck. Her fingers pressed around warmth, as if the crystal had a life of its own.

She had to tell Carys. Going to her dressing screen, she removed her nightgown and pulled on a simple white chemise and silver kirtle with blush-colored trimming. When she looked appropriate—no need to call for one of her handmaidens, she thought—she stepped out into the corridor and made her way to the courtyard.

By now, the sun hung high in the sky. She didn't need to look at a clock to know it must have been late morning. Her cheeks burned with the thought of it, realizing that to anyone who didn't know better, they might have thought the crown princess was lying lazily in bed far past an appropriate time for rising. If only they could have known she had spent the night facing a giant in an out-of-body experience.

Carys waited for her in the garden. After days of fight training and brandishing swords at one another, Elspeth had to admit it felt very ladylike and comfortable for the two of them to be meeting in one of the palace's lush gardens, surrounded by flowers and sparkling fountains, birds chirping overhead and trees spreading their branches to shade them from the sun. Both of them were dressed like ladies, in flowing gowns and jewelry fit for their station.

Seated on a stone bench with needlework to occupy her hands, Carys looked up as Elspeth came out through the archway leading from the hall. "Good morrow!"

"Good morrow."

Elspeth must have had an expression on her face or a tone to her voice that gave away the many emotions she was trying to hold back, because Carys immediately narrowed her eyes and smirked. "Any dreams last night?"

"Yes." Elspeth sighed, then looked around. A servant or gardener might be working nearby in the courtyard and overhear. Not that she was doing anything wrong by using her dreamsight—after all, she wasn't leaving the palace, strictly speaking—but she didn't think she was quite ready for anyone at court to know she had this kind of power.

She stepped closer to Carys and lowered her voice. "And not just a vision this time. I made contact."

Carys's eyes went wide. "What?"

"I made contact," Elspeth said. "I actually talked to Marin and Aster, and I was there when they completed the second task."

"The second task. They've done it?"

Elspeth sat down on the bench beside Carys. "Yes. We defeated a giant." She hesitated. "And...and we freed a prince and princess he had prisoner."

Carys gasped, then laughed, and finally stared at Elspeth wide eyed and open mouthed. "No! What? A giant?" She shook her head, almost as if she didn't believe it—as if she thought maybe Elspeth could be mistaken. "But there are no more giants left. They died off ages and ages ago."

"Well, one remains. Or at least, one did. Until Marin and Aster defeated him."

Carys set her needlepoint down beside her on the bench. "Tell me everything. How is their quest going?"

Elspeth shrugged. She knew the quest was going as well as it could, though no quest was ever simple or easy. She would be foolish to play down the struggles that Marin and Aster faced. "They're persevering," Elspeth said. "They're making progress, but it isn't without its challenges. I didn't know the Blood Mountains and the desert surrounding them would be so dangerous."

"King Donovan wouldn't hide his kingdom's sacred relics anywhere somebody could easily find them, I suppose," Carys observed.

"No, he wouldn't," Elspeth said. She smiled, changing her tone, trying to be more optimistic. "But now Marin and Aster have passed two of the three tests. Only one remains."

"Yes, you've already told me that, Elspeth, so stop teasing me," Carys said. "I need to hear what happened."

Elspeth paused. It wasn't that she was teasing Carys. She didn't want to admit how quickly the vision was fading from her mind, how much of it felt fuzzy and distant, as if it truly were a dream that didn't fully make sense and could be easily forgotten now that she was out of bed and going about her day. But this hadn't been a dream—and she didn't want to forget the experience of it.

She tried to remember how it started. "Well, I remember...I remember standing there along the mountain trail," Elspeth said. She closed her eyes and tried to picture it all again. "I could smell the moss and wood, and I could feel the tingle of sunlight on my face. I hardly had time to realize where I was or what was happening before I saw Marin and Aster coming up the path. I wasn't expecting them to see me, but they did—they did! It was like I was there!"

With that, she opened her eyes again and turned to Carys. Her sister stared at her expectantly. "What did they say? What did you tell them?"

"I explained everything as best I could," Elspeth said. "This isn't something that can be easily explained, especially when this is the first time I've actually made contact with somebody when I've seen them in my dreams." A small part of her wished she had told Marin about this part of herself before he set off for his quest. She could have told him that during her time in captivity within the goblin fortress, she had seen her father's mourning and the goblin's battle council.

But how could she have known that she would dream about Marin and Aster while they were off on their quest, let alone grow so much in this power that she could actually make contact, even though she still had no control over it? "I told them I have this power that has been letting me watch over them on their journey," she told Carys. "But I was just as surprised as they were that they were able to see me this time and that I was able to talk to them."

Carys nodded. "So…the second test?"

Elspeth opened her mouth to continue telling the story, but she couldn't remember what happened next. "Oh…"

"What's wrong?" Carys said.

"It's all a blur now," Elspeth said, standing and beginning to pace. "There was a princess named Hala, and she was under a spell that made her fall in love with the giant."

"But giants can't do magic," Carys protested.

"No," Elspeth said, turning back and returning to her seat on the bench, "I don't think it was the giant who put her under the spell."

Elspeth remembered that much. She and Marin and Aster had hardly finished their astonished greeting with each other before they heard singing coming from not far off the trail. They followed the sound and came upon a young woman dressed in nothing more than a tattered wisp of white silk. She brushed her flowing auburn hair as she sat singing to herself and looked up at them with a vacant, dreamy expression in her eyes as they approached.

"She told us that she was the bride-to-be of Sefvar the Great," Elspeth recalled. "It was clear from her first words that she was not right—that something possessed her. And then when her beloved Sefvar came thundering out of his cave to retrieve her, we had to run

318

and hide behind a nearby thicket. She didn't follow us or pay us any mind at all, almost as if she forgot about us the moment we were out of sight."

Elspeth's fingers twitched with the memory. She twisted her hands in her lap, remembering the way she'd held Marin's hand from their hiding place behind the thicket, horrified as the girl who'd just introduced herself to them as Hala was lifted up and carried inside the cave without any protestation or expression of revulsion, despite the way the great brute appeared, towering at a height of what must have been ten or twelve feet tall, with a twisted face, bulging eyes, and mangled teeth.

"But you didn't run away," Carys observed before Elspeth could continue the story.

Elspeth shook her head. "How could we? Not when somebody was in trouble." She paused. "I guess it should have been easy for us to run away, really, when there was no need to meddle in a conflict that had nothing to do with us. But Marin never even seemed to consider that."

That part of the dream remained vivid in her mind: Marin, holding her hand tight, looking her in the eye. *I know time is of the essence if I'm to finish this quest, but we can't leave this girl to such a fate*, he told her.

"I think it's in his nature, Carys," Elspeth explained, her heart hammering at the thought. "He can't help himself. Besides, he and Aster are no longer wandering adventurers the way they once were. They're princes now—and they have an obligation to help others."

Carys nodded.

"So, I told him we would do it together," Elspeth said. "I would be their aid in whatever way I could."

"What did you do?"

Elspeth hesitated. Again, the dream came in and out of memory. "The girl's prince—Prince Vaz—was imprisoned off in the woods. The giant had him chained up. He was going to be traded to the cult of sorcerers who put the spell on Princess Hala and made her fall in love with the giant."

She exhaled deeply, fidgeting in her seat. Carys leaned in close and put a hand on her shoulder. "It's all right, Elspeth," she said. "There's nobody around. There's no need to be so prim and proper here if you don't want to be."

Elspeth couldn't help laughing, then quickly calmed herself. She slouched, leaned forward, trying to relieve herself of some of the stress. She hadn't realized how much the night's adventure had taken out of her. Now all the emotions came rushing back to her as she tried to remember it and relay it to Carys. She was reliving it all over again.

"So, what happened?" Carys asked.

Elspeth straightened herself back up, folded her hands carefully in her lap, every bit a princess once again. "Marin…Marin was able to break Prince Val's chains with a swing of his sword. Then…" She paused, remembering. "We snuck into the giant's cave."

Carys grinned. "I can't believe you, Elspeth. You, alongside those men, infiltrating a cave to face a giant."

"Well, I couldn't let them go alone, now could I?" Elspeth said.

A memory flashed through her mind—Marin, gently cupping her face in his hand, trying to persuade her to stay outside the cave. *It'll be too dangerous*, he told her.

Whatever danger there is, we'll face it together, she replied. *There must be a reason I've come to you in my dreams like this. I can't wait out here and do nothing.*

She had to admit she loved the way Marin wanted so fiercely to protect her, that he wouldn't let her follow him into such danger. But when she insisted, he respected her. In truth, she thought, he might've even been a little grateful to have her there beside him for this peril.

"It's a good thing I was with them," Elspeth said. "Because we never would have been a match for the giant otherwise. I…I did something."

Something. That was the only word she could describe it. She had managed to work some kind of magic without even realizing what she was doing.

"What do you mean?" Carys asked.

"When we entered the cave, we saw that the giant was going to hurt Princess Hala," Elspeth said. "He had a greedy look in his eye and an unseemly smile on his face. We saw him reach forward to pull away the threadbare silks that Hala was wrapped in."

Carys looked sick at the very thought of it. "Oh…"

"Marin and Aster bounded forward together, both of them with their swords drawn, ready to fight this giant against all odds," Elspeth said. "It wasn't much of a battle—they didn't stand a chance against anything or anyone as big as this."

A chill went through her, one that belied the warm, sunny morning in the courtyard garden. She trembled and swallowed the lump in her throat.

"Carys, I stepped forward and did something. I made eyes with the giant and it froze momentarily. It stopped, as if locked in that moment in time. It was only a few seconds, but it was long enough for Prince Vaz to run forward and kiss Princess Hala and break the spell."

With that, Carys groaned. "Oh, true love's kiss breaking the spell? These evil magicians really must get more imaginative with their curses."

Elspeth couldn't resist smiling at that despite how much she was wrapped up in the memory. "I know, I know. But it worked, and once Princess Hala was freed from the spell, she recognized Prince Vaz— and she was horrified by the giant."

"And that's when you escaped?" Carys asked, excitedly.

"Well, not exactly," Elspeth said. "Whatever power I had over the giant, it broke at that moment. But when the giant saw that Princess Hala no longer loved him—and that Prince Vaz was free—he went into a wild rage. He started punching and kicking at the walls of the cave."

"Oh, no," Carys murmured, already understanding what

that meant.

"Oh, yes," Elspeth replied. "The cave came crumbling in. We ran, and we escaped—barely! The giant, however, was no more. Crushed by the rocks he brought down upon himself."

"So, that's it, then," Carys said. "The second test completed."

Elspeth nodded, smiling so wide it hurt her face. "Yes. The second test completed. We said goodbye to Prince Vaz and Princess Hala, and they departed to return to their home kingdom across the far reaches of Monte Prospera. Then…then, it was merely I and Marin and Aster again."

Warmth spread through Elspeth. Frightening though the dream had been, and upsetting as she found the experience of reliving it, she couldn't resist feeling proud of Marin—and Aster, too—for all they accomplished. Marin had been the one to rescue her from the goblin fortress, and he was the one to step up to accept the quest when nobody else in her father's kingdom would. Even the bravest of knights could not claim to be half the man this peasant boy was proving himself to be.

"Will you try to make contact in your dreams again?" Carys asked.

"I hope so," Elspeth replied. "I hope so."

She hoped. But there was no guarantee. Just as there was no guarantee Marin and Aster would succeed in this quest, Elspeth had to remind herself. She kept believing, holding onto hope, feeling confident. But did she have any true guarantee?

Maybe this had been the last she would see of them until they returned home, assuming they ever did return home. The first two tests had been easy enough for them, but what if the third test was the one that did them in? The third test would likely be most difficult of all. That's how it always worked in quests like this, or so the legends said.

Carys must have sensed Elspeth's need for distraction because she stood. "Come on, Elspeth," she said, walking toward the archway that led into the castle from the courtyard. "It's almost afternoon. What do you say we change out of these fine dresses and put on our training clothes for some sword fighting? I'm starting to get the feeling I might need to put my skills to use very soon."

Elspeth followed. *I'm starting to get that feeling too, little sister,* she thought.

CHAPTER 42

Marin still couldn't believe Elspeth had appeared to him. It was as if he'd dreamed it. But still, she had spoken to him. Aster had been able to see her and speak with her too.

Then she disappeared just as mysteriously as she had appeared.

"What do you make of that?" he asked Aster that night as they sat beside their campfire. They cooked two small fumble-bats they had managed to poach. Despite their small size, the creatures offered plentiful meat for at least one meal. The bats hung from toasting sticks, sizzling and popping over the blaze of the campfire. The rich smell made Marin's stomach groan.

"It was strange. I won't deny it," Aster said. "But I don't think we should put too much thought into it."

"Why not?" Marin said. *Did I sound worried?* "I wasn't worried," he added quickly. "I was just…thinking out loud. But do you know something I don't? Why shouldn't I be worried?"

Aster laughed. "You'll need to be a lot less anxious when you're a king," he said. "You can't be overthinking every little thing somebody says to you."

Marin stretched out his legs next to the fire. "You're right."

"I said that you shouldn't worry about it," Aster began, "because

I think that this is a very real ability. Maybe it's something Elspeth wasn't even aware she had. It's not foresight or prophecy—that's what happens when you're able to see the future. It's dreamsight—in your dreams, you're able to see things that are happening at that very moment. You can even have interaction with what you're seeing in your dreams, if your powers are really strong."

"And how do you know about dreamsight?" Marin asked.

Aster cracked a smile. "You weren't the only one who grew up reading a book or two. Ilth still had a few around the house, and I had a chance to peek into them from time to time. Don't look so surprised."

Marin opened his mouth to say something but had no reply. He nodded instead.

The fire crackled.

He couldn't forget what Aster had said a moment ago. It was going to nag at him if he didn't say something. "I don't think I'm fit to be king," he said.

"Why do you say that?" Aster said. "Of course, you are."

Marin looked away. Maybe Aster would think it was just the smoke from the fire making his eyes burn. "It's so much pressure. Don't you get it, Aster? I'm just some farm boy who fell into this position. I'm not anything special."

"You didn't just fall into this position," Aster said. "That's like saying our life is written out in the stars. Remember what the prophetess told you back on the first day after we ran away? If you hadn't taken the tide when it was in your favor, you'd still be there on Ilth's farm."

"But…"

"There are plenty of people who wouldn't do what you're doing here," Aster went on. "Going on this quest to rescue Elspeth. You do what's right even when it isn't easy. That's what makes a leader—not somebody who feels comfortable wielding power. You know, sometimes I think it's the people who like power the most who are the ones who shouldn't have it."

Marin shifted his position and leaned up against the tree behind him. The rough bark pressed into his back. "And you came with me," he said. "You came with me when nobody else did."

"I'm going to stick by your side through thick and thin," Aster said. "You can always count on that. I trust you. I trust your instincts. I trust your leadership."

Marin nodded. Aster always knew the right things to say. "How are you always so self-assured?" he asked.

Aster looked pensive for a second. "You know, I don't really know. I guess when I start to have doubts in my head, when I start to worry that I'm not good enough, I hear all of those thoughts in my head in Ilth's voice. She's the one who's telling me I'm not good enough or I'll never amount to anything—and it's easier for me to shove those thoughts aside that way, because who really cares what she thinks? She always put us down, and look where we are now. Besides, if I heard somebody talking about someone I cared about, someone I re-spected—like you, maybe—the way I'm thinking about myself, would I stand by and just let those things get said? Of course, I wouldn't. I'd stand up for you. You know that. Well, I deserve to stand up for myself, too."

Marin nodded. "Aye." It was all he could manage to say.

They ate their dinner, then settled back on the grass, talking long into the night as they watched the stars overhead. Marin pointed out a few constellations he recognized, recalling how some of them were heroes from myths and epics that generations before them had told. Even if the stars didn't spell out everyone's destiny, there might at least be a chance of being preserved forever in the heavens, where future generations could look up and admire you.

The sun was already high in the sky by the time they shouldered their bags and continued up the mountainside the next morning, having let themselves sleep in a few hours and rest after the past few days of peril.

"I think we might make it to the top today," Marin said, staring up at the highest summit. Just past an overgrowth of foliage, it looked like an opening in the rockface led into some sort of cavern. The vault they sought must have been just beyond there. "Maybe by this afternoon if we don't run into any surprises."

"Marin, when have we ever not run into surprises? I'd be surprised if we didn't run into any surprises. Oh, look—what's that up ahead?!"

Now I've spoken too soon, Marin thought. *Surprises to set us back a few hours. Of course!*

Several paces ahead of them, an expansive gulf divided the mountain landscape. A rickety bridge stretched from one side to the other, serving as the only connection between them and the next leg of their trek. The ropes holding the bridge bore years of grime, and the wooden boards forming the walkway were discolored and warped. The whole thing swayed in the breeze. If somebody breathed on the bridge too hard, it would likely snap apart and go hurtling into the deep gully.

They had to cross it.

"This is bad," Marin said. He paused a few feet away from the stony edge and looked down. Far below, rapid water heaved and churned between the two sides of the ravine, splashing up around sheer rocks where anyone or anything falling from up above was fated to be dashed to bloody shreds.

A sign stood posted at the entry to the bridge. Black letters splayed across its weather-beaten surface: *CROSS ONLY IF YOU ARE WORTHY.*

"Truly?" Marin murmured. "Truly, is this what we're up against?"

Aster must have had their conversation from the night before on his mind too. "It seems a little coincidental," Aster said. "Are the gods playing some kind of cruel prank on us?"

"What other kinds of pranks do the gods like to play except cruel ones?" Marin muttered cynically. *That is*, he thought, *if the gods actually deign to participate in the affairs of humankind.* "I guess we have no choice but to go across."

"Cross only if you are worthy," Aster read from the sign. "Say, that makes me think…I mean, I know this bridge looks rickety and everything, but maybe it's a lot stronger than we think. Maybe it's able to support our weight if we know that we're worthy."

"And if we have doubts about that?" Marin asked. A heavy lump formed in his throat.

"Marin. Don't tell me you have any questions about your worthiness. After what we talked about last night?"

Marin shrugged.

"Maybe it's best if you go second," Aster said.

"Thanks."

Marin wanted to insist on going first—after all, it was the sort of brave move he would need to make if he wanted to prove himself. Besides, he wasn't afraid. At this point, there was very little that could scare him or intimidate him.

But if the bridge's resilience depended on his own sense of worthiness…

Aster had already taken several nervous steps out onto the bridge, cautiously putting one foot in front of the other. The bridge's ropes creaked as he shifted his weight. "It's, uh…it's not as bad as it looks." His voice quivered as he said it. "I just can't look down. I can't look down."

One more step, then another. Aster moved slowly but never faltered.

Halfway across, he paused. He put his left foot out in front of him and the board underneath him slid along the rope.

Marin gasped.

But the board didn't give way. Aster pushed forward, taking two more steps, the bridge swinging back and forth as he moved. Three more steps. Four more.

When he finally set foot on solid ground again, Aster's sigh of relief was so loud that Marin could hear it from all the way across the ravine. Aster turned, his face alight. "Made it!"

"Good work!" Marin called.

"Your turn now!" Aster sounded so confident in him.

Marin nodded. "Right."

He approached the bridge and couldn't resist looking down into the gully beneath it. If the bridge snapped, he was done for. The sound of rushing water rose from all those feet below. The sharp points of the sheer rocks in the river looked almost as if they were snarling up at him.

"Remember," Aster said. "You're worthy."

Worthy. Marin tried to picture Ilth doing something like this. There was no way she would have it in her, not the old hag who depended on two boys to do everything for her, the old hag who never did anything for herself but always complained when the littlest thing wasn't to her satisfaction. He wouldn't give Ilth the satisfaction of knowing her years of abuse still haunted him.

With one careful step, he eased his way out onto the bridge. The sway of it surprised him. He grabbed the ropes by his side to steady himself. The whole thing shook under his weight. His breath caught in his throat.

This is what it means to be brave, he thought to himself. *Bravery's not about never being afraid. It's about what you do when you are afraid. It's about acting even when you're terrified. And Elspeth is counting on me. My father-to-be, King Hector, is counting on me. All the people of Blunia—my future subjects—are counting on me.*

As if cued by his thoughts, Elspeth's voice came from behind him. "I'm counting on you, Marin."

He turned his head. She stood there behind him on the side of the gully he had just left. Her gold hair shone in the sun—it was unmistakably her.

"Elspeth!"

"Keep going," she said. "You're halfway there."

Marin looked back at the expanse of bridge in front of him. He was only a quarter of the way there, but if believing he was halfway there gave him the strength and courage he needed, then he could tell himself that. Why not?

He took another step, then another. The ropes creaked as he moved.

"You've got it," Aster said from the other side.

"It's easy, Marin," Elspeth called from behind him.

Snap! The wooden plank under his foot gave way, broke apart from the rest of the bridge. It plummeted into the gully, cracking and splintering as it struck a rock. Fragments of it flew in all directions upon impact. That could be him—that could be him if he fell.

And if he fell, then his mission was forfeit. Elspeth would die, or the kingdom of Blunia would be destroyed by the vraotyr. He would fail everyone!

Whoosh! The ropes at his sides tore and whipped in opposite directions. The entire bridge gave out from under him. For an awful, prolonged second, he hovered in midair. Aster and Elspeth screamed.

The next thing he knew, driven by sheer instinct, his hand closed around one of the wooden planks that used to be the floor of the bridge. Feet dangling beneath him, he went swinging across the gully and slammed into the cliffside.

"Marin!"

Aster knelt at the edge of the cliff above him, extending his arm down to help. His hand dangled at least six feet away.

Down below, the river raged. The rocks glared up at him with their sheer edges, ready to tear him apart if he fell.

Marin's heart pounded in his ear. His stomach lurched. What would it be like to plummet to his death, to be broken into bloody bits on impact?

His grip weakened on the board he clutched. He pulled himself up to grab the board above it. Perspiration made his palms slippery. Heaving a deep breath, he strengthened his grip, then grabbed another board, clinging desperately to hold himself up.

It's because I'm doubting myself! What Aster had surmised about the bridge was right—the whole thing had snapped because somebody who didn't recognize his own worth tried to cross it. And here he was, paying the price for his folly.

How was he supposed to realize his own worth now though, while dangling from a broken bridge over a deep ravine?

He struggled to lift himself up and grab the next board above him.

"You've got it!" Aster called down. "Just a few more."

Marin's cheeks burned. It wasn't just the sheer terror that crippled him now. It was the knowledge that he wasn't worthy!

"You've got to climb," Elspeth called. "You've got to climb, Marin."

He looked over his shoulder to see her standing as close to the edge of the ravine as she dared get. Wind whipped at her nightgown. Her hair had fallen out of place and hung over her eyes. Her expression showed distress like he'd never seen, even when she found out in front of the entire court she had to be sacrificed. "Please, Marin!"

"You can do this!" Aster said. "Come on!"

Marin heaved a deep breath and grabbed at the next board up. He closed his eyes, blocking out everything—the expanse beneath him, the way the rough boards cut into his hands, the creaking of the ancient ropes, the pounding of his heart, the trickle of sweat down his temples.

"Don't doubt yourself now," Aster said. "I'm counting on you!"

Everyone is counting on me! The thought should have been overwhelming. But it wasn't. It gave him strength instead of despair.

People needed him. What would Ilth have to say about that? Ilth never would've wanted him thinking people respected him or valued him! If only she could see him now—overcoming dangers like this, saving the girl he loved, proving himself worthy of inheriting a kingdom he would do a damn good job of ruling.

He opened his eyes and grabbed at the next rung.

Aster stretched his arm down as far as he could go. "Come on!"

One more rung, then another. At last, Marin took hold of Aster's hand, and the next second, Aster was helping him climb up over the edge of the cliff and onto the soft grass and solid ground. The last of the bridge snapped free of the posts holding its ropes in place, and it crumpled into the ravine.

Marin gasped, heaved, trying to calm himself. "We made it!" he said. "We actually made it!"

Aster beamed at him. "And you're more aware of your worth than you would've let on. You wouldn't have been able to cross if you weren't."

"Aye," Marin said. "Aye, I guess so." Marin sat up. "It's as you said—I'm not going to listen to the voices that say the things Ilth would have wanted me to hear. She has no power over me. You believe in me. And Elspeth believes in me."

Elspeth. He leaped to his feet and looked out across the ravine. Elspeth stood on the other side, her smile shining.

"You passed. You passed. Marin, this was the third test. You're almost there!"

The air around her shimmered with stardust and she faded from view, leaving only grass and shrubbery where she once stood. Almost as if she had not been there at all.

"I'm never going to get used to that," Marin said. "Her sudden comings and goings, I mean. It's good to have her here, but I still don't understand how she's able to do it."

"Like I said. Dreamsight. Maybe she's guarding us—like an angel or something."

Marin's gaze drifted down the ravine. "Thank you," he murmured to Aster. "I couldn't have done that without you."

"It was all you. I helped pull you up at the very end, but you were the one who climbed up that bridge like a ladder. You should've seen yourself."

The third test. They'd passed. Now all that remained was entering the vault!

Marin looked up at the summit of the mountain above them. It wasn't a far hike away. They were nearly there!

Then it would just be a matter of getting back to Blunia in time—and facing the vraotyr.

A shiver went through Marin. After all their hardships so far, the real challenge was still ahead of them.

CHAPTER 43

These dreams made sleep difficult for Elspeth. Not that she likely would have been sleeping soundly anyway. The idea of being sacrificed to an ancient monster was enough to disturb the sleep of even the most exhausted princess.

But though she had been in bed, deep in slumber, unaware of anything that was going on around her physical body while she lay, Elspeth never actually felt as if she had been asleep. She returned from these adventures with Marin and Aster on the other side of the world feeling as if she had been awake all night long.

As the clang of steel on steel rang in the courtyard, Elspeth countering at her sister to the best of her ability, she found herself struggling more than she should have been. More than she wanted to admit.

"I may need a nap, Carys." She lowered her sword and ran her arm across her brow to wipe the sweat away.

Carys stepped back. "Of course. It would be good for you." She paused. "Did you see Marin and Aster last night?"

Still breathless from their practice, Elspeth nodded. She righted herself, sheathed her sword, and crossed over to the bench where they kept waterskins. "You won't believe what happened," she said, opening one of the skins and taking a long drag of water.

She explained everything that happened on the bridge.

"But they're all right?" Carys asked when Elspeth finished the story.

"Oh, yes, they're all right," Elspeth said. "They've passed all three tests the Blood Mountains had in store for them. The only thing now…"

The next words caught in her throat. How was she supposed to admit this? If she said it out loud, would that make it real?

Carys must have recognized her distress. "What? What is it?"

This was stupid. If she couldn't tell Carys, then whom could she tell? "Carys, I think…I think there's something guarding that vault."

"What?"

"I don't know—a dragon perhaps? It's a premonition I had. They're still going to have to face a horrible beast if they're going to get into that vault."

Maybe, she told herself, it wasn't worth believing what she saw. Maybe she had just dreamed about the dragon and that was all it was—a dream.

Her hand closed on the crystal around her neck. It felt warm. Tsema had given her the crystal so she would have greater control over her dreamsight—so she could move back and forth between time and space, and so she could see visions more vividly. Even so, it was still a struggle. She was still a novice at this magic.

Carys shook her head. "Maybe what you saw was the vraotyr. And you thought it was a dragon guarding the vault."

"No. I saw it guarding the vault at the top of the Blood Mountains. Marin and Aster are going to have to face it."

"Why hasn't anyone mentioned this up until now?" Carys said. "No rumors or stories have talked about King Donovan leaving a dragon to guard the Royal Vault of Grythium."

Elspeth put her hands to her temples. "I don't know. I don't know. I wish I understood. All I know is what I saw." She buried her face in her hands. "And I saw a dragon, one that was far too big for two men to fight off alone."

"What about two men and a woman?"

Dropping her hands from her face, Elspeth looked up.

"I mean it, Elspeth," Carys said. "I would've gone with them in the very beginning if I thought it would've helped. I stayed here to be with you."

Elspeth stammered. This must have been why Carys had such an instinct to improve her fighting skills over the past few days. All these hours slinging swords in the courtyard—Carys sensed deep down she had to be ready for something.

"You've been my strength these past few days," Elspeth said. "Truly. But Carys, you can do a better job of protecting me if you go join them. I can't leave the palace except in my dreams, but you—well, there's nothing that says you can't go. You don't have to stay here and waste your time while the men undertake quests on our behalf."

"The only problem is Father. He would never allow it."

That fired Elspeth up. "If we're to be queens one day, we need to take on some sovereignty and self-sufficiency." She touched the crystal, her mind racing. An idea flashed into her mind, fully formed. "I know! I'll make contact with anyone Marin and Aster met along their journey. I'm sure I have the power to do that—if I have the power to visit Marin and Aster, why can't I seek out those they have helped? I'll see whether I can get them to come to their aid now."

"This is madness," Carys said.

"Is it?" Elspeth said. "Don't you get it, Carys? This fight is much bigger than what we can see right now. If I'm given to the vraotyr, how long until the gods make you a victim of their petty games? What happens if King Donovan finds out Marin and Aster tried to steal his sacred relics, and he uses this as an excuse to launch an attack on Father? But if our men actually fulfill this quest—and we help them do it—then we're proving ourselves the masters of this whole land, and who out there can question our right to rule?"

"I see what you're saying, but…"

"Blunia is our kingdom," Elspeth said, "and we can't just sit here and let things happen around us." She paused and sighed. "Well, actually, I *do* have to sit here and let things happen around me. According to Terro's demands. But you—you don't have to. You can go to them and aid their cause. Even if they retrieve the sword from inside the vault, how are they supposed to make it back here in only a few days? There's a reason you've been training so hard with your sword, don't you see? It wasn't just some whim that you picked up. You're going to have to fight."

Carys reached out and took Elspeth's hands. "It will take a different kind of bravery to leave you here alone."

"I won't be alone," Elspeth said. "I'll be with you the whole time, just as I've been with Marin and Aster." The crystal around her neck glowed. The heat of it warmed her skin just underneath her muslin fighting tunic. "I have a feeling now that the four of us have bound our souls together through these kinds of adventures, there will never be an easy way to break us apart."

"If this is the role I have to play in the adventure, then so be it," Carys said. "I'll do it. I trust you, Elspeth."

Elspeth stood and put her hands on her hips, raising her chin imperially, looking every bit a queen. "Come, then. It's time to put our plans in motion."

CHAPTER 44

"**B**ring me the witch."

Sir Bricot nodded, his dark eyes never making contact with Donovan's. Something about the knight's somber expression annoyed his majesty. *He doesn't approve of witchcraft,* Donovan thought. *I don't like the old hag any better than my knights do. But she might be useful.*

"Now!" Donovan demanded, and Sir Bricot turned to slip out through the flap of the hunting tent.

Donovan slouched back in his chair, running one sweaty hand through his hair. The air in the tent had grown hot from all the candles he burned. He reached for the tankard of ale on his table and took a long chug. Drinking was the only thing that gave him reprieve from the torment.

Movement passed by the flap of his tent. He tilted his head, watching the light from a torch illuminate the darkness momentarily. Nobody would dare come into his tent right now unless he called for them. They knew. They all knew. Donovan had not accepted the company of anyone for three days straight.

Let them think what they wanted. They could whisper all night long about how the king kept to his hunting tent, brooding, raging, turning away meals but calling for copious amounts of ale, occasionally screaming and pounding his hands on his table with unrestrained fury.

So when he called Sir Bricot into his tent and told him to go fetch the witch, Sir Bricot obeyed.

"You called for me?"

The king looked up at the sound of the high-pitched, nasally voice. Ilth peeked her wrinkled face in through the tent flaps. When he met her gaze, she hobbled inside, leaning on her walking stick, her black robe trailing behind her. She always had an expression as if she were planning something sinister. Always.

"You've lied to me," Donovan said, his hands clenching on the table. "Now, I want the story straight and true. Your prophecy said that King Hector's child would rule my kingdom."

"Yes."

"And those boys who showed up in my throne room. You said they were the babies I told Sir Bedivere to kill—the baby sons of my queen and my sister."

"Yes."

The audacity of the old hag! Donovan gritted his teeth, holding back his anger. If he lost his temper with her, there was no telling what trouble she might cause. Still, he had to instill fear in her if he wanted to maintain the upper hand here…

"I have reason to believe that those boys are *not* actually the sons of King Hector. I visited Sir Hardegan and told him to shoot the bastard sons of King Hector with his magic bow. The arrow could find no such quarry. I visited the truth pond and demanded to see the bastard sons of King Hector, and it showed me no such vision. Somewhere along the line, your story does not hold up. Now tell me, witch, what is the truth?"

Ilth grimaced. "I don't like being challenged, your majesty. Do you really think you can push me around like this?"

"I am the king."

"And I am a witch. I am doing a service to my king by coming out of my retirement to help you track down this threat to your rule."

"Ha!" King Donovan rose to his feet. "You mean you are here to reclaim your servants. I have a feeling I would get no such help from you if there weren't something in it for you."

Ilth stared at him, blinking her pinprick eyes. "Why have you called me here tonight, my king?"

Donovan took a step closer to her. "Who are those boys? And why should I still believe this prophecy? It doesn't seem to hold much truth."

"Prophecy is not always easy to understand or figure out."

"How convenient," King Donovan said through gritted teeth. "What's the sense in telling the future if you have to waste precious time figuring out what it means? And even then, it turns out you still might be wrong?"

Ilth hobbled over and sat down in one of the chairs, leaning her walking stick up against the table and making herself comfortable. "Very well. Let's say, just for the sake of argument, those boys aren't Hector's sons. But I'm sure you've heard the news by now. It's all they're talking about in the outer provinces. Those boys have taken King Hector's daughters to wife."

Of course, he had heard the news. It made his blood boil. How could King Hector condone such a thing, allowing his bastard sons to marry his legitimate daughters? Was Blunia really such a vile king-dom? "They have not been formally wed," he said simply.

"Their betrothal has received the king's blessing, and that's good enough," Ilth said. "But no, they have not been married. Right now, they are—"

"I know where they are right now," Donovan fumed. "On a quest to retrieve *my* kingdom's sacred relics. And for all I know, they intend to conquer my kingdom after they have wed Hector's daughters. By the law of the land, that would make Hector's heirs the rulers of my kingdom. Hector, my sworn enemy." *She must be goading me into saying all of this just to see me angry*, King Donovan thought.

He's lost all sense, Ilth realized. *He's lost his ever-loving mind.* Donovan did not even seem to put it together that if Marin and Aster were not Hector's bastard sons, then that meant they were his rightful son and nephew after all.

Nor did Donovan seem to realize Hector was only his sworn enemy because Donovan believed Hector lay with his wife and sister. If Hector were innocent of the affair, then they would be friends and allies still. And their kingdoms would be rightfully united by the marriage of Hector's daughters to Donovan's son and nephew.

Instead, King Donovan was so consumed by fury and distrust that he would destroy all that was good around him.

"What will you have me do?" Ilth said. She tried her best to suppress the grin twitching on her lips. Oh, she liked where this was going so much. The crazier Donovan became, the easier he was to manipulate.

"Stop them," Donovan said. "What can you do to ensure they do not reach the top of the Blood Mountains?"

That was it. She could no longer resist grinning. Her wrinkled old face creased in half with a wide, thin smile. "I like the way you're thinking, your majesty." She stood, straightening her robes, and lifted her walking stick. "Come, let us go to my tent. I think I have the very thing."

King Donovan made a face as if he were about to protest, but he quickly let out his breath and held out his arm. *After you*, the gesture said.

Ilth pushed her way through the flap and into the cold night air outside. The crackle of campfires and the buzz of conversation among the knights and huntsmen had become as easy to ignore as the rustle of leaves or the hum of cicadas at this point—she spent so many nights ignoring the rest of the camp. King Donovan's footsteps on the soft grass was the only sound she needed to hear right now. It told her he was following her back to her tent. He would do what she told him to do.

Even if it means certain death for those boys, she thought. It would be a shame to lose two young, strong servants. They had always done good work for her. But this was the only true way to leave Grythium without an heir. The idea of the chaos was just too much to resist for her sordid little heart.

They reached her tent on the far edge of camp. Ilth pushed her way through the flap, sucking in the heavy incense that covered the scent of several other more unsavory things. The small fire she kept blazing day and night filled the tent with heavy intoxicating smoke. She strode over to the little table where spices and herbs lay beside her open spellbook. She had been preparing her tent for working spells if the need ever arose.

"It's time to conjure," she said. She waved her hand and summoned a small pewter cauldron from across the tent. It whizzed through the air and into her outstretched claw. Several splashes of water sloshed out of it as she indelicately set it over the fire. "Well," she said, uncorking a bottle from the table and emptying it into the cauldron, "conjure or *convert*, I suppose. However you want to think of it." She dropped the bottle onto the ground and tossed in a handful of herbs.

King Donovan hesitated at the entry to the tent, almost as if he didn't want to get any closer and be part of what Ilth did. His desperation would get the better of him though. "Convert?" he asked, taking a nervous step forward.

Ilth looked up from the cauldron. Smoke swirled in circles around her face. "Do you have a lizard, your majesty?"

Donovan's brow furrowed. "A lizard?"

"Yes. Small creatures. Scaly, usually green, often a little bit slimy."

"I know what a lizard is! I'm asking why you think I would have one. Do kings carry pet lizards around in their pockets?"

Ilth wrinkled her nose. "Don't patronize me, your majesty. I am trying to help." She glanced into the cauldron. The frothing liquid inside turned from gray to green. "We'll need a lizard to complete the spell. So, if you don't have one tucked away in your pocket, then you'll have to send one of your squires to catch one."

Donovan's fists clenched and his jaw tightened, but he didn't say anything in reply to that. Instead, he turned and strode out of the tent, expressing his anger only through the aggressive way he stomped his boots into the grass with every step.

Ilth peered back at her spellbook, using her finger to trace the list of ingredients needed for the potion. Yes, she had everything but the lizard.

She glanced back at the liquid in the cauldron. The greenish color grew brighter, glowing, sparkling.

King Donovan came back in. "I've tasked one of my footmen to go down to the creek and fetch us a lizard."

"Good, good."

"May I now ask what the lizard is for?" His voice no longer sounded angry. He actually sounded scared.

Ilth laughed. "If we're going to thwart those boys, we'll need to send a formidable enemy." Yellow-green smoke rose from the bubbling cauldron. It smelled of brimstone and sulfur. "There's no way your army can get there in time, so I'll have to conjure some kind of obstacle. I've found that thunderstorms and briar forests are easy enough to overcome if the hero has enough tenacity." She looked King Donovan right in the eye. "What you need is a dragon."

"A dragon?" Donovan said. "We need a dragon, and you send for a lizard?"

"Fool." Ilth waved her fingers over the cauldron, sending the liquid stirring in a clockwise motion. "Don't you see? I'm going to transform the lizard into a dragon."

343

"You can do that?"

"Ha! Do you really think I'm so out of practice I can no longer manage this kind of malevolent magic? I'm a better witch than that!"

Donovan stared at her. "This had better work."

A half hour later, the flap to Ilth's tent burst open and one of the king's valets stumbled in. Ilth recognized him. It was Clovis, the buffoonish valet who escorted his majesty to the truth pond only days before. Water dripped from Clovis's trousers up to his knees. He cupped his hands close to his chest.

"I've brought it!" His face radiated earnest pride. Stupid, undeserved earnest pride, but earnest pride, nevertheless.

Donovan strode toward the valet. "Give it to the witch!" He pointed at Ilth, almost as if he didn't think Clovis would know who the witch was if he didn't indicate her specifically.

Clovis held his cupped hands out to Donovan. "It's right here."

"I said, *Give it to the witch*." As if Donovan's had any intention of touching the slithering little creature himself.

Ilth reached out her gnarled old hands. "Yes, give it here, my good sir."

A little wary of getting too close to Ilth, Clovis didn't take any steps nearer to her or her cauldron. He extended his arms, placing the lizard into Ilth's grasp.

It was a puny thing, not much longer than her finger, its green skin dotted with blue spots. It looked up at her with beady eyes, unaware of any danger it was in.

"What a sweet little baby," Ilth murmured, stroking the lizard's back.

Clovis looked expectantly at Donovan, as if hoping for praise.

Donovan cleared his throat. "Leave us."

"Yes, your majesty."

Clovis didn't need to be told twice. He brushed his palms on his tunic, likely trying to dry them of creek water and lizard slime, and hurried out of the tent. The flap closed, leaving Ilth and Donovan alone again.

"Ready, your majesty?"

"Let us see this magic at work. And woe to you if this fails."

Oh, this won't fail. Ilth took a step closer to the cauldron, her cupped hands held out in front of her. Firelight danced on her liver-spotted fingers and crusty nails. She opened her hands and let the miserable little creature fall into the bubbling brew. It disappeared into the yellow-green liquid with a sickening plop, then a hiss of something burning. A heavy puff of smoke erupted from the cauldron.

"Be prepared, Donovan," Ilth said.

"I'm ready." He hadn't even realized Ilth addressed him by name instead of as *your majesty*. His eyes fixed on the potion as it changed from green to yellow to black and then to green again. The smoke rising out of it, now dark as a thunderstorm, flickered with specks of gold.

Two enormous claws emerged from the bubbling liquid, grasping at the rim of the cauldron, their nails clinking against the metal. A head followed, something almost resembling a lizard, but with two horns sprouting from its head and spikes rising from the back of its neck.

"That's your dragon?" Donovan asked. The creature barely outsized one of his hunting dogs! It would make an easy fight for two teenage boys.

As if it heard Donovan's remark and wanted to assert its own dominance, the dragon reared its head and hissed. It pushed its way farther out of the cauldron, revealing a long reptilian body, enormous bat wings sprouting from its back. It grew. The head, neck, and forebody extending out of the cauldron had doubled in size in the seconds since it first emerged.

In another moment, its outstretched neck grew longer than

Donovan's full height, and its head was the size of a carriage.

"Yes," Ilth sneered. "That's my dragon."

The dragon batted its forelegs in the air, flapping its wings. As more of its body pushed its way out of the cauldron, the part already in the air kept growing, thrashing back and forth at the constraints of the tiny tent around it.

Its claw met the fabric that formed the roof of the tent. With one horrific swipe, it tore through, giving a shrill scream as it fought its way out into the open night sky on the other side.

Donovan broke his gaze from the horrific sight and bounded through the tent flap, unsure in his panic whether he wanted to escape the confines of the tent because he was scared to be in such an enclosed space while this was happening, or whether he wanted to see the dragon rise up into the sky once it escaped.

At the sound of the dragon's screech, and at the sight of it tearing its way out of the witch's tent, the entire camp erupted into chaos. Donovan stumbled through a frenzied scene of knights and huntsmen dodging this way and that, dogs howling, swords coming out of their scabbards amid shouts and screams.

"Do not harm the beast!" Donovan shouted above the uproar. "Ilth has summoned this creature on *my* order."

If anyone heard him, they didn't respond. The entire hunting party pointed, shouted, fled into the surrounding forest to take cover, or hid themselves to play dead in the shadows.

The dragon rose into the sky, growing, growing, growing still, until it was nearly the size of the largest ship in his fleet back at the royal port of Grythium.

"I'll be damned," Donovan murmured.

The dragon circled overhead, flicking its tail this way and that. Its wings beat the air.

Ilth appeared at Donovan's side, her head tilted back in a cackle as

346

she observed the monster she created.

"Not bad, is it?" she said. "For a retired witch, I mean."

Donovan couldn't take his eyes off the dragon, its scales shining in the night sky. "Will it stop those boys?" he asked.

"Oh, yes. It will stop them. They don't stand a chance."

CHAPTER 45

Carys paused, taking in a determined breath of earthy, pine-scented air as she leaned against a nearby tree and observed her surroundings—tall trees, tangled underbrush, and shifting shadows. All of it looked the same as where she'd come from, where she'd been traipsing all afternoon, with nary a sign of anyone or anything that could help her.

"Oh, Elspeth, what am I supposed to be doing?" she murmured. "Who am I supposed to be seeking out here?"

The silence of the Blunian woods felt oppressive, no birds chirping or animals rustling in the undergrowth, as if the trees themselves were holding their breath in anticipation, not wanting to draw attention to themselves, lest they be drawn into this quest that the princess now undertook.

How was she supposed to catch up with the boys when they were so many days ahead of her? How was she supposed to help them when she was so many miles away and couldn't even rally help the way she'd promised Elspeth she would?

She had been so determined when she snuck away from the castle. But not anymore. Now she was just the scared little girl who had let a goblin army take her and her sister captive, a little girl who'd been unable to defend herself, even when she knew she could best any squire at swordplay.

Carys slumped, feeling the weight of her armor shift from one side to another, too big for her as it was. She'd borrowed it from one of her father's knights, and she hadn't expected it would be so heavy. Or so hot. She pushed her tangled brown tresses behind her ears, picking out a twig that had caught in one of the strands. "I can do this," she murmured. "I can do this. Now is not the time to doubt yourself."

She reached down and gripped the hilt of her sword. Just touching it made her feel more powerful. How many princesses before her could have claimed to be a trained warrioress?

"Carys."

She recognized the voice. Whirling around, she found herself face to face with Elspeth. Her sister stood only a step or two away, a shaft of light shining through the trees illuminating her from behind like some sort of halo.

"Elspeth!" Carys exclaimed, stumbling backward in surprise. Clumsily, she fell against a tree, then staggered to catch her footing. "What are you—oh, I didn't expect this!"

Except she had been expecting it really. Elspeth had promised her only a few hours ago, right before Carys set out. She'd told her she would assist her in rallying the support that Marin and Aster needed.

"Is this how your dreamsight works?" Carys blurted out.

Elspeth sighed. "Calm down, Carys," she said, the way she always did when Carys got rowdy or boisterous or excited. Carys would just have to get used to that, she supposed. Even when they were on a dangerous quest together. "Yes, this is dreamsight," Elspeth said. The wind gently rustled the silk of her dress, giving her even more of an ethereal appearance.

Carys stepped forward. "Elspeth, I'm so glad you're here." Not knowing how else to greet her, and feeling more like a knight addressing the crown princess rather than sister talking to sister, she dropped down to one knee. "I don't know where I'm supposed to be going, or what I'm supposed to be doing. I'm lost."

Elspeth shook her head. "Get up, Carys. There's no need for these affectations. You're a fighter, remember?"

Carys drew herself back up. "Yes, I know. But…"

"No," Elspeth said. "Now isn't the time to doubt yourself. You're ready for this, Carys, I know you are. I'm counting on you to help our men, and I wouldn't ask this of you if I didn't know you could do it."

Carys nodded.

"I have found the assistance you need," Elspeth said. She raised an arm, indicating for Carys to turn around. "At least my magic is good for something."

Rustling came from the foliage behind Carys as she looked over her shoulder to see the trees and bushes shaking. At first, the sight of the creatures startled her and she drew back. A whole pack of them emerged from the greenery, some of them crawling, others of them hovering in the air and winding their way through the trees. One or two of them crouched in the boughs overhead, leaping from one tree to another.

"What—what are they?" Carys asked.

She'd never seen anything like them, enormous beasts the size of bears, covered in thick fur with patches of shimmering scales. Expressive eyes peered over their wide snouts.

"They're called nulquins, Carys," Elspeth said.

Carys had heard the name before, but she'd not known what they looked like. Maybe she would have if she'd paid half as much attention to her royal tutors as Elspeth had. She marveled at their huge paws padding at the ground, felt the gentle breeze that came off their beating wings.

"Marin and Aster rescued one of their own in the first days of their journey," Elspeth explained.

Carys turned back to Elspeth, barely able to hide her confusion about all of this.

"Or, at least, that's my understanding, based on what the nulquins tell me," Elspeth continued.

"They talk?" Carys asked. She looked from Elspeth to the pack of nulquins gathered only a few feet away from her at the edge of the grove.

"No, but I understand them," Elspeth said. "And they can understand you, if you address them."

Carys swallowed any sense of fear she had felt momentarily before and stepped forward. It felt good to be brave even when there was so much uncertainty. A flood of excitement welled up inside her. She held out her hand to the nulquin, offering it to them to sniff as if they were dogs.

Elspeth fell into stride beside her. "The nulquins are loyal to Marin and Aster. They'll carry you up to the top of the Blood Mountains."

With a steady hand, Carys reached forward and stroked the fur on one of the nulquin's face. It cocked its head, staring at her with warm eyes expressing obedience and trust. Carys patted the beast's snout. She looked over at Elspeth. "How long do we have?"

Elspeth understood what she meant: Could these creatures get her to Marin and Aster before they reached the top of the Blood Mountains and found themselves up against a dragon? "They fly like the wind," Elspeth said. "They can carry you there in only a day. And they'll bring you back just as fast."

Several of the nulquins bleated and huffed, as if affirming what Elspeth had said. Carys couldn't help laughing. Then, realizing this called for at least some propriety—particularly given she was a royal warrioress on a mission assigned to her by her sister, the crown princess of Blunia—Carys stepped back from the nulquin she had just pet and made a low, sweeping bow.

"I am Princess Carys of Blunia, daughter of King Hector and sister to the crown princess, Elspeth," she said, trying to sound as courageous and dignified as she could. "I need your help," she added.

To her amazement, the nulquins seemed to understand her. In one unified motion, all the nulquins lowered themselves, touching their snouts to the ground in obeisance. These beasts were actually going to help her!

"They are at your service, Carys," Elspeth said, placing a comforting hand on the shoulder of Carys's armor. Carys reached up and touched Elspeth's hand. It was difficult to remember that Elspeth wasn't actually there—that this was merely a magical appearance on her part, and she was actually back at their father's palace.

The nulquin that Carys had pet stepped forward, and Carys stretched her arms up across the animal's back, pulling herself up, kicking her legs over one side, and mounting to ride. It wasn't until she was up on top of the nulquin that she realized how wide their bodies were. She leaned forward, placing her hands on the back of its neck to steady herself. The nulquin beat its paws against the ground.

Elspeth stepped forward and patted the nulquin again in a show of gratitude. She looked up at Carys. "There is one other who will join your mission," she said. "A creature called Frik. I will send him to meet you at the foot of the Blood Mountains. He is another whom our men helped, and he will offer his loyalty to you."

With a flap of its wings, the nulquin rose several feet above the ground. Carys gritted her teeth and raised her head, feeling ready for the journey ahead of her. "Then, I'm off," she said. "Thank you, Elspeth. I won't fail you."

With that, Elspeth faded away, leaving only an empty patch of grass where she once stood. Now the mission was up to Carys—and she had to be brave. This was her chance to prove her own valor.

She patted the nulquin on the back. "Take me to Prince Marin and Prince Aster."

CHAPTER 46

The old man sat outside a small lean-to built from rough wood, his bent body so gaunt and lanky that, from far away, Marin mistook him for a scarecrow set out on the stony ground. He climbed to his feet as soon as Marin and Aster approached, his eyes going so wide they practically illuminated his sunburned face caked with years of grime. He ran his gnarled hands through his mane of overgrown hair, then limped forward.

"Huh—huh—hulloh," he rasped. "Hello." His voice croaked in a way that suggested he hadn't spoken in years. *How long has he lived this far up the mountain?* Marin thought. He'd been all but certain they left civilization behind them at the foot of the mountain, but then there had been the orphanage, the giant's cave, the bridge…

All of those were tests though. Was this old man another test? This feral outcast living so deep in the brush that there was very little distinction between him and an animal at this point. The leaves and animal pelts he had assembled into clothing gave him an untamed, wild appearance, something no longer human.

But it was still important to be princely and respectful, no matter how unnerving this man seemed. "Good day to you, sir," Marin said.

"What are you doing this high up the mountain?" the man said.

"You're not supposed to be up this high. Nobody is supposed to be up this high."

He stepped back, turned, dashed into his lean-to and returned a moment later brandishing a longsword, one that was so rusted and damaged by years of neglect that it looked like it might fall apart in the man's hands at any second.

"Go back," the hermit said. "I pray thee—return from where you came! You're not welcome in these parts!"

The crazed look in his eye suggested he meant what he said. Marin held up his hands to show that his weapons weren't drawn. "We don't mean you any harm."

"It's not me I'm worried about," the hermit said. "Nobody ventures this far up the Blood Mountains unless they have a specific purpose. I'm here to guard the vault of Grythium, to ensure the kingdom's relics aren't stolen."

Marin glanced at Aster, who shrugged, as if to say, *What are we supposed to tell him?*

The truth. Marin would tell this man the truth. There was no use in playing mind tricks or being deceptive.

"Then I'm afraid we're the ones you're trying to protect the relics from," Marin said. "We are princes of Blunia, and we come seeking them for our own."

The man lowered his sword and glared at them. "So, the prophecy has come to pass. After all the years I have stood guard here, you have indeed come seeking the relics. I did not realize King Hector had sons. Are you legitimate?"

Marin didn't understand what he meant. "Huh?"

"Are you legitimate? Was your mother the queen, or was she some common wench the king dallied with on the side?"

"We are not the king's sons by blood," Aster said. "We're betrothed to his daughters."

354

The hermit sighed. Something had softened him. "My boys, I cannot let you pass. I pray thee, go back down the mountain and leave this place in peace. Too much pain and suffering has been caused by these relics." Then he added, "And this prophecy."

He stepped back and sat back down beside the entrance to his lean-to. He set his sword across his lap and closed his eyes, almost as if he were trying to will Marin and Aster to disappear.

Marin stepped forward. "I don't understand. You said you've been guarding this place for years? Who are you?"

The hermit opened one eye and looked up at him. "I was once a knight sworn to the kingdom of Grythium. They called me Sir Bedivere the Ironclad." He traced his long fingers over his sword. "I was a commander of the army, noblest of all who served King Donovan. Until the day he heard the prophecy."

The prophecy. The prophecy—the damn prophecy!

"We've heard the prophecy," Marin said. He didn't want to talk about this. Not here, not now. "Prophecies don't matter. Our fate is not something we're bound to. It's something we create ourselves. And we're not here to cause trouble for the kingdom of Grythium."

Except maybe he was. King Donovan wasn't fit to rule his kingdom—he was a madman who would kill babies if it meant maintaining power. If Marin could claim the relics of Grythium, then he could put a stop to that.

"If prophecy isn't real, then how do you explain yourselves?" Sir Bedivere asked. "Why do the heirs of King Hector come this far up the Blood Mountains seeking the royal relics of Grythium?

"Because we need them," Marin said. "We're on a personal quest to save Princess Elspeth from being sacrificed to the vraotyr."

Desperate, he sank to his knees, facing the old hermit, eye to eye. "I can't face this monster with any ordinary sword. I must have a magic one that will grant me the strength I need."

Sir Bedivere made no reply, gave no indication he even heard Marin. He stared off into the trees, murmuring to himself. "I tried. I tried so hard to thwart the prophecy."

Marin got to his feet. "You can let us pass." If it came down to it, they could simply walk past the old hermit. If he tried to wield his sword at them, they were surely strong enough to overtake him. Not that Marin wanted to fight...

"Don't you understand?" Sir Bedivere said, getting to his feet. "This is why I've resigned myself to this life. I need to guard this vault and ensure the prophecy does not come to pass. I let those babies live even when the king commanded they be killed."

His words froze Marin. There it was. Something Marin had long suspected...

Before he could say anything, Aster stepped forward. "What are you talking about?" But something in Aster's tone suggested he understood where this was going too.

Sir Bedivere cleared his throat and set his sword down. He lifted his hands, palms out, as if to tell the boys to stay calm. "Uh...well... when I was at court..."

He lowered his hands.

"When I was at court, I was regarded as the most loyal and noble of all his majesty's knights. King Donovan knew he could count on me for anything. And when he heard the prophecy saying King Hector's heir would one day rule his kingdom, he lost his mind. I've never seen the king so angry, so jealous, so dangerous. I wish Ilth had never said anything."

Ilth? Marin felt his stomach drop. "Wait, Ilth? The witch? She was the one who told the king the prophecy?"

"Aye. And she was the one I went to in desperation."

Marin hung on Sir Bedivere's every word. "Went to in desperation?"

This was it. The truth was coming out.

"When the king summoned me to private counsel in his throne room, he gave me his newborn son and newborn nephew. He told me his son and heir was a bastard begat by King Hector, as was the son of his sister, who was next in line to the throne after his own son. He commanded I take the babies out into the woods and kill them. He said it was the only way to thwart the prophecy. He also gave me a phoenix bone key and said he had sent for the sacred relics to his kingdom to be locked away in a vault—up here, far away from the world, at the top of the Blood Mountains."

"A phoenix bone key?" Marin said.

"Aye," the hermit affirmed.

Marin watched Aster lower his hand in his pocket to feel for something inside.

"I didn't know where to go," Sir Bedivere continued. "I couldn't kill those babies. I couldn't! They were innocent. But I was duty-bound to serve my king, and I knew if I disobeyed him, then it would mean certain death."

As he talked, Sir Bedivere raised his hands and gestured in front of him, as if he cradled an invisible baby. He spoke as if reliving the memories he described, as if the pain still haunted him to this day. The anguish he went through as he tried desperately to save the lives of two small babies.

"How could I betray the kingdom in such a way?" Sir Bedivere asked. "Defy the king?"

"So what did you do?" Aster asked. "With the princes?"

Sir Bedivere looked around, as if he still distrusted the notion they might be alone. He lowered his voice to a whisper. "There was only one person I could think of to keep a secret." He sighed, struggling with the confession. "I know witches have their reasons that others don't understand. I went to Ilth and I offered her the two babies to keep in hiding. I told her that they could never know who they were or where they came from, and neither must ever know about the other, lest they start asking questions or getting ideas. As long as they lived in isolation on her farm, there was no way anyone in the kingdom could ever find out who they were."

That was it. There was the confession they needed to hear. Even though the thought had gnawed at him for days, the formal pronouncement sent Marin's head spinning. Those babies. Sent away. Spared a terrible death. Given to Ilth to keep as servants.

"After I'd done that, I couldn't return to the royal palace of Grythium. I had betrayed the king's orders!" The knight closed his eyes, remembering. "I still had a duty. I might not have condemned two innocent babies to death, but I would commit my life to guarding the royal vault of Grythium and ensuring that nobody ever stole the relics. And that is how I came to live here on this mountainside, fending for myself all these long years. Living with the guilt of what I did."

Marin swallowed, trying to dislodge the lump in his throat. Aster exhaled a long, heavy breath.

"Sir." Marin struggled to find his voice. "I believe we are those babies." He gestured at himself, then to Aster, then back to himself again.

"What?" Sir Bedivere's eyes went wide again, lighting up his sunburned face. "But I thought you said you were the sons of King Hector by betrothal. How could two servants…?"

But he simply shook his head, unable to articulate the question.

Marin and Aster told him everything—how they grew up as servants to Ilth, how they learned about each other and ran away, how they rescued the princesses of Blunia, how they came to set out on their current quest. The outcast knight listened to all of it, nodding his head and gasping, but never interjecting a word.

When they finished, he leaned back against one of the beams of his lean-to. "You know," he said. "I don't think the prophecy was wrong—but I don't think you are the bastard sons of Hector either."

"I would hope not," Aster said. "Considering we're betrothed to marry his daughters."

"We know we're not King Hector's bastard sons," Marin said. "King Hector has never sired a bastard."

Sir Bedivere laughed. "Don't you see? You are the rightful heirs of Grythium. By marrying Hector's daughters, his heirs, then by the law of the land, they will become the rulers of Donovan's kingdom when the kingdoms are united. Based on the decree of Emperor Wiltyne IV, only a hundred and fifty years ago, women can inherit lands and titles, and queens can rule in equal measure with their kingly husbands."

"Aye, that is what Elspeth said," Marin replied.

The knight went suddenly very subdued, as if a memory suddenly occurred to him. He took a deep breath, choosing his words carefully. "King Donovan's son had a birthmark in the shape of a diamond," he said. "On the inside of his right forearm."

No longer did anything shock Marin. He glanced at Aster as he rolled up the sleeve of his tunic, revealing the dark diamond-shaped spot just above his inner wrist—he was indeed the rightful heir of Grythium.

Sir Bedivere climbed to his feet, his spirit now changed. No longer fearful, no longer inclined to fight, he appeared jovial—almost celebratory. "My good sirs, please. By all means, who am I to keep you from destiny?" He raised his arm and gestured past his lean-to, toward the path leading up the hill to the highest summit of the mountain. "I pray thee. You must go to the vault now. I cannot—nay, I will not—stop you. This is your destiny to fulfill."

Destiny. Marin refused to think he was living out some destiny that Ilth had foreseen. Still, he couldn't deny how nicely all of this fit together.

He got to his feet. "We'll fetch the relics because I need the sword, but there's no such thing as destiny," he said. "We are not here

359

because of some fate written in the stars. We are here because of our own choices."

Sir Bedivere laughed. His eyes twinkled now. "Whatever has brought you this far, I am grateful for it. I've lived far too long with the fear that I betrayed my kingdom. Now I realize that I have saved its rightful princes from an unjust death. And you have still found a way back to the royal court."

"We are not welcome in the court of King Donovan," Marin said. *King Donovan. Father. My father. Aster's uncle.* The man who sent them both away to be killed. All because he believed some foolish prophecy Ilth had told him.

"King Donovan will never renounce his claim on our lives," he said. "But...but court politics don't interest me at the moment. I am here to simply do what's right. I'm here to fetch a sword so I can protect the girl I love."

"Will you show us the way to the vault?" Aster said.

Before Sir Bedivere could answer, a vicious scream pierced the air. They looked up in the direction it had come. An enormous dragon emerged from the mist surrounding the mountaintop, cresting the sky, circling overhead, its green wings beating at the air.

Marin froze with dread as the dragon closed in on the summit up above them, then perched itself just above the entrance to the cave that led to the vault.

"Oh, what in the cursed netherworld!?" he said. "Not this."

CHAPTER 47

"Come on!"

Marin charged up the hill toward the vault, his feet pounding underneath him, kicking up dirt and dust as he went. This was one last fight they needed to undertake. A dragon. A confounded dragon!

By now, nothing terrified him. He didn't care about anything except facing down this beast. He drew his sword, holding it aloft as he ran.

Aster fell into pace beside him. "What's our plan?"

"We don't have a plan."

Oh, they were so close! All that stood between them and the legendary sword of Grythium was a locked door—and with that sword, he had hope of defeating the vraotyr.

But he didn't have the sword yet. And here was a dragon. All he had was his ordinary sword given to him by King Hector's royal smiths. A fine weapon, but one that felt like a pathetic shard of iron up against such an enemy.

The beast stared down at them, fiery eyes glowing, black smoke billowing from its nostrils. It snapped its jaws, revealing chisel-sharp teeth. It swiped a clawed foreleg at Marin just as he reached the top of the hill.

"Get back!" Marin shouted, holding his sword out. "Get back and trouble us not! We are the royal princes of Grythium, and these relics are ours to claim!"

Oh, I do hope I sound braver than I feel, he thought. But he hadn't been lying—he and Aster truly were the heirs of Grythium. These relics were rightfully theirs. King Donovan's kingdom was rightfully theirs.

Another gnashing of teeth split the air. Marin gagged on the putrid smoke unfurling from its nostrils and mouth—the smell of sulfur and brimstone. But no breathing of fire. At least, not yet.

The dragon leaped from the summit above them and swooped down, its wings beating the air. Marin and Aster parted ways, Marin confronting the beast from the front while Aster took a swipe at its tail.

Sir Bedivere followed them up the hill, moving with sudden agility despite the way his life as an outcast hermit had seemed to have weakened him.

Even three against one, it wasn't much of a fight. The dragon was too large, too fast, too determined to obliterate and destroy. Marin's grip on his sword loosened as his palms grew wet with perspiration. He heaved a deep breath, dodging the dragon's claws that swiped at him.

"Aster!" he shouted. "Go for its underbelly! Its underbelly if you can!"

Marin's books had talked about how a dragon's underbelly was always where its hide was the thinnest, where its otherwise tough scales were easily penetrated by mortal swords.

Goaded by Marin's words, Aster dashed forward, but the beast whipped its tail around and struck Aster right in the stomach, sending him tumbling to the ground.

Around the dragon's other side, Sir Bedivere raised his sword and landed it right on the beast's back. The sword clattered against the thick scales. Again, Sir Bedivere struck. This time, the iron blade snapped in half against the dragon's hide.

362

It's hopeless, Marin thought. *We're no match for this creature!*

But then a shout came from the sky above them.

"I'm coming! I'm coming, boys!"

Lying prostrate on the ground, Marin pushed himself back, out of the dragon's reach, and raised one hand to shield his eyes from the sun as he looked up into the sky. A shape descended from the clouds. "Aster! Marin!"

The voice was instantly recognizable.

"Carys!" Marin and Aster shouted her name together. "Carys!"

The shape came into view. Her brown hair swirling in the wind behind her, Carys perched on the back of an enormous animal, grasping a makeshift bridle of heavy rope tied around her steed's neck. Was it a flying bear she rode? Marin couldn't tell.

The dragon roared. It bucked its head back, inhaled.

This was it! Marin could tell just by watching the deep breath the dragon drew.

"Carys, watch out!" he shouted.

But his call was drowned out by the eruption of green flames bursting from the dragon's open jaw. The fire shot through the air in Carys's direction. Her flying steed swerved, avoiding the blast.

Aster stooped and grabbed a rock at his feet. "Hey!" He pulled his arm back and hurled the rock at the dragon.

At the sound of Aster's shout, the dragon turned away from Carys just in time for the rock to strike it between the eyes. It screeched, shaking its head.

But this gave Carys just enough time to descend. Her mount landed on the ground, its massive paws kicking up a cloud of dust as it settled on the mountain floor.

Now that it was up close, Marin recognized her steed. There was no way he could forget the humped back, the stubby legs, the long snout. It was the nulquin—the same creature they rescued from the tunnels underground! Or at least, it was *a* nulquin, if not the exact same one. He looked bigger now, stronger, more grown up.

Then again, Marin realized, he and Aster probably looked stronger and more mature as well. Life out in the great wide world would do that to you.

Another sound of gnashing teeth drew his attention back toward the dragon. Smoke unfurled from the beast's nostrils as it narrowed its orange eyes at Marin. It heaved another flaming breath at them.

Marin and Aster jumped back, barely dodging the fire's path, feeling its heat.

Carys stumbled forward, tossing off her velvet riding cloak with a flourish to reveal shining battle armor underneath. "I hope I'm not too late." She flashed them a knowing smile as she drew her sword and held it out. "And backup is on its way."

"Backup?" Marin said.

The nulquin bounded forward, barking and growling as he came. Marin could never have forgotten that bark.

This was echoed by other growls and barks coming from the sky, louder and louder still, until there was a massive chorus of creatures calling from the clouds. They appeared one by one at first, then as a crowd—a pack of nulquins, all of them stampeding through the sky, their leathery wings beating the air.

"Here they come!" Carys said.

Another familiar voice shouted from the chorus of barks and growls. "Sir Marin! Sir Aster!"

Who's that voice? Marin thought. *I know I've heard it before!*

It was Frik! His face bobbed up and down on the back of one of the creatures, his bulbous eyes wide, his mouth spread into an eager grin revealing sharp teeth and a wagging tongue. When the nulquin carrying Frik neared the ground, Frik leaped, landing stealthily on his feet and running toward them.

"I says I wouldn't abandon ya, didn't I?"

Marin couldn't have been more grateful to see this old friend, no matter how brief their interaction with him had been.

"You needed aid, and I've brought it," Carys said. "Good to see you, boys!"

Aster's jaw dropped. For once, he was speechless.

Marin wanted to ask how, but the answer was so obvious. *Elspeth!* She must have sent her sister because she knew they needed help. It really had been Elspeth who appeared to them—not a hallucination or an illusion. Really, truly Elspeth.

The dragon circled overhead, swiping with its claws and snapping its teeth at Carys. As its head drew close, she swung her sword, clomping it across the jaw. "Back! Get back!"

Where the steel blade stuck its scales, sparks erupted like flint on steel. This creature's hide would be impenetrable. Swords were no use here.

"Carys!" Marin shouted. "Carys! Your sword—your sword—"

But before he could finish, the creature swung its head, unleashing fire in his direction. Marin jumped back.

He looked the creature up and down, trying to locate vulnerable spots that weren't covered by the blackish-green scales. As the beast panted for breath, its soft underbelly heaved up and down. Soft as satin, unprotected by the same steely plates that covered its back, neck, and legs—vulnerable indeed!

But how were they going to get so close to a creature that breathed fire?

Frik ran toward the dragon, raising one of his paws clenched into a fist. "Pick on someones ya own size! Leave this princess alone!" Frik shouted this, seemingly unaware he was even smaller and less fit for a fight against this dragon than even Carys was.

The dragon swiped at Frik with its claw, baring its teeth.

"Carys!" Marin shouted. "Its underbelly! Look at its unprotected underbelly!"

Carys nodded. "I see it!"

She bounded forward, holding her sword out, prepared to plunge it into the monster's stomach.

Its tail appeared out of nowhere and knocked into her, sending her flying to the side. She hit the ground and skidded across the stony dirt. Aster shouted, his voice a mixture of dread and despair. He ran to her.

Carys tried to lift herself up off the ground. Shaken, distressed, disoriented, she couldn't maintain her balance. Aster fell to his knees beside her. "Are you all right?" He took her hand in his.

A group of nulquins surrounded the dragon, all of them shouting and spitting, trying to put up as much of a fight as they could. The dragon shook its head back and forth, like a spaniel annoyed by too many fleas buzzing around it.

"Aster! Carys!" Marin shouted. "Look out!"

Aster and Carys looked up just in time to see the dragon descend to the ground, towering over them. It lowered its head, growling, uttering a drawn-out guttural sound, spewing thick phlegmy slobber. Aster put his arms around Carys and drew her close, defenseless, terrified for both of them. Her sword lay across the stone yard, out of reach. There wasn't time to make a run to grab it, not with the dragon focusing its attention right on them.

"Hey!" Marin shouted. Just as Aster had done before, Marin grabbed a rock at his feet and hurled it at the dragon, striking it in the eye. The dragon shook its head, screeching in pain. It glared at Marin and heaved fiery breath in his direction. Marin fell, dropping his sword, the stony ground slamming into his back. His sword clattered across the ground and disappeared down the hill beyond.

"No!" He pushed himself back up and crawled to the edge of the hill. Any sign of his sword was gone.

366

Defenseless, he whirled around, surveying the scene. Where was Sir Bedivere? The old knight stood off to the side, hovering beside a tree, his sword drawn and pointed at the dragon, but making no sudden movements.

Another screech from the dragon. It leered at Aster and Carys, opening its jaws, ready to strike.

"No! No!" Marin felt himself driven by sheer impulse. Before he knew what he was doing, he ran forward—no weapons in his hands, no armor to protect him, no plan in mind—and stepped between his friends and the dragon. "Leave them alone! This fight is with me!"

And that was true. This dragon's fight *was* with him. Marin was the one who had to fetch the sacred relics of Grythium. He was the one who had created this whole mess, and it was up to him to resolve it. Aster and Carys were good enough to stand by him through all of it, but they were not going to die for him. No, he wouldn't let them!

"Your fight is with me!" Marin repeated, throwing his arms up above his head, as if that made any difference. Even if he made himself as large as possible, he was puny and insignificant up against the monster.

It all happened so fast he could hardly process it. As if the dragon understood what he shouted, it drew its head back and lunged toward him with open jaws. The long, slobbery tongue swept around Marin like a heavy wet blanket, pulling him up off his feet. Carys and Aster screamed together as darkness enveloped Marin. He bumped this way and that, falling into one hard surface after another, before he felt himself sliding down some slimy tunnel in utter blackness.

It ate me, he thought. *It ate me and I'm sliding down its throat!*

The dragon's esophagus emptied him into a cavernous stomach that resembled what Marin always imagined the inside of a volcano would look like. He landed on a pile of rocks and rubble, all of it warm to the touch. He scrambled to his knees, righting himself as much as he could, and stared around at a place illuminated by pools of glowing molten lava. Fires burned in some of the brightest spots of magma, their flickering light throwing shadows all around the sloping walls of reddish pink stomach tissue.

"Oh, this isn't good." Marin ran his hands across his face and through his hair, wiping away the heavy coating of saliva that clung to him. It fell in fat plops on the island of black pumice where he'd landed. "Oh, this isn't good at all."

Debris and carnage littered the lava pit—skeletons of animals the dragon had eaten, including those of what looked like they were once humans. Marin recognized the royal seal of Grythium on their breast-plates. Had the dragon attacked Donovan's army before making its way to destroy him?

He crept across the pumice, leaped across a pool of lava to anoth-er black stone in the middle of all the fire. The warm heat burned his cheeks, and heavy drips of something fell off him—it was hard to tell whether that was his own sweat, or whether that was dragon drool still clinging to him.

He stepped across the black solidness to a charred skeleton lying nearby. One of its scorched bony arms clung to a sword sheathed at its belt. *A sword!*

"I hope you don't mind if I borrow this, friend." It was so dumb to make apologies to a corpse, of course. But something about the pre-cariousness of this awful place—a dragon's stomach—made him feel a sort of kinship with this fallen hero. The knight didn't deserve this. Knights rarely ever deserved their fates. They were merely victims of politics, of foolish kings who had no qualms about sending other men to participate in their egotistical grabs for power.

But now this knight's sword might serve a better purpose. *If this plan works...*

If it worked, Marin not only would be free of the awful creature's belly but also would have slain it.

Marin gripped the hilt and raised the blade, just as a nearby pool of lava bubbled, splashing him with some acid-green liquid. It seared across his skin, sending pain through every part of his body. He winced as he tried to hold back his cry.

Don't give up now!

Gritting his teeth, he raised the sword and surged forward, hopping from pumice boulder to pumice boulder until he reached the muscley walls stretching up around him. He took a deep breath as he thrust the blade into the reddish tissue and dragged it, bringing forth an explosion of blood.

The cry of pain was so loud Marin could hear it even deep inside the dragon's stomach. The cut he'd made in the stomach wall flapped open, revealing a bright burst of daylight from outside. Fire and smoke erupted behind him, and he moved forward to push his way out of the stomach and into the outside world.

"Marin! Marin!"

It was Aster's voice. Marin shoved back the fold of shredded stomach tissue and emerged from inside the dead dragon. Warm daylight shone down on him again, even if he himself looked a little different. His body dripped with slobber and blood. Where the dragon's stomach acid had splashed him, his skin blistered black.

Aster, Carys, and Frik surrounded him. "Oh, Marin," Carys said. "You did it! You killed the dragon!"

Aster smothered him in a hug.

"Oh, don't," Marin said. "I'm all bloody and slobbery."

"I don't care," Aster said. "I thought we'd lost you."

"Of course, you didn't." Marin grinned. "My part in this story isn't over yet, is it?"

Aster laughed. "No, I guess it's not."

Sir Bedivere appeared beside them, reaching forward to take

Marin's blistered arm. "Is that...?" He hovered his hand above the burn marks and traced them along Marin's arm, down his chest, across his stomach. "Dragon stomach acid?"

"I...I think so," Marin said. "Is that bad?"

The knight's face switched from concern to fear. "Oh..." He stammered, his lips moving but no sound coming out. Then he said, "Oh, it's deadly poison."

"Poison?" Aster said. "Deadly?"

Marin swallowed the lump in his throat. "How long do I have?" For some reason, he wasn't afraid the way he knew he should have been. "Is there any antidote?"

"It'll work its full effect in an hour," Sir Bedivere said. "Whatever antidote there is, we would never be able to find it in time to save you. We're miles away from civilization, even by flying."

Marin swallowed, trying to suppress the searing pain from the burn. "This isn't the end for me. We'll figure this out." He looked around at the others. "But for right now, we just have to carry on."

Oh, I hope I sound a lot stronger than I feel right now, he thought. The world spun around him. Was he dizzy because of the burn? Or was it the thought of dying that put him off balance?

"Let's get to the vault," he heaved.

He pushed past them and powered his way up the hill. Just seconds ago, they had been overjoyed at the idea they had slain the dragon together. And now he was dying. The vault was theirs for the opening, but he might not live to actually carry the sword back to Blunia and face the vraotyr.

Aster would have to do it. He'd have to fight the battle in Marin's place, if he were willing. He *would* be willing. There was no question about that.

Marin choked back tears. He hated the thought of Aster having to go on alone. Elspeth, who awaited his return, would never get to see him again. In his effort to save her life, he was going to lose his own.

He reached the top of the hill where the rocky summit led into a shadowed cave in the mountain's peak. He waited for the others to catch up with him. Aster had Carys by the hand. Frik and Sir Bedivere brought up the rear.

"Ready?" Marin said. "Sir Bedivere, Frik—will you two guard the entrance?"

Sir Bedivere nodded.

"Yessss," Frik said. "We's will."

It was too dark inside the cave to see much from the outside. Marin stepped forward, disappearing into cool darkness. The craggy walls narrowed the farther he went.

There it was ahead of them, only a few steps away. The vault, its gold door catching the daylight that seeped in from just outside the cave. They were finally here!

Marin went forward, traced his hands around the edge of the door, searching for a place where it would open. Along the right side, enormous gold hinges bound it to the stone wall. Along the left side—no handle, only a simple keyhole lined with carved phoenix bone.

"Marin," Aster said. "That's it."

Aster reached into his pocket and pulled out the glittering key—the modest little treasure he'd been carrying around since finding it at the bottom of Ilth's sugar sachet. He handed the key to Marin.

"Here goes nothing," Marin said. For some reason, he always imagined this moment would be a lot more triumphant. Instead, it hardly felt good at all. Another stab of pain emanated from his burned side through his body. He gritted his teeth, choking back the agony.

I'm dying. I'm never going to be able to wield this sword I've come so far to claim.

With a deep breath, he inserted the key and turned it. The lock popped with surprising ease for one that had sat untouched for so many years.

The vault door swung open, revealing a small chamber inside, a rocky fissure where three objects sat on a mound of stone in the center. Three ordinary, almost boring objects—covered in a light layer of dust, but otherwise nothing above and beyond what might be seen in any castle in any country across the entire realm.

What had Marin expected? Some celestial moment of glory? A glittering shower of light emanating from above, illuminating the relics with sparkles and shimmers? A heavenly chorus of angels singing as the vault door opened?

None of that happened. Just a dark vault with three dusty objects.

Not that it really mattered. A glorious celestial reveal would've been impressive, but would it have saved him from impending death?

He stepped forward and lifted the sword from the stone. It was indeed beautiful. Age hadn't tarnished its shining blade, which was inlaid with ornate designs in the metalwork from hilt to point. He gripped the gold handle and held the weapon out in front of him. It was surprisingly light. He didn't even have to touch the blade to see how sharp it was. A worthy sword!

He looked back down at the stone table. A rose-colored cape trimmed in gold embroidery and white fur lay folded beside a jeweled crown. The other two relics—they were his to claim as well.

They had come for the sword, so did it really matter whether they took the other two? Would it really be so unworthy for him to send Aster back to Blunia with all three relics? After all, King Donovan had gone mad and tried to kill him.

Father, he thought. *My father went mad and tried to kill me.*

Didn't King Donovan's subjects deserve somebody better to rule their kingdom than a madman? By all rights, these relics truly were his. As Donovan's son, he was heir to the throne of Grythium.

Taking the mantle and crown, tucking them under one arm, he

turned back to the others. "Well, we have what we came for."

Carys nodded. "Good. The nulquins will carry us back to Blunia. It's a long journey, and time is short." She looked from Marin to Aster, hoping to see some hopeful enthusiasm from them, but there was none. "The gods will release the vraotyr at midday tomorrow."

Marin swallowed. "Aye. That's right, Carys. Time is short. And I am so grateful to you for your help—not only facing the dragon, but bringing the nulquin pack to carry you home." He looked at Aster. "Aster. Brother. I'll need you to fulfill this mission."

He couldn't believe he was saying these words. "See to it that Elspeth comes to no harm."

Aster's face fell. "No. Marin, you can't mean…"

"You heard what Sir Bedivere said. I'm not going to make it back." Marin hated that he had to say this. How could he send Aster and Carys on ahead of him, ask them to carry out this mission when they had already done so much? "I could be dead within an hour," he emphasized. His own voice held so much weight that even he himself could feel it.

Aster's eyes watered. "Marin…"

He stumbled forward and threw his arms around Marin. Marin held him tight, struggling to hold back his own tears. His cousin whom he thought of as a brother—everything they had gone through, how far they had come together. If it weren't for Aster, then Marin would still have been toiling away on Ilth's farm, waiting for his life to start.

He might be dying now, but at least Marin knew he had really lived. He wouldn't have traded any of this adventure.

It was a struggle to let go of Aster. "Come on," he said. "We can't dally here. Our mission isn't over yet. And I'm going to take advantage of every last minute I have."

With those words, he headed toward the entrance to the cave, back to the sunny world outside. His legs suddenly felt heavy under him. Each step became a struggle.

Sir Bedivere and Frik waited just outside, whispering back and forth to one another. They looked up as Marin, Aster, and Carys appeared.

Oh, what is there to say to them? Marin thought. It was time to give his last commands as a leader.

He handed the mantle and crown to Frik. "Good sir." He struggled to find his voice. "You have been a loyal friend."

Did he sound kingly enough? Dignified?

"Will you—will you carry these back to Blunia for Prince Aster and Princess Carys?" he said. "They will ride with nulquins. They'll need your service when they get back to the royal city."

Frik bowed. "I will do anything his highness commands."

Marin smiled despite himself. "Oh, I am no highness."

He was though. He knew it now. And for the first time, he felt it. Years of modesty and humbleness were hard to unlearn.

"Thank you for your loyal service, Frik," Marin said.

Another surge of pain went through his body. He stumbled forward. *Let's get down the hill,* he thought, his mind racing. *I want to see Aster and Carys safely off with the nulquins. I want to know they're safely on their way back.*

Moving grew difficult with sudden fury. Dizziness overtook him and he tripped. Aster's hands went around his arms, grabbing him, holding him steady. "Marin!" he shouted.

Marin fell back onto Aster, threw one arm around Aster's neck to gain his bearings. His legs no longer had the strength to carry him.

For a few hopeless steps, Aster helped him move forward, but Marin had little control left over his body. Aster knelt, helping lower him to the ground.

Feeling slowly drained from his body, all except for a rush of pain coming from that place where the dragon's stomach acid had seared him. Marin heaved, trying to choke back the throbbing agony. He just wanted it over. He wanted the pain to go away.

The world around him dimmed.

He mustered the strength to talk. "This…this is it…"

"No!" Aster knelt over Marin's prostrate body. He looked around at the others present—at Carys, Frik, Sir Bedivere. "I pray thee, there has to be something we can do to help him."

Exasperation overtook Sir Bedivere. His expression went abruptly stern, fierce, his years of resentment toward society showing them-selves. "What would you have us do? Work some magic to make every-thing right? Go back in the past to undo the dragon's attack? Go in the future to prevent his death?" The meanness in the knight's speech soft-ened just as quickly as it had appeared. "If there's one thing I know, boy, it's that you can't thwart fate," he said sympathetically. "This is what's bound to happen at this point."

Aster pounded his fist on the stony ground. "Oh! Oh, if only we had some of that antidote."

A voice came from behind him. "Your wish is granted."

All eyes turned. Even Marin, in his fading stupor, looked up to see who had spoken.

There she was—a familiar face, one they had seen only once, many weeks ago. Her white robes shone under the hot sun, giving her the appearance of an angel—which, at this point, she very well might have been. Tsema the prophetess.

Aster gaped. "You!"

"I." She smiled and held out a hand. In it, she clutched a small crystal phial. "The antidote. Just as you wished."

Aster stammered. "But…" His eyes went wide with realization, and he looked down at the ring on his finger. "Wait…"

Tsema offered her hand out to him. "Yes. But we must make a trade, Aster. That ring carries great power. Its magic is stronger than I think can be justified for common mortals." She bowed her head. "I will grant its power just this once more, but in exchange, you must give it to me."

Aster's other hand was at his finger, tugging the ring off. "Please. Here. You can have it." He held the ring out to her and eagerly took the antidote. "Thank you!"

Marin heaved several deep breaths. Aster put one hand on the back of Marin's head to help him tilt back, opening up his throat. He gently put the phial to his lips to get him to drink it. The precious cordial flowed into Marin's mouth.

Its magic took immediate effect. Fresh energy returned to Marin and the pain subsided. He sat upright as if he'd been pushed by some unseen force.

"Marin!" Aster and Carys shouted together.

Before he could fully register his recovery, Marin found himself buried in hugs from the two of them. He couldn't help laughing with sudden joy. He was saved. It had worked.

"I thought we lost you!" Aster said. "Again!"

Aster's embrace felt so good. Marin had never felt so safe, so relieved, so overjoyed.

Carys planted a series of kisses on Marin's cheek. "Oh, Elspeth would never have forgiven me if I didn't bring you home safe," she said. "Marin! Marin! I knew you wouldn't leave us."

Tsema stepped around them, coming in front of Marin, looking down at him. She had that same gentle expression that put him instantly at ease, just as she had back in her palanquin.

Marin tried to find the words to say, but they came out all wrong. "Who *are* you?" He shook his head. "I mean, I know who you are. You're a prophetess. I remember our visit with you. But...I mean..."

Tsema laughed. "I am a friend. And a guardian, you might say. This ring has served you well, but now it is time for you to be on your own."

Marin nodded. If he didn't ask now, he would never know, and the question would drive him crazy. "How does it work? The ring, I mean."

Tsema held the ring up, admiring it. "I created it with the intention that it would help desperate mortals from foolish plights when all other hope was lost. If they could conceivably wish for some better outcome than the one they found themselves in, then the ring could change the course of events to put them on the right track." She tucked the ring away in the gold sash cinching her white robe. "It was indeed an excellent gift, but I think it has done for you all that can be done. Your destiny is now in your hands. Now go—it is time for you to achieve greatness."

Destiny? Here she was, talking about destiny again! But if anybody knew the secrets of fate and free will, it would be a prophetess. He had to know.

Marin got to his feet. "I don't understand. Is destiny real? Is our fate written in the stars? Or is it something that we have control over? You never properly answered our question."

Tsema made no reply. She faded away just as quietly as she had appeared, leaving all of them standing there, dumbfounded. A gentle breeze shook the branches on nearby trees.

Aster looked at Carys. "We saw her once before," he offered, trying to explain. "When we first set out on our adventure."

Carys didn't seem the least bit surprised. "My sister has had visits from her as well."

That might explain a lot, Marin thought. Elspeth had some sort of magic powers, even though it didn't seem that she really fully understood the extent of them.

But figuring all of that out would have to wait until later. They had a mission to fulfill. "Well, are we ready?" he asked the others. He looked at Sir Bedivere. "You'll come with us, won't you?"

Sir Bedivere's jaw slackened. He looked both surprised and frightened by the suggestion, as if he had never actually considered this possibility. "But…"

"Your duty up here on this mountain is over," Aster said. "You came up here to protect the vault. But now the heirs of Grythium have come to retrieve the relics that are rightfully theirs." He looked at Carys, then at Marin. "The heirs of Grythium and the heirs of Blunia."

"We are still only three," Marin said. "Our fourth awaits rescue. Then the four of us will unite our kingdoms and claim the future that is our right by birth."

"So, what are we waiting for?" Aster said.

Carys put her fingers to her lips and whistled. The nulquins—she was calling for them. "We have to fly fast," she said. "It took me nearly a day to reach here, and the wind was in our favor. We'll reach Blunia in just the nick of time if we're lucky."

A pack of nulquins rose through the air, coming toward them, wind whipping at their fur as they hovered over the hills.

Aster held the hilt of the royal sword out to Marin. "Here."

Marin accepted it, feeling stronger now, holding the relic that was rightfully his. The relic that would help him destroy the vraotyr. The sword he would use to save and protect the kingdom.

He held it up and watched the sunlight glitter on the blade, then looked around at his companions, unable to resist the confident smile that spread across his face.

"Well, then. Let's fly!"

CHAPTER 48

E lspeth wouldn't be sacrificed looking anything less than her best. No, that wasn't it. She would look her best, but not because she was going to be sacrificed. She *wasn't* going to be sacrificed. She wouldn't look anything less than her best when Marin came to rescue her, bringing the royal sword of Grythium with him.

She had to look every bit a queen.

After bathing in perfumed water, she sat while her handmaids brushed her hair out and dotted her blond tresses with white flowers and glass barrettes. They dressed her in a shimmering gown of silver silk, with gleaming gold bracelets and anklets.

She stared at herself in the mirror. This was the kind of beauty they wrote ballads about. If only those bards knew there was so much wisdom behind the beauty as well. Did all those women in the myths and legends have the same potential she did, and the men who told stories about them just never recognized it?

It'll be different with me, she thought. *When I am queen, mine will be a reign to be respected and admired.*

She traced her eyes from the shimmering silk of her dress to the pained expression on her face. Did she recognize the fear in her eyes because she knew it was there, or would others be able to see it too?

She raised her chin. *He'll be here*, she told herself. *He'll be here.*

"I am ready," she said out loud. She turned away from the mirror. Her maid Nella waited in the doorway. She held a bouquet of flowers, as if those would do any good. *Why are women always expected to carry flowers at any important event?* Elspeth wondered. She loved flowers as much as anyone, but they were highly impractical when walking to her doom.

Nella held out her hand. "My lady?"

Elspeth placed her hand in Nella's. Oh, how comforting it felt. Besides Carys, Nella had always been her dearest companion and most trusted confidante. Without a mother, Elspeth had counted on Nella for next to everything.

Don't start giving up on yourself right now, she thought. *This isn't goodbye to Nella.*

Elspeth put on a brave face as best she could. She and Nella descended the stairs from Elspeth's private solar and along the open atrium overlooking the city below. The city that Elspeth had watched sleep every night for the past week when she couldn't bring herself to rest. Everything seemed so different by daylight.

The guards met her at the foot of the grand staircase in the palace's rotunda.

Sir Gifford stepped forward. Elspeth couldn't help noticing he wore his best armor.

"Your highness," he greeted her.

She tried to read his expression. He had never looked at her this way before. Was it pity? Or admiration? Maybe something of both.

"Sir Gifford," Elspeth said. She tried to sound brave. "So good of you to come to escort me."

Marin will be here. He'll be here.

Sir Gifford offered her his arm. "Come along, my lady."

Elspeth accepted. They led the way, the rest of the guard walking

380

behind them, descending the marble steps outside the palace's main gate. It was the same place where, only a week before, Elspeth bade farewell to Marin and Aster.

Their little procession moved through the streets of Blunia— Elspeth in front, escorted by Sir Gifford, followed by two lines of royal guards, and Nella finally at the back, carrying her foolish bouquet. As they kept pace along the cobblestones, Elspeth shifted her eyes from side to side, noticing the villagers who appeared at their windows and doors, peering out at her. At first, she didn't want them to know she saw them. She wanted to ignore them.

No, she had to show them she wasn't afraid. She turned her head and smiled at them, raising her hand to wave.

They arrived at the wall overlooking the forest beyond her father's kingdom. Trees stretched ominously upward. She loved those trees— so beautiful and so serene. She had so many happy girlhood memories of exploring the woods with Carys, getting lost, going on adventure after adventure.

Now those trees represented nothing but danger. *That's where the vraotyr will come from.*

They passed through the gate onto the greensward between the palace wall and the edge of the forest. A wooden platform stood erected, a thick column towering out of its center.

That's where it has to happen, Elspeth thought.

She let go of Sir Gifford's arm and strode toward the platform unaccompanied. Her father waited at the front of it, talking in a hushed voice to Udifeus, the wizard mentor to Marin and Aster. As she approached, they turned to face her.

"Elspeth," her father said. "My precious girl."

He wore his crown, the way he did on all formal occasions. Sunlight danced off the golden points around his head. He lifted his arms. A white cape draped over the shoulders of his blue robe. Like her, he was dressed in his best. He was suppressing his fear as much as she was.

"Father."

She didn't let her voice quiver. She moved forward and stepped into his embrace. When he pulled back, she saw so many emotions in his eyes. Those same eyes danced with joy only a week ago when Marin and Aster brought her home. Now those eyes showed so much pain.

"Oh, my little girl," he said.

"Father, don't be like this. You know Marin will be here. He'll be here." She hesitated, unsure of whether she should tell him. What harm would it do now? "Carys has gone to assist him."

"Carys?" Confusion twisted her father's expression. He hadn't even questioned where her sister had been for the past two days. "She's gone to…what?"

"Yes, we'll explain anon," Elspeth said. Her father might have had time for emotion and fear and doubt, but she wasn't going to let herself give into that. She reached a hand up and touched the crystal around her neck where it sat tucked underneath the silk fabric of her dress. She had to be practical. "Right now, it's time for me to be sacrificed. But don't worry. Marin and Aster will be here to save me."

She tiptoed up to kiss him on the cheek. It wouldn't be her last. This wasn't goodbye. She strode past him and ascended the stairs to the top of the platform where her sacrificial pillar awaited. Behind the pillar, the palace wall stood, its parapets dotted with statues of her father's ancestors. She'd always been told the ancient kings of Blunia protected the palace. They served as a reminder of the leaders of the past, as an inspiration to leaders of the present.

There are no women, she always thought. *No queens among these kings.* That would change with her. She'd be a queen to be remembered and revered.

But first, she just had to get through the threat of ritual sacrifice this morning.

Standing beside the pillar, she turned her back to the palace wall and faced the forest, then offered her arms out to the guards. "Bind me."

They didn't say anything in response. Their boots clattered on the wooden floor of the platform as they approached. She shivered at the cold metal of their gauntlets when they took her hands.

Head held high, taking deep breaths, she let them wrap heavy cords around her delicate wrists.

Courage, woman. Now is not the time to be weak.

"Well, well, well." The gruff voice took Elspeth by surprise. She couldn't easily turn herself around with the way her arms were bound, so she tilted her head as best she could to look over her shoulder.

Terro stood at the foot of the steps, leering at her father. He leaned his lanky, gnarled body on his walking stick, his mossy hair swinging back and forth as he cocked his head back to laugh.

"All is done according to my command," he said. "I do thank you, King Hector. It will be easier to appease the beast with your simpering daughter than to have it destroy the entire kingdom."

He laughed again, stomping his stony feet on the ground as he cackled.

Elspeth turned away.

"Do not taunt me, Terro," she heard her father say. "Do what you must do. I will not have you drag this out any longer just to torture me."

"As the king commands," Terro replied. "Release the beast!"

The small crowd of guards and knights stood silent. No motion disturbed the quiet serenity of the greensward in front of them, nor the stillness of the forest beyond. Elspeth held her breath.

The grass swayed ever so slightly. Was it the breeze? Or was it...

A slow tremble shook the earth. The wooden beams forming the floor of the platform creaked under Elspeth's feet. The quake strengthened until the trees in the distance swayed back and forth. Knights and guards started to shout, holding their arms out to maintain their balance as the ground trembled.

This is what an earthquake must feel like, Elspeth thought. She had never experienced one before, but this was how she always imagined them.

This was no earthquake though.

Far off in the woods, three or four trees went crashing down, their splintering and cracking sounds filling the air like thunder. A shape rose from the opening in the far-off leaves where the trees once stood, unfurling itself, stretching upward. Its serpentine body gleamed with a thick layer of muck across its scales. It opened its cavernous mouth, showing rows of razor teeth.

Elspeth tried to hold back the scream building inside her, but the terror was too great. She had spent days telling herself she would maintain her composure no matter what—and now all sense and reason left her. She pulled at the bindings around her wrists, trying to break herself free.

The vraotyr lowered its head and stared at her with raging eyes. It hissed, black fog emerging from its mouth, then dove back down into the opening in the leaves from which it had come.

The earth shook again as it tore its way through the woods, knocking down trees in its path as easily as if it were a dog trampling through garden flowers.

When it appeared again, it was on the edge of the forest, no more than a half mile from the palace wall where the sacrificial platform stood. The vraotyr bowed its head, slithered back to the ground, moving toward her, winding across the expanse of grass in front of the gate with breakneck speed.

Elspeth bit her lip. *Oh, Marin. Marin, where are you?*

Movement caught her eye up in the clouds. She broke her terrified gaze away from the vraotyr to look toward something descending from the sky out of the clouds.

Was it—was it too much to hope for? Was it too good to be true?

The spot against the clouds flew closer, taking form as it approached. Marin clung to the back of a hairy beast with leathery wings. Even from such a height as he was, the silver blade extending from his outstretched arm was unmistakable.

His shout commanded the attention of everyone in the crowd. "Auuuugggggghhhhhh!!!"

Even the vraotyr stopped, its serpentine body curling up, its head twisting in Marin's direction at the sound of the battle cry. It hissed, emitting a cloud of black smoke.

"*DON'T TOUCH THAT GIRL!*" Marin shouted. "*YOUR FIGHT IS WITH ME!*"

More shapes emerged out of the clouds behind him—more of the furry, long-necked beast he rode. It was a whole pack of nulquin, soaring through the sky. Aster and Carys rode two at the front of the pack, along with a shaggy-haired feral man and an orange creature with bulbous eyes.

It's them, Elspeth thought. *They're here!*

Her cheeks flushed. She was saved!

Marin pumped his arm in the air, jabbing his sword toward the heavens. "*BY ALL THE GODS, I COMMAND YOU TO FIGHT!*"

His steed landed in the soft grass, and in a flash, Marin was on his feet, sprinting across the ground, holding the sword out in front of him.

"Marin," Elspeth whispered to herself. "Oh, my Marin."

CHAPTER 49

Marin never completely fathomed just how monstrous the vraotyr was until he got close. Everything about this creature instilled sudden fear right into his bones. It arched its serpentine body, drawing its head up to tower over him, its full length still lost in the forest behind it. Glittering hematite eyes flashed as it opened its jaws, baring teeth like javelins at him.

His whole body froze up. His breath caught in his throat, and his arm clutching the sword of Grythium trembled, his grip loosening.

Just past the vraotyr, Elspeth stood bound to a column in the center of a high wooden platform. The midday sun sparkled on her silver dress, giving her the appearance of some celestial, otherworldly being, even in this terrible place where she'd been made a sacrifice.

Condemned to this terrible fate because of him. Because of his own arrogance and foolishness.

And now he was here to save her.

"I'm here, Elspeth," he called. "Everything's all right now."

If only he believed that! He held the sword out at the vraotyr, making eye contact with it despite his terror. This thing was far worse than the dragon. How was he supposed to win such a fight? Even a magic sword would be nothing more than a pinprick in this creature's thick hide.

Footsteps on the grass approached behind him, Aster and Carys appearing at his side. "What now?" Aster said.

Marin gulped. "I wish I knew." He glanced over at Aster for a second, then back at the vraotyr. Whatever they did, they had to do it fast. He had the vraotyr's attention for now, but that wouldn't last long. How long until the vraotyr realized he posed no real threat and ignored him? How long until the vraotyr killed Elspeth?

All King Hector's guards and knights stood in a line along the palace wall facing the platform. None of them moved. Of course, they wouldn't—they all thought this creature was invincible. None of them would go up against it, not even to save the princess.

"Aster, be my backup," Marin said. "Carys, you protect Elspeth. Fight the monster if it gets too close, but don't put yourself in danger."

Carys's eyes pleaded with him, almost as if she were going to protest, to insist that she be part of the fight. But she just nodded. It wasn't until that moment that Marin realized just how much she trusted him—she counted on him to lead this battle.

I can't let her down, Marin told himself. *I won't let her down.*

Carys took off sprinting toward the platform where Elspeth waited, bound to the column by her wrists behind her back. At least Carys was with her. There was no way of knowing how this fight would go, but at least Elspeth had her fearless sister there to guard her while Marin undertook this challenge.

Why did this seem so daunting? Legend said this sword could win in any fight. But was that certain? The stories around the sword might have held no more weight than prophecy—they sounded nice, but they meant nothing when put to the test.

Marin forced his body to move despite his fear, pushing forward and going full speed at the vraotyr. It narrowed its sparkling eyes, hissed, but didn't attack. Before he could even question his own choice here, Marin swung his sword over his head, planting the blade right in the vraotyr's hide. It pierced the skin with a sickening splat. Inky blood gushed out around the wound.

The vraotyr drew back, screeching in pain.

Marin kept his grip on the blade, holding tight. As the vraotyr recoiled, the blade loosed from where it stuck in the beast's skin, giving another slicing sound as it ripped away from the flesh. Marin, sword in hand, fell aside, sliding across the grass. The ground hit him with such force that the wind left him.

Aster dashed to his side. "Are you all right?" He fell to his knee to help him up.

Marin scrambled to his feet. Grass stains and dirt streaked his tunic. He took a deep breath, letting his dizziness from the fall subside. "Yes," he heaved. "Yes, I'm all right."

Am I though? Am I really all right?

"But this fight will be harder than I expected," he admitted. He watched the vraotyr slither away from him. It dropped its head to lick the wound Marin had given it.

"You've got to get its head," Aster said.

"Huh?"

"You'll never stab it to death. It's too big and your sword's too small."

The vraotyr reared its head back up, drawing the foremost part of its body up so high off the ground it towered at least twice Marin's own height—maybe even thrice his height. Marin dreaded the thought of getting close enough to find out.

"Uh, yes. Aye." He responded to Aster without even registering what he'd said. His heart pounded too loud in his ears.

"So, don't you see? You have to cut off its head. Your sword is still sharp enough to do that."

Marin looked down at his sword, understanding Aster's advice. Of course! Of course, that was it! Why hadn't Marin thought of it himself?

But how to get up that high. He stared at the vraotyr's full height. It hissed, emitting another stream of black smoke.

It didn't matter how afraid he was—Marin had to act. It was now or never.

He turned and put his fingers to his lips. The whistling pierced the air, and his nulquin steed responded immediately, swooping over in his direction. If the nulquin dreaded the vraotyr, it gave no indication. Its loyalty to Marin, its trust in Marin, overrode everything.

The nulquin bent its knees, lowering its back for Marin to climb on without Marin's even having to explain it. Bless these creatures! They understood everything!

One hand still clutching his sword, Marin gripped the rope rein around the nulquin's neck and squeezed his thighs into his back to hold himself on tight. This was it—he was going to do it.

He stared at the sword in his grip, watched the way the sunlight danced on its jeweled hilt. The inlaid gold in the etchings on the steel blade glowed. *Wielded by a worthy man for a worthy cause*, he told himself.

"For Blunia!" he shouted, raising his sword in the air. "And for Grythium too!"

The nulquin took off flying, circling around the vraotyr, which raised its serpentine body and lunged at them. The nulquin moved too quickly, swerving out of the way as if it predicted the vraotyr's attack.

Marin leaned forward, pressing himself against the nulquin's long neck. The vraotyr stared up at him, fangs bared.

But then it did something Marin never expected. The vraotyr whipped his head around and slunk its body back to the ground, slithering instead toward its initial prey—Elspeth.

"No!" Marin shouted. "No, you leave her alone! Your fight is with me!"

He pulled at the rein, sending the nulquin descending through the air toward the vraotyr, which closed in on Elspeth at alarming speed.

Carys, waiting at the foot of the platform for a chance to protect her sister, bounded forward, brandishing her own sword. "Not on my watch!"

She raised the blade with both hands and brought it down on the vraotyr's face, slicing it across its lips. The vraotyr drew back, its screech so loud that the branches on nearby trees quivered. Blood sprayed across the grass.

The attack only emboldened the beast. It lurched at Carys, snapping at her. She countered, rushed at it, sliced at its face again, sending it recoiling.

Marin tugged at the rein of his nulquin steed, swooping downward. "Hey! Hey!"

His shout caught the vraotyr's attention. The creature snapped its head in his direction and hissed. Marin's flying steed fluttered backward.

I'll never get close enough like this, Marin realized. *I have to make a leap for it.*

Before he could overthink it, he pushed himself off the nulquin's back. He plummeted through the air for only a heart-stopping second before firmness underfoot broke his fall. He landed on the vraotyr's back, planting his sword right into the creature's hide as he came down.

Another deafening screech tore through the air. The vraotyr thrashed, trying to throw him off. Marin grasped tight to the hilt, holding himself steady so he didn't fall. From this height, it was certain death—and certain death for Elspeth, too, if he died before taking the vraotyr out with him.

And Aster. And Carys. They were all counting on him.

The thought might have once intimidated him, overwhelmed him, made him feel unworthy. Now it just gave him strength he didn't even know he needed.

He pulled the sword out of the scaly hide, sending a mess of black blood flowing all over him. Teetering, trying to catch his balance, he set his feet between two of the spikes that lined the vraotyr's back.

He raised his sword again, looking at the deep gash he had already made. He could stab again, but what good would gash after gash do if it only made the vraotyr angrier, never weaker? Aster was right—he needed to cut its head off.

If the vraotyr even knew that a puny, insignificant human stood on its back, it paid him no mind. Instead, it straightened itself up, raising its head high, staring down at the sacrificial offering that waited below—Elspeth, defenseless, tied to the column in the center of the platform. The vraotyr hissed.

Elspeth screamed as the vraotyr made a sudden dive in her direction.

This was it. If Marin didn't do the deed now, then the vraotyr would do what it had been summoned to do—and Elspeth would be nothing more than a heroine in history, a sacrifice lost to vengeful gods.

The sword's strength was up to him, just like his fate and destiny were up to him. Legends might tell of how the sword would win any battle, just as legends would tell of which princes would grow up to rule which kingdoms. But in truth, it was up to him.

It wasn't about the sword. It was about the person who wielded it.

His heart pounding, Marin found his voice and shouted. "No! She's my queen!"

The vraotyr hissed. Elspeth held her head up, staring directly up at the monster. Her eyes went wide, and something extraordinary happened—the vraotyr slowed, hesitated, as if there were something about Elspeth's gaze that held it at bay.

Seizing the moment, Marin balanced his feet firmly between the spikes jutting out of the hide, raised his sword and swung it around with all his strength. The blade shone with blue light and chimed as it cut through the air.

That was when he knew the full extent of the sword's power. The blade sliced easily into the vraotyr's flesh, cutting through it like butter, severing the head from the neck in an easy stroke. The sickening squelch of severing flesh met his ears.

He stared in awe, almost unable to believe what he'd just done, as the head and neck separated from each other. The head tumbled to the ground, blood spraying in all directions. As the vraotyr's serpentine body went limp, collapsing lifelessly underneath Marin, he plummeted through the air before hitting the grass. He heard the booming thump of the monster's body hitting the ground right after him, making the earth shake one final time. Then all was still.

Applause erupted suddenly. All the people surrounding the platform cheered, their many voices sending shouts and hurrahs into the air. It all sounded so far away, so distant. Marin could barely register what had happened. He lay in the grass, trying to catch his breath, letting the realization wash over him.

He pushed himself up, first to his knees, then to his feet. His entire body dripped with black blood. He wiped a glob of it from his face and stared out at the crowd. He weakly raised the sword of Grythium over his head and tried to cheer with everyone else, but he was too breathless to find his voice.

Elspeth beamed at him from up on the platform. A wisp of her golden hair fell across her face. She really was impossibly beautiful.

"We did it!"

Marin turned to see Aster there beside him. Drops of black blood dotted his face, and the torn collar of his tunic hung loose at his neck. Still, there was no mistaking Aster's smile—it was a smile of triumph. Aster held out his arms and buried Marin in a hug, the two of them laughing and shouting, unable to say or do anything more coherent than stupidly celebrate right there on the greensward they had just made a battlefield against a legendary monster. Victory was theirs! They had done it!

Sunlight glinting off Carys's armor caught Marin's attention. He

392

watched her dash up the stairs to the platform and use her sword to cut the bindings away from Elspeth's hands. Severed cords fell away as Elspeth leaped into Carys's arms, the two sisters hugging as joyfully as Marin and Aster had.

In another moment, the girls descended the platform together, keeping pace with one another as they stepped out onto the grass and came running toward Marin and Aster, Carys's armor shining and Elspeth's silken gown trailing behind her in the breeze.

Elspeth, Marin thought, as she threw her arms around him. Her skin burned hot against his as he pulled her close.

And there, on an open field splattered with blood, beneath the heat of the midday sun, beside the corpse of the conquered vraotyr, the four future leaders of Blunia and Grythium embraced and shouted and celebrated together, practically unaware of anything but the love and relief they shared, while their proud subjects watched from afar.

CHAPTER 50

"Long live King Marin! Long live King Aster! Long live Queen Elspeth! Long live Queen Carys!"

The chorus of shouting and cheers rose through the air in the great hall as Marin, Aster, Elspeth, and Carys stood on the dais, facing a room full of courtiers just as they had on the night their betrothals were announced.

But tonight, they faced them as newly crowned kings and queens.

Marin's face hurt from smiling so much. Oh, did he ever in his life think that his face could hurt from smiling so much? The humble servant who spent his days tending to crops and arguing with grouchy livestock.

The past few hours had flown by in a blur. Earlier that afternoon, he'd been standing in a field, covered in sweat and blood. And now he stood in royal robes, crown atop his head, surrounded by gold and marble in a room lit by jeweled chandeliers, listening to the applause of richly dressed nobility.

He would never forget the look on King Hector's face after the fight as he strode across the greensward to greet Marin and Aster.

"Boys," he said. "Oh, my boys. My dear sons." He beamed with fatherly pride.

Marin fell into a bow at the king's words, unsure of how to properly react. "You…you honor me with your praise, your majesty." He just wanted to forget that only seconds before, he had been kissing the king's daughter right in the middle of the greensward in front of the entire royal guard. Kissing her with tongue, no less.

"Oh, Marin, there's no need for formalities." King Hector went to him and drew him to his feet. "You've saved everything. You and Aster. It is I who should bow to you."

With that, he made a low bow. He rose up again, laughing, his blue eyes twinkling, and he approached each of the four in turn to embrace them—first his daughters, then the boys. When he pulled away from Marin, blood and dirt covered the front of his royal robes.

"Oh, I'm very sorry, your majesty," Marin said, looking down at himself, realizing it had all rubbed off from him.

"Don't be foolish, Marin," King Hector said. "I'll wear this grime like a badge of honor. It is not every day I am able to embrace a brave hero returned home from a great quest—a hero whom I'm glad to call my son and heir."

Marin nodded.

"And please, call me Father. Remember?"

Aster clapped his hand on Marin's shoulder. "He remembers, Father."

King Hector winked at them. "Good. Now, I need to have a conversation with the four of you. Let's walk for a little bit, shall we?"

They strolled along the greensward, tracing the edge of the forest, as King Hector commended them over and over again. Elspeth confessed to him her part to play in what had happened, her ability to appear to Marin and Aster in spirit when they were half a world away. Carys apologized for going off without leave, but she admitted she worried her father would have forbidden it if he had known.

"Most likely, I would have," King Hector said, his tone repentant, as if to say that yes, he might have tried to stop her several days ago. But after what he just witnessed, he would never question her abilities again.

Marin and Aster took turns regaling the king with stories of everything they had endured on their journey, the dangers they faced, the tests they had to pass. "We never would have made it back if it weren't for the girls," Marin said. "Women, I mean. If it weren't for the women. Elspeth and Carys. We might have been the ones sent on the mission, but they were the ones who gave us support and aid when we needed it most."

"I would say you four work well together," King Hector said with a nod of his head. "That's good. Because I have something I want to talk with you about. It would be fair of me to wait, I think. This has been an exciting day for you already, and I know this will be a lot to take in. But I am so proud of you four, and I do not want to let it go any longer than it has to."

Marin glanced at Elspeth and Carys to see whether they had any idea what their father was talking about. Elspeth shook her head and Carys shrugged.

"I think it is high time I retire from the throne," King Hector said. "I am getting older now, and it would be better for me to turn the affairs of my kingdom over to a younger generation, so I can enjoy the sundown of my life in peace and relaxation."

Whatever Marin had been expecting, it hadn't been that.

"So soon?" Elspeth said. Her jaw hung open.

"Why wait?" King Hector said. "My dear, the four of you have proven you are ready for this. I have never felt more confident in any political decision I've made."

Marin couldn't believe what he was hearing. *Wait...does this mean...?*

"We'll be queens," Elspeth said. "And our husbands will be kings?"

"Are you agreeing to it?" King Hector said.

Elspeth jumped in the air and started to clap her hands. "Oh, Father, of course." How could King Hector not have known how eagerly his daughter awaited being queen? Had he really paid that little attention—treated his daughter like a trophy or a prize despite the fact that she could lawfully inherit titles and lands? Marin figured he had to grant the old man some grace for still thinking of his headstrong daughter as a little girl sometimes.

"We'll need to have a coronation, of course," King Hector said. "Tonight, if you still have the energy for it."

"Tonight?" Aster said.

"Why not?" King Hector said. "The people will expect some kind of ceremony after the victory the four of you just had."

The four of them exchanged looks with one another. *I'm willing if all of you are*, Marin thought, but the words wouldn't come to him. He was still processing all of it.

"But first," King Hector said, "I'm sure you'll want a bit of rest."

That was how it went. He sent them back to the palace for respite in the hours that followed. Marin thought he wanted nothing more than to rest, but when the valets showed him and Aster back to the private chamber where they stayed before—that all seemed so long ago!—his adrenaline still powered through him. He couldn't have slept or even lain down if he wanted to.

The servants drew a hot bath for him and let him soak, scrubbing the filth of the journey from his skin. He hadn't realized how caked with dirt his skin and hair had become. It was worse than even their first journey. The warm water soothed his sore muscles. He lay back, resting his head on the rim of the brass tub and staring up at the ceiling of the bathhouse. Steam swirled in the air. *Your life begins now,* he thought.

No. His life had already begun long ago. Everything behind him up until this point had made him who he was. Now it was just time for the next eventful chapter in the story of his life—a story, he realized, that was most definitely being spelled out in the Book of Records right now.

He and Aster dressed together, putting on the long flowing robes that kings reserved only for the most formal of occasions. When Marin unfolded the yards of velvet and satin, he gawked. It was like the robe King Hector had been wearing that afternoon, like the robe he wore for the grand ball when the betrothals were announced. Gemstones and stitched gold lined the brocade.

Marin slipped the robe on and cinched his waist with a leather belt. He crossed over to admire how it looked in the gold mirror standing on the other side of the room.

"You nervous?" he asked Aster.

Aster sat on his bed and adjusted the sleeves of his own robe. "No. Are you?"

"No. For once, I'm not. I've never felt more comfortable in my life." Marin stood in front of the mirror and straightened the seams of his robe where they rested on his shoulders. He looked broader than he had the last time he was in this room—stronger, more mature. Or had he always looked this way and never noticed?

"Good," Aster said. "It took you long enough to feel that way."

Marin turned around. He was about to protest, to argue, to insist Aster was just giving him a hard time. But Aster had a point. Marin spent plenty of time doubting himself. He deserved to feel self-assured at last.

"I guess Tsema meant what she said, didn't she?" Aster said. "When she told us she saw greatness in store for us."

Marin sat down on his bed across from Aster. "I wish she'd explained herself when she appeared to us back at the top of the Blood Mountains. I have so many questions still."

"Aye."

"Well—we're not actually where we are because of destiny, are we?"

Aster shook his head. "No, of course not. But…"

Marin knew what Aster was thinking. "There's that prophecy…"

Aster stood and leaned forward to adjust the collar of Marin's robe for him. "I think Tsema saw the potential in us, some future the gods had in store. Other people would not have done as well as we did under the circumstances we faced." He patted Marin on the shoulder.

I guess there are some things in life we'll never have control over, Marin thought. *And those things might as well be ruled by the stars in the heavens. But there are many things we do control, that are up to us, and we're merely sailors trying to navigate a vast ocean, hoping for the tide to move in our favor.*

A valet came to their door by eight o'clock to escort them down to the great hall where the ceremony would take place. Elspeth and Carys waited for them in the corridor just outside the oaken doors to the hall.

Elspeth raised her hand and twiddled her fingers at them in a delicate little wave as they came close. "Are you ready?" she asked.

"Ready as we'll ever be," Marin said. He stopped and took in the sight of his queen-to-be. She and her sister looked more beautiful than ever. Shimmering silk flowed from their shoulders to the floor, belted at the waist with strings of jewels.

Marin leaned in and kissed her. The scent of honey and lilac hung around her. He pushed a tress of her loosely curled hair behind her ear, running his thumb along the softness of her cheek. Here was the girl who loved him even when he couldn't love himself. *If only you could see yourself the way Aster sees you and the way I see you,* she had told him.

"Maybe you should save the romance for when you two are alone, eh?" Aster teased.

"He's right," Carys said. "You two can stare lovingly into each other's eyes later. Our coronation is starting soon. Or did you forget?"

"As if I could," Elspeth said.

The oaken doors to the great hall drew open. The four of them stepped into place and moved through the arched entryway into the dazzling grandeur of the great hall. The bright lights nearly blinded Marin for a second after the dimness of the corridor. He looked around at the marble walls lined with tapestries, the crowd of richly dressed courtiers staring at him, the jeweled chandeliers burning with thousands of candles.

A green carpet trimmed in gold led from the entry to the dais at the front of the hall. Four gold chairs overlaid with velvet awaited them. They would have to serve until formal thrones could be built for all four rulers.

Marin and Elspeth walked side by side with Aster and Carys down the carpet. King Hector stepped forward to stand before them. He was followed by four lords, each carrying a crown on a velvet cushion.

"My people," King Hector addressed their attendees. "It is my great honor to pass on my rulership tonight to four young people who have proven themselves worthy of leading this kingdom. May I present to you King Marin, King Aster, Queen Elspeth, and Queen Carys."

He crowned all four of them himself. He began with the royal crown of Grythium, cleaned and polished by the royal jewelers. He set the crown on Marin's head.

"Wear it well, my son," he said.

He followed with three more crowns. Finally came a lady-in-waiting, holding the royal mantle of Grythium. She unfolded it and draped it around Elspeth's shoulders, pinning the gold clasp around her neck.

Then Marin took Elspeth's hand, and Aster took Carys's, and the four of them went to their thrones. That was when the crowd cheered—and their cheers seemed to stretch on for minutes upon minutes.

A guard whom Marin didn't recognize entered the great hall and approached King Hector—or rather, just Hector, Marin figured, now that his majesty officially passed on the duties of rulership. Father. That was all Marin needed to know him as.

400

The guard leaned close and whispered something in Hector's ear. Joy faded to somberness on the retired king's face. He nodded, gesturing toward the door. In response to Hector, the guard bowed and went back out to the corridor.

Marin didn't like the way the exchange looked. He reached over and set his hand atop Elspeth's where it rested on the gold arm of her chair. He would need her strength if something were really wrong, if something serious actually threatened the joy and revelry of this night.

Hector climbed up onto the dais and whispered to the four of them. "Your majesties." He kept his voice low enough that the rest of the assembly behind him could not hear. "I'm afraid your first duty in royal office comes before your coronation is even over. My guards have captured Donovan, the disgraced king of Grythium, along with the witch, Ilth. They have brought them to stand trial before you."

"King Donovan?" Marin said. "Stand trial before us?"

"I could do this for you," Hector offered. "It could be the one last task I undertake in my role as king before I formally retire."

"No," Marin said. He realized the other three were staring at him, expecting him to handle this. "That is kind of you, my lord. But this is our grievance, mine and Aster's. It is our responsibility to oversee justice here."

"You forget that Donovan wronged me, too," Hector said. "He was my dear friend. For many years, we longed to see our kingdoms united." Hector cleared his throat. "Before he accused me of treachery and banished me from ever visiting Grythium again."

And all because of some foolish prophecy, Marin thought.

There was so much that needed to be addressed. Marin knew the law. He was Donovan's trueborn heir, and he had the royal relics of Grythium in his control. Grythium was legally his if he claimed it.

And Donovan had tried to kill him and Aster—twice. First when they were infants, and now when they were young men. Ilth might have been the one to conjure the dragon, but Marin was a fool if he didn't think Donovan commissioned her to do so. A mad king—a vengeful, murderous king—was not fit to sit a throne.

"Your kingdoms are united now," he told Hector. "Your heir will rule his kingdom. That may be the greatest punishment he'll suffer. As he is our captive—and guilty of egregious sins against heaven and earth—I will let him know that I will now be taking his kingdom, as it is rightfully mine. It belongs to me and my cousin, and by extension, our queens."

Marin nodded to Elspeth, then to Aster and Carys. Then he addressed Hector. "Send in the prisoners, your ma—I mean, Father."

Hector stepped down from the dais and walked down the crimson carpet to the hall's entry. Marin felt suddenly aware of all the eyes in the room looking up at him, expecting wisdom and leadership. He didn't expect his first task to come so soon. But there was nothing to be gained by shying away from it.

Two guards appeared in the doorway, escorting King Donovan by each of his arms. The man who once ruled Grythium looked far more out of his wits than he had when Marin and Aster saw him last. How the past weeks must have taken a toll on him!

Silver flecked his ebony hair. Though his hair lay matted in some places across his scalp, he also had patches of baldness, making Marin think he might have torn it out in a fit of madness at some point. His glassy eyes peered out of a sickly, sunken face with a greasy sheen of sweat across his cheeks and brow. His body looked fatter, bloated under his disheveled hunting clothes.

Two more guards followed, bringing in Ilth, every bit as mean and ugly as Marin remembered her. She didn't even resist the guards as they marched her down the center of the crowd. She held her head high, her lips pursed in an expression of stubborn, insolent arrogance, her beady black eyes staring around at all the present courtiers.

The guards reached the front of the hall and held Donovan and Ilth before the four rulers. Marin looked down from the dais at Donovan. "Welcome, Father."

"You're no son of mine."

The guard to Donovan's left clapped him on the back with a gauntleted hand. "Bow before your king."

King Donovan doubled over from the slap on the back. Halfway to the floor, he caught himself and tried to make the fall look like a low bow, but he wasn't fooling anyone. He raised himself back up. His face showed a mixture of emotions. Was it fear? Sadness? Anger? Marin couldn't resist feeling pity for the deranged idiot.

But he sent me and Aster away to be killed.

Marin cleared his throat. "Do you recognize your own son, Father?" He didn't like referring to himself in third person—it seemed so patronizing. But it felt appropriate in this case. "Or your own nephew?" He gestured to Aster. "You sent us away to die when we were just babies, remember? Completely innocent. Completely helpless."

Whatever strength Donovan had up until that point, it completely cracked. His face twisted into an expression of sorrow. "You don't understand," he said. "There was a prophecy…"

"I've heard about the prophecy," Marin said. "And I take great pleasure in telling you, sir, that it has come to pass." He raised his hand and placed it across his chest. "I am your son and heir, and I have married the daughter of your once-friend, King Hector."

With those words, he gestured to Elspeth, who looked from Marin down to Donovan. Her expression remained stoic.

"Queen Elspeth will now rule by my side," Marin continued. "And her sister, Queen Carys, will rule by the side of your sister's son, King Aster."

Marin paused. Just in case Donovan didn't understand, he added, "Your kingdom has been united with the kingdom of Blunia. A prospect that once might have brought you much joy."

A tear rolled down Donovan's face. He choked with gut-wrenching agony as he comprehended what he was being told. "My little boy," he said. "My nephew. Oh, you don't know how sorry I am. What joy this should bring me. I am so sorry. So very, very sorry."

It didn't heal any of the hurt Marin felt. He still had so many questions.

"Why did you send us away to die?" Marin asked.

Donovan thrust a finger at Ilth. "She tricked me," he said. "She was the one who told me a deceptive prophecy."

Ilth sneered. "Was anything I told you false? I told you the truth, your majesty."

Hearing her cold, snapping voice was more than Marin could stand after all the cruelty and chaos she'd caused.

"Hold your tongue, Ilth." Marin had waited a lifetime to speak to her that way. Now that the moment finally came, it brought him the satisfaction he always expected it would.

Just because it's satisfying doesn't mean it's right, he thought to himself. Kings had to be better than that. Kings had to be judicious.

Marin cleared his throat, then began again. "You are charged with crimes as well, Ilth. Did you speak deceptive prophecy with the intent of manipulating his majesty King Donovan, my father, the royal leader of Grythium?"

Ilth sneered, stomping her foot in anger. "What he did with the knowledge is not my fault." She waved her arm, indicating Marin and Aster. "What did I gain but two ungrateful servants for seventeen years? Who are you to command me, now that you simply have a crown on your head and scepter in your hand? You are still nothing."

There it is, Marin thought. *She should be begging for mercy, and still she taunts me.*

"I am not nothing," he told her, amazed at the steadiness of his own voice. "I have never been and never will be nothing. I might have

404

been your servant once, but I am now your king. I am the ruler of this land by all the laws of gods and men, by the outcome of the tide and stars. This throne and this crown are rightfully mine, and I will preside over the kingdoms of Grythium and Blunia."

Now was the time to show kingly wisdom. Now was the time to be judicious, no matter how angry he was. What would the nobles think—what would Aster and Elspeth and Carys think—if his first act was to seek petty vengeance?

"As for you, Ilth, I decree you will no longer practice magic again," he said. "You will stand trial beginning tomorrow, and we will determine a proper punishment for you. I hope you have a good defense for the crimes you have committed."

"I'll tell you right now." Ilth's mouth twisted into a cruel little smile and she cocked an eyebrow. "Having two servants in exchange for keeping secrets from the throne seemed like an ideal circumstance at the time, ungrateful and incompetent as you may have been while you were growing up." She shrugged, then flicked her eyes at Donovan. "But when it appeared you were no more use to me, and with a mad king so easily controlled by the idea of your death…"

His death. His and Aster's. Ilth really did intend to see the two of them undone. "I have heard enough from you for now," he said, ignoring whatever face the witch made at him and turning his attention to Donovan. "And you. I should address you as Father, should I not?"

"I pray thee, my boy." Donovan clasped his hands together in front of him. He was actually begging! "Show forgiveness."

"I will show forgiveness," Marin said. "But I will also hold you responsible." He paused, choosing his words carefully. "You will serve no punishment, as I think your current existence serves as punishment enough. But unless someone will speak on your behalf, I see no reason for you to continue to rule over your kingdom."

Overwhelming silence hung in the air like damp, muggy fog. It was almost as if nobody even dared to breathe.

Marin looked out at all the attendees present. *These people thought they were coming for a coronation, and they find themselves witnesses to justice,* Marin thought. *And my rule begins with challenges on the very first night.*

"We will begin Ilth's trial tomorrow," Marin said. His mind raced, trying to find the right words, hoping they sounded wise and judicious and fair. "Let her trial last for three days," he continued. "In that time, may any of Donovan's subjects—whether they be his high lords and noblemen, or the lowest of servants—come to speak up on his behalf, let them do it. I expect none of them will."

He turned his gaze on Donovan. The disgraced king was cruel and pathetic, but Marin owed him the respect that a leader owes everyone he meets. "Understand, Donovan, that I assume your throne as your rightful heir by birth, and as your overthrower who rightfully sought out your crown and sword."

With that, he reached a hand up and touched the crown on his head, making sure Donovan did not miss that he was wearing it.

"I have the claim to your throne by the laws of gods and men, by the outcome of the tide and the stars," he said. "It is time for the kingdoms of Grythium and Blunia to be united. We have a future of prosperity in front of us. But in order for us to have those years of prosperity, we must also have accountability."

Oh, if only Tsema would appear right then and there, right in the middle of the throne room. The way she had in the forest when he and Aster first set out as runaways. Or the way she did at the top of the Blood Mountains. If only she could appear to offer guidance and wisdom, to assure him that he was doing the right thing.

You can't rely on a prophetess to tell you what to do every step of the way, he thought. *She just appeared to you yesterday in the hour of your greatest need and saved you from dying. What more do you want from her?*

And she had taken the ring from them. She knew it wielded too much influence over the affairs of mortals. There were some problems that he would just have to solve by himself. There were some tides he would have to sail without any influence from the stars.

Even so...

Why couldn't she just appear to offer him advice on his first night as king? Why couldn't she assure all of those present that Marin was doing his best?

Because you can't learn to rely on prophecy any more than you can rely on magic rings. It's up to you.

After all, wasn't that clear by now? Marin thought of Ilth's prophecy. It had indeed come to pass, inevitably and unavoidably, despite Donovan's best efforts to thwart it. All of that had happened because of what he and Aster had done—and because of what Elspeth and Carys had done.

Marin stepped back from the edge of the dais. "Take them away, good sirs," he said.

As the guards dragged Donovan and Ilth from the throne room, the courtiers broke out into a chorus of conversation. All of them had something to say about what had just happened.

Taking his seat again, Marin sighed. His first duty as king was done.

He looked along the dais at Aster, the brother and companion who had stuck by him through everything. The one who had first given him the strength to leave Ilth's farm all those months ago.

And their queens—strong, courageous, good. True companions who would rule by their sides. The gold collar of the royal mantle glittered around Elspeth's neck, its stretch of rose-colored fabric falling over her shoulders. She was the matriarch born to inherit Blunia. Now she would inherit Grythium as well.

She reached over and took Marin's hand, then escorted him down the dais to greet their people. The shimmer in her eyes, the blushing smile on her face, was a look Marin would never forget. Even though all the prosperity of two kingdoms now belonged to him, she remained the best prize he ever could have asked for.

The celebration lasted well after midnight. When the festivities ended, the hour growing late and all the guests having gone home to their own private manors or palaces, the four rulers went out on the balcony just outside the ballroom, the one that overlooked the seacoast.

From where they stood, the full moon illuminated the expanse of ocean that stretched out for miles. Marin had never seen the waters looking so flat and calm. It comforted him. If their adventure had been a voyage over treacherous choppy seas, then now at last they might have found a safe harbor.

Except not. The sea would never be completely calm for a king. He had responsibilities he would have to see to. He would have people counting on him. But he knew that he now had a chance to make a difference for others, to lift them up and make their lives better, thanks to his own power.

All this time, I told myself I couldn't be a good king because I was nothing more than a servant, he thought. Now he knew the truth. *A good king must be a servant at heart. He is not born to be served by his subjects. He is born to serve them.*

"Would you look at that?" Aster said, staring out at the sea.

"Carys and I used to sneak out here as little girls to watch the full moon over the sea," Elspeth said. "We always wished for the mother goddess to send us princes who would make good kings."

Carys smiled. "The mother goddess was listening to us after all. She answered our wish." She pulled Aster close and kissed him on his cheek.

Marin stared down at his flute of champagne, swirling the golden liquid and watching the bubbles rise. His mood was the same way— fizzy, bubbly, and golden.

"We have so much opportunity ahead of us," he said. "A lot of work, yes. But opportunity too."

Grythium had suffered under the rule of a man driven mad by fear. Blunia was still not altogether made right after living under fear of goblin attack. Both kingdoms had so much hurt. Both kingdoms were in need of so much healing.

"It won't be easy to settle all the chaos that has fallen on Grythium and Blunia," he said. "I'll be the first to admit I'm intimidated by all of it. But I couldn't ask for anyone better to do it with me than all of you."

Elspeth raised her glass. "Well said, love." She laughed, then took a long drink from the flute, and leaned over to kiss him. "We'll do it together. The four of us."

"We have so much we have to learn," Marin said, indicating himself and Aster. "We didn't even grow up in a royal court the way you two did." He nodded at Elspeth and Carys. "We know only servitude. I know only what it means to work in the fields and sweat over hard labor."

"Oh, you aren't trained in silly formalities?" Carys asked. "Such a shame. You didn't spend years of your life being pampered and told you're better than others."

"What she means," Elspeth said, "is that our subjects—our subjects of Blunia *and* Grythium—are lucky to have a king—to have *kings*—who know what it means to work hard, who aren't afraid of doing instead of simply decreeing. And that's what will make our job all the more exciting."

"What do you think will come from all of this?" Aster said. "Do you think our days of adventuring are over?"

"Hardly!" Carys said, her voice rising. "I don't know about the three of you, but I'm not going to sit around a throne room all the time. Oh, don't worry, I'll be here for court whenever I am needed. But I don't think our days of quests and missions are behind us. They've only just begun."

"If there's one thing the histories and epics have taught me," Marin said, "it's that peace and prosperity rarely last uninterrupted for long. Oh, we'll set rightful laws in place and provide our people with what they need to find bounty and comfort. But there will be other relics to seek, other monsters to battle, other prophecies to fulfill. And I suppose when those adventures call to us, we will have to take heed."

"Yes," said Elspeth. "Yes, we will. The four of us. Together. The royal rulers of Grythium and Blunia."

Marin had smiled many times that night, but this one felt different. It came from a contented, proud, deep-down-inside-him kind of happiness. He raised his glass for a toast among the four of them. "To the rulers of Grythium and Blunia."

Aster raised his glass. "To the tide and the stars," he said.

"To the tide and the stars," the four of them chorused together, and they clinked glasses, the chime of crystal on crystal filling the night with a beautiful sound.

THE END

ABOUT THE AUTHOR

Dylan Roche is a novelist and award-winning journalist based in Annapolis, Maryland. His first book, *The Purple Bird*, debuted in 2019. He holds a degree in English from the University of Maryland, and his work has been published by nearly fifty magazines, newspapers, anthologies, and blogs.

When Dylan isn't writing, he can usually be found training for his next marathon or ultramarathon. Follow Dylan online at @dylaniswriting or visit dylanrochewriter.com.